MW00713191

Also by Fay Lamb

<u>Amazing Grace Romantic Suspense</u>

Stalking Willow
Better Than Revenge
Everybody's Broken
Frozen Notes

<u>Ties that Bind Clean Romance</u>

Charisse
Libby
Hope

and coming soon
Delilah

For authors:

The Art of Characterization: How to Use the Elements of Storytelling to Connect Readers to an Unforgettable Cast

Storms IN Serenity

FAY LAMB

Write Integrity Press
Storms in Serenity
© 2018 Fay Lamb

ISBN: 978-1-944120-55-9

This book is a work of fiction. Names, characters, places, and incidents are either products of the author's imagination or used fictitiously. Any similarity to actual people and/or events is purely coincidental.

All quoted Scripture passages are taken from the Holy Bible, New International Version®, NIV®. Copyright © 1973, 1978, 1984, 2011 by Biblica, Inc.™ Used by permission of Zondervan. All rights reserved worldwide. www.zondervan.com.

Published by Write Integrity Press

PO Box 702852
Dallas, TX 75370
Find out more about the author,
Fay Lamb at her website www.faylamb.com
Or at her author page at www.WriteIntegrity.com

Printed in the United States of America

Letter to Readers

Dear Readers:

I recently had to reorganize my home to allow room for the belongings in two other houses. While plundering through long-forgotten boxes and bins, I came upon a treasure. An entire collection of my handwritten scribbles, and among the pages, here and there, I discovered pieces of *Storms in Serenity* that I began at sixteen and continued when I was in my twenties, that I dallied with during my thirties, and when the Lord took my writing away in my forties, *Storms in Serenity* was the first story I returned to when He gave me permission to write. *Storms* is the story with which I unlearned all that I thought I had learned and I relearned the art of story as I edited and revised. Truly, *Storms* is the story of my lifetime. Forty years in the making.

My hope is that as you walk the streets of Serenity Key, as you meet the many residents and discover their conflicts in life, that you will come to know them as I know them: up close and personal.

When I began to revise *Storms* and to implement what I had learned from others much more talented than I, God whispered into my ear a truth that I had never considered: no sin, even those that we commit in the dark, is hidden from God. Most sexual sins somehow seem to be considered personal sins. "No one knows. Who's it gonna hurt?"

If you asked King David, he would probably talk to you for days about how his moment of pleasure with Bathsheba turned his life upside down. And so, *Storms in Serenity* is the story of one man's sin and how God, who makes all things work to good, caused this man to see how his sin impacted those he loved even thirty years later. *Storms* is a modern-day retelling of the aftermath of David's sin with Bathsheba.

Get ready. As you touch your feet on the sand of this island, you're going to meet a lot of folks who have danced in my imagination for years. To help those who are not as familiar with the citizens, my publisher suggested a Character Index, and I agreed. However, we've placed it at the end of the book because there are some twists and turns that are given away if you know the full relationship of the characters at the start of the story. As always, my desire is to create ah-ha moments for my readers and not exasperation. So, if you get lost at first, I have been told you will be found soon, and from that moment of discovery, the characters will soon become such a part of your thoughts and easily identifiable that you won't want to leave Serenity Key. I've worked hard to make that a truth, and I hope you enjoy your visit to the little island town that has captured my heart for all of these years.

My prayer is that you, dear reader, will discover the message of this story, the same message that I place into every novel I write: God's love overcomes every wrong we have ever done. Our Father in Heaven turns everything to good, and even though we sometimes find that goodness the hard way, the Father's arms are open as He waits to show us His blessings in our lives.

Dedication

On the riverbanks of an island much like the Gulf shores depicted in the pages of *Storms in Serenity* sits a home built by my grandmother's relative, Emma Thursby, a great opera star in her time. The place is called River Wind. The home is a duplicate of the house, now a historical landmark at Blue Spring National Park, built by Louis Thursby, my great-great-grandfather. River Wind is deep within my heart because there the wild and over-imaginative child was set free.

River Wind is a part of this story, tweaked by my imagination. My love for island life began there, where many of the characters in *Storms* were born and have grown with me through the last forty years. I am so grateful to my cousin, Sherri Thompson McCoy, and her wonderful family who have preserved the home where it sits proudly overlooking the Indian River.

On those banks also lived another treasure of my life without whom none of my stories would have taken flight. She is Nancy Blanchard. When I was twelve years old, Nancy learned that I had a burning passion for storytelling, and she asked me to share my stories with her.

Nancy taught English Lit, and the stories I shared with her were that of a twelve-year-old writing newbie. You can imagine what she endured, but Nancy took my passion seriously. She didn't discourage me by reciting all I'd done wrong. Instead, Nancy met the pages with enthusiasm and dared me to live my dreams. Through her, I learned that when my wild child is imprisoned, my imagination can take me on boundless journeys.

Nancy, you are so dear to me, one of the angels placed in my life. You not only encouraged me to write. You encouraged me to live.

Prologue

Outside Della Croix's home, a car passed. Its tires stirred the leaves on the road. She pushed back her living room curtains and peered outside, thankful the vehicle continued without turning into her driveway.

Della walked to the couch, and with trembling fingers brushed the soft strands of hair from the sleeping teenager's face. If only she could tell the girl the truth and save her so much pain.

Della sat without waking the young woman. The child's striking looks set her apart—her dark mahogany hair framing her face with delicate wisps of bouncy curls, the rise in her cheekbones, and the eyes of darkest blue, a deep rich violet. They marked her as Della's daughter, though Emilee never seemed to notice.

Della longed to say so much to the unsuspecting girl.

Now is not the time. She's in My hands.

Her own poor judgment and terrible sin of so long ago stood between them. It changed the child's life and separated them physically as well as emotionally.

"Della." Emilee awoke. "How long have I been asleep?"

"Not long." Della pushed away the deep remorse engulfing her soul. She could run with Emilee, just leave. They should have left the school together four years ago when Zack Ryan allowed Emilee back into her life.

Now is not the time.

I can take her home, tell her the truth, and confess I'm her mother.

She's in My hands.

Emilee sat up. "He'll be here soon, won't he?" She looked to the street beyond the screen door.

Della nodded. "He treats you well, doesn't he, Emilee?"

Emilee shook her head. "Mr. Ryan treats me with indifference. I think he uses me to keep John and Andy in line."

Emilee's uncanny insight never failed to surprise Della. The man who'd lured her into a trap in order to yank Emilee from Della's life seventeen years earlier used people like commodities. He only kept them so long as they offered him the advantage. He destroyed at will.

If only she'd recognized that in him before it was too late.

"Sometimes he'll talk to me, but mostly, he leaves me alone unless I cross him."

What could she say to Emilee to make her understand that she must never anger Zack Ryan?

Emilee lifted her chin in a sure sign of defiance. "I'd rather stay with you. I'll find a job, work, and pay my way through college."

Again, a car drove past. They both turned and, at the same time, released deep sighs of relief.

"He wouldn't allow that." Della stood and moved to her desk in the corner by the window, putting space between them. What use was there to dream? Zack would smash any defiance on their part. "You have to admit Mr. Ryan was nice to give us two weeks of uninterrupted time."

"And I had to throw a tantrum to get it. I asked him a hundred times if I could stay with you, and he always gave excuses. He said he didn't know you well enough. I tried to explain, but he became so angry when I told him you were my teacher and my friend."

Della bet he did—the liar. She opened a desk drawer and brought out a small box.

"Six months and he'll have nothing to say about it." Again, Emilee held her chin high. "When I turn eighteen, I gain my freedom."

"And your precious John and Andy, what would you do without them?"

Emilee would never leave Zack's sons. Just the mere mention of the two young men ended any impending argument from her daughter. John and Andy Ryan were Emilee's only family—so far as Emilee knew.

"You see, Mr. Ryan isn't the only reason you're going back." Della put her arm around the girl as she sat beside her once again. Emilee leaned into her embrace, and Della wondered how often she had received comfort from a woman since Zack's wife had died so many years before.

Oriana Ryan: the only reason she'd allowed Zack to win in his evil game.

"But I'll miss you."

Della lifted her eyes toward the heavens. Only the Lord could give her the strength to convince her daughter that they would see each other again soon. Even though she was no better than Zack— a liar.

Emilee leaned forward. Her gaze bore into Della's soul. "I know you feel it."

"Feel what, sweetie?"

"We have a bond." She flopped back in her seat, arms crossed. "You have to feel it."

If Emilee would only look at her, really look into her eyes. Della had been Emilee's mirror image at that age.

"Is something wrong?" Emilee asked.

"Nothing at all." She held out her closed hand, opened her fist, and revealed the object she had retrieved from her desk.

Emilee took the ring box and opened it. Two small diamonds were set on each side of a larger opal. Her fingers trembled as she removed the ring.

Della smiled at the pleased look on Emilee's face. "It's something I want you to have so you'll remember me."

"It's beautiful." Emilee turned it over in her hand.

"Someone very special gave it to me."

"A boyfriend?"

"It's a complicated story."

"Tell me, please. You never talk about your past."

Della hesitated until she recognized this moment for the opportunity the Lord presented.

Emilee held the ring toward the light, squinting to read the engraving on the inside. "*Beloved*? That's beautiful. He must have loved you very much."

"He loved my sister."

Emilee tilted her head and stared at Della with such child-like curiosity that Della laughed.

"My sister, Uma."

"You never told me you had a sister."

"Well, I did. We grew up on an island, a little rustic town on the Gulf. I haven't returned in a long while, but I can still smell the salt in the air and see the sun sparkling on the water. Our father was a fisherman."

"Where is Uma now?"

"She died." Della swallowed the bitterness that emerged each time she thought of that fateful night.

"And that's how you got the ring?" Expectant eyes widened.

"Uma gave it to me the night before she died. You see something happened between us that kept us apart until then."

Emilee did not question her.

"On the day she gave me this ring, I gave birth to a child after hard labor. I had suffered alone through much of the pain. Then I saw Uma standing over me. I thought I was hallucinating. The pain drove me near madness, but when my sister slipped the ring on my finger and kissed my forehead, the agony fell away."

"So, you were her beloved sister."

"Yes, but her husband gave her the ring. She was his beloved."

"Where was your husband?"

Della brushed the girl's soft hair from her face and tucked it gently behind her ears. "My husband died without ever knowing about my child."

"Della, I'm so sorry. Your baby ..."

Della stared into the violet eyes so like her own.

Now is not the time. The inner voice remained gentle yet strong.

"I made a decision, one I regret every day."

"You gave up your baby?" Her tone mirrored the pain Della held in her own heart.

"Yes."

Emilee drew back. "I wonder if my mother regrets abandoning me."

"Oh, Emilee, I know she despises the fact she had to give you up. Not a day goes by that she doesn't wonder where you are or what you're doing."

"I'm going to make something of myself. Someday, if I meet my mother, I'll be able to tell her it didn't matter that she didn't want me." Emilee's hand flew to her mouth. "Oh, Della, I'm sorry. I wasn't thinking. My mother couldn't be like you. You gave up your baby because you were all alone."

"Hush. Please believe me. When your mother let go of you, she had a good reason, and I know she'd be very proud of you now. You've just graduated from one of the best preparatory schools in the nation, and you have scholarships to college." Zack may have taken everything from Della, but when Uma arrived at the hospital, her sister had given it all back to her—despite what Della had done to her.

Then the unthinkable happened, and Della had nowhere else to turn.

If not for what she'd done to Oriana, for the fact that Zack's wife offered Emilee shelter, Della would never have given in to Zack, even though he made sure she had nothing left to offer Emilee.

Della had placed her husband, Owen's name on the birth certificate rather than the child's natural father, Owen's brother, David. She and David had done wrong, but Zack knew only the depth of the depravity that included him. He'd never learn about her sordid past that had brought her such joy in the birth of her daughter. In his controlling way, he had learned of David, but thinking him only Emilee's uncle, he had left off his threats in that regard. Instead, he held what she'd done with him over her head, always threatening to tell Emilee the truth and destroy any future chance for Della to connect with her daughter. Despite her indiscretions, though, the Lord had impressed upon her not to agree to Zack's demands that he and his now deceased wife, Oriana, adopt Emilee. Instead, she'd left Emilee in their custody with specific demands, including this four-year opportunity for her to see her daughter almost daily while she attended the prep school where Della worked.

"I hope Mr. Ryan allows me to go to college."

"How could he not?" Della jumped to her feet and stood over her. "You've been a very dutiful student. You haven't wasted his money." She pushed back the alarm with a wave of her hand. Her child was brilliant. Surely, Zack wouldn't let her education thus far go to waste.

"He tried to stop me from going to church with you, didn't he? If it doesn't suit him, it's not done."

"Furthering your education is up to you, Emilee. Don't you let him take your dreams away." She walked toward the screen door and looked out on to the street. *Not like he did mine.*

"I'm going to marry his son."

The sincerity in the girl's remark and the dramatic change in subject amused Della. Still, marriage into the Ryan family was serious business.

"I love Johnny." She slipped the ring onto her finger for the first time. "He's my beloved."

Della thought not of John Ryan but of the young man who often appeared at school during the many weekends Emilee had been expected to stay alone in the dorm because having her at home didn't suit his father. Those were the days that Della opened her home and enjoyed the presence of her only child.

Andy Ryan's warm, dark eyes mirrored his soul, and he

cherished Emilee. He loved her more than the child could ever understand. She suspected he continued living at home only because he knew Emilee would return, and she would need him. At twenty, the young man attended college and worked full time. They never really discussed his father, but Della's instinct told her his eldest son despised everything Zack Ryan represented.

"I would think Andy more your style," Della said.

"No." Emilee stared at the ring on her outstretched hand. "Johnny's the boy for me."

A triangle of love came back to haunt Della. "If you love him like you say you do, Emilee, be sure you love him well."

"Oh, I will."

"I speak from experience, so you mind what I say."

"You don't like Johnny much, do you?"

John Ryan, on the two occasions they'd met, seemed almost like his father. Aloof, he studied people from afar and never accepted anyone on first impression. John seemed to mistrust everyone. Zack Ryan trusted no one and only a fool trusted him.

Della had been a fool.

"He's so sweet, Della. I don't know how anyone could not love him like I do."

Rose colored glasses were a harmful thing. "I don't know him all that well."

"Johnny has an angel's soul."

The words brought an involuntary cough, but Della remained quiet otherwise.

"I love him." The girl closed the space between them, engulfing Della in a tight hug. "I just have to convince him he loves me."

"So, you've decided. You won't mind going with Mr. Ryan?"

"Only because of John and Andy," she declared. "If it weren't for them, I'd never go back. Mr. Ryan is such a hard man. He doesn't love anyone. I used to think he loved Johnny, and I couldn't understand why he didn't love Andy or me, but I don't even think he loves Johnny. It's just that Johnny listens to him, and he wants to please his father. Mr. Ryan likes control. He uses people. Sometimes I believe he wishes that Cameron Matrai could be his only son." Emilee winced as if in physical pain. "Andy and Cameron are close, but there's just something about him that isn't right, but if I told Andy, it would hurt him."

Hadn't Della just reasoned the same thing concerning John?

"Just keep God close to you. Listen to Him always. You're His child. Also, remember that Mr. Ryan took you in and provided for you. And Mrs. Ryan was a loving mother to you when she was alive. Just keep that thought close, and let it wash away the hurt he causes."

"I'll miss you. You've been like a mother to me." Tears welled in Emilee's eyes.

"And you, my daughter." Della allowed Emilee to cry against her. "We'll write. I'll call." She closed her eyes. *Forgive me for this lie, Lord.*

Emilee wiped her tears with the palm of her hand. "I pray that God will let me meet my mother and father. Do you think He will?"

"In His time. Remember what I've told you about attending church. Fellowship is important."

"Did you go to church when you were my age?"

Della led her daughter to the couch once again. The Lord had opened the door for another chance to plant a seed. When watered just right, Della prayed it would grow in Emilee's memory. "My sister and I attended a church with our friends. We grew up in that congregation with the men we would eventually marry, David and Owen."

"Which one did you marry? Which one was your baby's father?"

Now is not the time.

It's not fair.

She's in My hands.

"Those are secrets I keep in my heart."

Emilee blinked and shook her head.

This time the car approaching the home slowed. "He's here." Emilee wrung her hands.

"Go get your suitcase, sweetie." Della sighed.

Emilee obeyed without question.

Della took a deep breath, steadied herself, and stepped outside. The car was, in fact, a very handsome limousine. And inside sat evil.

Zack Ryan waited for the chauffeur to open his door. Then he stepped out of the car wearing a dark blue suit, white shirt, and an expensive tie. His shoes were of the finest Italian leather. The scent of his cologne touched her senses, bringing back memories of long ago, and Della wondered how she could have ever thought she loved him.

"Colleen." He spoke the name Della abandoned years before. "I trust you're ready to live with our agreement. We won't have a repeat of the performance two weeks ago, will we?"

Della did not answer, though his tone demanded one. She was as surprised as Zack when Emilee had cried and pleaded for two more weeks with her.

"If not, I believe your daughter is old enough for the truth you try to hide," Zack threatened.

Della fought for the control she needed to keep from lashing out at him. The truth could destroy her daughter. She looked behind her to assure Emilee remained inside. "I'm ready to live with your demands." The words flowed from her like ice forming on a wintry pond.

A tiny squeak from her front door indicated Emilee's presence.

Though the coldness remained in Della's soul, she put warmth into her voice. "I want to thank you for allowing Emilee to stay with me for a while longer. It meant a lot to us."

Zack forced a smile. "Of course. And you, young lady, no antics this time. You're too old to act like a child, and I will not tolerate it now or in the future."

"Yes, sir."

Della realized it took every effort for Emilee to keep moving toward the limo. Although she would not return Emilee to her prison if the girl chose to run, Della didn't have the key to unlock Emilee's prison. Her freedom came from choice, and Emilee would never agree to leave either Andy or John.

"We'll be going," Zack said.

There would be no time for a long farewell, not on Zack Ryan's schedule. Emilee stopped in front of Della, but she looked past her. Was Emilee thinking of running? Too late. Della shook her head. Emilee dropped her suitcase and threw her arms around her. "I love you, Della. I'll always remember this time together, and I'll write. I promise."

"You just promise me you'll go to college, and you remember to walk with God." Emilee started to pull away from her, but Della held her close. Now, her words watered the seed she planted earlier. "Remember something for me." Della kissed her cheek. "Remember, Serenity isn't only a state of mind. It's a place, a very real and lovely place." Her voice never rose above a whisper, but intent rang with each syllable. "Serenity, Emilee, remember it."

"I'll remember. Thank you for my ring. I'll treasure it always." Emilee's hands shook as she pulled away, holding to Della as long as she could.

"Get in the car, Emilee New," Zack commanded, the use of her child's last name obviously meant to cut Della. She'd bested him with the adoption issue, and that had to eat at Zack. Emilee always lived on the outside, out of his full reach.

"Mr. Ryan, be good to her. I love you, Emilee." She waved.

Emilee watched her from the other side of the car. The chauffeur stood behind her like a Roman centurion guarding the treasure of his employer.

"Get in the car," Zack demanded.

Emilee ducked inside, and the chauffeur shut the door.

Zack walked slowly toward Della. "You remember the deal we made. You had your four years with her all at my expense. The school where you chose to teach cost a pretty penny. Now, you'll stay away from her. You won't write her, and you will never call."

Della received only one chance. No voice spoke to her. She held nothing back except the volume of her speech. "In the four years God has graced me with my daughter, she's grown to love me more than you could ever understand."

"I don't keep her because I love her." No emotion showed in his pale blue eyes. "I keep her because you love her and because my sons love her."

"I can rest in that, I suppose." In spite of the situation, Della smiled. *Thank You, Lord. Thank You for this.*

"And with her near, I buy Andy's loyalty, and I earn John's devotion." He turned from her and walked back toward the car. "Good-bye, Ms. Dellacroix." He stopped and once again stepped back before the chauffeur could open the door. "Colleen, I'm very serious about this agreement. I think you know what will happen if you attempt any contact. You don't want Emilee to know the bitter truth." The chauffeur opened the door and closed it behind Zack.

Pain pricked Della's heart as the car drove away. The tinted windows prevented her from seeing the face of her only child one last time.

She entered her home and shut the door. Falling to her knees, she clasped her hands in front of her. Tears flowed down her face in a steady stream. "I'm sorry, Lord, that I don't even have the strength to believe."

She's in My hands.

Della stayed quiet for a long moment, reaching for the calming effect of the Lord's touch upon her life. Only then did she rise and move to her desk. She pulled out paper and pen and began to write. *Dear David ...*

Chapter One

Twelve Years Later – Serenity Key, FL

John Ryan slid his hands into the pockets of his blue jeans and shortened his stride as the older man closed the wooden door of the stately Serenity Key Baptist Church and fiddled with the lock. Look up *hypocrite* in the dictionary, and you'd find the face of David New. The word defined the man from the bottom of his feet to the roots of his graying hair. Church was over, and others who attended must have scurried away.

The church sign caught John's eye. *Established in 1875. Who Does the World See in Us?* The person who changed the sign must've made a mistake. What did John see in Christians? Gullibility. How could anyone believe some God loved them? One look at the world around them said otherwise.

"How you doing, son?" David stopped at the edge of the steps, shielding his eyes from the sun and squinting in John's direction.

Hot, tired, frustrated, and lonely. Not that David New would care.

The smell of hamburgers on a grill wafted in the air. John's stomach growled. He added hungry to his list. "I'm fine." He stopped, though this man was the last person in the small town he wanted to see.

Across the street, a row of white Victorian homes stood in brilliant array. Down the road and across an intersecting street, Stewart's Grocery was closed as usual on Sundays. Above him, the gray and white clouds gathering in the otherwise robin's egg blue sky announced a coming rain. John looked everywhere but to the old fraud.

When David didn't speak, John surrendered his attention to him.

The man's usual smile failed to break forth on his gray-bearded face. Maybe John's appearance on the small island shook David after all.

"How do you like the house?" David jingled the keys he held in his hand.

Yeah, David was worried all right. He'd never made the inquiry during John's negotiations for the purchase of the grand old home that had been in the New family for more than a century.

John gave one more look at the church's sign. David's family probably settled here before 1875, probably grew deep rich roots in the soil, but some of the fruit off the family vine wasn't good enough for David. That was okay with John. The fruit, despite everything, was worth more to him than all he possessed. "I like it very much."

"A lot of house for one man, John. That's why Seth and I never lived there. You never said. Do you have someone to share it with you?"

Games. The fool wanted to play more games. John didn't answer. As far as he was concerned, the old man could stand there and squirm.

"My mother always loved it." David stared at John as if he

thought he'd gain an answer.

Wasn't going to happen. "I'm sure she did." Elusiveness—his trademark. As a lawyer, John needed it. As a man on a mission, he'd use it to his advantage. "Well, I'm on my way to the office."

"Have a good afternoon." David gripped the wooden railing and leaned upon it.

John took note of the man's weakness and moved away. "Charlatan," he murmured.

John never ventured into a church because he wouldn't pretend to be something he wasn't. An evil, dark soul need not pretend to be good. David sure had a lot of nerve walking through the door of that building. If God existed, in His anger, He'd strike the old man—and John—dead.

They were alike, he and David.

John was just a little more honest about his shortcomings.

———～～———

I will never leave you or forsake you.

The portion of Scripture sprang into David's memory. The irony of his thinking of the verse amused him despite his worry. He sank to the top step of the walkway leading to the street. "Thank You, Lord."

...Be content with such things as you have, for He Himself has said, 'I will never leave you nor forsake you.'

David's smile faded. He'd sure stretched the truth of that verse to its very limit. Still, God never abandoned him. This gentle, loving reminder offered proof of an ever-faithful Lord.

"Why hasn't it been enough for me to bring my sins before

You?" He mouthed the inquiry. Years before, David had laid his sins at the Lord's feet with a certainty he'd received forgiveness. Still, courage never came with grace. He'd never asked forgiveness from those he wronged.

He looked to the blue sky dotted with clouds, their white tops lifting from gray bottoms.

A storm was brewing.

"I'm afraid." David lowered his head, mumbling his prayer. "John Ryan and his brother are the dynamite You're going to use to blow the doors off my deception. Father, I caused this sword You're wielding over my family. I'm begging for Your mercy. Let Your fury fall only on me, and let it all end soon." He sat in silence for some time until his memory brought forth the face of a beautiful little girl. Could so much time have passed so quickly? Yes, it had. His son, Seth, was proof of that.

If John Ryan wouldn't tell him the truth, maybe God would. "Where is Emilee? What has her life turned out to be? Is she married? Did You gift her with happiness, Lord? Did she escape Zack Ryan before he destroyed her like her mother's letter warned me he could?"

He'd done nothing for his daughter, failing her at every turn. Still, he longed to see her. *Lord, please bring her to me. And, Father, Seth needs to know. He needs to meet his sister. If You'll just let me see the woman my child has become, have my children together with me—if only for one moment—I'll die a happy man.*

The prayer failed to bring him peace. If Emilee ever visited Serenity Key, how would he explain the truth he'd buried so long ago?

He'd given in to John's negotiations, letting the homestead go—at a more than fair price—because the sale offered a very slim hope of seeing his daughter again.

Nothing in John's nature showed him to be any more generous than his father. David doubted John had purchased the home for Emilee. For all David knew, John had married a New York socialite. But, if by some chance Emilee was involved in all of this, why wasn't she here?

"Mr. New?"

David blinked and turned his gaze to Pastor Noah McGowan. The young man stepped off the sidewalk in front of his home and crossed the street. "Is everything okay?"

David nodded. "Closed up shop and thought I'd sit and have a talk with God. Sorry to have worried you."

Noah sat beside him. With his arms on his knees, he clasped his hands in front of him. Neither spoke for a moment until Noah turned toward him. "You look troubled."

David nodded. To say he wasn't troubled would be a lie.

"Well, I was ordered over here to invite you to dinner. Will you join us?"

The thought of sharing a pleasant afternoon with the preacher and his wife held appeal. Still, he declined. "Thank you but not today." He reached for the railing and pulled himself up.

"Is there anything I can do for you?"

David placed his hand on the preacher's shoulder as they both moved down the walkway. "Not right now, son, but I may take a rain check."

"I'm available anytime." The preacher stopped. "I'd be happy to say a prayer."

David halted beside Noah. He puffed out his cheeks and released the air slowly, measuring his words. "You know the story of King David, when God sent Nathan the Prophet to expose the sins the king thought he could hide?"

"I know it well." The preacher took his wire-rimmed glasses from his face, squinting until he cleaned them, and placed them back on his nose.

"Nathan prayed for King David, don't you think?"

"I'm sure he did."

"I'd appreciate your praying for me like you'd imagine Nathan prayed for David."

Noah nodded, but David's request had silenced him, as David expected it would.

"Noah, I've done some terrible things in my life, and God's reminding me I need to take responsibility. I don't have the courage. I stand to lose a lot, and I'm not sure I want to own up to my mistakes. Since I'm afraid to do it myself, I'd appreciate it if you'd pray for God to put me in a position where I have no choice but to obey Him."

"It'd be easier for you if you'd obey God's direction. He can put a hurting on us when we're willful."

"Believe me, son. God has been trying to get my attention for years. After covering up the truth this long, the dirt's piled a little too high for me to reach in and unearth the ugliness."

"Whatever it is, I'll pray the shovel God uses to uncover it doesn't harm you." Noah pierced David with a meaningful stare. "Or others."

David ambled toward home. How could he ever explain to the pastor how God had used His shovel six times since David's indiscretion? A short walk to the Serenity Key cemetery would reveal six gravestones etched with the names of his family. And yes, with each death, the shovel had dealt him some tough blows.

Chapter Two

John cursed the tropical climate that made October on Serenity Key feel like July in New York. When he could, he reviewed his cases in the evening on his porch, allowing the Gulf of Mexico to throw an occasional cool breeze his way. Other times, he'd sit here in his office, with the thermostat set as low as possible, though still not cool enough.

He removed his glasses, folded his arms on top of his desk, and lowered his head. He'd discarded his contacts at home. The strain caused his eyes and head to ache. Still, he'd rather be here in his office instead of lying in bed unable to sleep. He always reached for the softness that had not shared his bed for months. Usually, he drifted to sleep in the porch hammock where his brother would find him and guide him to the bedroom. There, when tiredness engulfed him, he gained relief from his loneliness.

The heat affected his mood. Anger and hurt spun out of control, and at the root of it stood the woman he loved most in the world.

"Good night."

John lifted his head.

His law partner stood in the doorway. Mickey Parker held his own files in his hands. "Don't stay too late."

John picked up a document from his desk. Mickey had already started down the hall. "I won't."

What else could he say? John had little in common with Mickey. John had arrived on the island with an agenda, and Mickey and his wife fit the bill. Mickey had worked for the public defender's office on the mainland, awaiting the day when he could reopen his deceased father's offices. John had shown up with his Florida Bar license in hand and excellent credentials. What more did Mickey need to know to form a business relationship?

John didn't have to coax Mickey to get onboard with his plans, especially when John agreed to pay for the renovations and the startup of the business—no strings attached for Mickey.

Penny, Mickey's wife, turned out to be a better than average office manager and legal secretary-in-training.

John continued to stare at the document in his hand as the door closed behind his partner.

Even now, after everything, his conscience still pricked him when he read it. The document didn't belong to him, and he should have relinquished it to its rightful owner long ago.

His actions were selfish. The certificate belonged to someone who'd never asked anything from John's father except to know the tiniest detail about her family. Zack refused her, and while his father had been alive, John could not mend the hurt Zack's failure to disclose the information had caused. After the old man's death, John found the birth certificate hidden in his father's safe. Zack never intended for the truth to be known, and John, like a dutiful son, continued the legacy of deceit.

"I wanted to give it all to you," he spoke as if the beautiful woman stood in front of him. In Serenity Key rested everything she had ever dreamed of: a heritage, a family home, relatives, an uncle, and a cousin. But she'd betrayed him. "You know I can't stomach betrayal."

And the two people he loved the most had trampled upon his heart. All his plans, the work he'd done to pass the Florida Bar, the information he'd learned from the private investigator, he'd done it all for her, so she could be with the family she longed to have.

He released the certificate and allowed it to float to his desk.

He needed to take some of the blame for her absence. Who would have thought when he sprang his surprise on her that she'd have one of her own? When he'd told her they were moving to Serenity Key, she'd refused to come with him. Instead, and much to John's astonishment, Andy packed up everything he owned, and the two brothers arrived in Serenity without a vital part of their lives.

"Emilee," he breathed his wife's name. He imagined her standing before him, the smoking gun in her hand and the bullet in his heart. The love he held for her was deeper than any emotion he knew, and she'd inflicted him with a mortal wound. He was a living, breathing dead man.

The telephone rang, and John reached for the receiver. "Yes, John Ryan."

Silence greeted him.

"Ryan & Parker, P.A. May I help you?"

"Johnny." Uncertainty muffled Emilee's voice. His past measures might cause her to fear his retribution, especially if she recognized Zack's nature in his actions. That thought even sickened him.

"Emilee." He tightened his grip on the receiver, closing his eyes. Endless weeks had passed since they'd last spoken.

"I turned in my notice here at Cornell. New York Downtown

Hospital offered me a chance to return and resume my residency there if I'd like." Her words were tentative, as if she feared what he'd say.

John rubbed his throbbing left temple. "Why would you leave Cornell? It's closer to home. We both decided it was a better place for you to complete your residency. I don't want you working so far from home. Isn't that why you left there?"

She answered him with silence, the way she'd often submitted to his father.

"Why would you want to go back?"

"I know you arranged for Cornell to accept me. They told me."

"Yes, I did." He made a mental note to locate the informant. Whoever it was would be lucky if John allowed him to find a job in the darkest slums of the city.

"I told you I wanted to make it on my own. We discussed it, and you agreed. Practicing medicine was my dream."

Was?

"I just—I need to know before I reach the point where I can't pull back. Am I still welcome with you and Andy?"

"You're my wife." He moved the receiver away for a second, controlled his emotions, and placed it back against his ear. She was offering to leave her residency, her medical career, something she'd worked hard to achieve. Still, the hurt pounded against his heart, and he could give her nothing more than the assurance she remained his. They both knew he'd never let her go.

Zack Ryan would rejoice in his grave if he heard the way John talked to his wife. He'd adapted well to the lessons the old man taught. *Hurt them before they can hurt you.*

"Andy said you haven't told anyone you're married. Why?"

"When did you talk to him?" he demanded, his curt tone used

purposely like a knife plunging toward her heart. He wanted to cut her deeply.

"This is ridiculous. You're still trying to keep Andy and me apart. Why?"

He offered no reason.

"Andy's home. He told me where to reach you. It's Sunday, and it's too late to be at the office. Johnny, you should go home."

"John," he snapped. She'd already called him Johnny twice. That pet name sounded hideous on the lips of an unfaithful woman. He'd never accept it from her again.

"Oh, yes. We've become formal in our relationship." The coolness in her reply surprised him. "John, go home and relax. Andy says you don't rest well."

"I'm busy. We opened the door, and the work flooded in. Mickey and I have a lot to keep us going."

"Is he in the office with you?" As only Emilee could, she made her point.

He'd taught her well. He sharpened his anger on her concern for him. "No, he's home with his loving wife." He pulled the imaginary knife from her and waited for the moment when he could plunge it once more into her.

"I do love you."

The make-believe weapon fell to his side. Those words were her shield. She always said them at least once or twice during their conversations, and he always waited to hear them. Why did he find them so hard to believe?

"I wish you would just tell me what I've done. You're so much like your father, and you don't even realize it."

"Leave Zack out of this." He held his hand hard against his forehead, suppressing the intense pain. Without even knowing it, she'd located his vulnerability.

"I just can't understand—"

"When can we expect you?"

Silence stretched between them again.

"Emilee."

"You knew I'd already made up my mind. You probably heard the news the moment I turned in my notice."

"I don't know anything about you anymore."

"What you're really saying is you don't care to know anything that's not strategic for you. When did our marriage become a battleground? You're hiding behind something you assume I've done, and every move you make is a tactical one. You want to win the war, but you won't let me know why we're fighting. I'd gladly surrender to you in a moment. Don't you know that? If I've hurt you, I'm sorry." She took a ragged breath. "We've never been separated like this since the day we married. Do you remember? You promised to love me. To care for me. To protect me. That's all I've ever asked of you."

Every word she said hammered against the shell of defense he'd constructed, but the walls held firm. "When will you be here?"

"I'll be there Wednesday afternoon. I've arranged for a car."

"I'll meet you at the airport. Cancel the car," he commanded.

"No. I'll phone you when I get into town."

"You know how to get here?" In his life, he allowed only one person to win arguments with him. Lately, he'd been intent on winning them all. This victory, he gave to her.

"I've studied the map for weeks." She began to cry, and he waited, hand against his own eyes, to squelch the warm tears touching his skin.

"I love you, John. I'm not going to let whatever it is destroy us. I know you still love me. Please just tell me you do. You haven't told me in so long." Another long moment of silence separated them, broken only by her cry. "Please, Johnny."

His grip tightened on the receiver. He closed his eyes and allowed one tear to slip past his hand. "Good night, Emilee."

The phone was a magnet to his ear, but he managed to yank it from the strong pull of his desire for her. Stopping the conversation was the last action his heart wanted. He needed to hear her voice. He longed to know she cared for him, but *I love you* was a well-worn phrase to her. Still, she was deep in his heart and the very tormentor of his soul.

He picked up the birth certificate. *Mother's name: Colleen New; Mother's maiden name: Dellacroix; Father's name: Owen Vincent New; Child's name: Emilee Colleen New; Place of birth: New York Downtown Hospital, New York City, New York.*

"I don't know how you ever got your hands on her," John spoke to his father as if Zack Ryan could hear the conversation from his grave, not that Zack would ever give the answer. "But I'm so glad you did." The sobs he'd managed to contain broke through. "I'm so glad you did."

FAY LAMB

Chapter Three

Andy Ryan walked up the steps and onto the pier that jutted out over the Gulf waters. Halfway down the wooden planks he stopped and peered through a glass door. A light shone at the end of the long hall to the left of the law office's main reception area. He pushed open the door and stepped inside, moving in the direction of the illuminated room.

His brother hung up the phone and wiped his hand across his face. Emilee had apparently wasted no time calling John after finishing her conversation with Andy. John's tears were useless if he didn't intend to make things right with his wife.

Andy made his way down the hall. John studied a piece of paper without looking up as Andy stood behind the chair opposite his brother's dark mahogany desk—the one John brought with him when he'd left the New York firm.

"Don't you think it's time to close up shop?"

John jumped. "How long have you been there?"

Andy looked into dark eyes that mirrored his own, with one big difference: John's always seemed so mistrusting. "Long enough." Andy leaned his forearms along the high back of the chair and searched John's face. The pain visible only a moment earlier vanished. "Is my favorite girl coming to town?"

"She never was your girl, Andy. She has always belonged to me." John visibly swallowed. "Or has she?"

Andy refused to argue. He'd never won an argument with John. Nothing would change this time. "Why don't you go home and eat?"

"I have work to do."

"You're making work to do." Andy slapped the back of the chair. "To avoid a situation you created. It's lonely without her, isn't it?"

"I could ask you the same."

"And I'd tell you it is. Look, if you want to stay here and work, go ahead. I'm going to The Billows then home."

"Why'd you come after me?"

"What kind of a question is that?" Andy tensed, his body's reaction to the challenge in John's voice.

"A simple one."

"John, you worry me. Truth is, Emilee called. She's upset. She never tells me what's wrong anymore so I came to see you. I didn't ask because you're sulking."

"She'll be here Wednesday."

Andy's heart kicked up a notch. They'd been separated too long. "Good. Maybe you'll be able to sleep nights, and your mood will improve. You're one lucky man. Not many wives would take what you've dished out and come back for more. Em really loves you."

John rounded the desk.

Andy blinked but stood firm. Facing John was a trained reaction. Their father often menaced him, but John never came this close to open violence before.

"Not many husbands would take the leftovers she's dished out and die at the prospect of more."

The words rang clear enough. Still, Andy failed to understand them. Unadulterated pain showed in every taut line of John's face.

"Get out of here, Andy, before—before I do something I'll regret."

"I'm sorry." Why was he forever apologizing? He'd given his life for John and Emilee. At times like this, he regretted it.

Andy threw open the office door with force and stomped onto the pier. The door barely creaked as it crept back into place. Anticlimactic.

Small drops of rain began to fall as Andy walked the island's pier back toward the street.

How John had discovered the island remained a mystery. He seemed to have pulled the name Serenity Key from the top of his head. Had John ever visited Serenity before? He said no. He'd just heard of it. Why did he want to move here and abandon his wife, not to mention a successful practice with his name on the logo? He'd said he wanted a change of pace. Did Andy accept the story? No more than Emilee had bought into it.

One thing niggled at him. David and his son, Seth, shared Emilee's maiden name. Any other time, he could put it off as a coincidence, but with John—no. Andy had kept quiet. The truth would come out soon enough. Pushing John would be about as effective as demanding information from their father. So, Andy waited. And promised that if John hurt Emilee, he'd make his little brother pay.

Two steps brought Andy's feet to the asphalt of Front Street, which created a small bay between the main portion of the island, and the unofficial commercial district with offices and shops on the dock and a few stores and two restaurants, one of them Andy's new toy. The other dining place was much different from The Billows.

"Hey, son." As if reading Andy's mind, David New stepped from the shadows.

Andy smiled and held out his hand as the older man approached. They stood in front of David's Place, a restaurant favored by the locals. The windows, always open during business hours, were shut and the establishment dark because David closed on Sundays. David's Place reflected the personality of its owner—down-home friendly. You could eat your food inside or take it out on the back dock. If so inclined, you could even cast your fishing line and enjoy lunch while you waited for something to bite. People spent hours at David's, not just minutes.

"Not the same around here when you close. Nobody's laughing. There's no music from the jukebox," Andy said.

"You should be grateful. I'm sure your business doubles on Sunday." David walked to the opposite side of the street, seemingly unbothered by the light rain. Andy followed, and both men leaned against the concrete railing. Behind them, the waters of the small bay, which separated the town from the dock area, lapped against the pilings.

"I don't know, David. It's like you said at the council meeting when I sought approval to open The Billows. I have the tourist trade. The locals visit your place. I'm still pretty much a stranger on Serenity."

On the wall of Andy's restaurant rested a photograph of the old house Andy had renovated into his own eatery. It contained an invitation of friendship scrawled in David's handwriting, *Thank you for restoring dignity to the old home. The best of luck, and come over to my place once in a while. Your friend, David New.*

Andy enjoyed several leisurely meals at David's each week.

One day, Andy hoped to return the kindness David had shown to him since Andy's arrival, a whale out of water, beached in a lifestyle he'd never even considered.

"Both you and your brother have added to Serenity in the short time you've been here. It's good to see Mickey's name on a shingle. His dad was an attorney. Did you know that?"

"No, I didn't. I haven't had much time to talk with him or his wife. Up until a few days ago, I've kept busy with the restaurant."

"Does John like it here?"

Andy shrugged. "Can't say he does."

"Any particular reason he moved to Serenity?"

"I've asked that myself."

"So, why'd you move here?"

Andy scuffed his feet against a small stone on the street. He didn't look up. "My brother needs me."

"Well, I hope he appreciates you." David slapped his shoulder. "This old man is going home. You walking that way?"

"I'm going by The Billows to handle any disasters." Andy raised his hand as he started toward the dead end where his restaurant stood tall and beautiful against the night.

Nearing his place, he listened to the clank of dishes in the kitchen, inhaled the aroma of the seafood as it cooked, and reveled in the thought that it all belonged to him. With all his experience managing expensive, well-known establishments, putting this place together seemed effortless.

The interior renovations had been the hardest challenge because he wanted to keep the inside true to its heritage. One lesson he'd learned was that the islanders did not welcome change. David had referred Andy to the town's handyman, Luke Crum, and

Luke had proved himself a master carpenter. For a solid month, Luke toiled over every bit of restoration Andy requested. No chore appeared too difficult for the carpenter who said he'd honed his skills by doing, not by sitting in a class and learning.

Renovations completed, Luke had put Andy in contact with the local commercial fishermen. In fact, at Luke's advice, Andy agreed to purchase his food exclusively from Serenity fishermen and processors.

Instead of tiring him, the long days refreshed Andy. John didn't welcome his company, and work kept Andy's mind off their separation from Emilee. Now Andy suffered from too much time on his hands. He stepped through the back door of the restaurant. "Everything going okay?" He looked to his chef.

"Just fine, boss."

Andy waved and started back down the street. The rain that had threatened before did not materialize, and the air seemed heavier. Passing back by the pier, he looked up toward his brother's lighted office. John remained behind both his office wall and the barrier of anger and mistrust he had built long before moving to Serenity. Andy shook his head and continued past.

On First Street, a light from Blanchie's Salon, a small business in the center of the street facing the bay, caught his eyes mainly because not too many businesses remained open late on Sundays, if they opened at all.

He peeked in the window. The woman inside surprised him with a wave. He didn't know her and turned to see if someone walked behind him. Finding no one there, he opened the door and leaned inside. "You're open late, aren't you?"

"One of my regular customers from church has to leave town on an emergency tomorrow. I opened for her." She picked up a broom and started to sweep up hair scattered around her station. "Need a cut?"

The thought of a trim never occurred to him, but this girl was something else. The petite blonde's crinkly curls cascaded down her back. Her smile wove a web of pure delight around his senses. As he stepped closer, the twinkle in her green eyes caused one word to come to mind. *Imp.* Closer inspection revealed no ring on her left hand. "Sure."

"Have a seat. I'll be right with you. I have some towels in the dryer."

He obeyed, and she returned within a few moments. Wrapping a plastic cover around him to protect his clothing, she picked up her comb and ran it through his long hair.

He pointed to the object sitting in front of her mirror. "That's different."

"It's very special." She leaned forward and gave the item to him. He turned it over in his hand. It appeared to be a green angel made from some sort of needlecraft. "What type of work is this?"

She wet his hair from a spray bottle and then pinned a portion of it to the top of his head. "Tatting. My friend gave it to me. His mother made it before she died."

As she alternated between cutting his hair and releasing the layers captured on top of his head, Andy read the typed message attached to the angel.

> *To everything there is a season, a time for every purpose under heaven ... a time to break down and a time to build up, a time to weep and a time to laugh, a time to mourn and a time to dance, ... a time to embrace and a time to refrain from*

embracing, ... a time to keep and a time to throw away...

"Interesting. I take it you had to keep or throw something away."

"Not away. Just aside. Or so I thought." She shrugged. "Anymore, I'm not sure."

Andy raised his eyebrows, but she didn't respond.

Silence stretched between them as she worked.

"I think what you've done, turning the old Ramsey place into a restaurant, is wonderful," she interrupted the quietness.

"You seem to have me at a disadvantage." He stared at her image in the mirror. "You must be Blanchie because that's the name on the window. Is that a nickname for Blanche?"

"I'm Blanchie, and yes, it is." She let the last strands of his uncut hair fall over those she'd already trimmed.

"So, you own this salon?"

"Along with the Mainland National Bank. And you are Andrew Ryan." She continued her work without looking up.

"No."

She stopped clipping and stared at his mirrored image. "I thought you were John's brother."

"John's my brother. How do you know him?"

"He's Mickey's partner."

"And?"

She frowned.

Was he supposed to know everyone on the island? If that were so, her name would top his list.

"My sister, Penny, is Mickey's wife." The complicated relationship rolled off her tongue as if she said it every day, and she left no time for him to mull it over before she continued. "So, does John have two brothers?"

"Only me."

She rested her hand holding the scissors on her hip. "And your name isn't Andy? Penny told me that was your name."

He smiled. "I'm Andy."

"Oh, for goodness' sake, you can tell I'm not the sharpest knife in the cutlery set. I'm terrible with puzzles."

"You're very sharp. My real name isn't Andrew, though. It's Andre." He scrunched his nose at the hated name.

She stared back at him, and Andy couldn't take his eyes away from the reflection of the beauty who would best any star on Broadway.

"I like your name." She finished the last of her cutting and laid the scissors on her stand before giving him a hand mirror and turning his seat to allow him to view the overall style. "I wasn't sure how you wanted it. You wear your hair pretty long."

Not anymore. He stared at the shorter look.

"You can still tie it back," she answered his unspoken thoughts.

"This is fine."

She spun him back around, and he handed her the angel and the mirror. She placed them beside the scissors, her eyes resting on the message for a few moments. "That verse talks to my soul every day." She lifted the plastic smock and brushed the stray hairs away from his collar. "Do you attend church, Andy?"

"No, can't say I do." He stepped out of the chair.

She shrugged as if her question held no importance, but somehow, he imagined she weighed his answer.

"You?"

She nodded. "Oh, yes."

He gave no response.

"Promise me when the day comes and you decide to get a stylish cut, you'll let me do the honors."

Andy coughed at the slight. "Excuse me. Stylish?"

She laughed, "I'm sorry. Shorter."

"I think I'm pretty much in style."

"For the big city where you used to live." She again hinted she knew more about him than she confessed.

"You do have me at a big disadvantage."

"Not really." She led him to the cash register where he paid for the cut, tipping her well. She thanked him and placed the money inside the antique machine. "You see, the object I set aside, he helped you make the Ramsey house into the restaurant you own." She held out her hand as if just greeting him. "My name's Blanchie Crum. I'm Luke's ex-wife."

Oh, man. Couldn't Luke have said something? Six or seven days a week they'd worked together, and Luke never mentioned he lost a beauty like this one. In this small town, how did he keep her a secret? Andy imagined Luke hadn't hidden the truth by happenstance.

Andy had intended to ask her out. One more second, and he would have blurted an invitation to dinner. "It's nice to meet you, Blanchie." He forced a smile. "And I promise once I decide on a more stylish cut, you'll be the one I come to see."

She followed him to the door. "Thanks, again, Andy. I hope I'll see you around."

He walked out the door with the scent of the woman's delicate perfume permanently affixed to his memory.

"Hey, baby, watch out for this guy." Luke leaned against his pickup parked at the curb.

"I think it would be a better idea to look out for you, sweetheart." Blanchie went back inside, closing the door.

Andy scrutinized the interplay. Had Luke come by to visit his ex-wife or had he seen Andy walking this way and decided to check out what was going on?

Luke's gaze followed his ex-wife. He shook his head before turning his attention to Andy. "Busy?"

"Why? What are you doing?"

Luke held up a Styrofoam box containing a takeout meal. "My weekly pay," he announced. One meal a week was part of the arrangement since Luke refused to take the large sum Andy offered for the renovations and his expertise on winning over the natives.

Andy pegged him as crazy, but Luke declared receipt of Andy's pay as robbery for doing work he loved. Luke had also added that too much cash in his hands was a temptation he didn't need. Whatever that meant.

"Hey, ditch work. Get a plate. Let's go back to my boat and sit."

Going back to Luke's boat meant sitting on the wooden dock in front of John's house, looking at the stars, and listening to the Gulf waters lap against the dock pilings. Luke had his "home" docked there when John made the purchase, and Andy's brother found no reason to make Luke find another berth.

"How'd you ever let her go?" Andy asked.

"I made it impossible for her to stay with me." Luke looked back toward the lighted window of the office on the dock and shrugged. "Your brother working late again?"

"Always."

"Well, I have something up my sleeve that may help him

relax." Luke winked but made no attempt to explain.

Chapter Four

Emilee Ryan stopped at Cornell Medical Center's emergency room's reception desk. Her laughter at her friend's joke evaporated like water on scorching asphalt. She grasped Dr. Yasmin Garcia's arm and took a deep, steadying breath at the sight of the man peering at them from the door. "I asked Johnny to keep him away from me. You'd think he'd grant me one little favor."

Emilee closed her eyes. Blood pulsed against her eardrums, her heart raging with the fire of hatred. Opening her eyes, she pushed back the feeling of building trepidation.

Yasmin fumbled in her purse for her keys and then followed Emilee's gaze to the area outside the hospital's staff entrance and the man pacing in plain sight. "You know him? I've been trying to learn his name for a month. He's around here all the time. Maybe he could join us for dinner?"

Stalking. Always stalking her. He probably paid someone to give him her schedule each week. Cameron Matrai's appearance couldn't bode well for anything his machinations could evoke.

She'd be gone soon enough, and the time had come to tell Cameron to get lost. "You want nothing to do with the likes of him." Emilee lifted her hand in a silent command for Yasmin to stay inside. With the yank of the stethoscope from around her neck, she stomped down the corridor.

Emilee stopped, waiting impatiently for the electronic door to slide open. "What are you doing here?" She skulked around him, just out of his reach.

Cameron smiled at her, that grin that told her something evil lurked inside his brain. "Now, Em, is that any way to greet an old friend?"

"An old friend, no, but you, Cameron … What are you doing here?"

He pushed sandy-blond bangs away from stormy-gray eyes. Movie star looks helped him to get by in New York and California. Too bad looks were deceiving. Cameron was a very ugly man on the inside, and sometimes Emilee imagined she was the only one who saw it. "I've come to see if the rumors I've heard are true."

Cameron had been groomed well by his mentor—the same one who'd groomed John. But she and Andy had been able to keep Zack from completely destroying John's once-loving heart.

"Well, are they?" Cameron pressed.

"I'm sad to say, the rumors of your demise have been greatly exaggerated." She stopped and stuffed the stethoscope into the pocket of her lab coat.

"Why do you say that when I love you so much?"

"Cameron, there isn't any room for love in that pit you call a heart."

He grabbed for her wrist so fast she didn't have time to pull away. Forcing her arm down, he squeezed hard, yanking her against him. She winced from the pain but refused to cry. Like John's father, he'd probably like to hear her whimper, but she wouldn't give him the satisfaction. Those days died along with Zack Ryan.

"Don't go there, babe. Don't do it," he menaced.

"I don't intend to visit your heart."

"Ah, Em, there it is, that delicious sense of humor. No one appreciates it more." He pressed down again causing her to bend forward to alleviate the pain. "Serenity, Emilee. Stay away." He released her.

"I'll go anywhere I wish, and I'm going to my family. You're not stopping me." Not smart, provoking a madman, but she'd never back down to another man, especially one to whom she owed nothing.

"Watch me." He reached out and patted her head.

Emilee pulled back.

He caught a lock of hair and yanked, causing her to lose her balance. Emilee fell into him, and he held her there, like a lover saying good-bye to his girl. "Asking your precious Johnny to keep me away from you, sweetheart, poor judgment on your part," he whispered and released her. Then he walked down the sidewalk as if nothing had occurred.

Since Andy's departure, keeping Cameron in check had been nearly impossible for her—something she hadn't anticipated when she allowed her husband to all but abandon her. At least, John had attempted to do what she'd asked. Whatever power John wielded over Cameron lessened with the distance between them.

"Everything okay?" Yasmin startled her. "It looked pretty intense from where I stood."

Emilee rubbed her sore wrist but remained silent.

"Who is he?"

"Cameron Matrai. My brother-in-law's best friend." She may have done the wrong thing in not telling Andy the truth. Fear ran the length of Emilee's spine, like blood trickling down one's skin from a wound.

———⁓———

Andy focused on the numbers in front of him. The restaurant had run short on oysters, a menu favorite. He hadn't ordered enough from the local oyster farms. The problem was a good one to have. Business continued at a steady pace. The Billows was a profitable enterprise, as all the restaurants he'd managed had been. Starting to pick up the phone, he noticed the time on the small digital clock on his desk. Too late. He scribbled a note to call the supplier in the morning.

"Another day gone and how many dollars have you made?" Luke's familiar voice made Andy jump.

He looked to his office door.

"I'm taking the boat out." Luke leaned against the doorframe. "There's supposed to be a meteor shower. If my weather instincts prove correct, the clouds will roll away."

"Speaking of showers, know anything about that tropical depression the news mentioned this morning?" Not too many hurricanes had ever visited New York City. Andy dreaded the thought of facing one on an island sitting out in the middle of the Gulf.

"They say there's little chance, but the ants and mosquitoes tell me a different story. I'll let you know."

"So, you talk to bugs, and they predict the weather for you? Does this insanity have anything to do with the reason your wife left you?" All day long, Blanchie's green eyes and impish face haunted him. Andy needed a clue about her relationship with Luke.

"They're biting a bit more and working a lot harder. Come on out and play. It'll be a nice party. I already have two other takers."

So, Luke wasn't telling him anything. Andy straightened the papers in front of him, prepared to refuse the offer.

"I'm ready. Are you coming?" John stepped behind Luke, his usually solemn nature replaced by a seldom-seen smile.

Andy sat in stunned silence. John had seemed unhappy for months, and somehow, Luke had worked a miracle.

"Well?" John pressed.

"Wouldn't miss it." Andy pushed his chair back and stood. As they moved through the kitchen, he called out a few orders and told his staff good night.

"I docked at David's Place. We have another passenger." Luke threw the comment over his shoulder as they walked to the end of the wooden structure. Andy didn't care who joined them or how Luke managed to get John on board. Seeing his brother's smile worked wonders on Andy's melancholy mood.

"I'm ready." A footfall sounded behind them. "Bible study ran a little late." Before he turned, the sweet scent of her perfume announced Blanchie Crum was joining the excursion.

David started for his restaurant's kitchen to prepare an order. The phone rang, and he looked at his watch. "Right on time, old gal," he muttered to himself. "Seth ..." He motioned for his son to take up where he'd left off.

Seth nodded.

David answered the phone and stepped out the back door.

"Is Serenity still standing?" Verity Stewart asked before he could even say hello.

"Serenity is fine. Stewart's Grocery is okay, too. Nothing has changed in twenty-four hours."

"People think time moves slow on the island, David. You and I know lives can change in an instant there as well as anywhere. Have you found out anything?"

"Nothing really." He watched the sailboat on the horizon and recognized the passengers as they moved about. "Why wouldn't Emilee be with them, Verity?"

"I can't say."

David wanted to see his daughter. Trouble was, he didn't think he could stomach seeing her in the hands of John Ryan. Andy? Now that was a different story. Anyone would be proud to have that young man as a son-in-law.

"There's a way to find out. Why don't you ask? Wouldn't that be easier than all this worry? I'm afraid the stress is going to catch up with you."

"You're so worried you took a vacation." He stretched his arm and braced against the side of the building.

"I'm on a mission, and I'm enjoying myself."

"John Ryan scares me." He dropped his gaze to the wooden planks of the dock.

"A snot-nosed kid with an attitude problem? I've seen you take them down a peg with one sideways glance."

"But this snot nose is the son of a ruthless thug."

"I think John Ryan's a lonely man who can't help his actions. He's been hurt, and I think the wounds he's suffered are deep. Why don't you begin with some compassion?"

Verity knew something. David was sure of that. Whatever it

was, David would never get it out of her until she was ready to tell. "You enjoy the rest of that vacation, old gal. I miss you."

"Oh, the words you say." She faked a girlish giggle. "Do go on."

David stepped back and peeked into the restaurant. Seth was leaning on the counter. His attention seemed to be riveted on his old friend, India Thompson, who sat in the far corner.

"Hannah getting settled into her teaching position?" he said.

His son and Verity's daughter had been close friends all their lives. India had captured Seth's attention for a while, and Seth never told him why he stopped seeing her. Then Linda came into his life. Seth had fallen hard, and they had married. How David missed that charming gal who made his son so happy. Seth's heart had splintered when they buried his wife, and he was no good for either Hannah or India until he could work through the grief of Linda's death.

"I left Hannah yesterday. I raised her to be independent despite her challenges, and she encouraged me by reminding me that God would not have taken her hearing if He didn't have a plan for her."

"She's wise like her momma." David smiled though Verity couldn't see. "See you soon." He ended the call.

The lights on the city pier towering above and to the side of his dock were off, allowing a view of the meteor shower. David flipped the light switch off just inside the door of his storage area and left the phone inside.

"Thanks, Mr. New," someone on the pier voiced gratitude. David waved and wandered toward the corner of his dock. He leaned against the railing and looked off into the distance.

Verity's instincts were always on target, but David had met

Zachariah Ryan, and on the surface, John seemed a mirror image of his father. *Lord, is there something I don't see? You've shown me Andy's nature. I want to know this other man I feel is so closely tied to my daughter.*

"I should have taken her back then, Lord," he whispered. But he'd cowered to Zack Ryan's strength. He shook his head. Truth was, he'd been swayed by more than that. Zack's wife, Oriana, loved Emilee, and it had been clear from the way her sons interacted with Emilee, they adored her.

He covered his eyes with one hand, letting the tears fall at the memory of the beautiful five-year-old child with eyes of rich violet and cheeks indented with sweet dimples. She had inherited her dark hair and olive complexion from her mother, a fact that broke David's heart. Ribbons and bows tied her long mahogany locks into pigtails as she played on the floor with a much younger Andy and John.

He'd met her and left her in the hands of the Ryans where Emilee's mother had abandoned her five years before.

But before he'd left, Emilee had gifted him with a picture. *A picture for the Nice Man.*

David's hand had trembled as he reached for the art, nothing more than a child's scribble. His throat had closed in emotion. He'd gently pulled her from Oriana's grasp, holding her tightly against him. "I love you, child." He'd brushed a kiss against Emilee's tiny forehead, handed her back, and rushed outside.

"Who is he?" Emilee's voice had reached through the door and into David's heart. He couldn't move, waiting for the answer from Zack Ryan's wife.

"A very nice man who loves you and thinks you're a very special young lady," Oriana had answered. "Couldn't you tell?"

"Oh, Emilee." David lowered his head and stared at the ripples in the water beneath his dock. Nearly twenty-five years later, and he was doing what he always did. Waiting.

"I failed you because I was afraid for myself." He scanned the dark horizon to where Luke's boat had sailed. "What did you or your father do with her, John?" The angry words circled his conscience, but he would not give in to the call for repentance. *Lord, I don't like that kid. Nothing You can do will make me like him. That's just the way it is.*

Chapter Five

Mickey Parker and his wife, Penny, sat at the counter at David's. The place was always slow on Mondays, so Mickey had been surprised when they entered to find India sitting alone in a corner booth.

The woman's presence frayed Mickey's last nerve. Would tonight be the night he'd lose everything dear to him? He cast a wary glance at his sweet wife and pushed his empty plate away. Holding up his glass, he indicated to Seth that he wanted a refill, although something stronger would be nice.

Seth poured the iced tea from a pitcher and set it down in front of him. "You've been fishing a lot lately."

Seth! Man, one day I'm going to ...

"No." Penny shook her head. "Our boat's dry docked."

Mickey forced a sheepish grin onto his face. Denying it would make his wife suspicious. "I've been playing hooky at Cutter's Bridge."

"And leaving me in the office with John?" Penny placed her hands on her hips and offered him a smile. "I guess you deserve a break." She turned the swivel chair and bounced off.

"Where are you going?" Mickey reached for her.

"To say hello to India." She threw him a puzzled glance and

moved beyond his touch.

A few minutes later, he studied the two women sitting together in the corner.

Penny smiled at him.

India avoided his gaze.

Mickey relaxed.

"I didn't want to mention who I saw fishing with you at Cutter's Bridge." Seth leaned close and whispered.

"Shut up."

"Do you want to tell me what's going on with you and India?" Seth pulled back, his eyes narrowed.

"I'm fishing," Mickey snapped. "Just fishing."

"I hope you haven't caught something you can't throw back." Seth walked into the kitchen.

If his friend only knew.

Penny strolled by and winked playfully as she made her way to the restroom. Mickey turned the swivel stool and watched the woman sitting in the booth. India looked up. Her eyes searched his face as if looking for answers. Without offering a hint of his thoughts, he turned around. She was the last person he wanted to see. He couldn't help her, not now.

"Tell me you aren't taking what every other man in town already has." Seth returned to the counter.

Condensation slid down Mickey's glass. "Let's just say, I'm in one room with two women: one I love and the other I started to hate just this afternoon."

Seth's mouth parted, but before he could speak, the restroom door opened. He busied himself with clearing the counter.

Penny sat beside Mickey, and the weight of his indiscretions bore down upon him. He placed his arm around his wife. "Mouse,

I know I promised you a night out, but I'm tired. Let's get out of here. I'm sorry." For more than he hoped she'd ever know.

"Let's go home." She looked at him, so trusting, so easy with the forgiveness he didn't deserve.

Mickey raised a hand in farewell to Seth. "See you tomorrow."

"Good night." Seth kissed Penny's cheek. "Take care." Seth spoke to Penny, but his friend's warning, no doubt, belonged to Mickey.

***

Seth busied himself with chores, hoping his father would return and finish waiting on India. When he could avoid her no longer, he picked up a tray and headed that way. "You okay?"

The woman nodded, and Seth began to clear her table.

"Playing busboy as well as fire chief tonight, Seth?" She turned her green gaze in his direction, almost bewitching him before he realized he'd been here before.

"Tell me, India, how does it feel to know you can't win Mickey?"

In silence, she picked up her purse and dug through it.

"Mick's having a rough time. He doesn't need you," Seth said.

"I tried to help you over a rough patch not too long ago, didn't I? Unlike with you, I was exactly what Mickey needed." India struggled to push herself from the booth.

He raised his eyebrows. Not like India to carry around a few extra pounds.

She stood and brushed her napkin to the floor and then held out her payment for her meal. "Keep the change. Your service was worth it." She dropped it toward his hand. He caught the currency as she knocked against him on her way toward the door. Dishes clanged as he fought to keep his hold on the tray.

Seth looked at the bill. Her payment left him a one-cent tip. Despite his anger, he smiled. Life with India tried one's patience, but life without her would be no fun at all.

Blanchie lay on the padded bench at the stern of Luke's boat, her hands clasped behind her head to buffer the hard surface. "Did you see that one?" She looked to each of the three men with her. John and Andy Ryan stared at the sky. Luke's gaze was on her.

She turned her attention back to the heavenly spectacle of the meteor shower above, where yellow streams of light fell and faded from view. The rocking motion of the boat and the water lapping against it brought total relaxation.

Luke climbed below and came back on deck with a pillow. "Here. Don't let it fall overboard. It's the only pillow I got in the divorce."

She lifted her head, and he placed the cushion behind her.

"Better?"

She smiled up at him. "Thank ya, darlin'." She gave greater panache to her already prominent Southern accent to hide her anger with him. He'd told her he'd stopped drinking. Why then, did he have a case of beer stored below? She never nagged him during their marriage, and she wouldn't start now.

Another stream of light, bolder and brighter than any before, crossed the darkness above them. "Wow," she breathed.

"Ooh, ah," Andy teased from his seat in the companion's chair.

"In Serenity, the cry is actually 'ooh, ouch.'" Luke laughed. "Our finest volunteer fire department is in charge of fireworks, and it's usually a disaster. Seth has his hands full with that bunch."

"That bunch?" Blanchie admonished. "Luke, you're the worst."

They laughed, including John. Andy's usually stoic brother sat alone on the bow.

Blanchie pointed. "Look, John. You can see the lights on your dock and my sister's house."

"Where'd they live before they built that place?" Andy asked.

"With Mickey's mom. Penny took care of her when she was sick. Mickey didn't want to stay there after she died. They sold her place to pay for that one. Dana's death affected Mick—"

"Blanchie." Her name left Luke's lips in a hushed whisper.

Gossip was the only vice her ex-husband didn't enjoy. He was right.

Blanchie closed her mouth and looked again toward John. He sat very still, his stare focused on the shore. She moved past Luke and fore, climbing onto the bow using Luke's captain's chair as a ladder.

When she looked back at him, Luke scowled.

Blanchie offered a haughty tilt of her head, and with the exception of a grunt of disgust, he remained quiet.

John startled as she sat beside him.

"You have the most beautiful home in town," she said.

He nodded.

"Granny New called it her earthly paradise. When she died, Doc New moved to town. He lived in the apartment over his office.

His grandson takes after him. When Seth's wife died, he moved out of his home and hasn't been back."

Luke slapped his palm to his forehead.

Blanchie lowered her gaze. She'd gossiped again, but annoying Luke was fun.

"How did Seth's wife die?"

John's interest surprised her, and it gave her another opportunity to aggravate her ex. "Ovarian cancer. Linda refused treatment."

"Seth hasn't had many breaks, has he?" John scanned the shoreline. "His mother died when he was a baby, and his wife died young."

"How do you know all that?" Andy asked. "Have you ever talked to Seth?"

"No. I have my ways of finding out truths about people."

"You a spy, John?" Luke ran his hand along the leather captain's chair.

"No." John looked to his brother. "I keep my ears open and my mouth shut."

Andy remained silent for a moment, teeth clenched, cheekbones raised. Then he relaxed. "Where do you live, Blanchie?"

"I bought my childhood home from my parents."

"Your home is in town then?"

"Yeah, Second Street," she nodded. "The blue house with the white shutters."

"On the corner." Andy smiled. "I love your wrap-around porch."

"I like it, too. I spent some of my best times in that old swing on the south side."

Luke nodded.

Was it possible that those memories were as precious to him as they were to her? She had hoped they would make new ones there. She'd filed for divorce only to make him see his need to change. Her ploy proved an agonizing and complete failure.

John slipped his arm around Blanchie's shoulders. "Look." He pointed upward.

A long stream of yellow with just a hint of red streaked above them. When she looked back to him, John wore a smile she could easily get lost in, one not at all in tune with his nature. She turned her attention to Andy, who watched them with a grin.

What she saw in Andy's face was love. He apparently loved his brother very much.

The blonde imp sitting beside his brother mesmerized Andy. Because of her, John actually seemed to let go and enjoy the heavenly scene playing out above them. Beautiful. That's all he could say about her. He hadn't felt this way about anyone, not since ...

Not since Emilee.

He let his mind wander, recalling the beautiful violet eyes, the careless way she allowed her dark hair to bounce over her shoulders.

Andy stared up into the heavens. As another stream of light passed through the night sky, he remembered that as children they would make a wish upon a falling star. "Bring her home."

"What?" Luke asked.

"Just making a wish."

John tensed, and he lost the smile he'd been wearing. Andy hated he'd caused that to happen.

"Who's coming home?" Luke asked.

"No one." The sharp tone of John's voice could've cut through steel.

Blanchie backed away from John. She slid off the bow and onto the captain's chair.

Luke raised his brows and widened his eyes, looking from his chair to his ex-wife.

She offered Luke a sweet smile that said she didn't care about his silent reprimand.

If she belonged to Andy, he'd never care what she did wrong.

Luke playfully swatted at her.

"I'm going to get another soda." She avoided his touch. "Does anyone want one?" She stepped past him. "Luke, a soda, or maybe a beer?"

"A soda," Luke smirked. "Thank you."

"I'll have a soda." Andy stopped her with a soft touch on her arm.

"Be right back." She backed the few steps down into the cabin with Andy's gaze following her.

Her foot hit hard against the case of beer beside Luke's refrigerator. She flailed backward. Andy slid down the railing, catching her in his arms before her head could hit the edge of Luke's table. "You okay?"

"I'm fine." She kicked at the container holding the flat of cans. "When is he ever going to grow up?"

Andy started up the steps. Would any woman ever notice him without looking through someone else?

"When are you going to ask me out, Mr. Ryan?"

Andy turned. He tried to read her expression while seconds ticked past with only her blatant stare. He stepped back down into the cabin and closed the short distance between them.

He had to have her. He lowered his head toward hers and kissed her lips tenderly and then he pulled away just a bit. "Would you care to have dinner with me tomorrow night?"

Her cheeks turned the color of a soft pink rose. "Very much." She pushed past him, stopping at the stair railing. "I'm sorry."

"For what?"

"My forwardness."

"Don't apologize. I like a woman who knows her mind."

She climbed the steps, and he opened the refrigerator. What was he thinking going after his friend's wife? No. She and Luke had terminated that contract. Then why did the guilty feeling linger?

He reached into the refrigerator and pulled out three sodas, one for her, one for him, and one for the unsuspecting ex.

The sudden close of the refrigerator door without any of his own effort jolted him. He swung around.

Luke stood behind him, his face absent a smile. "Just don't hurt her. I've done too much of that. If you treat her right, we'll remain friends."

Andy gave a curt nod. "I'll treat her like a lady."

"A very fine and chaste lady. Blanchie doesn't need any of your worldly New York crap. She's a small-town girl."

"So, why did you let her go?" Andy whispered.

"I didn't. She cut the ties." He pointed to the case of beer. "Because of my worldly crap." He stepped back to allow Andy room to pass. "I can't blame you for seeing everything I saw in her just a little bit too late to make our lives right. If it had to be one of you … When she climbed up there and sat beside John, I thought about throwing him overboard."

"John's thoughts are elsewhere." Andy started toward the steps and stopped. "Your friendship is important to me."

"Oh, yeah? That's why you kissed my wife?"

"Ex-wife, Luke. I'd never touch another man's wife."

Luke didn't speak for a long moment.

Andy held his breath.

His friend shook his head. "Divorce is man's law, you know. God gave it to us because of the hardness of our hearts." He looked away, pinching the bridge of his nose with his thumb and forefinger. "My heart was so hard for so long. I almost destroyed what little we have left. I might not have the license or the right, but I still love her."

"I won't …"

Luke held up his hand. "She asked you first." His smile trembled. "I'm still working hard to clean up my act. She waited as long as she could. And she deserves a chance to find happiness."

"I understand."

"No, you don't, but I do. And let me make it clear to you, I'm not stepping back into the shadows. I want her back, but I want her to want me as badly as I desire her. I could appeal to her sense of morality, but since I was very immoral in our marriage, I would be a hypocrite." Luke pinched his lips together then shook his head. "She deserves the opportunity to make her own choices, to decide what's right for her. That's all you need to know." He motioned for Andy to step ahead of him.

Andy couldn't wrap his mind around all that Luke had said. He was aware of only one thing: his own desire for the woman

Luke still declared he loved.

Andy climbed to the deck, handing Blanchie one of the sodas. "I forgot the reason I went down there." She laughed.

"A kiss can do that." Luke made his way on deck.

"Luke, don't go there," she warned.

"It's okay. Andy and I have an arrangement."

Andy punched Luke's arm. What could he say to the woman? They were two court jesters vying for her attention?

"And what was that?" Blanchie frowned.

Andy shook his head and released the picture of him in a three-pointed hat with jingling bells, the diamond patterned onesie and a stupid grin on his face. "I treat you like a lady or else." He narrowed the conversation down to give himself the edge.

"Or else?" Hands on hips, she faced Luke.

"Just or else." Luke shrugged.

"I got the gist of what he was saying," Andy winked. "And I promise I'll behave."

John stood from his seat on the bow. He stretched. "Oh, yeah? I trusted you with my life, and you led me right into my own personal hell."

An uncomfortable glance passed between Blanchie and Luke. Andy lowered his head. No. John wasn't kidding. "I'm afraid, little brother, you made that hell all by yourself. I've been trying to pull you out of it, but you just won't grab my hand."

Blanchie's soft touch fell across Andy's hand. "There's only One who can pull anyone out of hell. His name is Jesus." She turned to face her ex-husband. "Isn't that right, Luke?"

Chapter Six

The next morning, John jiggled his keys in his hand until he found the one to open the law office. Balancing the office mail and a cup of coffee in his other hand, he slipped the key into the lock and turned. He looked heavenward when it didn't work. How many times did he have to complain about the old lock before Penny would call a locksmith?

Leaving the keys hanging in the door, he knelt and put the mail on the pier's plank flooring. An advertisement slipped through the crack and floated into the Gulf waters below. John stomped on the papers with one foot to keep the rest in place. He put his coffee on the windowsill. As Penny had instructed numerous times, he pulled on the door handle to release the bolt from the frame. He then turned the key. Success.

"What are you doing?"

John jumped at the voice behind him. No wonder Mickey called his wife Mouse. She was as quiet as one of the small rodents.

"I'm trying to get inside." Roaring like a lion was more of a habit to him these days. The relaxing evening on Luke's boat had forced him into a brighter mood, not to mention Emilee would arrive tomorrow. "Where's Mickey?"

"He's at a hearing. Good morning to you, too." She picked up his coffee from the windowsill, handed it to him, and shooed him forward.

"Good morning." He pushed open the door and held it with his back, offering her a rare smile.

She'd bent to pick up the mail under his feet, but straightened, hands on hips. "I didn't think you knew the difference between morning and evening."

"I know the difference." He would've picked up the mail, but she was in his way.

"Do you have any interests outside of work? Anything that makes you happy?" The mouse did not cower from the roaring beast. Nothing in her behavior before this had indicated she had it in her to go toe-to-toe with him. This was going to be fun.

"Do you see me as unhappy?" He pushed further back against the door. His smile remained, if only for effect.

"Basically unhappy and very unfriendly." She stooped once again to get the mail.

Good. She wasn't too afraid of him. She stayed down, gathering the mail, but looked up at him. He let his smile widen, pouring on the charm he usually hid so well. "And I suppose my demeanor has rubbed off on you."

"Excuse me. Are you the same John Ryan who snarls at me daily, tossing around demands and hiding in his office? You can't be him. He has no personality." Her eyes widened, and she covered her mouth with her hand. "I'm sorry."

"No, you're not." He didn't move, didn't lose the smile. "And neither am I. And just so you know, the electric bill went into the brink."

"It's just …"

"Look, if you're not going to change the lock on the door,

here's another job for you. Buy John a personality." He laughed at his own joke. "I'll try to do better, Penny."

"You do that, Mr. Ryan, and maybe we can become friends." She pushed upward. "Oh." She doubled, her hands against her stomach, the remainder of the mail blowing across the pier and toward the water. Thank goodness it was mostly bills and junk mail. No pleadings or hearing notices. "Ouch."

John dropped his coffee. The lid prevented a major disaster, but some splashed on his pant leg and onto her black shoes. The rest ran through the slats in the wooden deck.

"Just a little twinge," she assured him. "I can handle it." She started to straighten but slumped down again.

John lifted and carried her into the reception area. He sat her gently in the chair at her desk. "Are you okay?" He touched her forehead to check for fever. Whenever he didn't feel well, that's what Emilee did for him. Emilee was the doctor in the family. She should know how to treat someone when they were sick.

"It's just a little pain. Here." She pointed to her lower stomach, "And I'm just a little queasy." She reached for his hand and held to it. She squeezed hard, her eyes shut. "Ouch."

"Maybe you should see a doctor." His fingers whitened under the pressure of her grip, but he swallowed his intense need to shake free and redirect the flow of blood into his fingertips.

"You think." She rolled her eyes.

"What's the number?" he demanded. "I'll take you."

"John, the doctor's on the mainland."

"I know," he snapped. "Far be it for this town to have a clinic." He picked up the phone and waited while she looked up her doctor's number. She read it aloud, and he dialed. When she reached for the receiver, he pulled it away and barked that he and

Mrs. Parker were on their way, and she needed a doctor immediately.

———

Mickey stared up into the clouds. He'd come to Cutter's Bridge to sort it all out alone, but India sat by the shore, oblivious to him at first. How had it come to this? And how could he tell Penny?

He tried to break off his relationship with India yesterday. India said she understood, but she had a small problem to discuss with him. Since when did a mistress becoming pregnant by the married man she was seeing rate as a small problem?

He was out of patience with her. After all, this is where it had started. She had sought him here, badgering him until he relented. At least that's how he wished it had happened.

Not so. On the day he'd given in, she wasn't badgering him at all. She had cried, and he had responded—badly.

"What are you doing here?"

At the sound of his voice, she jumped to her feet. "I'm just thinking. I thought you'd be working." She reached out to hold his hand.

He pulled from her touch.

She brushed the edge of his hair with her fingers.

Again, he put space between them.

"No one needs to know, Mickey."

"It doesn't work that way. What we've done is wrong. And now Penny isn't the only innocent one in this." He walked to the edge of the water. "How do I tell her?"

"You're going to tell her?" Jade green eyes widened.

"I've made a mess of our lives, and I'm about to lose the only woman I ever loved."

India placed her hand over her swelling stomach.

Soon everyone would know. He lifted his gaze and followed the single tear down her cheek. It fell onto her rose-colored top, leaving a stain. He swallowed, but the hard knot in his throat would not go down.

Even with India's reputation for playing around, he had no room to claim this child wasn't his.

He sank to the sand. This news would kill Penny.

The crunching sand whispered India's retreat.

Just as well. He couldn't stand to look at her. But he had no right to any anger toward the woman who said she carried his child.

"How could I be so stupid?" He buried his face in his hands, bringing his knees up close to his body, feeling like a child himself. He wished he could sit next to his mother and listen to her words of wisdom. Although he would see disappointment etched across her face, she'd read Scripture with him and counsel him with God's word. He'd leave still fearful but stronger in his resolve to take the right course of action.

"Mick?"

He hadn't heard Seth approach, but Mickey's friend lowered himself onto the sand beside him. Seth wore his uniform, and the fire chief's leather belt crackled as he sat. "I saw India leaving. From the tears on her face, I imagine you had it out with her."

"Spying on me?" Mickey stared out over the water.

"We're getting ready to do some controlled burns between here and the Bayou. I was on my way back, saw your car and India leaving. Thought I'd stop."

"She's pregnant, and it's mine."

Seth coughed. "Oh, man."

"Don't ask me what I'm going to do because I honestly don't know."

"Don't ask me what I'd do, because I couldn't tell you."

"Well, I've made a mess, and I deserve the wrath of God."

"I don't give lectures about God." Seth's voice deepened, growing cold, almost angry. "So, leave Him out of this."

"Problem is, Seth, even I realize if He'd been more a part of my life, this wouldn't have happened. I stopped going to church with Penny after Mom died and my sister left town. I guess I thought He abandoned me, too."

"Don't blame this on your lack of interest in God. This happened because you got involved in a situation you should have run from. God didn't push you into adultery."

"That's as close as you've ever come to defending God, but that's not what I meant. You're right. This is my fault. I'm the one who allowed it to happen. You know, India isn't even all that much to blame. I know right from wrong. I'm not sure she does."

"India understands right from wrong. She just likes to stretch the limits until they break everyone and everything."

"When did you start hating her so much?"

"When did you start loving her?"

Mickey closed his eyes. "I've never loved her." And that made his crime even worse.

"I don't hate her." Seth picked up a handful of sand and let it sift through his fingers. "I can remember a time when I thought the two of us might marry. That was an eternity ago before she started giving away so freely what I selfishly thought she should have saved for me."

"I don't know if I can tell Penny." Mickey didn't care about Seth and India. It didn't matter that he had taken what he assumed so many other men before him had taken from her. He cared that he had engaged in the act with no thought of his wife. "I don't want to hurt Penny."

"You already have. It started the first day you allowed India to get close to you."

"What can I do?"

"I told you. I don't know." Seth's jaw rose with the clench of his teeth.

Mickey had taken for granted what Seth lost so tragically— the love of a good woman. If Seth's wife were alive, he'd never look at another. Seth had acted badly at his loss, drinking and nearly losing his job, but would Mickey handle his any better? If Penny found out, she'd make him pay dearly for his mistake, his worse punishment being her presence, just out of his reach.

"I'm going to be a father, Seth, with the wrong woman. There's nothing I can do about it."

"I don't see her as the type to get saddled with a kid, at least not until she has the rosy picture of life her mother and father planned for her: nice house, big money, rich man."

"Then you don't know her that well, and that surprises me. I thought you knew India almost as well as I do."

"Obviously not as well as you. She isn't having my kid."

Mickey allowed the comment to pass. At least Seth was willing to talk to him. He'd let him win this fight. "Terminating the pregnancy has never been an option. She loves children." And he knew that how? She'd shared it with him and with Penny one day when Penny invited her for dinner. After India left, Penny had cried, wondering why God had not allowed them the child they so desperately wanted.

Seth peered out over the water. "Well, I can't tell you what to do about the baby or your marriage, but I can tell you what I learned when I almost lost my job."

Mickey waited, anxious for anything that would help him deal with the situation.

"Accept your responsibility. You can't lie your way out of it or pretend it never happened." Seth stood and helped Mickey to his feet.

Seth's deep blue gaze scanned the water that lapped against the sand. He stood a couple inches shorter than Mickey's near six feet. He wore his blond hair shorter than Mickey's hair of the same color. Now, Seth ran his hands through it, a sure sign that he was very troubled by Mickey's news.

His friend picked up a stick and tossed it with all his strength into the bayou waters. The fire chief gig kept him outside a lot, and the bronze of the man's skin made him look like a surfer, though the Gulf Island rarely gave them swells that would allow them to skim across the waters let alone catch a wave.

Mickey waited for his friend to speak. He'd learned that Seth liked to think out an issue. Maybe he'd have some wisdom for Mickey after all.

Seth turned, making unwavering eye contact, a silent demand that Mickey pay attention. "Sometimes accepting our own role in our downfall is the hardest part, but it made the rest easy for me. My friends knew my failings, and because I admitted them and worked to correct them, they accepted my apologies and stood beside me all the way. You stood by me, Mick. I'll stand by you."

Mickey ran his hand over his red-more than-blond mustache. "Yeah, but you only had to stand before the town council. I have to face Penny."

Seth walked with Mickey toward the clearing. "I won't abandon you, but I have to be honest. It's taking a lot of self-control to keep from decking you for Penny."

"Mickey?" India's voice unnerved him.

"I've got to go." Seth walked on.

"Seth …" India reached out for him.

Seth turned and held his hands in the air. "Nope."

"I—I'm sorry."

"Sorry doesn't cover it." Seth left them.

"I've got to go." Mickey took off after his friend.

"What have I done?" India screamed.

Mickey spun back toward her.

India fell to her knees in the sand.

Mickey stopped and moved back to her. She stared up at him, tears streaming down her face.

For the first time, the full weight of his situation settled upon him. He'd not only betrayed Penny. He'd broken India's heart. He bent and pulled her into his arms.

This was how it all began, and now, he intended it to end in the same way. "You haven't done it alone. I won't let you go through it by yourself. I just need some time to sort it out, to break the news to Penny, but India, the other—we can't be together any longer. I've hurt you, and for that, I'm so very sorry. I promise to be there for our child, but that's all I can offer you."

India pulled away from him. She struggled to her feet, her hands folded across her chest, her eyes downcast. Mickey waited for her to pour her wrath upon him. Instead, silence stretched between them until she took a deep, quivering breath. Her gaze met his and held him there. "It's not your problem, Mick." She swiped at a renegade tear. "Go to Penny, and you forget we ever had this conversation."

"I can't deny my child."

"But I can deny it belongs to you. Go back to Penny. What happened between us, it was a bad dream. I've had a lot of those lately, and I don't want any more." She turned away from him, her head held high.

Mickey heaved a sigh of relief.

Penny would never have to know the truth.

Chapter Seven

John's good mood had taken wings and flown as far away as the peacefulness he had enjoyed on Luke's boat the night before. Now, he paced back and forth in the doctor's waiting room where Penny left him alone. He lifted his arm to see the time on his watch. Only half a minute later than when he had last looked and only fifteen minutes since the nurse escorted Penny away. He silently cursed Mickey for not being in the office or the courtroom when his wife needed him most. John reacted terribly in these situations. Emilee would attest to that fact. He had been inept at nursing her through any illness.

The trip from Serenity to the mainland proved a long one. Twice, John had pulled off the road as nausea overcame his passenger.

"It's just the flu. I'm sure." He had patted her back when she leaned out of the car. "I don't think my driving is that bad."

As ill as she seemed, Penny had offered a smile for his lame joke.

In the parking lot of the doctor's office, he'd waited patiently, holding the door, standing out of the way in case she felt sick again. No need to ruin a good pair of Italian leather shoes.

She hesitated, remaining in the car. "I feel stupid." She looked up at him. "You're right. It's probably the flu. If I just went home to rest, I'd feel better, and I'd save the money I don't want to spend on this appointment."

"I didn't drive all the way here to have you turn around without seeing a doctor." He'd laced his voice with determination, but he didn't hurry her. She finally stood and walked inside.

He paced for a few more moments before catching the eye of the receptionist. "Is she all right?"

She smiled. "Your wife is dressing now, Mr. Parker. She should be out in a minute."

John started to correct her but decided to avoid the trouble. "Can I pay the bill?"

The receptionist left him and returned with the necessary information. When she announced the amount, John stared at her, mouth open, eyes wide. "He must be one of the best."

"Well, our records show you don't have insurance. If you want, we do offer a payment plan."

"Glad my wife's in the medical field," he muttered. "She'll be making more money than me soon."

The receptionist narrowed her eyes and then shook her head. "Your wife is working with our scheduler for future appointments."

He pulled out his wallet, took out his debit card, and slapped it on the counter. She ran it through. Handing it back to him, she studied the card and widened her eyes. "Oh, you're not—I'm sorry, Mr.—Mr. Ryan." Her face reddened. She slid the bill onto the counter holding out a pen.

John didn't respond to her sputtering. He signed the slip and laid the pen down. At least Mickey would have one less worry. He could help his wife get through whatever illness she had without wondering how to pay the physician. John folded the receipt and slipped it into his pocket without looking.

Penny walked into the waiting room a few minutes later and flashed him a broad grin. She definitely didn't look like a woman who needed the amount of care John had financed and nothing like the woman who had entered the doctor's office with him.

"What's wrong?" he demanded. "They said you were scheduling other appointments."

Penny laughed at him.

John headed toward the door, pushing it open and letting it fall back against the wall, leaving enough time for Penny to slip out behind him. No one laughed at John Ryan. No matter how sick they were.

"Oh, John, you're too much." She reached for his arm and linked it in her own. "I forgot to pay." She jerked him back with her as she turned.

John stopped her before she reopened the door, giving a brief glance to the plaque by the doctor's door. "You'll be back." Next time, he'd make sure her husband brought her.

He opened the car door for her, and as he did so, the letters on the plaque replayed in his mind.

OB/GYN.

"You're pregnant."

"We've been trying so long." She touched her stomach. "This baby is all we've dreamed about for two years. We were about to give up."

"I suppose we need to put a priority on health insurance to get Baby Parker insured upon arrival."

"Who cares?" She stepped away from him and threw her arms open wide. "A baby, John, is a gift from God. He wouldn't let anything happen to us, not more than we can handle."

He waited for her to sit. "I haven't had much experience with babies." And he had no experience with this God in whom she seemed to place all her faith. God never helped when he and his brother needed Him most. He closed her door almost a little too hard and found his way around the vehicle.

"I'm going to start decorating the baby's room right away." Penny babbled as he climbed inside and began the return trip to Serenity.

Will you have my baby, Emilee, after everything that's happened between us?

"What do you think of yellow for a baby's room?"

Can we go back to the love we shared before?

"I want bright colors. They say it stimulates a baby's thought processes."

Will I ever see you hold our child to your breast?

"I hope it's a boy, but I'll be happy with a girl that has Mick's coloring. Blond hair, blue eyes."

I want a little girl with your violet eyes and your dark hair.

"And tall like Mickey."

With your sense of humor, Em. I want a child full of your wonderment.

"Oh, John, I'm so happy. I feel like God has placed His arms around me, and He's smiling upon this life inside."

God doesn't smile on me much, does He, Em? John hit the steering wheel with his fist.

Penny jumped. "Something wrong?"

He shook his head and shrugged.

"I'm sorry to carry on so much." She sat back, arms crossed over her chest.

"It's not you, Penny. I'm very happy for you and Mick."

"You know what you need?" She uncrossed her arms.

She'd taken his words as an invitation, and John immediately wished he hadn't sent the welcome. "I can't imagine."

"A good woman. We'll have to find you a good girl; you know, the marrying kind, someone who thinks you're better than apple butter. I think you need someone to argue with you. You enjoyed arguing with me in the office earlier. You can't deny it."

John inhaled and let it out slowly. How could he make himself clear to her? "You don't want to involve yourself or anyone else in my life. It's a little too complicated."

"How can it be complicated? You always bury your nose in a law book, and you stomp around like a stormtrooper with a cloud over your head."

"Penny—"

"No. I saw a bit of humanity in you earlier, and you're not going to close the door on it. Everyone needs someone. Without someone to love, John, there's nothing."

"I do love." He turned from her and looked to the passing landscape of palm and scrub and water filling the space between the mainland and Serenity.

"You have a funny way of showing it." She touched his arm.

He pulled away.

She relentlessly reached for his hand.

This time, her warmth rested against his skin, and he let it remain there.

"Love isn't anger, John. I know you must love your brother, but when you look at him I see so much rage."

"I don't hate Andy." He turned toward her. "I don't hate him." Angry, yes, but after all Andy had sacrificed for John, how could he hate him? Even after what he'd done.

"I didn't say you did." She smiled. "And I believe you. I think your love for him is very deep."

He watched the road again. "Andy is the reason I'm alive, the reason for everything I have."

Penny turned with her back against the door and stared at him.

He continued to stare out the windshield. She didn't need to know his life story. Only four living people knew the truth; he hated one of them and the other two he loved more than life, though he had to admit, he'd not shown it lately.

"I still say a good woman would work wonders in helping you enjoy life."

Well, she'd changed the course of the conversation—from one dangerous direction toward another. Time to stop her childish romantic fantasies. "I'm married."

"What?" She laughed. "That's impossible. You've been here for months. Where is she?"

"She'll be here tomorrow."

"Where has she been? Why didn't you tell us?"

"She's been completing her medical residency in New York." He was proud of Emilee's accomplishments. He didn't care if Penny knew. "She's a doctor." Well, she was going to be one, but she'd given it up for him.

"But you never mentioned her. I can't believe you would keep this away from Mickey and me. Or does Mickey know?"

"I haven't told anyone."

"You and Andy are a long way from New York in more ways than one. Why are you here?"

John didn't answer. He gripped the steering wheel, beginning to wonder the same thing.

"Is she the reason?"

"For what?" He turned a heated glare in her direction.

"For all the pain you try to keep hidden? For your anger with Andy?" Penny pressed.

Touché.

"Are you happy she's coming?"

This time John nodded. "Can't live without her, Penny." And he didn't know how to tell her.

He slowed his car as they neared Cutter's Bridge and pulled to the side of the road. "Isn't that your SUV? Whose car is that beside yours?"

Penny didn't speak for a long moment and did so only after taking a deep breath. "He's fishing. It's probably somebody else on the bridge with him. Don't worry about it."

"There's a bridge out there?" John strained to see.

"It's not really a bridge." Her words were forced as if she couldn't breathe. John looked at her. Her face had paled worse than when he'd had to stop the car for her to vomit beside the road. "Do you want to make sure he's okay?"

"He's fine. Like I said, he's out there fishing. Judge Emory usually rules quickly. Mickey told me he's—he's been fishing a little."

"If you're sure ..."

"I'm sure," she nodded and stared ahead and then bowed her head. "Don't tell him about the baby. Promise me, John." She lifted her gaze back to him, her nose turning a soft pink and her eyes pooling with tears.

"If you promise to let me help you both with the baby's room after the secret gets out," he offered.

"I didn't think you were listening."

"I heard every word, and despite my lack of manual dexterity, I'll help in any way I can."

Her smile clashed with the sadness in her eyes. "I'd appreciate that. Like Rick said at the end of Casablanca, John 'I think this is the beginning of a beautiful friendship.'"

"Don't fool yourself, Penny. I'm actually the other guy, not the one with you now, but I'll try to act friendlier." They were still holding hands. "You and Mickey will make good parents," he assured her, pulling from her grasp.

"I hope you and your wife can work out your problems." When she touched his hand again, hers trembled. "Let's get out of here, please."

Chapter Eight

Mickey sat at the table, watching as Penny continued to work on the dinner that had been cooking when he walked through the back door of their new home. The place still had the distinct smell of the pine-cut cabinets. Another pleasing aroma that reminded him he was a blessed man filled the room: Penny's spaghetti. There was nothing like it.

He smiled at her before opening the copy of *The Serenity Serenade* he'd picked up at Stewart's Grocery.

"Were you fishing today?" Penny asked.

The hair on his head would have reared straight up if not covered by the baseball cap. Instead, his back stiffened at Penny's seemingly naive but, oh, so meaningful question.

He held the newspaper close to his face hoping she wouldn't see the evidence of his burning cheeks. He pretended inattention but clung to her every word, even those unspoken.

"I thought you were going to a hearing before Judge Emory. Apparently, you wrote it on your calendar so John and I would think so. I caught you." Penny's words loomed over his head like a sword ready to cut him in half.

He wasn't ready for this, but he lowered the paper and laid it on the table. "I'm caught. I told you about the fake hearing because

I wanted to get away for a few hours." He stood and moved to the counter where she now chopped vegetables for their dinner salad. She used their sharpest knife.

He brushed the soft reddish curls that fell down her back and kissed her supple neck. She tensed at his touch. Penny was all he needed. So why hadn't she sufficed?

She turned her hazel eyes to him. Sternness hardened the curve of her lips, those precious crescents that reminded him of a country mouse, especially when she smiled and her petite nose wrinkled. He stepped back out of the way of the knife. "Mad?" He stole a piece of carrot as she moved to check the spaghetti.

"Was India with you?"

He felt the punch to his gut although she never moved toward him. The invisible blow made him bow as if hit. He remembered a law professor who once told him the best defense was to deny everything. "No."

She nodded and stepped back to finish the preparation of her salad, knife still in hand. Penny was way too calm. She didn't believe him.

"How'd you know I went fishing?" He closed his eyes, realizing immediately he was a fool. You never ask a question if you don't want to know the answer. David New passed that adage on to him. The old man declared it often. In trial, it kept Mickey out of serious trouble. Why hadn't he remembered it now?

Penny never ceased her task. "John took me to the mainland to see Dr. Giller." She placed the carrots on top of the other vegetables and slowly tossed them. Then she returned to the stove to check the simmering spaghetti sauce.

Mickey bit into the carrot he stole. It kept his mouth from hanging wide open.

"On our way back, I saw your car. Remember when we used to go there? What has it been now, four years? You're there a lot lately."

He nodded. She didn't see.

"That used to be our spot. No one ever found us there." She wiped her slender hands on the towel hanging on the oven door.

Funny, just today, he'd thought of how they used to wrap themselves in each other's arms, hiding away from their friends, talking, laughing, and kissing.

"I guess," she continued, "we've just gotten too busy. We haven't taken much time for just the two of us."

"Penny." He stole another piece of carrot from the salad. "We have our new home. We're married now. We don't have to hide away." He winced at his choice of words and tensed as she drained the spaghetti and prepared one plate.

He retrieved two bowls and placed them on the table along with the big container of salad she had prepared. When he sat, she placed the plate of spaghetti before him and brought him the pitcher of tea. She poured him a glass before setting it on the table.

Once he settled, she took a deep breath, and for the first time, Mickey noticed the strain on her face. "Mouse?" He carefully used his term of endearment for her.

She pulled out her chair and sat. "We need to talk."

"About what?" Without a doubt, the seams of his world were about to unravel.

"Oh, Mickey, if you would have just told me. I gave you every opportunity."

"Tell you what?" He continued to play the game, trying to save himself, but from what? The truth would eventually come out. He couldn't hide a baby for long, no matter what India had said.

"When I saw your car, I was so excited. I thought about the days before we married, and for a minute, I thought it would be a good place for my surprise."

He jumped up. His chair fell backward with a loud crash. "You saw us."

She waited, her hands clenched into tight balls, her long fingernails cutting crescents into her skin. He stared at them, afraid to look up.

"Penny, I don't know why. India just—please forgive me. I love you. I love you!" He reached for her, grappling to hold to her in more ways than one. She was the queen, and he the traitorous peasant. She held his fate in her hands. Off with his head—as long as she'd still keep his heart intact.

Penny shook her head and tears fell down her cheeks. "I didn't see anything." She rose, untangling her slender body from his, pulling from his hands as he grasped for her. "I didn't see anything but your car and hers. I only suspected." Her breath was ragged. "You must have thought it very amusing, me speaking with your lover last night."

His wife bent to pick up an overnight bag he'd failed to notice until now.

"You know what gave it away the most?" she asked.

"What are you doing? Where are you going?"

"I mentioned seeing the obstetrician, and you didn't even blink an eye. You were so wrapped up in protecting India." She stamped her feet and choked on the words through her sobs. "Mickey … it hurts … so … much." She straightened, seeming to grow stronger as her sadness turned to anger. "How could you put India before me? Was what I offered so terrible? I thought my gift to you on our wedding night—Now, you stupid, stupid fool, you can have all she has to offer." Her pitch strengthened as she spoke each word.

"Mouse, please?" He followed after her. "Please don't leave me."

She opened the door. "I need time. I don't even know how I feel right now. This should be one of the most joyous days in our lives. Instead, it feels like the end of all my hopes and dreams."

"She means nothing to me."

"I'm not so sure about that. See, I know you have a heart. However, you mean nothing much to her, not after she got what she wanted from you."

"Let's work it out. Here. Now."

Her lips curved into a surreal smile as though she were his mother and he the scolded child. "Some wrongs can't be worked out with a hug and a kiss."

"Don't leave me," he begged.

The smile vanished. "You have a lot of nerve. I didn't cheat on you. I'm not walking out of this house because I found another man." She stared over his head for a long minute.

Maybe she would give him another chance.

"I never thought … until today …" She shook her head. "I would never do that to you."

"I'm sorry. I'm so sorry."

"Tell that to our baby." She slammed the door.

"Mouse!" Mickey opened the door. "Don't go."

She turned, and he fell before her. "Please, don't leave me. I can't live without you. I'm sorry."

"I told you. John took me to the doctor. He took me because you were busy with India. I'm not sure you understood me." She kicked dirt at him. "God help me and your baby, Mickey, but you're going to be a father."

She ran, turning only when she reached the dirt road leading from their home. Mickey couldn't find the strength to rise. He remained on his knees, his hands reaching out toward her, silently begging.

Penny turned and walked away from him.

He clutched at the grass and stared up into the heavens. Penny was having his baby. She was right. This day should be one in which they could rejoice over the blessing they'd been seeking from the Lord for so long.

He lowered his head and clenched the loose grass he held.

For the first time since he'd walked away from the church of his upbringing, Mickey got a glimpse into what life had been, despite the sadness of his mother's lingering death and his sister's abandonment.

Penny had been his greatest blessing, standing beside him through all the pain—the long-term care for his mother, his sister's rejection. Penny even kept in touch with her.

She'd never let him down.

And now, he'd done the unthinkable, and his wife only knew the half of it.

The shadows of the tall pine danced in the natural light illuminating India's bedroom. She lay across the bed holding her pillow close. Today the roller coaster that had become her life veered off the tracks when it collided with the lie she'd told Mickey and the look of disappointment on Seth's face.

94

What had Penny Parker ever done to her? She always treated India with a kindness reserved for a true friend. Just the night before, hadn't Penny joined her at her table, and in all sincerity shown an interest in her life? She'd asked India how she kept herself busy these days.

If Penny only knew.

"Oh." India bit her lip and rolled into a tight ball, pulling the covers up to her chin. Her lies failed to make the situation better. They only made it worse. Now she had to deal with the guilt.

Her ploy had not been easy. Mickey loved his wife. The irony was that on the day India planned to give up her plan of seduction and confide in Mickey, ask for his help and the help of his wife, he had comforted her, held her, made her feel safe. She no longer wanted to tell the truth, no longer needed Penny's help. Mickey became all she needed for the moment, and she wanted to hide there in his arms. If only ...

Then if only had occurred.

India was thankful her parents were on their yearly trip to Europe and would be gone for at least two months. Telling them was a problem she'd handle another time.

Her mother had begged her for years to leave Serenity Key. "You're meant for a better life." Chelse Thompson would whine. "You can't find the sort of man you deserve on this island."

"But you found Daddy, didn't you?" She had thrown her arms around the man who seemed unable to return such emotion. She dreamed of being Daddy's little girl, but Xander Thompson lacked the skills necessary to relate to her. Maybe all those years cowering to her mother's demands had zapped Daddy's ability to cope with anything outside of his business.

India wanted to prove to her mother that she could find a

winner without leaving the security of home. Security meant a nice car to drive, food to eat, and household staff to clean up after her. So, when he stepped out of his Mercedes with the New York tag, she knew she had found a trophy to show Mother.

At first, he'd been attentive, well mannered, and caring. He appeared even wealthier than her father. They began to spend time together, and India fooled herself into thinking she'd found something special.

She never knew when the something special turned into something dangerous. She hadn't seen it coming. They were walking by the water in the woods beside the Ryan home. He'd picked up a stick and bashed it against the palm there. "One day, I'm going to show him what it means to cross me. He thinks he can treat me this way, take from me what's mine."

In spite of his unsuspected fury, India saw a tortured soul and tried to soothe him. She sat on the rough coquina rock and patted the spot beside her. "Whoever's made you mad, this sunset will take the anger away."

"You don't know anything about my anger." He'd rushed at her. She'd scraped her hands on the rock trying to get away. When she'd fallen in her haste to escape, he'd picked her up and thrown her on the sandy ground, treating her like nothing more than a rag doll. She fought him, but he held her down and forced himself upon her. Her cries for him to stop went unheeded until he had taken all that he wanted from her. Then he left her lying on the ground devastated and confused.

India closed her eyes to shut out the memory. Lifting her head toward the heavens, a low guttural scream started in her soul and found its way to the surface. "Why? Why did this happen to me? Why?"

"Maybe because you asked for it?"

She bolted upright at the man's voice and tumbled off the far side of her bed, putting space between herself and the intruder. Why hadn't she locked her front door?

"Seth." She let out a breath as the sudden adrenalin rush drained. "What are you doing here?"

He moved inside, remaining quiet as he stepped toward the framed photograph on her nightstand, picking up her treasured picture of him. Finally, he looked up at her. "I was outside on your front porch trying to figure out how I could talk to you without putting my hands around your pretty neck and choking the life out of you. I heard you scream and thought someone beat me to it. I wanted to save Mickey from a life in prison."

India moved around the bed. Seth, she need never fear. Oh, they often quarreled and battled with words, but Seth would never harm anyone. Still, she stood at the foot of the bed beyond his reach.

He held out the framed photograph taken on one of the most important days in Seth's life. "Mickey wasn't the first married man to catch your eye, I see."

"That picture was taken before you married. And you're not married now, are you?"

He continued to gaze at the photograph for a long moment. His failure to fight back surprised her.

"I never thanked you for being there for me after she died. I had my gun loaded. I planned to ..." He rubbed his eyes with the heel of his hand.

Why did he think she stayed? "I didn't do it for your gratitude." She'd remained there because she loved him.

"You wanted more from me than I could give to you. I knew

that."

"No, Seth. I only wanted you safe."

He set the photograph back on the stand and stared down at his hands. "Tell me how you could do this to Penny? She's the only other person in this town besides me who cared enough to call you a friend. Despite our little squabbles, we were friends, right?"

India moved to the dresser. Truth was Seth's most powerful weapon. She stared at the letter on top of her jewelry box. The vision of her attacker's handsome face, the cold darkness that took hold of him, like a wolf stalking its prey, invaded her memory, and she trembled. Since the day he'd raped her, she'd not seen him. He never returned to explain his actions, and even if he attempted to come close, she would hide from him.

Two weeks after the attack, his not-so-apologetic, vaguely written letter had arrived. Still, her fear of him remained.

"Tell them," her attacker taunted. "Go ahead. Who are they going to believe? A tramp or me?"

Seth would believe her. He'd help her through this. Seth had to understand that the baby was an innocent victim. He would help the baby, even if he didn't want to help her. "Seth." She turned toward him, letter in hand.

He stood and glared at her. "You're no better than a harlot."

She lowered her head, and her tears fell onto the paper. Her last bastion of ethical hope exploded into nothingness.

"A real little home-wrecking tramp."

She took a ragged breath and released it. "Maybe if you told me how you felt back then I wouldn't have tried to find comfort elsewhere. It's only three words—I love you—and maybe if you whispered my name after you said them, I wouldn't have been so insecure. I needed to know your true feelings for me."

Storms in Serenity

"Did the other men tell you they loved you? Did they all declare their undying adoration?" He walked toward the door and turned. "If my respect didn't prove my love for you, well, that's your problem. I take two issues seriously. Death and infidelity. Both cause final separation."

"Seth ..." She started toward him.

He held up his hand, commanding her to stay away. "If you had remained faithful, I never would have married Linda, and I sure wouldn't have killed her."

Despite his rejection, India stumbled forward. "God took Linda." At least that's the way she saw it. God didn't care if His children were the most wonderful people on earth; He took them away just the same. *If I became Your child, God, would You take me away? I'd like to go now if it's all the same to You.* "Linda would still be dead today whether you married her or not."

Seth closed the space between them. "I caused my wife's death."

India shook her head. "I know that's not true. You're forgetting I was there the night she died. The hospice nurse stayed by her side the entire time. You didn't kill Linda."

"That's right. You were there." His eyes held a shadow of cruelty India never noticed in him before, even at his lowest point when he had been drinking to ease his grief.

She braced herself for what would come next.

"Like a vulture waiting for my wife's last dying breath. Trouble is, they buried my wife and left my carcass. I wasn't much good to you, was I? Even on a night when I was most vulnerable, I couldn't give you what you wanted because I couldn't see past your infidelity."

His words stung, but she steeled against them. He thought he'd killed his wife. She'd never again use his love for Linda against him. "I went there the night she died because Linda asked for me. She asked for Hannah, too. Do you remember? She told us both she knew we loved you, but she assured us no one could love you as much as she did. She said you were the only person on this side she would miss."

Seth stared through her. "There was someone in heaven she missed more, and if I'd only realized how important—"

"Seth, don't you see, you and me, there's got to be a chance." She moved closer to him.

"I don't want what nearly every man in town has had."

She slapped him—hard—but he didn't flinch.

"You're so self-righteous. I don't know how I ever thought I loved you!" she screamed.

"I'm thinking the same about you."

India ran to the bed stand and picked up the framed photograph. She hurled it toward him with all her might. She missed her mark. The frame slammed against the bedroom wall, the glass bursting into tiny shards.

Seth bent down and picked up the frame. He knocked the remaining glass out and pulled the picture free. Slowly, he ripped it into little pieces and let them flutter to the floor. "I never want to see you again." He started away.

"Go on. Run to Hannah. But you'll never have with her what I could give you. She doesn't know you like I do. I understand your pain, and I know how you think, Seth. We have a lot more in common than you realize. Did Hannah ever watch you cry like a baby knowing you wanted to end your life and if she left you alone, you'd blow your brains out?"

The door slammed behind him.

She fell to her knees and covered her face with her hands. "Seth!" She balled her hands into fists.

This would be the last time Seth New or anyone pushed her away because she wasn't good enough. She was better than this. She'd made a mistake or two, but she was not the kind of person who would destroy two people she loved. Mickey and Penny didn't deserve what she had plotted for them.

India remembered her attacker's smug sneer as he hovered over her, taunting her with her bad reputation. All the while, she had wished the dirt would enfold her, take her away from Serenity forever.

"We're going to survive. It's you and me, kiddo." She never imagined a child born of such ugliness could become the most important part of her life. She might have gone about it all wrong, but everything she'd done since she'd learned of her pregnancy had been meant to keep the child inside her safe from the monster who was its father. Still, seeking to destroy Mickey's marriage for her own gain ...? She stood, keeping her hand poised over her small, swollen stomach. All her life, she'd been selfish, looking out for what best served her.

Tomorrow, she'd start doing things the right way, take responsibility for her child, and right the wrongs she'd done to her friends.

And Seth—she'd forgive him.

Someday, maybe he'd forgive her, too.

Chapter Nine

Blanchie stood in her hall behind the stair railing, out of Andy's view as he sat on the porch swing. Would she awake to find this evening had only been one fantastic, out-of-reach dream? Well, standing there wouldn't make the dream any better.

Andy smiled as she pushed open the screen door and concentrated on placing one foot in front of the other, careful not to spill the beverage and make a fool of herself in front of her debonair date.

Compared to Andre Ryan, Luke was Huckleberry Finn.

No. No. No. Why couldn't she just push thoughts of Luke aside for two minutes?

"I enjoyed dinner." Hadn't she already said that, maybe three times now? She sat beside him.

"Thank you for joining me." He ignored her repetition, his politeness shining through as it had the entire evening.

From which of her Christian romances had she borrowed him? Absolutely none. She was in the secular aisle, flirting with danger. Andy was no more obedient to God's will than Luke.

And just like that Luke returned, standing between them like a ghost from her past. But Luke was no ghost. He was flesh and blood—handsome and manly.

Andy's warm hand brushed against hers as he took the glass, and Blanchie pushed aside thoughts of his spiritual condition along with her memories of her ex.

She focused her attention on the street while sipping her tea. Andy did the same. She recalled the way his brown eyes danced when he teased her and the turn of his lips when he had smiled at something she said. The simple but determined kiss he had given her on Luke's boat the previous evening would linger with her forever.

If only he'd put his arm around her or at least touch her hand, anything to assure her this would not be their last date. Words formed in her mind, but they failed to come forth with any intelligence, something to make him want to stay. "Your restaurant is very …"

"Snobbish," he teased.

Blanchie brought a closed fist against her leg. They'd already had this conversation as well, her attempt to laugh off the fact she'd never eaten anywhere as fancy as The Billows. Why was she so nervous? Taking a deep breath, she turned, closing the distance between them. "No. Elegant."

The lime in his aftershave tickled her nose as it had done all evening, and her desire for him took over every sense God had given her.

He turned toward her, resting his arm on the back of the swing. His hand brushed the strands of hair falling from her French braid, and Blanchie leaned into his touch.

"If The Billows is elegant, it still doesn't do you justice."

She stared into his eyes. If possible, they had grown softer.

"You are a very beautiful woman."

Blanchie had taken every effort to dress so he would notice, choosing a slender black skirt with a matching jacket. She spent hours on her hair and applied her makeup to perfection, all for Andy Ryan, to hear him say those words.

"Thank you." She reached up to brush his long hair away from the side of his face. "Remember when I told you your hair wasn't stylish?

"Uh-huh."

"I stand corrected. It suits you."

"I'm thinking of having it cut again." He drank his tea and placed the glass on the wooden porch floor. She handed him her glass, and while he lowered it next to his, she situated herself more comfortably in the swing. He straightened. "I know a nice shop in town where the stylist does a great job. Think she'll cut it for me?"

"If that's what you want."

"I want …" He leaned toward her. "To kiss you. I've wanted to kiss you since we left this porch for dinner."

Blanchie smiled. "I've wanted you to kiss me."

His lips brushed against hers, and then he hesitated. When she moved against him, he pulled her close. He released a soft sigh, and she rested her head against his shoulder.

"Am I too forward, Andy?"

He laughed soft and low. "You're the least forward woman I've ever known."

She pulled away from him. "Do you mean other women have asked you out and begged you to kiss them?"

"All the time." He shrugged.

Was he joking? Somehow, she doubted it. His words flowed like simple truth.

"Is that how this happened?" he asked.

"I asked you on this date. I practically left you no choice."

"I had a choice." Again, he caressed her hair.

"You're not just being polite?"

He shook his head. "I value my friendship with Luke. That's why I didn't ask you out. So, I'm very happy you took the initiative."

"Luke doesn't have any say in it."

"He cares a great deal for you."

"Don't bring him here," she whispered. "It's too perfect."

But Luke was here, his memory standing in the shadows, waiting to pounce. In all her life, Luke had been her everything.

"Come here." Andy made her settle into his arms once again.

Blanchie breathed in the scent of his aftershave. His kiss against her hair sent shivers up her spine and quickened her heartbeat. Is this how Luke felt in the arms of all those women who'd come between them with his cheating?

When had she last felt this way? Not since high school. Not since ... No, she again put up the blockade, refusing to allow Luke to invade this moment. Her ex-husband represented the past. This date was with Andy, and she wanted to go on another.

She was being silly. Andy wasn't from Serenity. He'd traveled the world. Didn't he talk about his worldwide trips as if it were no big deal to jump on a plane? She'd never left the South. Huckleberry Finn was more her speed, but what would she do if Andy never wanted to see her again?

"Blanchie, can we be honest?"

She pulled from his embrace and prepared to counteract his verbal punch. "Andy, I know you don't want me to think this is leading anywhere. I'm not some naïve girl who believes a first date is next to a marriage proposal." She hated lying. Why, then, did this tactic of self-preservation come so naturally to her?

"I understand. You're not ready. You and Luke still have issues."

She and Luke would always have issues.

"I don't want to be the one who catches you on the rebound."

"What?" She uttered a half laugh.

"I may be out of line asking you this."

"Go on." Amusement vanished, and in its place stood overwhelming optimism.

"Are you on the rebound?" His gaze would not release her.

"If I said yes?"

"I'd leave now."

"If I said no?"

He turned his head slightly and bent toward her. As if thinking twice, he inched away again to look into her eyes. She allowed him to see all of her emotions there, and he tugged her to him and kissed her long and hard. She wrapped her arms around him, wanting to hold him there forever. When he put space between them, she refused to release him, holding his strong forearm in her grasp. He'd saved her from lying about his question by not demanding an answer, but the outcome was worth it.

"Andy, I don't want this date to end." She looked into his eyes. "And yes, when it does, I want to do it again." She released her hold. "See how forward you make me."

"I wouldn't like you any other way." Again, he settled back, Blanchie in his arms, words unspoken.

The ringing of the phone intruded on their moment. "Let it alone." Andy kissed her hair.

"It's late. Something could have happened." Unable to erase the habits of the days when she worried for Luke, she ran inside and answered.

"Blanchie, Penny there?" Mickey asked.

"No, Mick. I haven't seen her. Why wouldn't she be with you?" She paced, mobile phone in her hand. Then she ducked and looked out her closed window, holding up her index finger to beg Andy to wait for her.

"I—I've made a terrible mistake. India …"

Blanchie straightened, thankful for the wall that kept her from falling.

"I messed up with India, Blanchie."

With India that could only mean one thing. "How could you? Are you an idiot?"

All the times Mickey had counseled Luke, and now he had fallen as well.

Silence stretched between them until Blanchie blinked back to reality, trying with all her might to get a grip, to prevent an emotional downslide. Seldom in life's tragedies had she been able to empathize with others, but she could feel her sister's pain all the way to her core. Broken trust could shatter a heart into near nothingness, leaving you to pick up the splinters and go on with life.

Mickey hadn't spoken, and Blanchie steeled her voice, thankful that Andy could not hear this family drama. "You don't have to answer. You are an idiot. When did Penny leave?"

"I don't know. An hour, maybe two."

Footsteps on her porch told her Andy was drawing near, but when he stood in front of her door and then started toward the porch steps, Blanchie's gaze followed him. Penny stood at the base of the porch, carrying an overnight bag, her red hair wind-tossed, her eyes moist with tears, and her nose rosy as if she had cried for hours.

"Are you okay?" Andy asked, helping Penny up the steps.

"Mickey, she's here. I'll call you back." Blanchie slammed her phone down on the foyer table and flew to the porch. "Oh, honey." She engulfed her sister in her arms. "He just told me."

"He told you about India?" Penny cried.

Blanchie cast a glance toward Andy. "Yes, honey. He told me."

"Is everything all right?" Andy asked.

Even in the midst of turmoil, she found his clumsiness with the situation endearing, the first misstep he'd taken all night.

Blanchie released Penny and moved toward her date. "They've had a fight," she whispered. "As much as I hate—"

"No." He caressed her cheek. "She's not well. You take care of her."

"She's upset. That's all."

He bent and kissed her one last time. "If you need me, you know my number."

"I do." She hated to see him go, hated that life had intruded on the first bit of happiness she'd had since her splintered heart separated from Luke, but her sister needed her. "Good night, Andre."

Andy stopped. He said nothing for a moment. If possible, she thought both desire and pain flickered in his eyes. "Only you ..." He pointed at her. "Only you can get away with calling me by that name."

Darkness greeted Andy as he entered the home through the

back door. John's place had become so familiar to him that he didn't need a light to walk the hall leading past the kitchen to the left and the dining room to the right. At the end of the long entryway, the house opened up into a large room. To the left lay a comfortable living room. To the right, John had created a study complete with shelves lined with law books and an occasional good read. An upstairs light offered soft illumination as Andy climbed the steps.

Every man dreamed of a woman like Blanchie—sweet, funny, engaging, charming. He could easily fall in love with her.

When she called him Andre, it opened new worlds to him. Her voice caressed his ears. Not since before the death of his mother had his proper name been spoken without hatred lacing the sharp voice spat between his father's sneering lips.

"You're home early," John spoke, and Andy jumped.

"Scare me half to death, will you." He stopped in front of his brother's opened bedroom door.

John sat in bed, his laptop open. Sensing his brother had awaited his return, Andy entered. "What did you do tonight?"

"Worked."

Andy leaned against the footboard of John's bed. "I trust with Emilee coming tomorrow you'll work less."

"What'd you and Blanchie do?"

"Dinner. And I walked her home."

John turned the computer. A picture filled the screen. Andy edged nearer as if pulled by a magnet. He smiled. "That's Em's favorite picture."

John touched the screen. Andy had snapped the photograph of Emilee and John building a sand castle. Between them, a small girl played. They had stopped on the beach at the little one's request.

She had wanted someone to play with her. Andy had captured the moment perfectly. The child beamed at the camera, a real little ham, while Emilee and John gazed into each other's eyes.

In a moment not too dissimilar to this one, Emilee had gazed upon the photo in much the same way John was doing. "Do you know why I love this picture?" she'd asked. "Because of the love in John's eyes." She'd touched the photograph over John's face. "When I look at this picture, I know with all my heart your brother loves me."

"She loved me back then." John broke through Andy's memories. "Can you give me that?"

"She has always loved you, John, even when you least deserved it." Andy walked out the door. John had destroyed his marriage to Emilee. How did he expect Andy to give that back to him?

Andy walked to his own room where he sat on his bed and stared at his image in the mirror. Even though he accepted Emilee's love for John, the woman never left his mind, and without a doubt, she never left John's heart.

The phone rang, and Andy grabbed it. Maybe Blanchie needed him after all. "Hello."

"Johnny?"

Not Blanchie, but Andy smiled. "No, Em."

The line clicked. John had picked up. The mistrusting pain in the rear.

"Andy, John's told you?" Emilee started.

"We'll be seeing you tomorrow."

"My plane arrives at two o'clock," she advised.

"We'll meet you."

"I arranged for a rental." Was it his imagination or was her voice strained? Didn't she want to be with them?

"Do you need John?"

"No. I don't want him to say something that will make me regret my decision. But I'm coming whether he wants me there or not."

Holding the phone, he moved to the door and closed it, although it didn't make a difference.

"I hope he isn't working too hard." She sighed.

"He's in his room now." And he was listening in, but Em knew that. This wasn't the first time they'd played this game.

"I'm sacrificing my pride, Andy. Do you think John will appreciate it?"

"I know he will."

"I love him." Good words for his brother to hear. "I just want to see his face. I thought before he left here I couldn't stand to see the contempt in his eyes any longer, but this separation has to end."

"I'm glad one of you is taking the step to end the breach."

"I used to think practicing medicine was so important, but I've learned my marriage—my husband—should be my main focus. I've asked God to put us back together again."

God? Was every woman he knew familiar with this invisible entity? He had never known Emilee to pray. As far as he was aware, Emilee hadn't stepped into a church since the summer after prep school when she'd stay with her teacher—Della Croix. He often had to wait until the afternoon to see her when he visited on Sundays because of the woman's insistence that Emilee attend church with her.

Enough with these God thoughts.

"I think if John wanted to, he would tell you he loves you very much."

Silence filled the line. Three desperate people treading water. John failed to take the lifeline Andy had tossed to him.

Andy's head started to ache, an indication he would soon have a migraine. "He loves you, and so do I." Let John hear that. If his little brother didn't understand how much he cared about both of them, John could suffer.

"I love you, too," she whispered.

"You okay, Em?"

Emilee took a deep breath. "He can push me away a million times over, but I'll never let him go. I've fought most of my marriage for him, Andy. I'm not going to end the war with a loss."

Not that John would ever let her go—the possessive jerk.

"Andy, some things are going to come out—truths that will hurt you. I won't let lies stand between John and me any longer. He never tells the truth, not even to you. When I get there, I'm talking to John. I'm telling him everything I know."

"Em, what did John lie about?"

Over her phone, the doorbell rang. "Andy, I have to go."

"It's late for visitors, isn't it? Let me hold on while you answer. Where's the doorman?"

"Who knows? He's still as unreliable as ever. I'll be okay, though. Some of the staff from the hospital heard about my resignation. I gave one of them my entrance key. They wanted to say good-bye."

"Don't stay up too late. Love you." Andy held the receiver until he heard one click, then the other. He fell into bed, his headache lingering along with his thoughts of Emilee. Then he drifted off to sleep remembering Blanchie's beautiful eyes and the touch of her lips against his.

FAY LAMB

Chapter Ten

Penny stared into the darkness beyond the window of her childhood bedroom. She never liked the dark. Only since her marriage had she slept without a nightlight.

Since her wedding night, she'd never slept away from Mickey.

India? God, why her?

Why anyone?

The door hinge squeaked as it had always done, and Blanchie entered. Penny could see her in the reflection of the window. Blanchie closed the door and stood with her back against it. What was her little sister thinking? Was she happy Mickey wasn't the perfect man Penny thought she'd married? He was just as flawed as Luke.

"Sissy, can I get you anything?"

Sissy. Blanchie used that name only when she pitied her. Penny didn't need sympathy. She needed a gun with two bullets. One for Mickey and the other for India.

"No, I'm fine." She wouldn't cry another tear over this mess.

"We both know that's not true."

"Don't!"

"Don't what? Care? I love you. I don't like to see you hurting." Blanchie stepped toward her.

Penny held up her hand. "Don't dole out your pity on me. I

don't need it."

Blanchie stopped. "I just want to help."

"If you want to help me, then answer some questions for me. You're an expert on cheating husbands." She hadn't slapped her sister, but Blanchie's head jerked back as if she'd been struck.

"If I can."

"Wasn't I good enough for him? Did he need someone with more experience? Did I do something wrong?"

"Those are questions I still ask myself today. I don't know why Luke did the things he did. I just know I got tired of trying to be what I thought he wanted. I turned my life over to God."

"And divorced him—God never said to divorce him, Blanchie."

Blanchie shook her head. Words formed on her lips, but at first, Penny heard only a few mumbled phrases. Then Blanchie straightened. "No, God didn't tell me to divorce Luke. Melvin was my pastor as well as my father-in-law. He loves Luke and me. He sat us down, and Luke wasn't ready to do what his father asked of him—what God required of him. He didn't want to save our marriage. Melvin said Luke's carelessness could cost my health. He suggested we separate, and when Luke continued to cheat on me, Melvin suggested a more drastic step." Tears crept into Blanchie's voice. "The separation was never meant to be permanent, but after I got away from the hell Luke made of our lives, I couldn't go back. I prayed and prayed for him to come around."

"You don't divorce!" Penny screamed. "God doesn't say divorce."

"No, but if I hadn't divorced him, I'd be a widow today, or I might even be dead myself. He slept around, Penny. And he came back to me, and like a fool, I so easily forgave him and let him have his way with our money, with our lives, with me. I haven't seen him drunk in months. No. God doesn't say divorce, but he can turn my mistake around and make a blessing from it."

"I don't care. I really don't care."

"So, I suppose you're going to forgive and forget. Go back to him and let him use you."

"I don't know what I'm going to do. I don't know how long he's been with India. How many times they've—how close they are—when he plans to leave me."

"He's not leaving you." Blanchie crossed her arms. At least the pity was gone. Anger stood in its place.

"That feeling of intense love or just lust, it's powerful."

"He doesn't love India. What man in their right mind would think she's worth loving?"

"I felt that power tonight." For the first time since Blanchie entered, Penny turned from the reflection to face her sister. "I used to actually think I could hate John Ryan. Until today. He drove me to the mainland to see Dr. Giller. John, not Mickey, was with me when I learned I'm pregnant. I saw a different side of him. He was kind and thoughtful. He listened to me."

Blanchie's eyes filled with tears she somehow managed to keep from falling. "You're pregnant?"

Penny nodded. "Before I came here, I sat on the rocks overlooking the Gulf on the Ryan property. The thought of John joining me intoxicated me. My body hasn't tingled like that since before ..." She paused to keep her vow. No more tears for her. "I saved myself for Mickey, letting those feelings build until our honeymoon." She would not cry. "I would have allowed John Ryan to release those feelings if he'd given me a chance."

"You can't mean that." Blanchie gasped. "Penny, you've got to stop thinking like that. It's in the heart where lust begins, and if you're not careful, it turns into action."

"Stop your worrying. John wouldn't. He's married."

The shock on Blanchie's face pleased Penny. "From the look on your face, I can see that your date hasn't told you."

"That's his business. One date doesn't mean you tell your family's entire history." Blanchie started toward the door.

"You know," Penny stopped her with her words, "I'd feel better if Mickey had died."

"Penny!" Blanchie spun toward her. "Don't talk like that. Even after all Luke's done, all those nights I spent awake, listening for him to come home, I was scared to death a highway trooper would knock on my door and tell me he'd been killed in an accident."

"Or by some woman's husband."

Blanchie stared at her for a long moment. She huffed out a sigh. "I'm not your punching bag; I'm your sister, and I love you very much. You're angry at Mickey, and I understand I'm the closest person to you, but if you say one more thing like that to me tonight, or ever, I'll kick you out on the street."

Penny lowered her head. "I'm sorry, Sissy."

Now, who pitied whom? From the moment she married Luke, Blanchie had talked of nothing but having a child. Penny hadn't missed Blanchie's reaction to the news about the baby. Penny's words stung her sister, bringing those tears to her eyes. By God's grace, Blanchie had never gotten pregnant, but Blanchie wouldn't see it that way. She'd often mentioned how a child would fill the void left by Luke's unfaithfulness.

Blanchie was wrong. With this child inside her, the void

threatened to turn into a black hole and swallow Penny alive.

"I'm sorry, too." Blanchie's arms went around her. "What are you going to do?"

Penny pulled out of Blanchie's embrace. "I'm going to get on my knees, and I'm going to pray. I'm going to ask God to forgive me for thinking of John Ryan. I'm going to ask Him why my husband thought so little of the vows he made to God and to me. Then I'm going to pray for God to direct the paths of my child, my husband, and me." She walked past Blanchie to retrieve the suitcase she'd left by the bedroom door.

"I admire you for being so strong."

Losing in her battle not to cry, Penny swiped at the tears falling down her cheeks. "I've given Mickey everything I have. What do I do now?"

"You pray. You shower. You sleep. You wait on God." Blanchie brushed Penny's hair back from her face. "If you only do the first three steps, you'll end up like me."

Within his dream, the lights on the stage nearly blinded Andy, and he turned away from them. Loud and obnoxious music flowed through the core of his being. In his teenage years, Andy had used the music to escape the truth of his life. He had penned the tunes and sat in the garage for hours, the chords blaring throughout the estate. He had hoped his father would challenge him.

When Andy played heavy metal, something indescribable gripped his soul. If Zack Ryan had approached Andy after he had worked himself into a frenzy, his father would have met a formidable foe, and not the cowering youth Andy became. After a while, when Zack failed to take the bait, Andy gave up his music and concentrated on life in the real world.

Now, the music he created so long ago haunted him in his recurring nightmare. He placed his hands over his ears and tried to shut out the noise, but he couldn't block the sound. At the touch on his shoulder, he pulled away, crouching from the figure he knew stood beside him. The touch came again, and Andy whirled around to confront the enemy.

As always, a figure in a monk's cloak towered over him, but when Andy stared up into the creature's face, he met only void and nothingness, a black hole. A bony hand stretched out and pointed. Andy turned and saw the familiar scene from his past. The dream always carried him along the same path. "This isn't fair. I can't win. I never win."

The creature pushed him forward, and Andy planted his feet, refusing to step closer. The next push proved more forceful, and Andy fell to his knees. The lights around him dimmed. When he looked up, he stared into the frightened brown eyes of his little brother. Seven-year-old John stood outside the door to their mother's room.

"I'm scared," John cried.

"I know, buddy." Andy stood.

"I want Momma." John's chin trembled.

From behind the door, their mother's pleas for their father to stop his beating of her began. Andy closed his eyes. This time he would allow John to scream.

Lightning lit the stage and a burst of thunder drowned out the incessant blaring music. Against his will, Andy clasped his hand over John's mouth, cutting off the scream that should have pealed against the storm outside.

The doorknob turned, and Andy pushed John behind him where his younger brother crouched in fear. The door opened, and Andy stared into eyes empty of any emotion. Zack Ryan reached out and grabbed Andy by the arm.

John shrank back against the wall, out of their father's sight.

Zack pulled Andy into the room. "She fell, Andre. She fell." His father shook him. "Your life and the life of your brother and your precious little Emilee depend upon her falling. Do you understand what I'm saying to you? Do you, Andre?"

Why couldn't he just say it? He tried, but the thoughts failed to meet with his voice. *I'll tell everyone what you've done. Murderer. I'll keep us together. I'll find a way.*

"Answer me." Zack shook Andy so hard his teeth bit his tongue.

Andy tasted the blood. He looked into his father's eyes intending to tell him he would never let him do this to him again. "Yes, sir," he whispered.

The music turned up a notch. Andy winced as a loud bell sounded above the din around him. The cloaked figure raised his bony hand and pointed to the scoreboard above his head. For the first time in his life, he noticed the name of the being controlling his nightmare. God received the first point. A zero remained under Andy's name. So, this was the god in whom Blanchie placed so much faith and to whom Emilee petitioned for John's love. This god had controlled Andy's life and made it a living hell for the last time. If the prize was this entity's banishment, he would win.

Andy turned back to face the next stage of the game. He blocked out the thunder of bass and treble and concentrated on the waters flowing in the fountain appearing before him. Emilee stood on the other side of the pool. He turned back toward the creature. "We don't have to go any further. I win this round. Her love for John doesn't bother me any longer. Next round."

The creature's bony finger jabbed the air several times in the direction of Emilee. Andy turned back in time to see John wrap her in his arms. Andy closed his eyes against the feelings of unbearable loss engulfing his soul. When he opened them again, he watched as John kissed Emilee for the very first time with passion, which Andy could tell had been pent up inside his brother for some time. "I love you, Emilee. I love you so much, babe," John declared.

"I said I win this round." Andy forced a smile that vanished as his thoughts flashed across the bottom of the scoreboard. *I could have protected her much better than you, John. Zack hurt her, and you never noticed.* A second win posted for the god controlling his life.

Andy braced himself for the rest of the game. His life depended upon it. Voluntarily, he opened the door that appeared before him and stepped into the apartment he had shared with John and Emilee. They were newly married and unable to make ends meet. In retaliation for Emilee's marriage to John, Zack refused to support Emilee's schooling. John took on two jobs and his school to help Emilee pursue her dream. Seeing them struggle to maintain their jobs and their studies, Andy had moved into their apartment to help alleviate some of the burden. "Hey, Cameron." He smiled at his best friend already standing in the living room.

"Andy," Cameron Matrai greeted.

"Where's Em?"

Cameron nodded in the direction of the bedroom. A familiar sound reached Andy's ears and just as quickly, Emilee cried out. Andy cast a look at Cameron. A slight smile turned his friend's lips. Andy ran toward the room.

His father stood over a fallen Emilee as she cringed close to the bed. Andy grabbed his father's arm and twisted it behind his back while at the same time pushing him out of the bedroom. "I'll kill you, old man. If you ever touch her again, I'll kill you. You will never do to her what you did to my mother."

Behind him, Emilee emerged, her hand covering her already swollen cheek.

"Get out of here." Andy pushed his father forward. Zack fell against Cameron who prevented the older man from falling.

Emilee pressed a warm hand around his upper arm and gave a slight squeeze. "Make him leave, too. I don't want Cameron here."

"Go, Cameron. Emilee's upset. I'll call you later."

Above him, the loud ringing began. Andy looked up to see the cloaked figure again score a win.

"No," he argued. "I stopped him. Zack never hit her again."

The hood over the creature's void face moved in slow motion, side to side, in refusal of Andy's plea.

"He never hurt her again. You're a god. You know it's true. You know everything. I win this one. Put up the score for me."

Again, the creature refused.

Andy swallowed the truth before admitting it. "It's not Zack. You don't mean Zack. You're saying Cameron. That's not true. Cameron's my friend. He wouldn't hurt Emilee. I want this win."

The bony finger once again pointed, and Andy turned. Nothing hindered his walking toward the coffin appearing before him in the funeral home. He looked inside and allowed the relief to wash over him. Zack had died quickly and too easily. The heart attack hit him in the middle of a board meeting—a stockholder's conference at which John refused to accept a seat on his board, opting instead to remain with his law firm where his star had risen quickly.

He heard sobbing. John sat in the pew in front of the coffin. Andy sat beside him and pulled John close. "Let it go, buddy. Let it go."

John continued to cry like a child, reminding Andy of the small boy outside their mother's room. John didn't remember what Zack had done to their mother. Andy could excuse John's grief only by reminding himself that John had been too young to understand. Andy never wanted his brother to remember that night.

Andy looked to the side door. Emilee stood just outside the room. She turned and caught his stare. Tears flowed down her beautiful face. His heart pounded as he turned to look at the scoreboard. The creature had four points to his zero. His gaze again fell upon Emilee. She stretched empty arms toward her husband. All the while, John sat with his back stiff and turned away from her. Emilee won the first battle for John with her love, but Zack conquered with his death.

Andy conceded the win. He stepped away from the scene like a dutiful soldier. "I'm ready." He indicated, and after a moment's darkness, a new room appeared. Andy walked inside and stared out the windows of the high-rise office he inherited after his father's death. He couldn't allow John to give up his position at the law firm. Someone had to run the company and doing both would take John away from Emilee.

Still, each day, he stared down at Broadway below him, wishing for a return of his old life, managing one of the fine establishments there. "I won't cry. You can't make me."

"Mr. Ryan, you have a call on line one," the voice sounded over the intercom.

Andy answered the phone on his desk. A smile crossed his face as his friend's voice greeted him. "Really? Man, that'll be a blowout. I'd love to go. It'll be like old home week at the restaurant. Let me check my calendar." He flipped through the book on his desk and stopped at a date. "No can do." He swallowed. "I have a meeting in Paris. No. I can't miss it. No. I've already discussed it with John. He doesn't know anything about the Paris division. Sorry, Cameron."

Andy hung up the phone. In one swift motion, he knocked everything from the desk. "I hate you, John. This is not my life. I want nothing to do with Zack's work."

John pushed into the room seeming oblivious to Andy's distress and the mess he'd made. "Thirty-five percent, Andy. That's what Dad left you."

Andy stared at him. "I don't believe you."

"Well, these prove it." John laid several certificates of stock on the desk. Andy's name appeared in bold letters on each document.

"You hold them, John. I wanted nothing from the old man." *Nothing but his love, but he didn't have any to give me. It all belonged to you.*

"Andy." Hurt filled John's dark eyes. "I'm sorry you had to do this. I'll make it up to you."

Andy lowered his head. "Just keep making Emilee happy, and it'll all work out. You can't leave the law firm. You've worked too hard."

This round could go either way, and he wasn't surprised when the creature received another point. John had stopped making Emilee happy. Everything Andy had sacrificed meant nothing to his brother.

"You win. Let me go." He spoke to the god controlling him. Traditionally, the nightmare ended here.

The hood nodded forward, and Andy caught his breath as he faced the unknown. The heavy metal music resounded, causing Andy's head to pound. His heart thumped in his chest, and sweat broke out on his forehead. Terror gripped him, held him firm. He stood now in John's law office in Serenity. The back of John's chair greeted him, and the cloak of the monster rose above the high seat. He could handle most everything else. This dream was as much a part of him as his soul, but the master now pushed him further into worlds he didn't want to explore. He couldn't face losing, not in this place he now considered home—not in Serenity, free of all the troubles of the past.

The chair turned. The creature lifted his bony hand to the hood keeping his face in darkness. He pulled it away slowly as he stood. "I won, Andre. I always win." His father's evil laughter mixed with the very music Andy had created in rebellion against him.

Andy screamed and bolted upright in his bed. Sweat soaked his hair, and he searched the room, making sure he was completely out of the nightmare. He closed his eyes against the pain in his temples. Taking a very deep breath, he stood and made it into his bathroom. Opening the medicine cabinet, he fumbled for the prescription he knew would offer him relief. His fingers found the covered syringe, the only help for his cluster migraines.

The pain blinded him. A light would do no good. He popped the lid from the needle and hesitated. Leaning hard against the sink, he sobbed. "Why can't you just leave me alone, Zack?"

Without taking the injection, he threw the needle hard against the far wall and heard it fall into the ceramic tub as he fell to his knees and vomited into the toilet.

Chapter Eleven

Blanchie listened outside Penny's bedroom door. She couldn't hear a sound. Penny had finally drifted off to sleep.

Her phone rang, and Blanchie rushed downstairs to answer, picking it up from the table where she'd left it earlier. "Hello."

"Is she okay?" Mickey asked.

"No, you idiot. She's not okay." Blanchie leaned against the banister.

"She's pregnant?"

"She says she is, Mick, and you're a wonderful husband to care, especially now that you've taken all her joy away."

Mickey's heavy sigh came across the lines. "I want to talk to her."

"She needs to rest. I'll tell her you asked about her and the baby. She thinks you're protecting India, and you couldn't care less about the baby she's carrying."

"I tried to protect Penny."

If he were in front of her, she'd slap his face. "You wanted to protect yourself, and you know it."

"You may be right, but I care for my child. I care for my children."

The pain in Blanchie's soul deafened the click of the phone

line. *Twins. Oh, Lord, forgive me. Penny's having two babies to love, and I only wanted one—one little boy or girl to stave off the loneliness of Luke's rejection. Please take my jealousy away.*

She pushed the screen door open and walked onto her porch. The glasses she and Andy drank from earlier remained under the swing.

An October breeze cooled the air. Nature teased Serenity at times. While getting ready for her date with Andy, she'd heard something about a late-season tropical depression—or was it a storm? Big difference. She'd have to remember to ask Luke. He could out-forecast the weatherman.

Even when he was the cause of the storm.

"Stop it." The last two areas she wanted to focus upon were the weather and her ex-husband. She also wanted to separate herself from Penny's problems. Before Mickey's first call when Penny had appeared on her porch steps, she'd enjoyed a wonderful date. Holding to the swing's chain, she lowered herself onto the seat.

She wanted to think about Andy Ryan. He gave a new meaning to an enchanted evening.

Luke stood out of view, watching Blanchie as she rocked in the porch swing. He'd love to travel with her wherever she was right now. Only, he'd forfeited his ticket.

When she stood and started inside, he stepped forward. "Hey."

"Luke." She opened the screen door. "It's late, isn't it?"

He followed her down the front hall, past the stairs, and into the kitchen. "Yeah, listen. Is Penny here?"

She nodded. Luke despised this wall between them. Once upon a time, she shared everything with him—his favorite little gossip.

"She okay?"

"She's fine. She's asleep."

People he loved were hurting, and he hated it. "Mickey messed up, huh?"

She placed the glasses in the sink and turned, leaning her back against the counter, one eyebrow raised. "Yeah, he did."

He didn't move. The tea cart by the archway was a safe distance from her. He stayed there. He'd always known they would eventually come to this. Too much separated them, and Blanchie deserved answers. As divorces went, theirs had been civil. Yeah, he'd done everything she listed in her Petition for Dissolution of Marriage. No, she didn't want to reconcile—not until he changed. And he hadn't been agreeable to the changes she wanted to see in him. Until recently.

"And?" she coaxed. "What do you have to say about that?"

"Been there. Done that more than once."

"Yes, you have." She shook her head, and he winced.

Blanchie never admitted to him she knew the entire truth. Even in the divorce, the intimate details, the names of the women, all his vices, went unspoken.

"Did Mickey call you? Is that how you knew?" she asked.

"Yeah, he sounded frantic. He thought maybe she came to see me."

Blanchie scowled at him "I hope he didn't call every home on the island."

"No." Luke examined the palm of his hand. Maybe he'd get out of this situation without a confrontation. "He called me and said he was calling you. I don't know why he thought Penny might seek me out."

"He was afraid. It's nice to know he can turn to you." The open disdain lacing her voice completed her obvious, unspoken thought that she never could.

Luke chose to ignore her. "Man, he's in a pickle." If he'd done this to Blanchie, he would never be able to stand before her now. When he'd been unable—no, unwilling—to give her a child, if another woman had carried his baby because of his carelessness, any shred of civility they held now would have unraveled.

"Why did he turn to India?"

Luke swallowed hard. The truth in big bites was hard to chew, but he could no longer avoid the subject of his infidelity. "Why did I turn to other women, Blanchie?"

She gasped. This cleansing himself of his sins was a part of his self-rehabilitation. Still, he had to remember to deal a little more gently with her.

"Because I wasn't enough." She turned from him and ran her slender fingers across the dishtowel folded and lying on the counter.

He nodded though she couldn't see. He didn't want to hurt her with his words. She was everything, but she still hadn't been enough.

As if she read his mind, she spoke, "I don't understand. I tried so hard to be everything you needed."

If he could only take her in his arms and reassure her that he loved her now more than he'd ever loved her, but she would kick and scratch in an attempt to avoid his pity. He pulled out a chair and sat at the small kitchen table, the one he'd made, the one that used to sit in his cabin where they lived before the divorce. He ran his hand over the wood. He'd sure love to have them back—the table and Blanchie.

"You have nothing to say?" she demanded.

"What can I tell you?" He lifted his gaze to her, determined to face the music, but she had her back to him, busying herself with the dishes. "How was your date?" he asked.

"Andy behaved like a gentleman just as the two of you agreed he would." She still did not turn to him.

"Good."

"You know he didn't ask me out. I asked him," she taunted.

"I heard. I saw." Luke hadn't wanted to hear. He hated seeing their kiss. He played with the salt and pepper shakers on the table. She had snagged them along with the table when she left him. "When you kissed him, I wanted to wring your neck and his."

"But …?" She swung around.

Now he had her attention. "Even though I think that in the eyes of God you're still my wife, it would have been a little hypocritical, don't you think?" He raised his eyebrows.

She started to open her mouth, but then she pursed it tightly, staring at him for long seconds before shaking her head, a familiar reaction for him. His little gossip did know how to hold her tongue on occasion, especially when it came to defending herself. "Who are you seeing now?" she finally asked.

Still toying with the shaker, he tilted his head. He readied for her reaction. "I haven't seen anyone since a month before the divorce became final."

"Not because of me?" She dried her hands, walked toward him, pulled out a chair, and sat. The look on her face dared him to step into the deep waters she pulled them toward.

"Yes, because of you." He locked his gaze with hers. All the times before, when he had lied, she'd known because he couldn't look her in the eyes. He would never lie to her again. "Since I can't have you, I don't want anyone else."

She shook her head. "You know, if you had only given up the gambling, the drinking, and the women, we'd still be together."

"I'm glad you left me."

"Luke." She jumped to her feet. Fire lit her eyes, but at the same time, her mouth twitched, and she fought back tears. "Did you come here tonight to torment me?"

"I think you may have saved my life. I had to learn the hard way. Wasn't that your plan all along?"

"So, have you learned?" She softened.

"I have, but I can tell that you're having trouble believing it. Isn't that why you went out with Andy tonight?"

"What?"

"You didn't like the beer sitting on the floor, and when you fell over the case, you were angry with me. Andy was pretty convenient." Yeah, he'd seen it all.

Her fingers grasped the back of the chair in front of her. She picked it up, hesitated, and then set it back down gently.

Luke relaxed. That could have gone one of two ways. Thank goodness, she'd not chosen to bash it over his head.

She bent close to peer into his face. "I asked Andy Ryan out because I'm attracted to him."

"Of course, you're drawn to him. What girl wouldn't be? More than a few women in town have commented on his looks. He's rich. That makes him even more eligible. You ought to see the tokens he tries to keep hidden."

"Jealousy is beneath you, Luke, and you should be ashamed. Andy said your friendship is the only reason he didn't ask me out.

I thought you hated gossip, and I thought you considered Andy your friend."

She always had a way of getting through to him—eventually. The task had grown a little easier since he'd sobered. "True. I owe you an apology." He accepted her reprimand. "Listen, those tokens—the autographed pictures, the presents—he isn't very comfortable with them, if you know what I mean. I only saw them because I helped him put them away in storage at The Billows. And you're right. The only reason I mentioned them is because I am jealous. Not going to hide that from you."

"I know what you mean." She nodded. "And you were right, I don't like the fact you're still drinking. You lied to me. You told me you quit."

"Did you see any opened cans?"

She hesitated. The gears in her mind were turning. "I don't care. You can do what you want."

"No, I can't, not if it means I might lose any hope of you loving me again."

Blanchie studied his face. She once told him his eyes were the color of the Caribbean. If only she would swim in them now.

"I love you," she whispered, cleared her throat, and spoke a little too loud, "You know I love you, but I have to move forward. It's true. I thought when we first divorced you'd come right around and realize what you lost."

"I do."

"That doesn't mean I'm going to drop everything and try to rekindle any kind of relationship with you, Luke. When you'd stay gone, the worry was too much, and many times the relief from my growing terror wasn't your return but Kurt Davis standing on our porch in his uniform, telling me you needed bail money. I'm not putting myself through that again. I can't do it. Can you understand?"

He stood and touched her face. "You keep watching. This old lump of coal you tried to shine up, he's going to be a brilliant gem, like the song says."

"I can't wait." She smiled.

"I hope Penny can forgive Mickey. I know it'll be hard for her. You forgave me for a lot of my indiscretions, but I don't think you would forgive me for bringing a baby into this world by another woman."

Blanchie's smile vanished. "What?"

He thought she'd known. He hated gossiping, and he'd just stumbled into a mess of it. "India's pregnant. Didn't Penny tell you?"

She shook her head. "I don't think she knows."

"He says he doesn't love India. I believe him."

"How can you be so sure?" She planted her hands on her hips. She obviously waited for his answer—one he didn't want to give.

"Do you really want to know?"

"Of course."

"Because, baby, I never loved any of the women I cheated with. I was too stupid to realize it then, but you're my only love. They held my body. You own my heart." He struggled to get his voice above a whisper. "I prayed to God, and I vowed no more women, vowed to be the man you need. Only you. If you don't take me back, I'll live alone with what I've done to us."

She straightened, tugged at the top of that sexy black dress she'd worn for Andy—and not for him. Then she held his gaze. She'd never been one to lie, and Luke was sure that whatever she said would be the truth. "That's a wonderful confession, but don't hold your breath waiting for me to return to you. I can't see you keeping to that vow."

He'd poured out his heart, and the love he had for her failed to flood over the wall she'd built around her heart. What had he expected? His actions had been the cement holding the bricks in place.

He forced on a smile. "Just watch me," he challenged.

She shook her head as if dismissing the thought that he could be faithful. "What is he going to do about India's baby?"

Blanchie's mind would choose to ignore him, but her heart would take it all in, over time, just as it had his infidelity.

"I don't think he knows." He started toward the hall. "Penny." He stopped short, and Blanchie ran into him.

Penny sat on the stairs.

She stared up at him with red, swollen eyes, full of hurt. Her body trembled. "Tell me it's not true, Luke. Tell me she isn't pregnant with his child. I don't think I can stand it if she is."

He moved around the banister to her. "I thought you knew."

"This can't be happening to me. What did I do to deserve this?"

He sat beside her and let her cry against him, holding her close. "You want me to go beat him up? Remember I did that when he pulled your ponytail in third grade. I can do it again if you want."

She looked at him, her green eyes brimming with unshed tears, and he received the smile he hoped his ridiculous remarks would bring.

She leaned back against him, and he rocked her back and forth. "I will, you know."

"I know."

"It would pay him back for the time in fifth grade when he hit me with the rock."

"You deserved that rock." Penny sniffled.

Luke looked at Blanchie.

She stood against the wall, her hand covering her mouth.

"You and I know I deserve most everything I get and don't get." He held his free arm out, and Blanchie moved into his embrace. Two of the most important women in his life were hurting, and he didn't know what to do for them.

Chapter Twelve

John sat on the seat of his bedroom's bay window as the early morning darkness surrendered to light. On his schedule for today: life. Overhearing Emilee's discussion with Andy on the phone last night left him sleepless but exuberant. Her admission to Andy that she would fight for their marriage proved to John the depths of her love. He stared at the empty bed, the one he planned never to lay in alone, not for one more night of his life.

Emilee deserved an explanation for his actions. She told Andy she knew John lied to her, but she hadn't told Andy the extent of those lies. She had to be aware her family was here in Serenity and that John had kept the information from her. Still, she offered him absolution. If she could pardon him, he would forgive her everything, and yes, he'd forgive Andy, too.

John looked at the digital alarm clock. In approximately eight hours and fifty-three minutes, he intended to take Emilee in his arms and beg for her understanding and forgiveness. Then he planned to introduce her to the family she never believed she'd meet.

Out of view, India watched the couple from the foot of the city pier before climbing the steps.

"Get away from me!" Penny stomped her foot down on top of Mickey's.

He winced and pulled back from her. "Penny, we need to talk. Baby, I'm sorry. I don't know what else to do. Tell me. I'll do anything to make it right again."

Penny clenched her fists at her sides as if trying to keep from lashing out at him. "I gave you that chance last night, and you blew it."

"What did you want me to do? Lie?"

"I wanted the truth, Mick, without having to force your hand. You aren't the man I thought I married. That Mickey would tell me if I failed him in our marriage."

"You didn't fail me. I failed you."

"Is there anything else you have to tell me?"

"Penny, I think you need to know something." India moved from the shadows. Lodged in her throat, her heart threatened to cut off her breath. Penny obviously knew about the affair. If Mickey told her about the baby, she needed to tell them both the truth.

"You!" Venom spilled from Penny's lips. "You have the nerve to show up here after what you've done—what you both have done to my marriage!"

Penny's claws slashed toward India, stopped only by Mickey's quick grasp of Penny's wrist. "India, not now."

Penny jerked free. "Keep protecting her. Go on. You do it so well."

"Penny, you have to know the truth." After what she'd done, would Penny ever listen to her?

"You slept with my husband, you tramp. You took something valuable to me and made it worthless."

India glanced toward the street where people stopped and watched with sudden interest. She took a deep breath and accepted her retribution as just and Mickey's undeserved. "Let me explain."

"You need to go." Mickey nodded toward the gathering crowd.

"This is important. Please let me explain."

"Let her have her say, Mick. I'm waiting," Penny baited. "Air out the rest of our dirty laundry, India. Let everyone know you slept with my husband."

A collective gasp came from the onlookers.

"Penny, I'm—" Mickey turned toward his wife. His face met with her open hand, the angry sound eliciting another communal intake of breath.

"Stop it." India tried to move between them. Could she rip her heart into two pieces and hand one to each of the people she'd wronged? "I've hurt you, and I'm sorry. I didn't understand how wrong I was—not until—I don't want this."

"You caused it." Penny started toward her, but again Mickey managed to come between them. He wrapped his arms around his wife and lifted her up, turning her in the opposite direction.

"Go, or I'll let her have you." Mickey threw the words over his shoulder. "Please, just go."

India backed away, and Mickey released Penny, who stormed into the law office. Mickey cast India a stern look of warning and followed his wife.

India turned toward the crowd, aware of how a Christian in the coliseums of Rome might have felt. But she was no Christian. She was the lion that devoured a marriage.

"Tramp," someone hissed.

She stopped and straightened her skirt and blouse. India allowed very few people to see her pain. She wouldn't start now. She'd try again later to explain the truth to Mickey and Penny. "Excuse me." She pushed past the onlookers.

Hoping no one would follow, she moved up the steps leading to the back of David's restaurant. There, out of the sight of those who condemned her, she leaned against the wall fighting for air as sobs racked her body. With eyes closed and head bent, a picture of a story from her teenage years flashed in her memory. How ironic that Mickey's mother had been the one to teach her about the woman caught in adultery and how Jesus had commanded that one without sin should throw the first stone. Then Jesus had stooped down and busied himself writing on the ground.

If I open my eyes, Lord, will You look up at me and ask me where my accusers have gone? I've done something terrible. I'm that woman caught in the very act, and it's not the first time I've done something evil. I believe in You, and that makes me afraid of You. Still, I'm alone, and I have to believe that You aren't going to do something terrible to me. All I have is this baby within me. I've shamed my child and myself. No one will love us now. No one will listen. No one will care.

We love Him because He first loved us.

Dana Parker had long ago assigned the verse to her for memorization, and until this very moment, India never understood its meaning. Opening her eyes, she almost expected to see Christ looking up at her from his writing. Her gaze met only the dock's wooden planks, but she knew God was near enough to touch, yet just out of her reach.

Andy's office door creaked, and he forced his eyes open, raising his head from the couch cushion. He should have taken his medication. In his case, hindsight would have gotten rid of his blurred vision, at least.

"Mr. Ryan." The Billows' hostess scanned the room until her eyes rested curiously on him as he laid there, his head throbbing. Her blue hair spoke of her age, but Maude always wore a smile, and she always had a kind word for everyone who entered his restaurant. "Line two is for you. Said his name is Cameron, and he needs to discuss negotiations for the arms you want him to smuggle into Serenity."

"I'll smuggle his arms." Andy eased his body upward.

"You're a popular man today. Ms. Crum stopped by, but when she saw Ms. Thompson waiting for you, she said to tell you she'd come back later."

"Ms. Thompson?" He staggered to the phone and picked up the receiver, not yet hitting the button with the blinking line. He pressed his thumb and forefinger on each side of his head trying to push the pain in his temples aside so he could recall Ms. Thompson. He snapped his fingers. "Oh, you mean, India. Did she say what she wants?"

The woman shook her head.

"Show her in, and would you mind doing me a big favor?"

"Anything."

"Could you give Ms. Crum a call and ask her if she's free for a late lunch?"

"And if she is?" A twinkle gleamed in the older woman's eyes.

"I'll see her around ..." He brought his watch up before his eyes and tried to focus on the blurred dial. "Let's say one thirty. Thank you, Maude." He pushed the button on the phone as she exited. "I told you the takeover of this island depends upon absolute secrecy," he barked into the phone and wished he'd remembered to keep his animation to a low roar. He held his head, wondering if Cameron's laughter rang as loud and as insincere as it seemed. "What have you been doing? You left here, and I haven't been able to reach you."

"Been busy," the voice boomed. Andy held the phone away from his ear. "How is life in Hickville?"

"Be careful what you say about my town."

Maude pushed the door open, and Andy motioned India to have a seat. "This is good timing, Cameron. Would you like to speak with India?"

"No." The answer resounded both from over the line and in the room. Andy turned away from India, embarrassed. The thought never occurred to him that a misunderstanding with her had brought about Cameron's sudden departure from Serenity Key. It wouldn't be the first time a dalliance caused Cameron to rush out of town.

"Look," Cameron said. "She started getting too serious. What was I supposed to do?"

"No problem. I'm sorry." He looked at India who sat, back stiff and head bowed. When she looked up at him, he mouthed the same apology. He offered her a smile and then spoke to Cameron, "You must be busy. I thought we'd see you a lot more."

"I've been on the road," Cameron advised. "Life isn't so wonderful when you have to sell yourself every day."

"Oh, self-pity doesn't suit you, my friend. The life of an actor, beautiful women telling you how perfect you are. I've been there, and I've seen you in action. A terrible life." Andy rubbed his temples.

India moved as if uncomfortable in her seat.

What a moron. Could he have been any more insensitive?

"You aren't seeing India now, are you?"

"I may be. You never know," Andy teased while trying to remain discreet. Mentioning his date with Blanchie was out of the question. How many women had Cameron stolen from him over the years? Those hadn't mattered, but if Cameron so much as looked at Blanchie, Andy suspected his lifelong friendship with Cameron would end. "Look, I need to go. Why don't you call me at home? Em's flying in today." He looked at his watch. "She's on the plane right now."

"Are you sure? When I saw her last night, she said she wasn't going. She wanted nothing to do with John or even you."

"When I spoke with her late last night, she said she'd be here." Andy held the phone away once again but this time looked at the receiver in disbelief. He put the phone against his ear. "You must have misunderstood."

Andy refused to live with John if Emilee decided to stay in New York. John seemed almost like his old self as they shared coffee this morning. Andy picked up his smartphone from the desk and opened his contacts, locating Luke's number. He might need the carpenter to start right away on the third-floor renovations of the restaurant where Andy planned to take up residence.

He placed his mobile phone on the desk, and for the first time, wondered why Cameron had called him on his business phone.

"I'm sure I did misunderstand." Cameron broke into Andy's plan of escape.

"Must've been you knocking on the door when I was on the phone with Em last night."

Cameron began to cough, and some time elapsed before he spoke. "What?"

"You okay?" Andy laughed.

"Yeah." Cameron cleared his throat. "What did you mean, knocking on the door?"

"When I spoke with Em, someone knocked at the door. She said her friends planned to stop by for a farewell party. I assume you did the knocking."

"Wasn't me." He continued to cough.

"What'd you do, swallow a bug?" Andy smiled once again at India.

"Hope it's poisonous." India looked out the window.

India had spunk. Cameron never liked spirited women.

"You know," Cameron said, "I think she mentioned they were coming over. She must have forgotten to tell you I stopped by. I'm glad she changed her mind."

"So am I." Andy breathed a sigh of relief. "Look, I really have to go. India didn't stop by my office to hear me shoot the balmy Florida breeze with you."

"Be careful, Andy. She'll cling to you like a bougainvillea vine, thorns and all."

"Well, you know me, old friend. I'd be very happy in that situation. I'll tell John and Emilee you called." Andy hung up the phone.

"He's not coming here, is he? I mean, not anytime soon." India scooted to the edge of the chair.

"No." Andy found the strength to get up and close his office door. His headache had moved in cycles all morning. At this point, the pain caused nausea.

"Would you mind leaving it opened?" India visibly tensed as she turned in his direction. Her knuckles whitened from the tight grasp she held on her leather purse.

"Sure." He left it cracked. Except for her obvious discomfort, India's presence amused him. He had seen her often when he first moved to Serenity. She was a constant companion to Cameron after he arrived to help with the moving.

India wore her dark hair long and straight, allowing the strands to fall over her shoulders. Her lips were lush and curved. Jade eyes now studied him as if she thought him capable of great harm. Her look presented vulnerability not matching her fiery personality.

"Please accept my apologies for my friend's behavior." He cocked his head just a bit to indicate his sincerity.

"I said you don't owe me an apology. I'm glad he's gone."

"Just a minute." Andy stepped into the bathroom adjacent to his office. He ran the water until it flowed as hot as he could stand and then took a washrag and soaked it. Wringing it out, he returned to his desk and pressed the heated cloth against his forehead.

"You aren't looking too well," she commented.

"Migraine," he muttered.

"I thought only women got those."

He nodded, deciding not to take the remark as an insult to his manhood. "What can I do for you?" He surveyed her clothing. He'd been on the small island too long. He'd never have looked twice at what any woman wore, especially when he lived in New York City, but India's dress was definitely overkill for mid-morning on a Wednesday on Serenity Key. She was here after something.

India settled back into the chair. She fidgeted, looking at her hands. Whatever she wanted, she found it hard to ask.

"I need a job." Her voice became louder with each word.

"You? I don't mean to be blunt, but you don't strike me as the type to work as a waitress. I even got the idea you—"

"You have to understand. I need to work." Her fingers gripped the arms of the old Victorian chair, a valuable piece of furniture he had purchased as part of the Ramsey estate. "If I need to, I'll beg. I wouldn't come here—" She swallowed hard. "I wasn't coming here—but no one else is hiring. This ... thing ... with Cameron ... I know you're the last person to ask, but please, you have to have some kind of job, any position. I'll do anything."

"Have you ever ...?" He stopped, shook his head. He wouldn't be so cruel as to inquire about experience she obviously never had. "I don't have any openings for a server."

Andy was no stranger to total devastation, and that was what he saw written all over her fallen face.

"I'm sorry I took up your time." She started to stand.

"Slow down. Not so fast." He leaned forward, elbows on the desk, his hands pressing into the cloth. "I do have another opening," he lied. "It requires more hours, but you'd be a salaried employee." He made the position up as he went along, and it began to sound good to him. "Of course, since you have no experience and you'll require extensive training, I'd start you out at a lower salary." That sounded very good to him. "Are you interested?"

"Yes. Anything." She hadn't stood all of the way. Now she sat, fingers still tightly grasping the furniture.

"India, you're hurting the chair." He let the rag fall onto the desk.

For the first time, she relaxed.

"You'll learn to manage this place, be my right-hand man—

woman. It'll free me up for the paperwork."

He already had enough time for paperwork. Maybe India could work him right out of a job. Maybe he would just visit his restaurant from time to time to say hello to the employees. Maybe when Luke finished the renovations for his apartment upstairs, people would remember him as the eccentric who opened a restaurant to live alone above it.

"Manager." India seemed pleased. "Andy, I'll do my best. I won't disappoint you."

Andy rose and moved toward the door.

India jumped to her feet whirling toward him as if picked up by a cyclone. Her eyes grew wide. "Please, leave it open." Her voice rose somewhere between a cry and a scream.

"I'm just closing it for a second. I'll stand here. I have a personal question."

"Don't, Andy." She backed away.

"Don't what?" He left the door cracked and started toward her.

India held her hand out as if to stop him from approaching. "Don't give me this job and make me pay for it, too. I'm already paying."

The woman wasn't only vulnerable. She seemed truly frightened of him. "All I want is to ask if you need any other help?"

A whoosh of air left her. She straightened and put her hand to her chest. "The job is enough," she whispered. "But thank you for asking. It means so much."

"I'm glad you came to me. I mean, I've been wondering whom I would find to take on that job." The lies made him uneasy, but he saw their worth when the fear left her eyes, and the smile broke through.

"I know you're inventing this position for me, and I appreciate it. When do I start?"

Was he that transparent? His temples throbbed. "To tell you the truth, there's a lot going on this week. I won't be around much until Monday morning. I'll see you then. Ten thirty sharp." He led her to the door and held out his hand. "I offer benefits, too, and I'll tell you about those on Monday." He surrendered his first truth, wondering why the information was so important.

"Thank you." She edged closer to him. With her hand resting on the outer doorknob, she rose up and kissed his cheek. "I won't make you regret this." She left, and he closed the door.

He moved back to the couch and lay down. If Cameron had mistreated her, why did Andy feel he had to make it right? He sat up quickly. "What if it isn't Cameron at all?"

Last night, hadn't the sisters mentioned India? Could her desperation stem from whatever troubled Penny? Blanchie's sister had obviously fought with her husband. What if it had nothing to do with Cameron and everything to do with Mickey? Any relationship he might share with Blanchie Crum could already be in trouble.

What did he always receive when trying to make amends for others? He got a nightmare visit from Zack Ryan and a migraine.

Chapter Thirteen

Midday found Serenity's Chief of Police with a phone at his ear as he rolled his pencil back and forth along the table with the flat of his hand. Kurt Davis listened as the New York detective continued to provide information.

Kurt's officer entered the station, and Kurt covered the receiver with his hand. "Give Seth a call and get an update on the storm," he said before returning his attention to the call. "What do you suspect, Detective Brighton?"

"Without a body, she's simply a missing person." The heavy Brooklyn-born accent traveled across the line. "A neighbor in the co-op found the door ajar. When she entered, she found evidence of a struggle."

"Such as?" Kurt scratched the side of his head with the pencil.

"Overturned furniture, blood, other DNA evidence in the living room and master bedroom."

Kurt balled his fist around the pencil. "Does she have a job? Did you check with her employer?"

"A resident-doctor. The hospital tells us she resigned, effective yesterday. She left her forwarding address, and that's where you come in. Her colleagues planned a small farewell party at her place last night, but our doctor never answered the door.

They assumed something came up, and she was unable to contact them. An airline ticket found in the apartment by investigators proved a dead end. She didn't catch the flight, but we have an even bigger question."

"What?"

"Why would a doctor with so little time left in her residency and with an ample salary package on the table—hers for the taking—just up and move to a nowhere place? You don't work that hard to throw it away."

Nowhere place? The detective probably imagined a small-town force of five or six. In actuality, Kurt, Tank, and their dispatcher, Brittany, were the only protection for the small island. They were all the town needed. Nowhere places were generally safe locations. "I see your point," he said. "Was she close to anyone there?"

"Yeah, she had one good friend at Cornell, another resident, a Dr. Yasmin Garcia. Trouble is, she's missing, too. She left the hospital early, and no one has spoken to her since. One of the residents thought he recognized Garcia's car in the garage when he arrived. When we went back to investigate, we found no vehicle fitting that description."

"Did they remember seeing the first doctor's car?"

The detective's sigh was so heavy Kurt felt its weight. "Her vehicle is missing, too."

"The other woman, what can I tell her husband?"

"As little as possible, Chief. He's a suspect."

"Easier said than done. He's an attorney."

"I know John Ryan; I know his brother, too. Knew their father." Disdain laced the man's tone.

"You don't like these men much."

"Son, many years ago, I investigated the death of Zack Ryan's wife. She was the belle of New York, a philanthropist, and a real gem of a woman. I tried to prove her old man beat her and tossed her off the balcony, leaving the rain to pound her body until we arrived. My efforts fell short. The Ryan brothers—and the doctor—were children then, but I think Andre either witnessed the incident or knew about it. He refused to say anything. When their old man died, I met with the brothers and asked if they were willing to tell the truth now that it couldn't touch Zack. Andre said very politely that he couldn't. John Ryan threw me out of the house. In my opinion, Dr. Emilee Ryan is married to the devil's son."

"Are there any incident reports, noted abuse?" Kurt touched his face, feeling the scars there.

"None. They're a tight-lipped bunch, those Ryans. I guess powerful people value silence."

Obviously. How many months had the brothers lived among them, opening businesses, making friends? And not once had either of them mentioned this woman—a wife who'd lived with them since she was a child.

"Here, let me give you the vehicle information." The detective rattled papers on his end of the line.

Kurt scribbled the tag and identification number for both missing vehicles.

"That should do it, Chief," Detective Brighton said. "Let's hope this is a big mistake, and John Ryan appreciates his wife more than his father appreciated his mother."

"When did the neighbor enter the apartment?"

"Between seven thirty and eight this morning."

"So, foul play possibly occurred between last night and 7:30 a.m.?"

"Precisely."

"Well, I think that's all I need. I appreciate your taking the time to fill me in. Makes my job a lot easier. I'll get right on it and keep you apprised on this end. Please do the same with your investigation." Kurt put the phone down. He eyed the clock and shook his head.

His officer, Tank Williams, drew near. "What's up?"

"New York has a missing woman from an upper-class co-op. Sign of struggle, blood, and other evidence." Kurt moved the point of the pencil to each of his notes as he spoke.

"What does a missing woman in New York have to do with us?" Tank's muscular black frame moved even closer.

Kurt tapped his pencil lead against her name.

Tank stood tall, tossing a sharp look in Kurt's direction, eyebrows raised.

"It may have nothing or it may have everything to do with us." Kurt leaned back in his chair.

"Come again."

"Have you ever heard either of the Ryan boys mention John's wife?"

Tank straightened his holster, and the leather crackled. "No. Can't say I have. Should we go see the Ryans now?"

Kurt nodded. He rose and moved to the dispatch desk and handed Brittany his written notes. "Call the sheriff's department. Ask them to issue an APB on this vehicle. Here's the description of the owner. She's reportedly missing, foul play expected. The car could be stolen so they should approach with caution." Kurt turned away for a moment before he could look at the young woman who was such a valuable employee. "I'd like the courtesy of a call if they find her or her vehicle."

"Sure." Brittany's blue eyes fought back tears. He wished he'd never shared his story with her. He hated the pity in her eyes.

Brittany had needed a friend who understood the tragedy of abuse. Kurt had been that one. "I'm okay." He forced a smile for his dispatcher's benefit. "And so are you."

He motioned for Tank, and they walked out into the bright afternoon sunlight. "What'd Seth say about the reports on the storm?"

"All forecasters say the weakest tracking device is the only one forecasting landfall in our direction. They told Seth to listen for the reports and check with emergency management if he doesn't hear from them."

"And Seth said?"

Tank laughed. "We'd probably learn more by checking in with Luke from time to time."

"I agree." Kurt nodded. "Luke's saved lives before. I'll trust him again."

But a tempest of another kind was beginning to brew over Kurt's island. He squinted against the bright sunlight. "The investigator paints a different picture of John Ryan than I've seen."

"He's a no-nonsense attorney."

"A former corporate lawyer and member of the board of directors for a Fortune 500 company, since the death of his father. He's now practicing criminal and civil litigation in Serenity? Why?"

"Probably wanted something most everybody wants when they come here—a change of pace?" Tank opened the driver's side door of the patrol vehicle.

Kurt claimed the passenger seat. "Let's hope that's all it is. I'll know it when I look into John Ryan's eyes and tell him about his wife." Kurt clenched his jaw. He couldn't stomach this. If John Ryan did anything to harm his wife, Kurt wouldn't be responsible for his actions. More than once, Tank had been the only person standing between Kurt and a man who thought his wife or child was a punching bag. "I'll meet with John. You see Andy."

"Kurt ..."

Kurt shook his head. "If I find out he's had her hurt or killed, I don't want you in my way."

"Spoken like a true law enforcement officer," Tank smirked. "If he's guilty—"

"He's a dead man."

"I have another plan," Tank offered.

"You want to meet them together? Is that it?"

"Sounds like a pretty good idea to me."

"Ain't going to happen." He motioned for Tank to put the car in motion.

The wind blowing across the third-floor balcony of The Billows caught Blanchie's hair, and she brushed it down before reaching across the table and touching Andy's hand. "We can do this some other time." He looked miserable, as if all he wanted to do was to find a bed, pull the covers over his body, and hide from the world.

"It's obvious, huh? I hope eating will help. Penny doing okay?"

"She's at work. I haven't talked to her since she left the house."

"She and Mickey haven't kissed and made up?" He shuffled in his seat, seeming uncomfortable about more than the headache. The way gossip flew from perch to perch on the island, he'd probably learned about Mickey's tryst with India.

"Not so simple." She gazed out over the water. They sat on the third-floor balcony of The Billows. A mess of construction materials filled the apartment inside. Outside, where they were, the breeze flowed clean and smelled of salt.

The glass door slid open, and the waitress brought their meals—seafood salad for both and water for Blanchie. Andy had asked for a large soda and a bottle of aspirin. "Thank you, Katie." He gave her a smile Blanchie knew he didn't feel.

"Anything else before I head down?"

Andy deferred to Blanchie.

She shook her head.

"No, thanks," he said. "We'll be okay."

"I hope you feel better, Mr. Ryan." The young waitress blushed as she left them without another word.

"I think young Ms. Katie has a crush on you, Mr. Ryan," Blanchie teased.

Andy popped the lid on the aspirin bottle, poured four into his hand, and then threw them into his mouth, downing them with the soda. "I thought these migraines were over."

"You get them often?" Blanchie touched his hand.

"Not since I came here."

"Poor baby. Eat."

He wore his long hair loose today. The wind caressed it, tossing it carelessly into his face. She offered him a sympathetic pout and brushed the strands back.

He closed his eyes at her touch, causing a shiver to run down her spine. Gentleness shined so brightly in his nature. Opening his eyes, he reached up and held her hand.

"India came to see you today. Did she want anything in particular?" She hated to interrupt this second date even as flawed as it was by his headache.

"Yes." He closed his eyes tightly then opened them.

"She's bad news. Be careful."

"She's in some kind of trouble." He rubbed his temples.

"A fix she placed herself in on purpose. With no thought of anyone but herself." How could she warn him of the danger he faced with India near—the danger she faced if India turned her ploys toward Andy?

"I heard Penny mention her name last night."

Either he didn't know, or he was fishing for answers.

Blanchie nodded. "Penny always treated India with respect. My sister doesn't deserve this." Blanchie leaned back in her chair.

Andy pushed his plate away and rested his head on fists, elbows on the table. "So, what did India do to Penny that's so awful and ...?" Before he got the question out, illumination flickered in his caramel eyes. "She and Mickey?"

The town's gossip must not have lit on the Ryan's perch. "She's pregnant, and she told Mickey it's his baby. He isn't denying it."

To his credit, or discredit, Andy showed little shock at the town's newest scandal.

"You can see why I want you to be careful where she's concerned."

Andy closed his eyes and covered them with his hand.

"I'm sure John told you Penny's pregnant."

Andy looked at her through the slits he made with his fingers.

"John didn't tell me."

"I shouldn't be mentioning it either."

"Probably not." He rubbed his eyes now. "But I'm glad you did. Now, I need to tell you something."

"Okay." She placed her napkin on her lap and smoothed it with her hands.

"I hired India today."

Blanchie gasped. "How could you?" She tossed an angry gaze at him.

"She seemed desperate, but if I'd known this would cause problems between us, I wouldn't have given it a second thought."

"But you did." Blanchie leaned back in her chair.

"There's something more going on with her. She's frightened. Before today, I only spoke with her when we first moved here. She made fast friends with my buddy, Cameron. The thought crossed my mind that …" He shook his head. "It doesn't matter what I thought."

Blanchie pursed her lips. She fought against saying her good-byes and not getting tangled in anything that included India Thompson.

"Will you trust me?" he asked.

Not the question she expected.

"I'll be very careful. I gave her my word, and keeping my promises is very important to me."

She'd once thought her heart hardened like stale bread by Luke's smooth words and soft eyes. The sincerity in Andy's tone and in the tenderness in his brown eyes made her feel like fresh, soft dough, right out of the oven—and her body warmed, too. "You're a kind man, Mr. Ryan. I can't be mad at you for caring about someone, even if it's India."

Andy stood and patted her shoulder. "Excuse me." Before he could reach the glass door, it slid open.

"Mr. Ryan." Officer Tank Williams blocked the entire exit.

"Hello."

Though Tank shook Andy's outstretched hand, Blanchie knew from experience with Luke that Kurt's second-in-command was there on business. Still, as Tank stepped onto the balcony, Andy pushed past him. "Right back."

Tank started to follow.

"Give him a second. He's not feeling well, and I don't think you want to go where he's going, if he's as sick as I think he is." Blanchie motioned for the officer to take a seat.

Chapter Fourteen

Kurt paced outside the law office of Ryan and Parker. Innocent until proven guilty, that's what the law said. He couldn't let his past get in the way. John Ryan might know nothing about his wife's disappearance.

Kurt breathed deeply before swinging the door open and stepping inside. "Afternoon." He nodded at Penny.

"Kurt?" Penny stood.

"I'm here to see Mr. Ryan."

The flash of fear crossing Penny's features touched him somewhere deep inside. They were old acquaintances, and he knew how much she loved her family and friends.

"John? Why?"

John stepped out of the conference room. "Chief Davis. What can I do for you?"

"May we speak privately?" Kurt motioned toward the room John had just exited.

"Sure." John waved him forward.

Legal books adorned the walls on each end of the room. Three Florida Statute books lay open on the table. Once, Kurt thought he'd study law, but he found law enforcement the quickest way to stand between the innocent and the criminals who could change their lives.

"What can I do for you?" John moved to the head of the table. He remained standing. Leaning forward against the chair, he tilted it forward, the back legs off the floor. A very relaxed action Kurt honestly didn't expect.

"John?" Mickey swung into the room. "Everything okay?"

"Chief Davis needs some legal advice," John told his partner.

Kurt studied his old friend. Mickey's eyes flitted from him to John. Had John confessed to his partner, and did Mickey expect to represent John for whatever crime he'd committed? If so, John played it far too cool.

"Mr. Ryan," Kurt spoke. "You have a right to have a lawyer present."

John released the grip he held on the chair. It fell forward against the table with a loud bang. "Excuse me. I thought you came to see me about a legal matter—your own."

"I'm in the middle of an investigation."

Mickey froze.

John did not ask Mickey to leave.

The lawyers stared at Kurt.

"Mr. Ryan, do you have a wife?"

"Yeah, right." Mickey chuckled.

Kurt's gaze remained fixed on John. What emotions would he see play across the man's face?

John hesitated then nodded. "Emilee."

"What?" Mickey took a step forward.

"Have you heard from her within, say, the last twelve hours?"

"Not directly. She talked to Andy last night around ten thirty, maybe eleven. Why do you ask?"

"Are you legally separated?" Kurt glanced at Mickey, whose

gaze hadn't left John's face.

"My wife remained in New York when I wanted her to move here. I guess you could call it a separation of choice."

"And she made the choice? Why?" He now gave John his full consideration.

John looked at his watch. "She should be landing at the airport in about twenty minutes. She'll be here within the hour. You can ask her."

"Mr. Ryan." Kurt leaned forward, hands on the table. "Dr. Ryan's apartment …"

"Our apartment." Steel laced John's voice.

Kurt winced at John's possessive tone but pressed on. "A neighbor found your apartment door open this morning."

"Maybe Emilee didn't close it all the way when she left. I can't imagine her doing something like that, but it could happen."

"This occurred at approximately seven thirty. Your wife's plane wasn't scheduled to leave until much later."

"Em's the only person I know who likes to sit in airports." John stroked the top of the chair and then stopped. He lifted his hand and brought it down.

Buying time or grasping for comfort? Kurt couldn't be sure.

"And security is heavy. She'd need to get there early."

"Those would be fine explanations, but your wife never made it to the airport."

John struggled to pull out the chair and sit. When he did, he folded his hands in front of him and stared at them for a long, uncomfortable few moments. He reminded Kurt of a small, disappointed boy rather than a confident lawyer. "She decided not to come." He bowed his head.

"Is there a reason she would change her mind?"

"Too many to name."

"That's not specific enough, sir. Why didn't your wife make the plane?"

"Kurt." Mickey took one more step forward. "You've got John worried now. Why don't you tell him why you're here?"

"The neighbor found blood in the living room and master bedroom. There was evidence of a struggle."

"Blood?" John's question hung in the air between them much the way a scream remains in a room once it's been released.

"The officers entered her—your—apartment. They found enough evidence to start an immediate investigation."

"No one saw her leaving? What about her car?" Mickey took another step into the room. "The airport. Has anyone checked with them?"

Kurt nodded. "I told you. She never made the plane. Her car is missing."

"She told Andy some friends were coming over to tell her good-bye." John's fingers pressed into the leather arms of the chair.

"She didn't answer the doorman's call. That's the story her friends are telling."

Any shred of confidence John had held dissipated when he stared up at Kurt. "But the doorbell rang while Andy was on the phone."

"He told you this?" Kurt's interest was piqued. Had John just blown his alibi?

"No." John shook his head. "I listened on the other line. I heard them. Andy wanted her to wait and make sure it was safe before she hung up, but she said it was all right. She expected them. He let her go."

"You make a habit of eavesdropping on your brother's calls?" Mickey questioned.

"When Emilee's on the line, yes." John blinked as if waking from a nightmare. "They gave me a chance to tell her what I needed to tell her, and I didn't take it."

"Excuse me?"

John shook his head. "No one saw her?"

"NYPD is trying to locate another woman, Dr. Yasmin Garcia."

John nodded. He obviously recognized the name.

"She was supposed to join the party. She left the hospital early, and someone recognized her car in the parking garage. No one has seen either Dr. Garcia or your wife since they left the hospital at different times."

"You think their disappearances are connected?" Mickey pulled out a chair and sat, turning his back on his business partner.

"They're not sure."

John's face twisted in silent anguish, but sometimes remorse appeared much the same way.

"Do you know, John?" Kurt asked.

John blinked as if to clear his mind. "How could I know? I've been expecting her call to let me know she arrived. She planned to rent a car and drive here from the mainland."

"Any reason you're not meeting her there?"

"Because she didn't want me to drive her."

"Was she coming here to end your marriage, Mr. Ryan?"

"Kurt?" Mickey shook his head.

"I can speak for myself," John snapped.

"I think you're wasting time here." Mickey ignored him. "We need to find John's wife and make sure she's okay. She could be hurt and in need of medical attention."

"She could be dead. Are you here to tell me she's dead? Is that what you think?"

"I don't think anything. New York asked me to speak to you about the whereabouts of your wife." Kurt turned his attention to Mickey. "Let me ask you one question."

"I can't help you."

"Because you didn't know Mrs. Ryan existed?"

"John's personal life is his business." Mickey's lips spoke the words with conviction, but his flitting attention, searching between Kurt and John, screamed betrayal.

Kurt looked back to John. "Let me get this straight, Mr. Ryan. You're telling me you know nothing about the disappearance of your wife, a wife you never saw fit to tell anyone on Serenity about even though you've lived among us for some time now?"

"I know about her." Penny stepped into the room. "She's a doctor, and she's coming here to live. John told me. What's the big deal, Kurt? Some men don't like to talk about their personal lives, especially marriage trouble." She glared at her husband. "Tell them, Mick. You know about that, don't you?"

"Penny." Mickey slapped his hand down on the table.

Kurt turned his attention back to John. "I find it hard to believe a man who exhibits your kind of possessiveness doesn't know every move his wife makes."

John pushed the chair back and stood. "I may seem possessive, but I never owned her. If I did, she'd be here with me. You get out of here and find my wife. Don't you come back and tell me anything except you've found her." John rushed forward. He brought his face close to Kurt and placed his pointed finger against Kurt's badge. "Think anything you want about me. I don't care.

Your job is to protect Emilee. She's missing, and there's a good chance she's injured. You may think I'm some deranged husband who wanted to teach his wife a lesson. I don't care. You do your job and find her."

"We'll find Emilee, Mr. Ryan, and if you've hurt her in any way, rest assured, you will pay. I don't like men who mistreat women. You might even say I've had my fill of it. By the way, don't leave town." Kurt walked out of the office, nodding his good-bye to Penny.

Kurt walked over the office threshold but held the door open, waiting.

"Oh, God, what have I done? Emilee, what did I do to you?"

Kurt walked off the pier and met Tank at the patrol car. "What'd you get?"

"The man is nursing a terrible headache."

"Has he spoken to Dr. Ryan?"

Tank nodded. "Last night. Emilee Ryan called. He said his brother would probably tell you the same. John eavesdropped on the conversation. Before you ask, he said that's normal behavior for his brother."

"Was he expecting Dr. Ryan to arrive today?"

Tank walked to the driver's door of the patrol car. "He said that's what she told him when he talked to her on Sunday and again last night."

"A planned alibi or the truth?" Kurt spoke more to himself than to his officer.

"From the reaction I saw, Andy Ryan isn't hiding anything. Emilee Ryan's disappearance was a shock. I'm glad Blanchie Crum was with him. He fell apart. What did you get from the other one?"

Kurt shook his head but said nothing. John Ryan was guilty of something, but of what, Kurt didn't know.

Chapter Fifteen

The conversation David overheard through the open window of his restaurant's office landed first on his heart then penetrated his soul. Pain sliced through his chest. He grasped his shirt and fell into his desk chair. What were the chances that John Ryan would marry another individual with the same name as the child David had left behind? Could his daughter be lost to him forever?

Lord, don't let it be so.

He fished in his pocket for his keys and opened his desk drawer to pull out a small metal box. With shaky hands, he fought to find the keyhole and turn the lock. Lid opened, he ran his hand over the well-worn stationery.

He continued to run from the truth, keeping his sin buried in his soul much the same way he kept the letter from his sister-in-law and the drawing given to him by his little girl entombed in the box.

His hands shook as he laid the paper on the desk—Emilee's gift from so long ago. "Child, what have you done? How could you marry that man?"

He unfolded another paper, a letter written by his sister-in-law twelve years earlier. She'd done the unthinkable, giving their daughter to Zack Ryan, but he couldn't harbor any animosity toward her. Colleen may have left Emilee with the Ryans, but it had been David who'd left her there after he found her.

I didn't much care about anything after I left Serenity, David. I got involved with a terrible man. Zack Ryan took everything away from me, and in the end, when I felt I had no other choice, I gave him our child—yours and mine. Zack wanted Emilee, and he made sure he got her. But I didn't let her go without a promise from him. I went to school, I got a job teaching, and I waited long years for my daughter to enroll so that I could be with her for a short period of time. Zack kept his end of the bargain, and he sent Emilee to the preparatory school where I teach and allowed me to befriend her for the four years she stayed. Now with her schooling over, I had to live up to my end of the bargain, but it breaks my heart. I wanted to tell her the truth, but the Lord impressed upon me she isn't ready.

Yet Zack is a hard man, too hard for our daughter's soft heart. If not for his two sons, I would fight heaven and earth to keep her. Those boys, especially the youngest, hold her heart more than I ever could. And with the lie I've lived, how can I expect her to choose me over them when they obviously love her so much?

She's a smart girl, our Emilee. She wants to be a doctor. Your father would have been so proud. I just hope her heart doesn't deceive her and leave her dreams in ruins.

David closed his eyes against the truth. Kurt Davis had referred to the woman as Dr. Ryan. Emilee had fallen in love with the wrong son. With a shaky breath, David turned his attention back to the letter.

Though I felt the Lord holding me back, it seems that with my silence, I have betrayed her again. God is not so cruel as to keep me from telling her the truth without His having a wonderful plan for her. Maybe that plan is for you to bring us together at last. I ask only that you pray for God's guidance to do what is best for Emilee. Please forgive me for all of the sorrow I've caused in our lives.

The letter's words remained engraved in his memory along with the artistic signature that followed, *Colleen Dellacroix New.* She'd asked his pardon when David needed to fall at her feet and beg her forgiveness. He should have gone to New York again after receipt of the letter. He should have demanded that his daughter be allowed to come with him. After all, she would have been nearing adulthood.

He shook his head. "She wouldn't have left with a stranger. Oh God, if anyone ever understood the truth about adultery, would they enter into it? I've harmed so many with my actions and my silence, and now Emilee."

Seth. He would have to be told. The man David had always tried to portray to his son was a fraud. He lifted his hands toward the heavens. "What do you want from me?" He fell forward as another pain crossed his chest. God couldn't kill him now. He had to know if his daughter was dead or alive. Heavy sobs racked his body. "A wise man will hear, and will increase learning; and a man of understanding shall attain unto wise counsels." He choked out the words as God poured the verse, like balm, into his hurting heart.

Time was wasting. God had given David His answer. He picked up the phone and dialed. When the familiar voice reached him, he again broke into sobs. "I need to talk. Please meet me in the cemetery."

Noah McGowan nearly fell onto the old granite bench while David New remained standing, sharing his sordid tale. Noah looked away from the gravestones to the moss-covered oaks shading the graves. Four generations of David's family lay buried throughout the cemetery, but here, under the oaks and surrounded by a black wrought-iron fence, rested those David had known and loved: his father, his mother, his brother, his own wife, and Linda, the wife of his son. Noah forced his gaze back to the cold, hard stones.

David touched Linda's headstone. "You know, with the exception of Seth's beautiful wife, everyone here was crushed by the weight of my secrets and my sin. I should have admitted what I'd done to my brother, and I should have asked his forgiveness. Truth would have stopped all of this before it got out of hand."

"You didn't know what consequences your actions would have." Was he actually trying to excuse David's behavior? Why? Because good men like David didn't fall? But they did. All the time.

"That doesn't matter, Noah. Every bit of what I did was sin."

One of Noah's mentors had fallen. God had placed Noah in the position to help. With a resolve to treat David no differently than anyone else, Noah looked up into the face of a tortured man who awaited a response. What did you say when all you had were questions?

"Seth once told me his aunt, Colleen, and his mother died around the same time. Now, you're telling me Colleen didn't die? She actually spent time with your daughter?"

"If I hadn't tried so hard to hide the affair, if I'd just told the truth, Uma and Colleen would both be here, and I'd have both of my children with me in Serenity. My mother wouldn't have gone to an early grave, and my father wouldn't have left us as soon as he did. Her passing broke his heart."

Since the day David had asked Noah to pray, he'd faithfully done so. Though Noah would have preferred another way for God to get the older man's attention, he trusted God.

"Why, Mr. New?" The question came from deep inside. Noah needed to know.

David ran his hand along the top of his brother's headstone. He tilted his head back and looked up at the branches of the old oak. "The weight of what I was doing to my brother never hit me until Colleen told me she was pregnant, and Owen couldn't be the father. Though they loved each other, they hadn't been intimate for a long time. When she told me, I did everything I could to get them together."

"Like the king calling the faithful Uriah home from war."

David shot him a look, and Noah met his stare.

Finally, David nodded. "I wonder, to this day, if he didn't know the truth. Owen knew me better than I knew myself."

"Was Colleen really so willing to play along?"

"The lives we'd built depended upon her going along with it."

Why did Noah's thoughts meander to Kurt Davis and the most precious gift God had given to Noah—his wife, Belle?

Noah stared at the grave of the long-dead Owen. He prayed that the rumors of Colleen's action had not reached her husband's ears.

David ran his tennis shoe clad feet over the dry oak leaves on the ground, bringing Noah from his own thoughts. "We told ourselves we were trying to keep from hurting everyone we loved. Owen actually asked me at one point if I wasn't up to something. He told me to come clean."

"Didn't you wonder why he offered you the opportunity?" Owen had to have known. The knowledge of it ripped out a piece of Noah's heart. If Owen stood before him, he'd hand him the ragged edge. They were kindred souls. Kurt hadn't taken Noah's offer either.

"Noah, Owen's question scared me to death."

"So, what did you do?"

"With Owen's suspicion of me, I had to seek an ally. I asked Xander Thompson for help, told him Colleen had needs Owen wasn't fulfilling." David coughed. "I'd like to say that's how I fell into this mess—wanting to help my sister-in-law feel loved, but truthfully, I was a selfish fool. My wife and her sister were the most beautiful women I'd ever known, and one of them wasn't enough. I wanted my brother's wife, too."

"Did India's dad know the truth?"

"No. He always believed he was helping Owen's marriage. Xander told Owen he wanted to celebrate a big promotion. He and his wife invited Owen and Colleen to dinner and drinks. Xander had gotten a drug from someone after hearing it was supposed to help a man get his appetite back. He mixed it in Owen's drink, and a man who'd never said an ugly word turned mean. He picked a fight with the wrong guy and ended up dead. Colleen left town right after the funeral, and we didn't hear from her until just before she gave birth."

"Maybe it wasn't the drug that turned your brother mean, Mr. New."

David stared at him.

"Maybe the truth and the emotions that go with it are what angered Owen that night." Anger still fueled Noah on occasion. He had to fight to keep it under control. All he faced were rumors, unsubstantiated words that God had pressed upon him to forget. God wanted him to walk in faith. Why? For such a time as this? No. Because Noah had not forgotten. His broken relationship with Kurt was testimony to that.

Noah stared ahead, reading each letter of Owen's name, taking time to gather himself. He'd come here to offer David counsel, not relive his own mistakes, but David's failure to make things right with Owen echoed Noah's own stubbornness.

"Do you know what the saddest part of all of this is? If I'd only confessed to Owen, he would have raised my daughter without saying a word, loving her as his own. All his life, he'd covered for me. I think he asked me to come clean so he could bury another one of my mistakes."

"Could his wife have lived with her adultery?"

"Colleen has lived alone with it all these years." David pointed to the grave of his own wife. "Uma was willing to live with it, but she died in a car accident returning from New York where she went to care for her sister during the birth. My wife went there when I didn't have the courage to go myself."

Noah started to utter platitudes of sorrow, but he didn't feel sorry for David. Instead, he remained quiet. He couldn't offer his condolences to Owen, so he'd save his compassion for his friend, Seth. This news was going to kill him. Seth had already been through enough.

"After we lost Uma, Colleen disappeared. When I couldn't locate Emilee, my mother seemed to die a little each day. I think she stayed alive as long as she did for Seth and for the hope of seeing Emilee, whom she thought to be Owen's child, a part of the son she'd lost."

"Isn't there anyone you shared this with?"

David rubbed his hand along his gray beard. "Verity Stewart knows all my secrets. And now you."

"But Uma knew."

"True. Colleen called. She had a difficult time throughout the pregnancy, and she told Uma she wanted to make things right so God would spare her child. Uma packed an overnight bag, got in our car, and said she'd bring her sister and my child home, and we'd never say another word about it."

Noah placed his hands on his thighs and pushed himself up. "And when Uma died and Colleen didn't return, you stayed quiet." Had his voice sounded as condemning to David as it had for him? "Didn't you wonder what happened to Colleen and your daughter since Uma said she would bring them home?"

"When I learned about the accident that killed Uma, I didn't care much about anything. After the fog of grief cleared and I sought and found my daughter, I was told by the man who had my daughter that Colleen had died in childbirth and meant for him and his wife to keep my child. Colleen had named Owen as her father and not me. As far as this man knew, Emilee was my niece." David lifted his head to the heavens. "Back then I didn't really want my daughter. She represented a Pandora's Box, and the man—he had a wonderful wife. She loved Emilee, and so did their sons. I let her talk me into it for one reason." He closed his eyes. "I was afraid to tell the truth and accept the blame." David stood and walked to the wrought-iron gate before turning back toward the graves of his family. "Now, when I want my daughter ..." David sobbed, his body quaking with overt emotions.

"I get the feeling there's more to my being here than hearing your confession."

David covered his eyes with his hand, and silence stretched between them. Noah gave him the space and the time to form the words.

Finally, the older man looked him in the eyes. "My daughter's missing. I overheard Kurt and Officer Williams talking with her husband and brother-in-law. My unwillingness to obey may have cost my daughter her life."

Just after David had called Noah, Kurt phoned him. They hadn't spoken in months. Kurt told him they were investigating the disappearance of John Ryan's wife, and John and Andy might need some spiritual comfort. Was David speaking about the same woman?

"The family Emilee lived with never adopted her." David broke into his thoughts. "Today, I learned she married one of the couple's sons. He's here in Serenity."

"Your daughter is married to John Ryan?" Noah asked, and when David turned curious eyes to him he explained Kurt's call.

"He's married to my daughter, and she's missing. I feel like the biblical David watching the Lord wield the sword over my family."

Noah wanted to shake David. If only the man had obeyed God.

If only Noah would obey.

Noah couldn't judge this man when Noah was doing no better?

Noah grasped David's shoulder. "The Lord didn't stop loving David, and David never lost faith, Mr. New. He leaned upon the Lord whatever came his way."

David nodded. "Keep praying for me, Noah, and for Seth and

Emilee."

"How is Seth going to handle this?"

"I don't know, son, but I suspect after he learns the truth, John Ryan and I may be in his line of fire."

"David had a son named Absalom," Noah said.

"He killed his brother to avenge his sister." David opened the gate.

"He tried to destroy his father."

David stumbled, and Noah reached out to prevent him from falling. Instead, both men fell to their knees. David covered his face with his hands. "Oh, Lord, protect my family from my sin. Please take Your sword away, but whatever You do, Lord, I will obey and will abide."

Chapter Sixteen

John touched the porch screen and looked beyond to the Gulf waters lapping at the edge of his property. Luke's sailboat, tied at the dock, rocked with a gentle motion in the soft tides, and the early morning sun sparkled like small diamonds on their ripples. The long night had passed with no word from Emilee.

Andy finally left him to get some rest. John hadn't wanted him to leave, but he hadn't told Andy so. The injection John had given Andy only took the edge off the migraine. Those headaches registered first in his brother's eyes. Then his brother would begin to move slowly as if every part of his body ached. John always recognized the symptoms when they were younger. Lately, though, he'd ceased to care—until they'd heard Emilee had vanished, and the evidence did not look good. Now the insecurities had returned, and he needed his older brother much the way he'd needed him in their childhood.

A man moved around the side of the house, using the old brick pathway. John didn't care to know who was here to offer him condolences, but when his visitor stepped to the screen door, John came face to face with Pastor Noah McGowan.

A preacher had arrived after Mom died.

A cold shiver ran down John's spine. He opened the door to

allow the man inside then fixed his gaze on the waters once again.

"John, I'm Noah McGowan."

"I know who you are, Preacher." John braced himself and turned his gaze to the pastor. Noah carried a Bible.

Emilee read her Bible often in their room at night—a look of pure peace shining in her eyes. His wife clearly treasured each word. She once told him she was God's child. It didn't matter where her earthly father resided.

John wrapped his arms against his body. He closed his eyes, trying to keep the remembrance close. He hadn't found her father, but he'd found her uncle and her cousin.

"Have you heard anything?" Noah asked.

"No." John's voice barely rose above a whisper. If the preacher asked, it meant he came for some other reason. He heaved a sigh of relief and dropped his arms.

"I'm here to offer you some support, to pray if you'd like."

John stared. He wanted to see into the preacher's soul. Never before had he given this man the time of day. What would make a stranger come into his home and offer him anything? "I'm fine."

"Excuse me, John, but you look like you're deep in the pit of hell."

John rubbed his hand over the stubble on his face then through his oily and limp hair. Although he still wore the clothes he had donned the day before, his tie was missing, and the shirttail hung out. "I look right at home. What really brings you out here, Pastor McGowan?"

"Call me Noah, and I told you." The preacher shifted the Bible from one hand to the other. "I want to offer my support and to pray with you." He held out a hand in greeting.

"I don't worship God." John remained sure of this one fact.

He wanted nothing to do with God and didn't want to shake hands with His preacher. John kept his hands at his side.

"Well, I believe God sent me here to you, so maybe you should listen." Noah lowered his hand.

John gave a hoarse laugh. "God isn't going to do us any good." He watched Noah's face for any discomfort. None showed. John couldn't hold his gaze, uneasy with the man before him. They were not on even ground.

What was wrong with him? He could destroy this guy. He could make him run out of this house and never look at him again, leave him to the devil.

But you're going to listen, if only for the fact he came.

At first, John thought Noah spoke. He threw a sharp glance at the preacher standing in silence beside him. The words had come through his own tired and weary thought process—a powerful voice deep inside telling him he had no choice.

"No," he spoke aloud. "I'm not listening."

Noah stepped back and gave his head a slight shake.

"I'm not His child." John winced at that plain and simple truth. He was no one's child. His mother died long ago, and his father, well—that story made him cringe.

"It's obvious."

Was that bitterness etching the preacher's tone? John relished just a little of this victory over his unwavering foe. Noah McGowan had human frailties after all.

"So leave me alone," John demanded.

Noah shook his head. "I promised a friend I would be here for you. I'm keeping that promise."

"I could throw you out."

"Yes, you could."

John turned away from him again. "If God exists, Preacher, why does he let good people suffer?" Why had Andy and Emilee suffered all their lives?

"Delving right into the meat, are you, John?" Noah chided.

John didn't turn to look at him.

"Bad things can be looked upon as blessings, too."

John couldn't care less about the mysteries of this God he didn't care to know, the God whose people called a curse a blessing. He pushed the screen door open and stepped off the porch onto the pathway leading to the water. He walked at a brisk pace to the end of his dock where Luke's sailboat continued to bob in the water.

"Morning." Luke stepped from the vessel's cabin, his hair mussed. He held a cup of coffee. "Morning, Noah."

John turned with a start, unaware the preacher followed until Luke greeted them both. If nothing else, John admired the man for his tenacity.

"Any word?" Luke asked.

Noah must have shaken his head because Luke nodded his understanding.

"The preacher just came by to comfort me." John swallowed against the dryness in his voice. "I can't get your friend to leave."

"Noah just wants to help you, John. Why don't you listen?"

"How often have you listened?" The anger and the question flowed out against John's will. "Wasn't your father the preacher before him? I don't know much about religion, but doesn't your God frown on divorce? Why is it you've lost your wife? Couldn't God keep you together?"

Luke smiled, and John was relieved to know he hadn't taken as many scales off Luke's hide as he first hoped. Still, he refused to apologize.

"Well, yeah, John, but sometimes He allows His kids to grow up the hard way. I'm the stubborn one. I left Blanchie no choice."

The time had come to put an end to this farce. John turned on Noah. "If your God can bring my wife back to me, I'll fall on my knees and worship Him for the rest of my life."

"Be careful what you promise to God," Noah warned.

"I'm promising you."

"No." Luke shook his head. "You're challenging God, not His preacher, and God won't be baited. Heed Noah's warning. God has a way of bringing us to our knees when the occasion calls for it."

Were they all out to get him? Couldn't they see his misery? Okay, he'd deal with their mythical being directly. He took a deep breath and looked to the heavens. "Bring her back to me, God, and give me a second chance to make life right, and I promise I'll worship You forever." He raised his fist. "Do it and prove me wrong. Prove to me there is a God because I don't believe You exist—and if You do, I think You're a God of anger and hate, and not one of love. If You love me, You wouldn't let my yesterday turn into this nightmare."

"Do you usually talk to those you don't believe exist?"

John stared at Noah. Either the preacher had spunk, or he didn't realize with whom he dealt. John was the devil's son. He'd heard other people say those words behind his back. Almost everyone thought it. He might as well claim the truth. "Yeah, I had an imaginary friend once. My father ran him off."

"Do you mind if I add my prayer to yours?"

The preacher actually thought he'd talked to God. Yeah, right. "You go ahead. Give your God a chance to work it out." He stared out over the Gulf.

"Father, look upon John Ryan and show him You are a God of mercy and longsuffering."

On the boat, Luke bowed his head. John saw it from the corner of his eye.

"Let this man know You see into his hurting soul. Knock on the door of his heart and let him know You're there. We pray You will guard Emilee Ryan and keep her safe until she's home with her husband; and Father, make her husband ever mindful of the promise he has made to You."

"Amen," Luke said.

"John, they have something," Andy called from the porch. He held a phone in his hand.

The world spun in slow motion as John took one heavy step and then another up the dock. His legs wobbled, his heart raced. He could hear nothing except the roar in his ears.

Noah reached to steady him, and with the preacher's assistance, he managed to stumble up the hill, his hand outstretched for the phone for what seemed an eternity before he took it from Andy's grasp.

"This is John Ryan."

He listened as Kurt Davis apologized for reporting over the phone. The officer's words sounded far away.

"No. No. No. No. No." John sank to his knees. He dropped the phone to the ground. Sobs burst forth—large, uncontrollable, breathtaking sobs. "God, I can't do this. I can't do this alone! Em— Oh, God, I don't know what to do. Emilee!" He screamed her name, the muscles in his throat aching from the strength of his guttural plea. Then, energy spent, he slumped forward, his hands covering his face. "Em," he whispered her name over and over.

Seth held the items his father had kept hidden inside the metal container. The box remained a mystery to him over the years. Now, he discovered it held Pop's deepest, darkest secrets—truths that seriously affected Seth's own life. Pop had blubbered that he only wanted to protect him, but Seth didn't buy the story. By hiding the items away, his father protected himself at the expense of a daughter—Seth's sister—someone Pop said he loved.

Seth stared at the portrait of his mother. All the days of his life, Uma New watched over him from her vantage point above the fireplace mantel. Though he couldn't remember his mother's touch, he possessed a deep love for her. After Linda's death, he stood here before her and poured out his heart. All the while, Mom looked down upon him with her loving smile. He felt in his heart that she heard his secrets. This belief was the sole reason he didn't denounce God entirely. Heaven must exist because in his dreams both his mother and his wife lived there together watching him daily.

"Aren't you going to say anything?" Pop asked.

Life in the aftermath of Linda's death taught him to stay calm when hit with surprise. Now, though, his composure ebbed.

His father had told him everything. He then shared with him a child's drawing and the letter supposedly written by Aunt Colleen. The letter, Seth smashed into a ball and tossed on the ground at his father's feet. The drawing, he held tightly in his hand. "Where is my sister?"

"Right now, boy, she's lost."

"The family that kept her, this man and woman you went to

visit, where are they?"

"Gone. They're both dead. All that's left of her family are the two boys."

"How do you know they're dead if you never saw her again?"

"One of the boys in Emilee's family told me."

"That's the second time you've said that. They aren't her family. I am. Where are these boys?"

Pop took a deep breath. "They're here. I just learned today your sister married John Ryan."

Seth squeezed his eyes shut, allowing the truth to settle against him. "John." He opened his eyes and shook his fist in his father's face. His past boiled down to one truth—John and Andy Ryan were a part of his sister's life, a life he was not privileged to enter.

"I overheard Kurt talking with them on the dock today." Pop paced away from him and back.

"How is this possible? They've been here for a while." Then truth dawned, adding fuel to the raging fire within. "You knew who they were from the start, old man. You sold Grandma and Grandpa's house to John and didn't even blink an eye doing it. Did that give you any peace?"

"Your grandparents left it in my hands to give to her. Nanna and Dandy Dellacroix left you their place. If John had not arrived before I died, the house would have been yours. Your grandparents all hoped—"

"They knew about her, too?" He walked toward the screen door, kicking it with his work boot. The door crashed against the outside wall and sprang back with a solid force. "Everyone knew about my sister but me." He whirled toward his father.

Pop followed him onto the porch. "Death is a very hard subject to explain to a child. In order to tell you about Emilee, we would have had to tell you about Owen."

"I haven't been a child for a number of years. I faced the death of my wife and managed to survive. Next excuse." But he really hadn't survived. When he didn't think about Linda every minute of every day, then he could call himself a survivor. But that would never happen.

"I have no excuse. I wronged you, son. I wronged your sister. I wronged everyone."

"Well, how does it feel to know you sold your childhood home to the man who killed your daughter?"

"We don't know she's dead, Seth. We don't know anything. I've asked Noah McGowan to stay with John. I want to believe John didn't harm her."

Had he heard his father correctly? "I can't believe you told Noah before you told me. What right does Noah have in our business?" The anger boiling to the top threatened to scald everyone and everything around him.

"He's a man of God. I needed to talk to him. He offered me the kindness, and I took him up on it."

Seth shook his head but lowered the heat on his ire. He would not cast blame upon his friend. It belonged on the shoulders of the man standing in front of him, a man he once admired. "And you allowed John and Andy to play their games, knowing they could bring her home."

"I knew they were the boys she'd been raised with, but I didn't know she and John married. We've never discussed Emilee. I'm not even sure what John and his brother know."

"They obviously know something—at least John. He had to know. Otherwise, why is he living in my grandparents' house? When they arrived, didn't you think to ask, 'Hey, boys, where's the daughter I abandoned? Did you throw her away like I did?'"

"Seth!"

"You know what makes me the angriest?" Seth pointed an accusing finger. "Do you?"

"Tell me." Pop lowered his head.

"The fact that you've been such a hypocrite all these years. You told me I needed to get my life right with God and that I can't run from Him. You, of all people, lectured me. You haven't gotten right with God. How can you expect me to do it when you haven't?"

"I have."

"Liar!" Seth stepped in his father's direction but then backed away, terrified at how close he came to knocking him to the ground. He pointed through the screen to his mother's picture. "There's no way on this earth you ever deserved her. You deserved her sister. You're both filthy, cheating liars who killed my mother. And you—you let Mom go to her sister alone, knowing she went there to help bring your child into this world. I can't imagine how she handled that. And because of you, my mother died and my sister and I are strangers. I may never get the chance to know her."

"She had a better life." Pop raised his hand as if asking for a pardon. "Can't you understand? Emilee had it all—a mother, John and Andy. They loved her. I know. She went to the best schools."

Seth studied his father for a long moment. Was he serious? "Do you think my life is so bad? Up until today when I found out what kind of person you really are, I thought I lived a charmed childhood. Did you feel sorry for me all my life because I didn't live in a fancy home, wear the finest fashions, or go to the finest schools? Did you think that by living on Serenity Key I missed out on something better?" Seth pounded his fist against his own chest.

"I had Grandpa Isaac and Grandma New. Nanna and Dandy Dellacroix loved me. You raised me. I had you." His words flowed between clenched teeth. "What did my sister have? You're a fool if you think I buy your story. And now I know why I've always felt incomplete. Yeah, Pop, I've never thought of myself as a whole. I thought it was the loss of Mom, but maybe I picked up that feeling from you. Knowing she was out there somewhere, didn't it leave you feeling empty inside? Maybe not. You just didn't want her to share our life. You're a selfish, lying hypocrite, and you deserve everything you get." Seth stormed off the porch.

"Boy!" David followed.

The voice reaching out to Seth held the same commanding tone of a father still in control of a situation. Despite his real desire to keep going, Seth spun around in the middle of the street.

"Where are you going? What do you plan to do?" Pop stood on the porch.

"I'm going to do what you've never done. I'm going to figure out what's in the best interest of my sister." Seth brushed away the tear on his cheek. Intense anger always made him cry, and he hated himself for the weakness.

The color drained from Pop's face, and he looked ill. He turned and walked into the house.

Seth took one step and then another back toward his father before he stopped. "You deserve this, old man. You pretend to be so close to God. Well, I don't need you or Him."

Andy picked up the phone and allowed Noah and Luke to

walk John toward the house. "Kurt, what? Is Emilee …?"

"The highway patrol in North Georgia received a call from a man concerned about a woman. He stopped to help her late yesterday and found out she'd run out of gas."

"Em?"

"We believe it was your sister-in-law. We know it was her—your brother's—vehicle."

In spite of it all, Andy allowed the smile to come. "Kurt, John wouldn't correct you on that one. That car is definitely Em's baby. A black BMW with gray interior. Her college graduation present from John. Why was the man concerned?"

"He used some gas he had in his truck to get her started. Then she followed him to a station. He indicated she was somewhat disoriented, and she didn't have identification or a wallet. He filled up her car and paid for it. When she realized what he'd done, she tried to offer him her diamond watch as payment. He refused."

Andy's smile faded. "For John to be so upset, there had to be more."

The man said that your sister-in-law acted confused and a little fearful of his approach."

Andy closed his eyes tightly. "That doesn't sound like Emilee at all."

"She doesn't have a mental illness either of you failed to mention?"

Andy shook his head. "Of the three of us, Emilee is the sanest."

"Has she ever mentioned a resident getting a little physical with her?"

Now, Kurt was worrying Andy. "No. No one."

"What about the person who knocked on her door? Did she

mention the name of anyone she expected?"

"Again, no. She said some of the other residents wanted to get together to tell her good-bye."

"I think the key to all of this is the person who stood on the other side of that door."

Andy caught his breath. Kurt seemed to be holding some information close to his Kevlar vest. He rubbed tired eyes. "Why don't you tell me what this man in North Georgia said that has you concerned?"

"When the man opened her car door to help her inside, he said he noticed a moist red spot on the back of her coat. He asked your sister-in-law if she was injured in any way. She seemed not to understand his concern, almost lost."

Andy held his breath.

"When she left him, she got back onto the interstate. He called the authorities, followed her for a bit, but he suspected she got nervous because she sped up, and he lost her. He met up with a trooper at a rest stop and filed his report."

"She was headed south on the interstate?" Andy prayed that was the case. Any small sliver of hope he could give to his brother would go a long way at this point.

"She was a good 450 to 475 miles from us. That's close to seven hours away. If she's headed our way, that car would have to get exceptional gas mileage to get her this far."

"She might squeak it out."

"To get to where she was, she'd been driving for twelve hours," Kurt said.

Andy ran his hand through his hair. "She couldn't have. She'd need to fill up one time—at least."

"Unless someone took her money or in her disoriented state

she left it at the last place she stopped and someone took a golden opportunity."

Andy's headache, which hadn't truly left him, threatened to return with a vengeance.

"Who knows? She could have rushed away and thought quickly enough to grab some money and place it in her pocket. Maybe she used it at the first stop."

Andy closed his eyes and waited. "Is there anything else I should know?"

"The man was an off-duty EMT. Though the blood loss didn't seem significant, he was worried that her injuries may have sent her into some type of shock. He wasn't sure she'd be able to find her way to where she was heading."

Andy took a deep breath as a mournful wail rang from inside the house, mimicking the fear in Andy's heart. "Aren't they looking for her? Wouldn't the police be on the lookout for her car?"

"There's an APB for her and her car, but it's possible for her to slip by."

"That's encouraging," Andy growled. "So, they wait until she passes out and has a serious accident and harms herself and others. Even if her cell phone is in her purse, she could have called one of us, and we'd make sure ..." Who was he kidding? Between late yesterday and this morning, Emilee could have made it to or close to Serenity. He didn't want to think about it.

"I don't have anything else to tell you. I'll keep you informed. I'm sorry it isn't better news for you and your brother." Kurt ended the call.

Andy clicked off the phone. Before he could calm his brother, he needed a moment to himself. He stared out over the waters.

Emilee had to have left New York yesterday in the early morning hours.

Serenity wasn't located near the interstate. Emilee would have to take some lonely stretches of highway. He hated to think of her alone and out of gas, bleeding, and frightened. "Where are you?" he whispered.

Chapter Seventeen

Seven hours later, Andy's sanity ebbed away with each tick of the clock. Lying on the couch, he'd slipped into sweet oblivion where Emilee resided, alive and well, and John, happy and carefree.

A voice broke through his dreams.

Someone had turned on the television. Andy lifted his head and focused on the image. A woman meteorologist brushed her blond hair back before clicking a remote to show a tropical storm skirting the Florida Keys and moving into the Gulf of Mexico.

He stood, his attention riveted to the screen. Weather girl pushed a button and six lines appeared on a map of the Southern United States. Each gave a different scenario of the storm. Five of the lines curved away from Serenity Key. "We have one model that insists the front will not stall. So, for folks in this area ..." she pointed directly at the island, "keep watching for the latest coverage on Tropical Storm Pauline."

The aroma of roast beef reached him. His stomach soured. He couldn't eat with Emilee in danger.

In the kitchen, a female voice hummed what Andy suspected was a hymn. He scratched his head. Blanchie.

John and Noah McGowan sat in each of the two high-back

chairs on either side of the fireplace. Their eyes were closed.

Andy moved to the door and peered through the glass to the lighted dock where earlier in the day, he'd watched his little brother melt into nothingness. Since then, John wavered between despair and agitation.

Noah hadn't left John's side. His brother might not want to admit it, but John obviously took comfort from the preacher's quiet and persistent presence.

A strong knock sounded on the back door. John bounded to his feet. Noah sprang up and motioned them to stay put.

Blanchie came to stand beside him. "It's Kurt." She braced him.

Andy offered a smile he did not feel.

The police chief was dressed in jeans and a pullover shirt. Kurt had been here once before, questioning John about his relationship with Emilee. John told it like it was, the relationship, that is, but he never gave Kurt the reason for his separation from Emilee. Something Andy desperately wanted to know.

"What is it?" John demanded.

"Nothing new."

Andy reached out and held to John as John swayed. His brother couldn't take much more of this.

"It just doesn't make sense." John looked at Andy.

Andy's mobile phone rang, and he fished it out of his pocket, glimpsing the ID. "Cameron, we're in the middle of something now."

Andy took a deep breath. Cameron might have been the last person to see Emilee in New York. "Hold on." He lowered the phone. "Our friend Cameron Matrai visited Emilee the night she disappeared," he told the chief.

"How do you know?" John's eyes flashed anger.

"He called me at the restaurant yesterday." Andy placed the phone back to his ear. "Cameron, the police chief's here. Emilee's missing. I don't have time to go into it now, but he'd like to ask you a few questions. Cameron? You there?"

No response. Cameron had hung up or the call had dropped.

"That's strange." He started to dial his friend.

"I don't want him around Emilee." John edged closer to Andy. "When he was here, I told him she didn't care for him. I warned him to stay away from her."

Andy abandoned the call. "That's ridiculous. Cameron's like a brother to me. Emilee loves him."

"Emilee hates him." John spat the words.

"How would you know?"

"You can't stand there and tell me you haven't figured it out. Cameron let me in on what you and Emilee did."

"What did we do?" Andy ran a hand through his hair. "I'd love to know what's made you treat us like your enemies."

They all watched them now: Kurt, Noah, and Blanchie.

"Tell me, John, so we can move on. If you want me to believe Cameron spread lies about Em and me, tell me what they are." He grabbed John's shirt collar. "Emilee's in danger, and the spring load on my patience with you is shot. Tell. Me. Now."

Inane thoughts seeped through Andy's anger. John needed to change his clothes. He needed a bath and a shave.

John yanked free. "I know what he told me; I know what Emilee told me about him."

"Start with Em."

"No." John turned away.

"No?" Andy's laugh rang false.

Blanchie's soft touch met his skin. In his agitation, he shrugged free of her. "What did Cameron have to say?"

"The truth. Cameron told me the truth." John stared back at him with pain so deep that for a moment Andy wanted to embrace his brother, tell him he was sorry for whatever atrocity John imagined he'd committed.

"You're a lawyer. I have a right to know what accusations have been brought against me." Andy placed a hand on John's shoulder. "How can I respond to allegations when I don't know what they are?"

John shook his head, but the pain remained etched on his face. He wiped at his eyes with the back of his hand. "I'll take the blame for why it happened. I wasn't there for her. I let things come between us. I left her alone." His lips trembled. "Andy, why? We've gone through so much. Zack ..." John looked around as if remembering they weren't alone. "Emilee's my wife." John patted his chest. "You and Em—you're all I've ever loved."

"Tell me!" Andy demanded with a force that shocked even him. He backed away and cast a wary glance around the room. When all they'd ever done was hold the family truths close to their vests, John was showing all of them the fragile seams held together by fear of everyone on the outside. Their lives were about to unravel because of John's suspicion.

"Just admit it to me! Don't make me tell you what you know!" John screamed the words.

Kurt stepped toward them. "Okay, boys."

"What did I do? I gave up my life to keep you together. Have you forgotten? I gave up the work I loved to run a company created by a man I hated just so you could practice law and Em could attend med school. I gave up my fancy place in the city to move into a place that you and Em could barely afford when Zack refused to pay her way through school. I moved here because Emilee was worried about you being alone." He needed to shut up. He'd said too much.

"Andy, please." Blanchie tugged at his arm.

He cast a warning glance her way, not that he would hurt her, but his emotions swirled, gaining momentum, spinning him out of control. He could feel it in the anger raging inside of him. John's vague accusations whipped him into much the same kind of frenzy as the rock music of his youth.

Blanchie stepped back.

"What did I do?" Andy demanded.

John's lips trembled, and he couldn't seem to speak through the emotion. His brown eyes, one minute filled with pain, now filled with hatred. "You … slept … with … her." He choked out the words. "You slept with my wife."

Andy's fist slammed into John's face.

John hit the floor. Blood ran from his nose and a cut on his lip.

Never had Andy raised his hand in anger toward John. They needed each other. John had always needed him. Andy looked at the fist he balled in front of him.

John held his jaw as he fought to stand. He fell back to the floor, and Noah helped him to his feet.

"Does the truth make you angry?" John taunted.

Andy didn't have to answer. His fist had said it all: Outrage. Anger. Pain. Sadness. Not because of the truth, but because of the absurdity of his brother's claim.

Andy heaved a heavy sigh. "Cameron wouldn't lie to you like that." He looked at his knuckles, clenching and unclenching his hand before shaking off the pain caused from the impact with

John's face.

John wiped the blood that trickled from his busted lip and nose. Red smeared the side of his face.

Andy slumped forward. He lowered his gaze to the floor, shaking his head. "I'd never do that to you or to her. I've never been anything to Emilee but—"

"You've been everything to her."

Not everything. If he had, John wouldn't be married to her today. She wouldn't be missing because he'd never have thrown her away like John had done.

Andy met his brother's stare.

Tears pooled in John's eyes. "Don't you know that? You're everything to her and to me. You're the only reason we survived. That's why it hurts so much."

"But I'm telling you, John. It never happened." He raised his hands in defeat.

"I don't believe you."

Andy stuffed his anger into his jeans pockets along with his fists.

John moved away from the group. He fell onto the couch and leaned forward. "All I want is my wife back, Andy. Can you give me that?"

"Can I give you?"

John had asked the same question when he looked through the photos on the computer. Now, Andy understood the paranoia, the listening in on conversations, the drive to keep Andy away from Emilee, all the anger from his brother. "It's not up to me to give you anything," Andy reasoned. "I told you. She never saw me because of her love for you. I'm what I have always been: Emilee's friend. I'm not even her best friend. You own that title, too. She and I both watched as her best friend and her lover became a madman."

"But what if she doesn't come back?"

Fear kept Andy from answering. Nothing happening to them made any sense. Of the three of them, Emilee had always been the rational one. And she was lost somewhere between North Georgia and Serenity, bleeding, and in need of medical attention she had failed to seek.

Andy closed his eyes. An image playing before him: Emilee, the life ebbing out of her as she lay in some forested area where they'd never find her. Other than that visual, Andy had nothing to give to his brother, so he gifted John with silence.

Nothing Kurt could say would give the brothers comfort. He nodded to Noah who followed him down the hall to the back door.

"She's alive." Noah pushed the door open. "At least she was a few hours back."

The sun was making its descent. Darkness would be on them soon enough. Kurt remained silent. Noah didn't often speak to him, and Kurt wished their conversation now could be over something more pleasant.

The Ryans' circumstances were a mirror into their own lives. Suspicion caused the strain in Kurt's relationship with Noah. Doubt had been planted by Belle's Aunt Queen, someone Noah and Belle should be able to trust, though, for some reason, Queen never liked Kurt.

"You're not keeping anything from them?" Noah crossed his

arms over his chest. "They're suffering."

Kurt slapped a mosquito that had the misfortune of trying to suck his blood. The night was heavy with them. "I told them all I know. Are you staying?"

Noah nodded, waving a hand in front of his face, scattering the persistent parasites. "I promised I would."

"What's going on here? Do you have any idea?"

Noah shrugged. "I can't tell you. I think John feels responsible for his wife's disappearance, but I don't know why."

Kurt motioned Noah further away from the house, at least out of the mosquito-drawing white porch light. "What do you know about Cameron Matrai?"

"Never heard of him before that call."

"Why spread gossip like that, especially someone Andy says is close to them?" Time had come to dive into long troubled waters. "Maybe you have an insight. Why'd Queen do that to us?" Like John and Andy, a woman and a fool's gossip stood between Kurt and his best friend.

Kurt recognized his friend's don't-go-there warning in the narrowing of Noah's eyes. "The first question to answer is whether the gossip is true or false."

"What do you think?" Kurt pressed.

"I think there are a lot of reasons someone would make those accusations: jealousy, love, protection …" Noah walked to the ancient stone cherry tree planted at the edge of the patio. He stared up at the spindling arms and dying fall leaves. "Wanting someone, no matter how much it hurts that person, to know the truth."

Which one of those did Noah attribute to Cameron Matrai? What did Noah believe about Queen?

Noah stretched up and with both hands held to a heavier limb on the tree. He stretched forward. "We'll never know the why unless we know what really occurred. Andy's fist backed up his denial. I don't think he slept with Mrs. Ryan."

Kurt pursed his lips. Noah was good at talking three-dimensionally, and Kurt had long since learned to counter his friend's ability. "I can't tell you what really occurred, Noah."

Noah brought his arms down. "Then we're still at a stalemate, aren't we, Kurt? How can I understand when you won't let me in? Either of you." He held up his hand, showing Kurt his wedding band. Two dimensions of their talk disappeared, and they were down to one, the personal part. "I'm Belle's husband."

"And I'm her—"

"What are you, Kurt? How did you keep her company when I was away at seminary?"

"If you don't want your face to look like John Ryan's face, you'll stop right there, or my fist will speak to you as loudly as Andy's did to John."

At Kurt's blunt reply, pain sliced across Noah's face. Without another word, he walked toward the house.

"Noah?"

Noah made it to the door stoop before turning. He looked like a tired old dog, kicked and beaten.

"Why don't you think about the reason Andy pummeled his brother? The truth of Belle and me, it lies in there somewhere. You've got to trust your wife. Me, too."

"I've got to have faith in God, and He says to love my wife. Once upon a time, I would have trusted you with Belle's life. Now, I don't trust you or her aunt. I'm her only protection. That's it."

"You know what I think?" Kurt smirked.

"What?"

"You're a lot like John."

"In what way?"

Kurt pointed a quick finger at his friend. "You want to stay angry with me. You can't be angry with your wife because like you said, God told you to love her. By taking it out on me, you're keeping me and Belle at a distance from each other. Is that the way you want to protect her? Look what happened to Emilee Ryan. It doesn't work."

Without another word, Noah stepped inside and closed the door.

"You stubborn, pig-headed preacher. One day ..." Kurt rid the world of one more mosquito and stomped toward his car. He was tired, and he was angry, and that didn't make for a good combination.

Chapter Eighteen

Mickey turned at the sound of footfalls on his dock. As his wife approached, he looked back to watch the sun glisten against the water as it made its descent into evening. *Lord, just let her say she's forgiven me.*

"Mickey?" Penny's voice flowed soft, almost soothing.

He closed his eyes. He had loved her forever. He couldn't face her—not after what he'd done.

"Mickey?"

"Yeah." His tongue weighed heavy with the effort it took to speak, and he continued to stare out over the water.

"You haven't eaten today, have you?"

He shook his head. His last meal had been the spaghetti she'd fixed before she left him.

"Come over to the Ryans'. Blanchie prepared too much food."

"Have you eaten?" He swallowed hard. She needed to take care of herself and their child.

"Yes, but I'm worried about you."

Good. She wasn't as mad at him today as she had been yesterday. He turned, reaching out for her. "I'm fine, Mouse."

She stepped back. "John feels bad about the misunderstanding."

Mickey lowered his arms. "Misunderstanding? I couldn't misconstrue what he never shared with me."

She glared back at him, her green eyes dark and stormy. "Exactly. So, maybe you know how bad he feels, or maybe you don't."

"Don't you take his side. I jeopardized our future believing in him." He searched her eyes for any reprieve from her anger for the real cause separating them, his only desire to have her tell him that they had a future together no matter what he'd done. Truly, if he'd done anything right, it had been trusting John Ryan. The man knew how to run a law office. As a government employee, he'd never had that experience. John's success had been Mickey and Penny's gain.

And Mickey, having gained so much, had lost it all with his own actions. He'd give back every cent he'd earned if Penny would come back to him. John hadn't ruined Mickey's future with Penny; Mickey had tossed it away as if she weren't the most valuable blessing God had bestowed upon him.

"John didn't ruin our future, Mickey. You and your affair with India did that. When is your other child due? Maybe India and I will be in the same hospital room. Won't that be convenient for you?"

At least they were still in sync with each other, though he liked it better when their thoughts were both on happy things. He grasped Penny's shoulders. "I love you, Penny. I don't care if I ever see India again."

She struggled to free herself from him. "I won't let you abandon your child. I'll see to it you're a part of your other baby's life."

Her words pierced his heart, and he released her. Was she

thinking of forgiving him? Or was it her child she was thinking of? She'd allow him to be a part of their child's life but expected him to stay with India. The thought made him want to retch.

Too bad the thought of holding India in his arms, giving to her what should have been only Penny's, hadn't made him feel this way until it was too late.

"I'll make sure India's child doesn't feel the burden of what the two of you have done."

He closed his eyes and gulped in a deep breath.

He deserved to pay.

But Penny had played her hand. And within it, she held his heart. "I pray you do. More than anything in my life, I want you to make sure I do right."

"John isn't well. I think you could drop your ridiculous pride and stand beside him. He didn't kill his wife. She's still alive. At least the last report said she was. She may be hurt, though."

John deserved what he was getting. He wanted to scream the words at her, but the thought came back and pricked a hole in his conscience.

"So, are you going to stand beside your friend?" she asked.

"I'll be there in a minute."

"Good. He's nearing exhaustion. No one can get him to rest. You've been his friend up until now, Mickey. Don't fail him."

"What about his brother?"

"Andy and John aren't talking."

"Why?" He faced her again.

She shook her head. "I didn't see what happened, and it's not my place to say, but it wasn't a good scene. He needs you. And if you won't do it for John, do it for Noah. He's been there since this morning, and he needs to go home. He's dead tired."

As if on cue, John, silhouetted against the lights at the back of his home, exited his porch next door and walked toward the dock. Noah followed close behind.

"You go on inside before the mosquitoes eat you up." He stared into her beautiful green eyes. He'd do anything for her. And Noah. "I'll see what I can do."

———✧———

John ran his hands through his oily hair and stared out over the horizon. Emilee was somewhere close. He could feel it. All their lives, he had an uncanny ability to sense his wife's presence, and she was near. And with that knowledge came the all-too-real feeling of danger. Was it just the idea that a squall was entering the Gulf? No. The forecasters gave it only a slight chance of becoming a hurricane and an even slighter chance it would hit the island. Then what?

He didn't want to contemplate the answer.

"John." Noah dared broach him again. "You need to go in and shower, rest, maybe eat something."

"It's getting dark," John whispered only because he didn't have the strength for anything else. "She's all alone. She's afraid. I feel it, and I can't help her. Where is God? I don't see Him answering your prayers." He watched a mosquito land on his arm then watched it take his blood. He didn't care.

Noah swiped at the bugs circling him. "God works in His own way, not yours. You can't bully Him around like you do everyone else."

John took out the mosquito with a loud *whap* and lifted his hand. Blood covered it.

Just as Emilee's blood was on his hands. He'd left her vulnerable and easy prey for whoever had harmed her. "I think you know where your God can go." John cast an angry glare at the preacher.

Noah stepped backward away from him.

"What are you doing?" John barked.

"He's waiting for the lightning to strike." The voice came from behind Noah. "It's a no-no. You don't blaspheme God." Seth New stepped from the shadows.

John would have been amused at the way Seth winced when he saw his face, but John didn't have it in him. "You don't believe?"

"I believe," Seth said. "I just don't care. God doesn't have much use for me. He's shown me how little He cares."

"Then why should I believe?" John turned toward Noah.

"Because Seth's wife believed, and Seth once believed. Despite anything Seth does, he can't run off God. He can be angry with God all he wants because he knows God is ever-faithful to forgive."

"I don't know much of anything, Noah." Seth looked down at the toe of his shoe and kicked at a pebble on the dock. The small stone plopped into the water. "Didn't Melvin Crum always say assurance comes from God and not from individuals? How can you be so sure of my standing with God when I feel so far away from Him, especially now."

Was Seth challenging the preacher? Good luck. So far, John had lost every argument.

"Don't muddy the water here with your grievances against the Lord. Emilee Ryan is in trouble, and she needs intervention. Would you deny her our prayers?" Noah sparred.

Seth shifted his weight from one foot to the other. "If I thought God would listen, I'd say my own for her."

With his eye that wasn't swollen after Andy's perfect punch, John peered through the darkness. Did Seth know the truth, or was he simply concerned for a woman he knew nothing about?

Noah clutched John's elbow. "Your wife will need you when she arrives. Why don't you at least go up and lie down until—"

"Until when?" John's entire body stiffened. He dropped his arms to his side and clenched and unclenched his fist. Then he turned his head toward heaven, his voice an uncontrolled scream. "I can't! I can't lie in that bed we're supposed to share. I can't do it." He covered his battered face with his hands, but his cries continued. "I can't do it. If I do, it's like saying this is okay. I'll get used to her not being there. I'm not going to let that ha—"

Strong arms encircled him, cutting off his cries. The force took him off guard. He struggled at first, but whoever held him wouldn't release him. "Oh, God!" he screamed. "What am I going to do?"

"You're going to go into my room, and you're going to rest." The soft, soothing voice reached into his agonized mind.

John looked into the face of his brother and then leaned his head against Andy's shoulder.

"I'm sorry, buddy." Andy called him by the seldom-spoken nickname—the one he used the night of the storm when Mom had been killed.

Like the small child that once clung to Andy, he allowed his brother to lead him up the hill and into their home. Somewhere along the path, Mickey joined them, placing a firm hand on John's shoulder. "I'm here, John, and I'm sorry."

John nodded and sobbed against his brother.

⌘

Seth started toward the house—once the place where he felt at home most in this world—his grandparents' home.

Noah blocked his way. "He doesn't need your doubts. He needs God's love." He pushed past him.

Seth grabbed Noah's arm and motioned him to wait until everyone moved out of sight.

"What more do we have to say? I'm tired, Seth. I want John to rest. He can't hold up much longer."

"You know the truth," Seth spat the words. "You knew before I did."

Noah said nothing.

"Do you think he loves my sister?" Seth leaned in.

"I have no doubt about it, but sometimes when you love someone, you don't think straight."

Seth nodded. "Yeah."

"Where's your father? You didn't take this out on him, did you?"

Seth gave a half-nod, not yet convinced Pop didn't deserve everything Seth had dished out to him.

"He feels bad enough. This has been a burden he's carried for too many years."

Seth pinched the bridge of his nose, fighting the emotions that pummeled his chest. "He should have told me first."

Noah sat on the dock and dangled his feet over the water.

A lecture was coming.

"Haven't you ever done something that shamed you,

something you didn't want anyone to know, and your silence caused the whole situation to fester and take on a life of its own?"

A memory sprang to Seth's mind, something harbored in the blackness of his soul. He sat down beside Noah, continuing to battle his emotions. Would putting words to his indiscretions make the burden he carried over Linda's death weigh less?

"Don't lie to me. We both share a secret no one knows," Noah lifted a brow.

Seth closed his eyes, thankful for Noah's words that quelled his confession. Then he laughed at the memory of their boyhood secret.

"If they find out you and I shot Sheriff Tompkins in his rear with the BB gun, we'll be crucified." Noah laughed.

"You two shot him?" Luke's sailboat rocked, and he stepped outside. He rubbed his hand through his unruly mop of brown hair and yawned. "Everyone blamed me. My dad grounded me for a year, and I didn't even own a gun. I hate them."

"Look what you've done," Seth accused Noah.

Luke's feet hit the dock. "You owe me. You guys owe me big." He started toward the house. "Not only did I get grounded. I got the belt, a big leather strap, and I think my dad purposely let the buckle hit me a few times." Luke headed up the hill. "I smell roast beast."

"So, up until now, we kept it a secret." Noah touched the toe of his shoe to the waters below, making a tiny wake.

"Not the same."

"Isn't it?" Noah leaned forward, peering downward. Then he moved one shoulder up and the other down, clicking his finger and breaking out into song, "We shot the sheriff."

"Yeah, but we didn't kill the deputy." Seth sang.

"Ha-ha." Noah laughed then sobered. "We worried about Sheriff Tompkins and promised to say special prayers for him. We both felt sorry, and we agreed to ask God to forgive us."

Seth remembered well. They had been very frightened, and they could turn to no one else. So, they agreed they'd pray, but twelve-year-old boys didn't pray together. Seth did pray in the privacy of his room, and he knew Noah did the same. "Like we thought his fat rear couldn't survive a BB?"

"Not the point, Seth. Do you remember how your grandfather and his friends sat on his office balcony calling out jokes? I don't think Tompkins drove into Serenity after that without someone laughing at him. The barbs went on for years, and there's Luke. Didn't you hear what he said? He wasn't kidding. I remember how mad his dad got when the sheriff accused him. I'm sure his dad used a very wide belt."

Seth shrugged. "It wasn't the first time."

"We know Luke pulled a lot of pranks in his life, but what if this one, the one he didn't pull, was a turning point in his life. What if you and I caused Luke to start making the choices he made? Now imagine if you and I came clean back then. The shooting was an accident."

"A mishap of that proportion would have ended my life if Pop had found out."

"And I think Melvin borrowed the belt he used on Luke from my dad." Noah smiled. "Life might be a lot different if you and I had taken our punishment. Maybe the people still would have teased the sheriff, but Luke wouldn't have been blamed, and maybe he would have made wiser choices." Noah used Seth's shoulder to stand and pulled his childhood friend to his feet. They walked toward the house in silence broken only when they got to the screen door. "You're guiltier than I am, you know." Noah held to the door handle.

"Oh yeah? How?" Seth laughed.

"Because Luke's your best friend, and you let him take the fall."

"Not true." The voice came to them from the darkness of the porch. "I always figured you were the one to blame the most, Noah."

"And why's that?" Noah asked as Luke came into view.

"Because the sheriff mistook your dark hair for me."

"You've known all along," Seth barked.

"Yeah, I did, and Noah's right. You two are the reason for every bad choice I've ever made. You should be ashamed. I blame you."

"Oh, shut up," Noah stomped past him.

Luke laughed and followed, his voice mimicking a younger kid. "Oh, Seth, what if Sheriff Tompkins dies? It'll be our fault. We need to pray for God to forgive us and for Sheriff Tompkins to get better."

So, Luke had overheard his conversation with Noah many years earlier. The truth only made him admire his friend more.

"I couldn't believe the two of you didn't pray for me," Luke complained. "After Dad got done with me, I couldn't sit down for a month. No wonder I turned out like I did."

"Do you always listen in on our conversations?" Noah opened the house door and walked inside, Luke behind him.

"When the two of you get together, I come out on the losing end. What do you think?" Luke challenged.

The door closed, leaving Seth on the outside.

Seth stood alone in the darkness and looked out over the yard filled with lush tropical vegetation planted by his grandparents and before that, his great-grandparents. Now, it belonged to his sister. He sat on the porch steps and stared into the darkness through the tears in his eyes.

"Emilee, please come home to me."

Chapter Nineteen

Noah walked with Penny toward the back door of the Ryan home. Though a heavy weight lay on his shoulder, he still managed a smile. Penny looked as if she'd lost her only friend. "Are you okay?"

She shook her head. "But you have more important things on your mind. Belle will be worried about you if you don't get home soon."

"Pastor McGowan," Andy called to him from the living room. "John wants to see you."

Noah's smile waned. "You know, Belle and I are available anytime you need us." He stepped back inside where Andy was waiting. "I thought John was sleeping."

"He promised to rest after he spoke to you." Andy led him upstairs. "He's in my room."

At the top of the landing, Noah followed Andy and when Andy pointed inside, Noah pushed open the door. One lamp on the nightstand offered a dim glow. John lay staring at the ceiling. He looked much better after shaving and showering, although Noah winced, thinking of the torture he must have endured while running the razor over his swollen and cut face. John draped his right arm over his eyes as if to shut out the light.

"I'll be downstairs." Andy closed the door behind him.

"I'm sorry." John dropped his arm and turned his head. "You've been here all day, and I've treated you with nothing but loathing."

"I'll live." Noah sank into the chair beside the bed. He would never admit that, thus far, John Ryan had been the most difficult of persons to handle. Yet, John had a reason—an overriding fear that he may never see his wife again.

"Don't stop praying for her," John said.

"I won't."

"You talk about Him as if He's your best friend, like you know Him personally." John's stare penetrated Noah's soul.

"God?" Noah nodded. "He's my best friend. He's my Father, my Savior, and my Lord."

"So, you really believe He exists?"

"If not, why preach?"

"And you think He cares about Emilee and me?" John reminded Noah of a small boy questioning the greatest gift in the world.

"I know so."

John turned his eyes back to the ceiling. "I hope I haven't run you off. I don't handle stress well."

"Nah, really?" Noah smiled.

John's face remained unchanged. "If God is as powerful as you say, I could use Him in my corner. You'll come back?"

"I'll be back, but God will be with you whether I'm here or not. I'm headed home to spend some time with my wife. I hope you'll rest."

John nodded, and as he did so, the tears streamed down his cheek and onto the already damp pillow. "Who is it?"

Noah stood. "Who is what?"

"You said earlier you made a promise to someone to stay here." John looked at him. "Who was it?"

"I think you already know."

"Emilee's uncle?"

"Uncle?" Noah raised his eyebrows.

"David New, Emilee's uncle."

So, John didn't know the entire truth, but he did know something. "David asked me to check on you, yes." He couldn't reveal David's truths, so he skirted them a bit. "And I'm sure he'd like to be here, too. He isn't a man to visit if he's not wanted."

"For a man who abandoned her, he seems to care a lot now."

"Think how people might perceive your actions, John, before you doubt David's intentions." Noah clenched his teeth and took a deep breath.

John grew silent for a long moment then nodded. "I'd like him to come. Once Emilee's safe, we can all talk. I'll take what's coming to me."

"I'll tell him. Listen, everyone downstairs has my number. If you need me before I get back ..." He stopped. "John?"

John's eyelashes rested against his swollen cheek, and Noah almost hated to disturb him.

"Yeah."

"The problem between Emilee and your friend, Cameron—"

"He's not my friend."

"Why did she ask you to keep him away from her?"

John opened his eyes.

Noah waited. Would God part that heavy persona of aloofness John showed to everyone and allow him to answer? When John didn't speak, Noah turned away.

"She never told me her reasons, but I've suspected trouble between them for some time. I thought that maybe she was worried that he knew about her affair with Andy."

Noah drew closer once again. "And you believed Emilee could be unfaithful to you, that your brother would do such a thing, only because Cameron said so?"

"What would you do? He's Andy's best friend. He said he wanted to let me know because he didn't want to see Emilee come between us. I love them both."

Noah took another deep breath. "To be honest, I wouldn't push my wife away. I'd hold on to her like precious gold."

"I'm beginning to think Cameron lied, that maybe she had other reasons for wanting me to keep him away. She asked me because she knew I could make him do it."

"She had reason to think Cameron would comply with your request?"

John closed his eyes again. "She knows I hold some sway, but she doesn't know why. My father left me in charge … of a trust … for him." His voice became a whisper, and his words slowed. "Andy … doesn't … know. I … don't … want … him … to … know."

"He won't hear it from me."

No answer came, and Noah walked out of the room. He made his way downstairs. "He's asleep," he announced to the small crowd gathered in the living room. Mickey and Seth each held a plate filled with roast beef, potatoes, and carrots. "You have my number if he needs me. I'll be back in the morning."

"Noah." Andy stopped him. "It's okay. I can—"

"I know you can," Noah assured. "He needs you, but he did ask me to come back."

"I'll drive you home."

"No. I'm fine. You stay with your brother." He nodded toward the living room. "Blanchie looks pretty tired."

Andy blinked as if the thought of Blanchie's tiredness were a revelation to him. "Thank you." He held out his hand.

Noah took it securely in his and gave it a hearty shake.

"You've been a good friend today." Andy opened the door.

"You've been a good brother."

"You can say that after what I did to him?"

Noah studied the man's face. How would Andy take his words? "I think you knocked some sense into him. He's beginning to have some doubts about what your friend said about you and your sister-in-law."

"Did he say that?"

"He said he believes Cameron lied to him," Noah said.

"Trouble is, I can't believe Cameron would say that."

"Get some rest."

Andy swallowed hard. "Kind of hard when a piece of your heart is missing."

Cameron hated this part of the world. How Andy could have followed John here was beyond him. Even Emilee had stayed behind.

And that had worked for Cameron. All he'd needed to do was bide his time, wait for her to let down her guard.

Emilee thought she knew him. She'd kept him at bay.

Smart girl.

Until she'd gone and got so sure of herself that he'd been able to get to her without a problem.

Behind him, his suitcase lay open on the motel bed, clothes still inside. With Emilee out of the picture, his plans were falling into place.

No need to unpack. He wouldn't be in this mainland motel for long. He'd wait it out, make sure Andy suspected he'd hurried to Serenity to help the brothers get over the loss of their precious Emilee. He'd gotten a flight out of New York after leaving Emilee as bruised and beaten as he could without killing her.

A neighbor had exited an apartment when he knocked on Emilee's door. He'd met the beauty before, had even flirted with her. Her recognition of him had thwarted his original plans to leave Emilee dead. Little did he know at the time that the twist in his intended fate for Emilee saved him when he found out that Andy had been on the phone with Emilee when he'd knocked.

He'd always been good at making quick decisions. He'd pummeled her enough to leave some cuts and bruises, even restraining himself when she fought back. With the witness, he couldn't afford to leave her dead as he'd planned. Instead, he left her well enough to flee, certain that his promises to kill both the Ryan brothers would keep Emilee away from Serenity Key. If his menacing words hadn't given her the message, the truth he'd shared about what her wonderful husband had kept from her had definitely been fruitful. Emily hadn't been able to hide the emotional pain he'd inflicted any more than she could conceal the physical pain.

Cameron liked the idea of watching John suffer, never knowing where his precious Emilee might be and all the while Cameron would know she was alive, living in fear for her husband

and at the same time hating him for keeping her family a secret—just like old Zack.

Not knowing what had happened to Emilee would slowly drive Andy's brother insane.

Cameron laughed aloud. His plans would fall into place.

Cameron had blundered, though, when he'd later placed the call to Andy's cell phone. He never thought John or Andy would call the police in for help—not the way they guarded their secrets.

Well, Cameron had a few of his own, and he was going to make John pay for some of them.

He ran through his list. *One: John must hate his wife and his brother; two: Emilee must be taken out of the equation; three: John must spend the rest of his life wanting what he can't have. Search John. Search. You won't find your precious Emilee.*

He brushed a hand along his arm. The cuts her nails made there and on his chest were deep and painful. Emilee sure offered him a good fight.

Tomorrow, he would begin to face the dreary days on Serenity Key, pining along with John and Andy for the woman who simply didn't love them any longer. Oh, yes, and he would find more ways to make John suffer. Andy would survive. Andy would get over the loss, but Cameron would never allow John to forget her. Never.

Cameron slid his suitcase to the far side of the bed. He had time, all the time in the world. He wouldn't arrive on John and Andy's doorstep at first. Other business on Serenity needed tending. She had jade green eyes, dark hair, a wicked sense of her own beauty, and she could be very dangerous to him if he didn't take care of her.

Once he finished with India, she'd never open her mouth. Sending her the check to buy her silence had failed. She never cashed it, and that could only mean that she was smart enough to hold on to it, to use it against him. Oh, he would see India Thompson again, and he would make certain that she didn't speak to anyone about anything.

He smiled, thinking of his conversation with Andy. His friend remained very secretive about the woman in his office. Yes, Andy was seeing India. That frightened him at first, but now he realized India sought only Andy's money. After Cameron, the most likely candidate for her to pursue would be Andre. She wouldn't besmirch Cameron's name because she knew how close he was to Andy.

That would work in his favor. He'd just have to save his friend from India the same way he saved Andy from Emilee and would soon save his friend from John.

Maybe he should pay a visit to India now. He'd be careful. Get the job done. Leave the island without anyone knowing, come back to the mainland and arrive tomorrow, playing the part of a concerned friend, full-well knowing that he'd already made sure Emilee would no longer seek to be a part of the brothers' lives.

Despite the late hour—ten o'clock—David thanked Blanchie for allowing him entrance through the familiar back door. He walked with her down the long hallway that opened into the vast living room of his childhood home. Now, it belonged to the husband of his daughter, the son of Zachariah Ryan, the wrong son.

Andy sat in one of the high-backed chairs in front of the cold fireplace. A growth of beard was beginning to peek through the skin of his usually shaven face. His long hair hung loose against his shoulders. Andy wiped his hand across his eyes. The man's chin quivered, and Blanchie stepped forward, but David motioned her to stop. Instead, he cleared his voice. "Andy?" This was the right son, the one who could love his daughter. Why hadn't Emilee married this one?

Andy straightened and quickly covered his eyes. "David." He did not look up.

"Have you heard anything?"

Andy shook his head and looked at his watch. "Not since the last report several hours ago."

"Nothing else?"

"Nothing. The waiting is killing me."

David sat in the matching chair opposite Andy. "How is John?"

"He's resting," Blanchie offered. "I just checked on him a short while ago. He's restless, but he's asleep."

"I have to be strong for him," Andy spoke.

"You have to be strong for yourself," David told him.

"I don't understand why she would be so careless. Why did she let the car run out of gas? It just doesn't make sense. Emilee is never rash. She's a physician. She doesn't overreact."

David's daughter, a stranger to him, became less of one through Andy's words.

"She's level-headed, not stupid. There has to be a rhyme to her reasoning."

"What do you think is going on?"

Andy stood and walked away from where David remained sitting. Blanchie moved beside him. "I spoke to our friend, Cameron, and he told me she didn't want to come here. She'd changed her mind."

"No, she wouldn't do that." John stood at the bottom of the stairs. "Emilee would face me first. She'd tell me she planned to leave me."

The gruesome sight of John's swollen face compelled David to his feet. "What in the world happened to you?"

John blinked and stepped back. Surprised or frightened, David couldn't tell which. John stepped off the staircase and into the living room. "My brother decided he'd had enough of me." He lowered himself onto the couch.

Andy motioned David to again take one of the seats in front of the fireplace, and David did so. "Have you seen a doctor, boy?"

John stared at the floor. Without looking up, he shook his head. "I don't need a doctor, Mr. New. I need my wife."

If he needed her so badly, why did he ever let her go?

Judge not that you be not judged.

But, Lord...

For with what judgment you judge, you will be judged: and with the measure you use, it will be measured back to you.

This man is so much like his father. He's capable of anything.

And why do you look at the speck in your brother's eye, but do not consider the plank in your own eye?

David said nothing, listening as the Lord poured wisdom upon him.

"David, are you okay?" Blanchie placed a hand on his arm.

He nodded but again gave his attention to the forlorn man sitting on the couch. "I know exactly how you feel, John."

"I don't think you do." John lifted his swollen face. "How could you?"

"Because thirty years ago, give or take a few months, my wife left and I waited for her to return to me."

"David," Blanchie pleaded. "Don't go there. I know how your story ended."

David ignored her. "And, John, I hope you haven't done or said anything to your wife that you'd regret if you don't have the chance to make it right."

John gripped his hair and rocked his body back and forth. For a few long moments, his mouth moved, but no sound came. With each breath, his words grew louder. "Johnny. Johnny. Johnny! My name is Johnny!" He sprang to his feet, rushed toward the door, shoved it open, and ran off the porch.

In the darkened path leading toward the Gulf waters, John fell upon his knees. "Oh, God, let me hear her call me Johnny." He hugged himself tightly, his body again rocking with his grief. "Emilee!" he screamed her name. "Em, don't leave me."

Andy started toward his brother, but David held him back. "He needs this, Andy. Let him go."

Beside them, Blanchie cried. Andy pulled the young woman into his embrace, and David watched as Andy gave way to the same emotions engulfing his younger brother.

They could both cry for John, but only those who had suffered a loss of this kind could understand the strength it took for John just to breathe.

Lord, I see. John didn't hurt my child—not with physical violence—not intentionally. Both these men love my daughter desperately. Please give us all the chance to show her we love her—again.

Chapter Twenty

Emilee didn't think she could take another step along the dark, deserted highway, but the signs telling her she was approaching Serenity Key kept her on her feet.

She'd stopped several times on her trek, too weary, or too wary, to go on. The fog in her brain grew cloudier. At her last stop, she'd wavered in and out of consciousness, dead tired, but she'd heard Della Croix's voice. *Remember, Serenity isn't only a state of mind. It's a place, a very real and lovely place.* Serenity was her destination. She'd fought to get this far, even walking more miles than she thought possible from where she'd pulled her car out of sight as it started to sputter to a stop. Out of gas.

Now, that she was here, the doubts returned. Her arrival would place both John and Andy in danger. She'd have to figure it out, but first, she needed to take care of her injuries before they took care of her.

She found her way into what looked like the heart of the town. Swaying as she stood, she opened her coat and touched the wetness on her shirt. Wincing, she pulled her hand away. The bruising was worse than the bleeding, causing pain with each step. She fought to keep her balance but in her tiredness, she lost the battle, landing hard against the concrete sidewalk. Pain pierced her bruised body.

She cried out.

For some time, she sat, her legs straight, head tilted back trying desperately to get a rhythm to her breath that would help ease the throbbing. She clenched her eyes shut. When she found the courage to open them, nothing around her had changed. This endless nightmare was reality.

She smoldered beneath the lightweight trench coat. Her attempt to shrug it from her shoulders met with more pain, bringing her movement to an abrupt stop. "Cameron." The name hissed between her teeth.

She resisted the urge to stand, the thought of the agonizing pain too much, but she couldn't sit on the sidewalk in the middle of town forever. The soft hum of a vehicle's motor made her decision easy.

She placed her palms on the coarse concrete and pushed to her feet. The car neared, its lights just visible. A tall hedge to one side afforded her a place to hide, and she struggled forward to duck behind it.

The car passed, and she stared after it, her mind playing tricks on her. It couldn't have been him. Had Cameron realized she couldn't heed his warning? Was he looking for her? Cameron had wanted to kill her. The fact that he'd left her alive surprised her. She covered her face with her hands. He'd done so much more, and she'd been powerless to stop him. Even the scratches, her fingers clawing for release, had not halted his attack.

She stepped back onto the sidewalk. She took a deep breath, and the cry of pain caught in her throat. Even if she knew where to find John and Andy, would it be safe for her to go to them? Cameron was more than capable of carrying out the threats he'd left her with. She lowered her head. She wasn't good at living life without her husband. And Cameron had said she had family here. An uncle and a cousin. Her greatest desire. "They're all I have." With each whispered word, she released her breath. With each step, her body throbbed. She tightened her coat. October. And so warm.

She managed to walk the block and turned right. Older Victorian homes, many dark inside, lined the avenue.

She came to a corner and stopped before an old wooden building, its steeple reaching to heaven. She drew close to the sign. Tears flooded her face. *Remember, Serenity isn't only in your mind. It's a place, a very real and lovely place.*

"Serenity Key Baptist Church," she whispered the name in awe. "Serenity ... Serenity Key Baptist Church. Della may have attended church here with her sister ... her husband ... her friends."

Serenity Key.

That couldn't be a coincidence. She stumbled backward.

She didn't think she could withstand one more act of betrayal, especially by her friend, Della. If her uncle and cousin were here, Della must have known them. Maybe she'd been friends with her parents. Why hadn't Della told her about them?

She straightened as far as the pain would allow, refusing to believe that Della would hurt her. After they married, Emilee had mentioned to John that she missed Della. Had he found her? Had he wanted to move here so that he could gift her with a meeting with her old friend and had he stumbled upon her family?

"Do you know where your precious Johnny lives, Emilee? He's in Serenity, sweetheart. Look how much he hates you. He's there and you're here. He's with your uncle and your cousin. Just like Zack, he's kept the truth from you. But Zack told me."

Cameron had spoken the ugly words close to her ear as he'd held her down.

She shut her eyes against his ranting. "John doesn't know," she said aloud to dislodge the evil in Cameron's voice. "He doesn't know, and if he does, he didn't tell me because he's hurting. He wanted me to see Della again. That's all. I know it."

She staggered a bit but kept her balance. "Why didn't you kill me? Anything is better than facing Johnny's pain, or even worse, his pity," she whispered to the unseen villain of her living nightmare.

"I'm going to kill your precious Johnny if you ever see him again." Cameron's words continued to invade her thin grasp on sanity. "Don't think I won't, Emilee. What I've just done to you is just a small bit of what I plan for him if you insist on returning to his life. Andy won't even be safe if you go to them. I promise you."

The pain was enough to convince her that Cameron Matrai would kill John and maybe even Andy if she ran to them.

"Your uncle, he's a big man about town. Owns a restaurant. Your cousin, Seth, he's a fireman. Runs the Serenity Key Fire Department, and Johnny's with them pretending you don't exist." Her mind spun with Cameron's taunts, and she fought to understand why she'd decided to chance the lives of her husband and Andy.

If only Cameron's voice would leave her alone.

"Zack told me about your mom, too." He'd gotten in her face when he'd finished with her. "She didn't want you either."

Now, she started to walk, but her legs refused to move. "God, I don't know how to find any of them. I'm afraid." She slipped to the grass beside the sign. Lying on her side, the one that received the least of Cameron's anger, she closed her eyes. The tears slid from her face onto her hands, which cradled her head. "Help me, God, or let me die."

Blanchie sat on the swing. She liked it here on John's back porch. Music drifted up from the radio on Luke's boat, and she could hear her ex-husband singing along. A smile crossed her face as she remembered how he used to sing throughout the cabin where they'd lived.

"What's that smile all about?" Andy interrupted her thoughts. "You looked a thousand years away from here."

"Just two or three." She leaned against him. "And I shouldn't have gone there at all. The future is so much better." As she spoke the words, something deep whispered that the future she had planned was wrong.

"Do you want me to walk you home?" He helped her settle against him, his actions belying his words.

Not that she wanted a future with this man to be wrong. Andy was just so right. "In a little bit." She lifted her head to look up into his face.

The salty breeze fell across them, and Blanchie thought of John sleeping restlessly upstairs. She knew the terror of lying in your bed, wondering if the one you loved would ever come home to you again. She'd cried and begged God every time to bring her husband home safely.

And God had never let her down.

"Ooh la la," Luke sang.

Andy chuckled.

"He really is a clown, isn't he?" She shook her head.

"I can't say I've ever known anyone like him in my entire life."

"They don't make them like Luke. God broke the mold, probably on purpose."

Andy laughed. "I think the world needs more like him." Andy kissed the top of her head. "He's honest, hardworking, and a real friend."

Blanchie nodded. Yes. Luke had developed all those attributes. Why hadn't she noticed? He could be telling her the truth about his drinking. The case of beer was full. As far as his work, she had noticed him laboring every day at some task, and he had mentioned to her that he was ready to settle down for the winter and write. Luke was a prolific writer, a published author. If he'd handled the other seasons of the year as steadfastly as he protected what he called his "writing time," perhaps they would have had the perfect life Blanchie had longed to have with him. Now, though, Luke worked daily, and he hadn't borrowed money from her or anyone else in a very long time. Even shortly after their divorce, those to whom he owed money had knocked on her door wanting to be paid. She'd recently found an envelope filled with cash slid under her door. She'd never asked for alimony. They had no children, but Luke had written on the envelope. "I owe you so much more. This is payback for the times you got me out of trouble." Luke appeared to have stopped gambling and spending his money on other vices.

His friendship with Seth also spoke volumes. He remained quietly strong for Seth during his mourning, keeping Seth from hurting himself.

"Where did you go now?" Andy tugged her even closer.

Blanchie shook her head to clear her thoughts. "I was thinking that we all see situations the way we want to see them."

"And what brought that about?"

She lowered her head, ashamed to look Andy in the face. Her thoughts had betrayed him, and she struggled to return to sharing this moment with only him.

He made her face him. The palms of his hands rested warm against her cheeks. "I haven't said thank you."

"For what?" she asked.

"I couldn't bear up without you. You've been very understanding. I nearly beat my brother to a pulp, and you remained beside me."

I hope you'll let me stand beside you for a long time. The words had been on the tip of her tongue, but she couldn't bring them forth. Luke had become an open book to her, but the man she sat beside hadn't told her he had a sister-in-law. He'd never really talked about himself. John had thought Andy could have cheated with John's wife. Andy declared the accusation a lie, but how could she be sure?

Her silence must have bothered Andy. He stared at her for a long while. "Tell me what you're thinking."

"I was thinking about what's important in any relationship," she offered.

"Did you come to a conclusion about that?"

She stared out at the yard beyond. The sliver of moon that shined in the sky sparkled upon the Gulf waters. "Trust. Relationships can't endure if there isn't trust."

"I agree." He brushed a kiss across her forehead, looked into her eyes, and slowly began to lower his lips to hers.

No. The voice inside of her was low and deliberate. Although his kiss from their first date had been all she could think about, she pulled back before his lips could touch hers again.

"Whoops." The screen door banged shut. "Sorry."

Blanchie stood and straightened her clothing. "Don't you ever knock?" She faced her ex-husband.

"I had no idea you two would be making out like teenagers."

"No. You and I made out like teenagers. Andy and I ... Andy and I are talking like adults." She turned toward the man she wanted to love. "I'll be ready to go in a minute. I want to clean the kitchen." She stormed past the man she had never stopped loving.

Luke raised his hands in the air. "What'd I do? I wanted to see if you've heard anything. I sure didn't come over to see you kissing my wife."

"Ex-wife," Andy's voice echoed with hers.

Blanchie moved to the kitchen where she stood in the darkness. Why, when she'd decided to move on, did she feel that Luke was supposed to walk beside her?

"Em. Emilee," John called. "Emilee." The cries grew louder.

Blanchie rushed upstairs hoping to stop them before Andy could hear.

The call from Dr. Yasmin Garcia surprised Kurt, but he soon learned it came at the request of NYPD. The information she had would prove valuable.

"I knocked on her door, and it opened." The doctor's voice quivered.

Kurt held tightly to the phone. With his right hand, he

clenched a pencil.

"I found Emilee unconscious in the bedroom," she added. "Her clothes were torn and her body badly beaten. She awoke in terror. I couldn't calm her for several minutes. I tried to call the ambulance, but she wouldn't let me. She seemed so frightened, Chief Davis. More than anything, she was afraid that John would find out."

"What do you mean?" Kurt questioned.

"She believes John won't be able to live with what this monster did to her."

"Does she have reason to fear John?"

"I don't know him too well. The first time we met, he acted like a man truly in love with his wife. At our second meeting, I thought the exact opposite."

"What happened next?"

"I checked for broken bones, cleaned up and bandaged some open wounds, tried to ascertain if she could have internal bleeding, but that's a little difficult without the proper equipment."

"So, you took care of Emilee without reporting the crime?"

"I promised her I wouldn't. I told myself it was one friend helping another."

If he could only block out her words. He rubbed his chin until he realized the unconscious act. The scars on his face weren't so deep now, but the scars on his heart always bled when he heard stories like this one. "Dr. Garcia, why didn't you come forward sooner?"

"The authorities contacted me after I returned from a trip out of town, taking a break after some grueling shifts. I didn't even know that my whereabouts were a concern to them. They asked me to provide a statement with regard to what I saw when I walked in, Emilee's behavior, and her injuries. I've done that."

"Fair enough. Did Emilee happen to tell you the name of her attacker?"

"No, she didn't, but I have my suspicions."

"Would you mind telling me?"

"I saw Emilee with him outside the hospital. I couldn't hear what they said, but I know he threatened her, maybe even hurt her."

"When was this?"

"A few days ago."

"Do you know his name?"

"Cameron—Cameron—oh, I can't remember."

"Cameron Matrai?"

"That's it."

With a muttered curse, Kurt snapped his pencil in half.

"Do you know this man?" she asked.

"Vaguely. Dr. Garcia, I'm sorry you were involved in this. I'd advise you to call the police if you see Matrai again. Do not approach him or allow him to get close to you."

"Chief, I'm afraid Emilee can't deal with what happened to her as easily as she believes. I've treated a few rape victims in my short career. Emilee is suffering from post-traumatic stress. She wouldn't agree to go to the hospital with me or to report the incident. I tried to stay with her for as long as I could, but she grew agitated and asked me to leave. I'm not sure at that point if she knew what she was doing."

"She wasn't lucid?" Kurt rubbed a hand over his face.

"Not completely. She was functioning, but I believe she could only do that because of the long hours we clock in and the way we function in our residency."

Kurt remained silent.

"Emilee drew blood from him, too." Dr. Garcia said.

That got his full attention. "How do you know?"

"Blood under her nails. She said she left deep gashes on his arms and chest. Emilee's physical scars will fade, but the same can't be said for the emotional ones."

"I know that only too well." As a child, the scars on his face had shamed him. His embarrassment, his broken heart, and his anger kept him separated from all but a few. Now, he only remembered them at times like this when duty caused him to face his past.

"Emilee is a level-headed, decisive doctor," Dr. Garcia said. "This behavior is uncharacteristic. Either her attacker came back, or she's alone, and she's confused."

Kurt stared at the broken pencil. "Thank you, Doctor. I'll advise you if we find your friend."

"I pray you find her alive." The doctor ended the call.

FAY LAMB

Chapter Twenty-One

Seth woke with a start. He looked around the small space he called home and then laid his arm across his forehead, trying to remember what had startled him awake. The waters lapping against his sailboat threatened to lull him back to sleep. Then, he remembered.

In his dreams, a woman cried.

Linda? He didn't think so. He had only one re-occurring dream about his wife.

Who then?

He'd been searching for something—maybe someone. The whimpering began, low at first but growing louder. He'd started walking, looking under bushes. The cries continued until he'd found himself in front of the Baptist church.

And that's what woke him.

He sat up, threw the thin sheet from his body, and swung his feet over the bunk. He stood and stumbled from the back of the cabin toward the front.

Unopened mail cluttered the booth that served as his dining room table, and as he reached to pull his jeans over the seat, some papers fell onto the floor. He slipped the pants on and bent to pick up the parcels.

Since he'd given up drinking, Seth's cure for a sleepless night was a nice walk around the streets of Serenity. The late evening or early morning hours were always so peaceful. He stepped out of the cabin and onto the dock.

Gentle waves lapped against his boat. He breathed in the scent of rain and looked past the bay and over to the buildings on Front Street. The clouds far out in the Gulf illuminated as an unseen lightning bolt cut through them. The storm would travel down the coast and probably never hit land. He prayed the hurricane coming into the Gulf of Mexico would do the same.

Seth always took the same route—down C Avenue past Noah McGowan's house on one side and the Baptist church on the other. Then he'd turn left and walk the block to where his vacant house sat dark and lonely. He hadn't stepped inside the two-story Victorian since the day he'd buried his wife.

A raccoon scampered across Noah McGowan's yard, turning its bandit eyes toward Seth as if to say he was beyond the law. The critter had left his calling card strewn across the curb in Noah's yard. Mr. Raccoon had enjoyed a feast in the McGowan garbage. Seth picked up the trashcan, replaced the refuse, and secured the lid. He wiped his hands on his pants and looked around for some way to cleanse them more thoroughly. Noah's spigot glistened in the moonlight, and Seth made his way to the side of the house to wash his hands.

The sound of footsteps came from behind. He spun around.

A lazy armadillo stopped his march across the grass and gazed up at him. The animal turned its beady eyes to the running water and then back to Seth before plodding toward the street. Seth turned off the water and started for the road.

In the light cast by the church sign, Seth caught sight of

something lying on the ground. He squinted.

The thought of an alligator crossed his mind. On rare occasions, one would find its way out of the channels and into town.

With a cautious step, he moved across the road. Then he stopped.

He didn't have Luke with him. Luke was the only person stupid enough to lead the beast back to where it belonged and save it from certain death if they summoned a trapper. No one could ever convince Luke that by attempting to save the creature's life, he jeopardized his own.

Seth edged closer. That was definitely not an alligator.

"Johnny?" A woman sat up and stared in Seth's direction.

Dare he hope?

He moved forward, and she scrambled up against the sign, holding her hands out as if to brace against some terrible evil. "No." Her hushed plea stopped him.

"I'm not going to hurt you. Are you all right? Do you need help?"

She lowered her arms.

Eighty degrees and she wore a trench coat. The breeze blew, and a trace of an unforgettable scent touched his nose. He recognized the odor. "Are you hurt? Are you bleeding?"

She said nothing, and Seth moved closer. Her eyes grew wide in the semi-darkness, and she tried to back closer against the sign.

"I'm not going to hurt you. I'm a paramedic. I'm here to help. My name's Seth New."

"Seth?"

"Yes, that's right, Seth. Where are you hurt?"

"I'm not hurt."

She was either lying or disoriented.

"You're Seth New? You're the fireman?"

Once on the grass in front of the sign, he stooped in a non-threatening manner, looking at the woman. "You know me?"

"David is your father?"

"That's right. David's my father. You know about him, too?" He needed to keep her talking and gain her confidence.

She shook her head.

The three separate lights placed over the sign provided a bright glow around her. Her eyes—her glassy and unfocused—were deep violet. They were mirror images of the eyes he'd inherited from his mother. "Emilee?" he whispered.

Her lips began to tremble, and her eyes pooled with tears. "Johnny told you?"

"He's very worried about you." He'd tell her whatever she wanted to hear to gain her trust. "I can take you to him right now."

She seemed to think on that. Then she shook her head. "No." She shrank from him.

"Okay." He stood and backed away, hoping the space would make her feel safe. "You're hurt. I'm a paramedic," he repeated. "Let me help you?"

"I need to go." She struggled to stand.

Seth did not move. Reasoning with her was the only option left to him. "Don't be afraid of me. I'm your brother."

She spun toward him, losing her balance but managing to stay on her feet. "Who are you?" she screamed as if never seeing him before.

"Your brother. Seth."

"Liar." She backed away from him. "Seth is my cousin."

"No." He took a step forward.

Her scream pierced the air, and she bent forward as if in terrible pain. "Get away from me."

He raised his hands to indicate he would advance no further.

Lights cast illumination behind him. "Seth?"

Seth motioned Noah back, but he came alongside, clad in pajamas, his hair mussed and glasses crooked. Seth turned back.

His sister had vanished.

"Around back." Noah pointed.

"Call Kurt. Tell him Emilee's here. She's injured." Seth ran after her.

———— ⌇ ————

India sprang awake.

Something scraped the concrete downstairs underneath her bedroom window. She ran to look out. Pulling the drapes back just enough, she peered downward. The pool's lights illuminated the screened area. The silence filled her with a sense of security. She started to pull away, chiding herself for letting her nerves get the best of her. Then she caught the shadow.

The silhouette grew more defined—the dark outline of a man, his head tilted upward. She looked in the direction of her parents' open bedroom window. Why had she not closed it?

The man stepped into the light.

"Oh." She stifled the scream. "No, God, no." She fell back onto her bed, fumbled for the phone, then dialed the police station. "Brittany," she whispered to the dispatcher. "This is India Thompson. There's a man on my porch. He wants to kill me."

Andy placed his glass against the refrigerator's water dispenser. The small light brightened the area around him. When the cup filled, he pulled it away and the kitchen fell into darkness once again. He didn't like the quiet, but he was thankful John and Blanchie slept.

After Luke's visit, Andy went to find Blanchie to walk her home. She'd fallen asleep in a chair beside the bed, holding John's hand. Andy had placed a soft kiss on her forehead hoping to wake her, but the gesture failed to reach through her exhaustion, and he left her there.

Lights entering the drive to the house drew Andy to the kitchen window. Kurt's patrol car. Andy discarded his glass and met Kurt at the back door. "Any word?"

"You got a minute?" Kurt motioned him outside.

Andy followed Kurt into the yard by the patrol vehicle.

The chief faced him, his features grim. "I have a few questions, and I figure you can answer them better than anyone."

Andy shrugged. "Anything."

"Your friend, Cameron, he stayed on the island for a week or so after you moved here?"

"Yeah, he helped us move."

"He left suddenly, didn't he?"

Andy nodded.

"Do you think he left because John asked him to stay away from Emilee?"

Andy shrugged. "Maybe, but I think there was something else."

Kurt raised his eyebrows. "I'm listening."

"India Thompson. He likes his flings, and he can make a woman believe she means the world to him."

"And?" the officer said the word between clenched teeth.

"Well, I think when it got a little too real with India, he left."

"And you don't believe Cameron told John you and Emilee were having an affair?"

Andy had done a lot of thinking since he'd punched his brother. John kept truths hidden, but he never outright lied. "Truth is, I believe John."

Kurt didn't press, and silence stretched between them.

Andy walked into the shadows. He leaned against an ancient mango tree. Its leaves rustled in the wind as if conjuring up the dead. One dry, hard leaf fell against the back of his hand, and he picked it up. "My father was a cruel man. He took a lot of his anger out on Emilee."

"I fail to see what this has to do with Cameron." Kurt leaned against his patrol car.

"Marrying John made it worse." Andy ignored the officer. "He saw Emilee as an adversary, and believe me, no one wanted to make themselves an enemy of Zachariah Ryan." Andy ran his tongue over his lips. He hated exposing the family skeletons.

"Go on," Kurt urged.

"After John disobeyed Zach and married Emilee, the old man refused to help with Emilee's college, so I moved in with them to help with expenses." He looked down at the leaf. "Often when I arrived home, Cameron would be waiting for me. We'd make plans to go out."

"Yeah."

"I didn't think it so strange back then, but Emilee never played hostess to Cameron. She either stayed in the kitchen or behind the closed door of the bedroom."

"John said she hated him." Kurt straightened the ball cap he wore.

Andy shook his head. "Emilee's heart isn't capable of hate."

"What happened?"

"I came home early one day—a migraine. When I opened the door, it bumped Cameron. He seemed nervous. If you know Cameron at all, he's a little too self-assured. He stuttered when he said hello, and I laughed at him. It's so clear now, almost as if I'm replaying that portion of my life over and over to discover the significance." Andy threw the leaf away. It turned in circles as it made its way to the ground.

"Keep going."

"A loud slap and Emilee's cry alerted me that Cameron wasn't alone in the apartment."

Kurt stepped toward him out of the light and into the darkness. Andy recognized anger when he saw it. Kurt's jaw remained clenched, raising his cheeks. The officer balled his hands into tight fists.

"My father had pinned Emilee in the bedroom, slapping her, and cursing her for marrying John when he had other plans for his favorite son. I reached them before he could hit her a third time. I pulled Zach's arm behind his back, pushed him away from her. I threatened to kill him if he ever touched her again."

Kurt opened his fist and took a deep breath. "Not afraid of making an enemy, huh?"

"From the moment I entered this world, Zack made me his enemy. My father hated everything about me."

"You were his natural son?"

246

"Firstborn, presumed heir to his kingdom, spitting image. What can I say?" He focused his attention on the dirt beneath his feet.

"Did your father kill your mother?"

Andy jerked his gaze upward. "What does Mom's death have to do with this?"

"Just curious. I guess it's true about money not buying happiness."

"Money can buy a lot, but happiness is just an illusion if you think it can be bought. Zack Ryan did everything to make Momma regret the day he came into her life, but she blossomed. He never got it. Momma stayed happy because she didn't need him or his money." Andy massaged his temples with his thumb and forefinger. With Emilee in danger, he couldn't afford another migraine. "Let's not go there, Kurt. What my father did, it's over, and I don't like to think of the past."

"Sure. About Cameron?"

"Cameron stood there the entire time, and when I threw Zack out, he stayed. Emilee begged me to get Cameron out of the house. So, she probably did ask John to use his influence in keeping him away from her."

"Could she be upset over Cameron's knowledge of your affair?"

Andy raised his fist, intent on showing Kurt what those same accusations cost his brother. The officer held up his hands as a sign of truce, and Andy backed away.

"I love her, but I would never—I could never—take Emilee's love from John. I don't appreciate anyone saying I tried."

Kurt remained silent.

Andy heaved a deep breath. He was about to betray his best

friend, but what else could he do when Emilee was in danger? "The fact that Emilee asked me to have Cameron leave isn't what's bothering me."

"No?"

"I'm beginning to wonder if Cameron's fear of my father wasn't the only reason Cameron just stood there and didn't help Emilee when Zack hurt her."

Kurt moved toward him. "Andy, I'm going to tell you the truth, and if you come at me the way you did a second ago, I'll arrest you. Do you hear?"

Andy jammed his hands in his jean pockets and braced for the news. "Don't keep me in suspense. What has my friend done?"

"Chief?" Kurt's car radio crackled.

The officer ducked inside. He and the dispatcher shared some technical jargon Andy didn't understand then the woman said, "It's going crazy here. India's on the line. She's scared to death. Says she has a prowler. Pastor McGowan called. I dispatched Tank to the church. Noah says Seth found an injured Emilee Ryan. She ran and Seth's combing the area."

"Seth?"

"Ten-four. Seth found her."

"Have Tank keep me posted."

"India?"

"I'm right around the corner. Keep her on the line." Kurt waved Andy forward. "Get in."

Andy moved toward the car. "Kurt, the dispatcher said Em's hurt. Why are we going to India's house?"

"Tank's on it, and believe me, India needs our help more than Emilee does right now."

Chapter Twenty-Two

India cowered against the wall of her bedroom, her hand covering her mouth to stifle the screams churning up from the pit of her stomach and straining her throat for release. What was keeping Kurt?

"India," Brittany's voice came over the phone. "Are you there?"

"Yes," she whispered. "He wants to kill me. Please tell them to hurry."

"Kurt should be turning down the drive now. He'll probably have his lights off, and you can't see him. He'll let you know when you're safe."

"Don't hang up. Please don't hang up," she begged.

"I'm here."

India strained to listen. The noises on the porch vanished. A drop of courage seeped into her. She pushed away from the wall, the phone in her hand, and walked with one cautious step in front of another to her window. With timid fingers, she lifted the curtain. Two figures lurked just outside the screen around the porch. One wore a baseball cap, and the other—the other had long dark hair. Andy Ryan. The man with the baseball cap looked up toward the house, and India let her breath out. "Kurt's here, Brit. I see him in the backyard."

"Any sign of your prowler?"

"I don't think so."

Brittany conversed with Kurt. India could hear none of their muffled words.

"India," Brittany said to her. "Listen to me. Is there any way your prowler could have entered the house?"

Air rushed from India's lungs. Where had Cameron gone?

"Are you there?" Brittany's loud inquiry reached her over the wire.

The earsplitting knock on her front door rattled through India's body. An involuntary scream pealed from her. She threw the phone away and hunched down in the darkness, still screaming. Suddenly, arms engulfed her, and she struggled to get away from their grasp. "India. It's Andy, Andy Ryan. It's me." Andy held her. "It's me," he repeated, holding his hands against her cheeks, forcing her to look at him. "Are you hurt?"

"Kurt." From somewhere a voice sounded as if in a tunnel. "Kurt, are you there?"

"You're safe." Andy's voice broke into the wall of fear surrounding India, and she blinked up at him.

Kurt entered the room and picked up the phone. "She's fine, Brit. Good job. Tell Tank I'm waiting for an update."

"Are you sure you weren't dreaming?" Andy asked her.

"No." She buried her face against his warm chest. "He wants to kill me."

"Who?" Andy asked.

"Tell him." Kurt replaced the phone on the bed stand. His fingers moved the ragged pieces of the picture Seth had torn to pieces, but he said nothing about them.

"You know?" she asked him.

He nodded. "I believe so. Why don't you tell us?"

"Is it Cameron?" Andy tightened his hold on her. "India, did Cameron harm you?"

Andy would never believe her. "I don't know what you mean."

"Did he hurt you?" Andy demanded. "A woman is missing, and Kurt believes Cameron may have something to do with her disappearance." Andy turned his attention to Kurt. "That's it, isn't it?"

Kurt nodded and left the room. She pulled away. In the darkness, she hoped Andy wouldn't see her tears. "What would it matter? No one's going to believe me."

"I will."

"Yeah, right. You'd take the word of the town tramp over your friend."

Andy reached toward her.

She flinched, stepping backward.

His hand brushed against her forehead, pushing her bangs from her eyes. "I've never called you a tramp."

"Get to know me long enough, and you'll join in with the general consensus."

"I'm not that shortsighted."

"Cameron told me what everyone believes."

"Cameron is a fool, and if he's hurt you or anyone else, he'll answer to me."

The weight of his words threatened to pull her down. If she learned anything from Cameron in the short time they were together, Andy was someone important to him. What had changed Andy's similar opinion of him?

"Tell me the truth, India, and I'll protect you."

Should she test these waters, find out if he'd still care when she told him? "You'd stand by me and tell everyone you believe me?"

"You won't find a better friend, but you have to tell me the truth. My sister-in-law's life may depend upon it."

"What sister-in-law?" India gawked.

"John's wife. Kurt thinks Cameron's harmed her." Andy bent his knees to bring his gaze level with hers. "Could he hurt her, India?"

India hesitated and then moved to her dresser. She turned on the table lamp there and grasped the check Cameron had sent to her in the mail along with his letter. Bringing it back to him, she held it out. "Yes, he could."

Andy took them from her, studying them. After a moment, his hands trembled. He turned away from her, slamming his open hand against her wall. "Why?" He started for her bedroom door.

Betrayed, again. When would she ever learn? India grabbed for him. "I'm sorry, but you asked me. I had to tell you, but don't leave me here alone."

He stopped. "I have to help Kurt. My sister-in-law is out there somewhere. If Cameron's in town …"

"I'm afraid of him. If he hurts you and Kurt, there's no one to protect me."

Andy nodded. He tucked the papers she'd given him into his pockets.

Before she could question him, he wrapped her in the warmth of his protection. How had she managed to handle all the fear alone for so many months? Even Mickey failed to make her feel this secure. Whatever he wanted to do with the evidence, she didn't care.

She didn't have to manipulate Andy. He believed her. He cared.

A bright light circled the house. "Kurt's got his flashlight out." Andy released her.

After a few minutes, the light went out. Kurt opened the front door and called to them. Andy led her downstairs.

"I found a slice in the screen. That's how he got inside the porch. There're some footprints around the tear, but other than that, there's no other trace." Kurt stomped his feet on the welcome mat before stepping into the foyer. "Did you know your front door was unlocked?"

That Cameron hadn't tried that door first was a miracle. "Kurt, I swear it was Cameron Matrai."

Kurt tapped Andy on the shoulder with his flashlight. "Did you forget to tell me he planned on making a visit?"

"I had no idea he would come back. You were there when he phoned. He hung up on me." Andy released India but slipped his hand in hers as he led her to her mother's couch. She sat, and he moved into a chair opposite her. "Will you tell us what happened?"

Everyone in town knew her exploits. They had tagged her with ugly names. Seth had called her by some of them. Yet, how could she tell two men about the horror of rape? She searched for the words, starting to speak, but her heart battled against her mouth.

Neither man pressed the issue.

Finally, she swallowed and took a deep breath. "He seemed so nice at first, a real gentleman. I don't know what happened, but something made him angry."

"John." Andy turned his head upward and studied the ceiling.

Kurt nodded. "John has a knack for that, doesn't he?"

India studied her hands. "I tried to talk to him and suggested we walk to the west side of your property."

"John's property," Andy corrected.

"I thought maybe the sunset would get his mind off whatever bothered him. I used to go there a lot when I needed to think. But when we got there, he turned into an animal." Her hands trembled. She laced her fingers and rested them in her lap, pushing down to keep them still. "He held me down and smothered my mouth with one hand, and he tore off my ..."

Her body began trembling with a force she could not control. "I couldn't get away no matter how hard I struggled; he held me tighter and tighter. My mind keeps replaying the scene. He knew how to do it too well. How many other women has he hurt? Tell me, Andy. You know him better than anyone. Is it his habit to violate women?"

Andy stood and paced back and forth, stopping in front of Kurt. "You didn't tell me it was rape." He blinked. "It's my fault." He began his pacing once again.

India followed him with her eyes. How could she hurt him like this? Why did she have to make him feel responsible? She stood and stepped in front of him, stopping his nervous movement. "I apologize, Andy. I know you had nothing to do with what Cameron did to me."

"I had everything to do with it, India. I brought him here." His warm hand touched her face for the second time this evening. "And I'm very sorry."

"I don't hold you accountable. You shouldn't either."

"What made you put it all together?" Andy asked Kurt.

"Go get some clothes together." Kurt stood behind India and placed his hands on her shoulders. "We'll wait down here."

Kurt waited for India to make her way up the stairs. The old saying that someone looked like they'd just lost their best friend held true when he looked back at Andy. "Dr. Yasmin Garcia put the pieces in place for me."

"Emilee's colleague." Andy nodded his recognition of the name.

Kurt fought against asking if the Ryans had ever considered anyone a real friend—other than Cameron Matrai. Instead, he nodded. "Dr. Garcia confirmed what the evidence in the apartment already showed. She ID'd him as someone who'd had an altercation with Mrs. Ryan outside the hospital. Your sister-in-law didn't say, but Dr. Garcia is relatively sure your buddy violently raped Emilee."

Andy paced up and back before reaching for one of Mrs. Thompson's expensive crystal vases. He thrust the valuable above his head, poised to hurl it across the room. "Why?" The lips of his tortured face let forth the agonizing cry. "Why?" he asked again, coughing out the question, lowering his arms without throwing the crystal. "All my life I've tried to protect Emilee. I should have stayed with her in New York and not babied John by coming here." He collapsed on the couch clutching the vase and stared up at Kurt. "Emilee's running from Cameron, and he's here chasing her."

Kurt cut his eyes to the stairs. "I think he has additional business to tie up on the island. Wouldn't you agree?"

Andy breathed in and released the air slowly. He set the vase down and dug into his pockets. "India just gave me this upstairs. I suppose that since she didn't cash it, Cameron realized she wasn't like most of the girls he's known."

Kurt glanced at the substantial amount of the check. Then he read Cameron's letter. Though not an admission, the evidence was deprecatory. His stomach churned. "You suspected that he could have done this before?" Heat surged from somewhere deep inside.

Andy blinked. "What?" Recognition lit his brown eyes. "No. Not like that. Cameron is used to dealing with women who cling to him. I've never liked it, but many of them are easy to buy off."

"Is that how you operate?" Kurt narrowed his eyes. "Will you do the same with my friend, Blanchie?"

Andy held up his hands. "I don't deal like that with anyone in my life, especially not Blanchie. I—I'm falling in love with her."

Kurt stared at Andy. He'd never met anyone like the Ryan brothers. He still hadn't figured them out. Why did he suddenly feel sorry for Luke? His old friend, with the ways of his past, could never compete with the man before him. Sad. Kurt, and probably everyone in town, thought Luke would eventually triumph and win his ex-bride back.

"He couldn't buy India off, though." Andy broke into Kurt's thoughts.

India came into view at the top of the stairs. He thought a lot of things about India Thompson in the long years he'd known her. Now, more than ever, he admired her spunk. No matter what anyone said about her, she was tough.

India's gaze rested on the evidence in Kurt's hand.

"I'd like to keep these," he said.

She nodded her agreement and cast a look of what could only be considered gratefulness in Andy's direction.

"Can we go find Emilee now?" Andy asked.

"Why wouldn't she come to you or John for safety?" Kurt asked.

"It doesn't make sense."

A knock sounded at the front door, and Kurt's officer entered. Tank cast a cautious glance in Andy's direction.

"Any luck?" Kurt asked.

"Can I speak with you?" Tank held the door open.

"It's all right," Kurt advised. "Whatever you have to say, he deserves to know."

"There's no sign of Dr. Ryan, but Seth's adamant he saw her."

"And how can he be so sure?"

"He said she looks just like his mother."

"What?" Kurt allowed a nervous laugh to escape. "What does that have to do with anything?"

Tank shrugged. "Seth says his mother is her aunt."

Kurt turned an accusing eye toward Andy, but Andy stared back in wide-eyed silence.

If Seth knew this, if it were fact, why hadn't he told anyone? And what of John Ryan? How did a man keep a secret like that from his own brother—and from officers investigating his wife's disappearance?

Tank pulled a notepad out of his shirt pocket and flipped a couple of pages. "I'm still trying to get it straight, but Seth says David is her father. He says his aunt, David's sister-in-law, is her mother. From what I can figure out, that would make Dr. Ryan Seth's cousin, I think."

"No, sister," India added. "If David is her father. Right? A half-sister."

"Is Seth drinking again?" Kurt demanded.

"Sober as a hanging judge."

"This true, Andy?" Kurt voiced his question this time.

"How do I know if he's sober?"

Kurt took a step forward. He meant to appear intimidating. He wanted the truth. "I mean is Seth related to Emilee—brother, cousin, third-cousin once removed? You Ryan boys sure like to keep secrets."

Andy shrugged and shook his head. "We've always had to keep secrets, but we always kept them together. John, me, and Em. My brother has become a stranger to me. We used to be everything to each other, but now ..."

"John never said anything to you about David and Seth?"

"No." Andy again shook his head. "He bought the house from David. I had some suspicion. Emilee's maiden name was New, and it isn't that common of a name."

Kurt faced his officer. "You get Seth and David and have them at the Ryan house in fifteen minutes. I want to see for myself if Seth's sober, and if he is, I want answers—if I have to jail John Ryan to get them."

Chapter Twenty-Three

Seth gave a terse nod to Blanchie when she opened the back door. With determined steps, he walked the familiar hall of the home once owned by his grandparents and now owned by a monster.

The object of all his anger stood when he entered the grand living room. Seth paid no attention to Blanchie as he ran at John Ryan, gripping John's shirt in his hands. "What did you do to her? Did you pay to have it done?"

John blinked. He offered no resistance. Rather than tensing, John seemed to lose his strength. "I don't understand."

"Seth, John's been right here. What could he have done?" Blanchie asked.

"Seth, let the man go." Officer Tank Williams barreled into the room like a steamroller ready to flatten any riotous behavior.

Seth shook John. His adversary's body moved like a rag doll in his grasp. "There's a scent that's hard to describe, but once you smell it, you'll never forget. Emilee's bleeding, John. How do I know? I smelled it."

"You—you've seen her?" John stammered.

"Seth." Kurt exploded into the room, like a bomb dropping onto the situation. "Release him now."

Others entered behind Kurt: Pop, Andy, and India. Why was India involved in any of this, and why was she with Andy Ryan?

John's brother stood behind India, his hand on her shoulder. Andy whispered something in India's ear. She nodded, placed her purse on the floor, and stepped back into the corner of the hall like a spider waiting for her prey.

Blanchie's gaze followed India's movement and then returned to Andy. Seth had once felt the emotions he could see playing across Blanchie's face. They'd come by way of India as well. Blanchie's eyes held the look of one who'd been betrayed.

"Son." Pop placed a hand on his shoulder. "This man is not your enemy."

Seth pulled back, ready to punch John with a heavy right fist. Whatever Emilee suffered, she'd gone through it because of John Ryan.

Pain in his shoulders and down his back brought his attempt to pummel John to an abrupt halt. "Tank, man, let me go. You're protecting a criminal."

Andy pushed around Kurt and started in Seth's direction. John stepped between them. Andy sidestepped, but John grabbed his brother in a stronghold similar to the one Tank kept on Seth.

Andy strained against the grip John held on his arms, jerking one way then the other.

"He doesn't know the truth, Andy. He's behaving the same way we would if the situation was reversed." John pulled back on his brother.

"Tell me why she didn't want to come to you, John," Seth demanded. "She ran at the thought."

Now, facing Seth, Andy struggled to free himself. "John's not some animal who'd harm his wife. I'm tired of everyone judging him. Let me go, John."

"Just remember, Seth and David are family."

John's words brought quiet to the household, but Seth gave him only a momentary reprieve. "I'm not your family. Have you ever smelled blood? I have. And Emilee is bleeding."

John blinked and released Andy, then bent at the waist, covering his stomach with his arm. "No!" He rose up, screaming the word, reminding Seth of a wolf howling at the moon. Lon Chaney. Maybe, like the werewolf, John's demons held him captive.

"Did you go crazy on her, John?"

Andy brushed past John, his arm back, ready to deliver a punch.

Kurt moved in front of Seth "I'll arrest you." He kept his hand on Andy's chest. "Think about it. Your sister-in-law is out there afraid and in pain, and you won't be able to help her."

From behind him, Seth baited the brothers. "They don't care about Emilee. If they did, why would they leave her alone in New York?"

"Because she wanted to stay!" Andy yelled. "She begged me to come here with John. You don't know her, Seth. Don't presume to know the situation."

"Will I ever know my sister, John, or will I be attending her funeral knowing nothing more about her than I would a stranger?"

"Get him out of this house." Andy sprang forward.

Kurt shoved the angry man away. "Andy, look at my officer. You and I might be an even match, but Tank has an advantage on you, and both of us have the law on our side." He pointed at Seth. "And, you, shut up."

"I didn't hurt Em," John spoke. "I love your cousin with all my heart."

Pop's head snapped upward at John's words. He opened his mouth to speak but clamped it shut.

"Pop, don't you think it's a little too late to continue with the lies?" Seth closed his eyes and took a deep breath. "Look where they've gotten Emilee so far."

David offered a slow nod. "John, your wife is my daughter."

"She's my sister, you idiot." Seth once again struggled within Tank's hold.

John closed his eyes and gave a slight shake of his head as if trying hard to take hold of a situation completely out of control. "I don't think so. I have her birth certificate …"

"You have what?" Andy spun in John's direction, eyes flashing with anger.

"I found it in Zack's personal papers after he died," John explained.

"And how long has it been since our old man keeled over?"

"Not now, Andy."

"Why not?" Seth demanded. "We're family after all. Why don't you tell us why you kept Emilee in the dark? Didn't you think it a little sick to live among your wife's family without telling her—without telling us."

"I planned to surprise her. Then Cameron told me about the affair, and when I announced our move …"

"Emilee and I never had an affair." Andy sent a book flying off the end table. "Cameron lied."

Despite Tank's hold, Seth clenched his fist. "Announced? You didn't ask her? You told her? What kind of husband tells his wife he's moving her a thousand miles away from the life she's known?"

"I planned to give her a life with her family. It's the one promise I never kept."

Andy let out an angry growl-like sound. "No. Not just one promise. You promised to love her, to protect her, to cherish her, to trust her. You never had to believe me, but why couldn't you believe in her? When she looks at you, John, all I see is love, even at your cruelest." He slumped forward. "You condemned Em and me for a wrong we never committed while you kept the truth from all of us." Andy walked toward the front door, opened it, and turned back. "I always knew that you had some part of the old man in you, but I never thought you were so steeped in his hatred and vindictiveness." He patted his chest. "I tried—I tried so hard to protect you from that, and I failed."

Blanchie moved beside Andy. She slipped her hand into his.

"I am not our father." The words flowed from John like agony might flow from someone destined for hell. "I am not Zachariah Ryan."

Seth relaxed, and Tank probably sensing the fight going out of him, released his hold. Seth turned and gave him his angriest look.

Tank narrowed his eyes at him. "I'll …"

"Let it go," Kurt told his officer. "There's a lot of emotion in this room."

As if Andy had not seen the brief confrontation, he continued to stare at his brother. "Then why all the secrets? All our girl ever wanted was to know her family, to understand why she was abandoned and left with us. You never told her. You never told us." Andy pointed to David and Seth.

"David knew," John accused, pointing at Pop. "He probably knows much more than I do."

"Yes, Andy, that's true," Pop admitted.

"But I didn't." Seth moved into the circle of men who had the most to lose if Emilee came to harm. Blanchie stepped away, allowing him entrance. "She's my sister, and I didn't know."

"I'm sorry." John left the circle.

Seth rubbed his sore arms and cast another angry glance in Tank's direction, but he didn't care to challenge the glare the officer returned.

"Sorry doesn't cut it." Andy ran his hand through his long hair before raising his hands toward John in a gesture that told them all Andy wanted to strangle his brother. "I don't know what to do with you anymore, John. Everything you touch, everything you love, you destroy. It's like looking at Zack in the mirror. I can't live like this any longer. I'm so angry—I've never felt this much anger." Andy shook his clawed-shaped hands toward his brother before letting them fall to his sides.

"Andy ..." India stepped from the corner and reached for his hand.

Blanchie stepped back as if slapped in the face. She tossed a sharp look at Andy. To make matters worse, Andy didn't pull from India's touch.

"What right do you even have to be here, India?" Blanchie asked.

"Blanchie." Andy sighed.

Blanchie pushed past him. "I'll start some coffee. It's going to be a long day."

"I need to look for Emilee." Andy pulled from India's hold and moved toward the door.

"I know you didn't have an affair," John said.

Andy stopped.

"And even I don't believe Cameron would hurt Emilee."

"He hurt her, John. Believe it." Andy moved toward his brother, his eyes on Seth. "We need to stop bickering and find her before he has a chance to do it again."

"Andy's right," Kurt agreed. "Tank, get this organized. Andy, I need to talk to you, Seth, and India alone."

Seth looked at India. What had she done now? With much reluctance, he followed the other two men into the kitchen.

"Blanchie, will you excuse us for one minute?" Kurt asked.

Blanchie surveyed the group, her attention resting on Andy. He smiled and bent to kiss her cheek.

She pulled away before he could. Then, as if apologizing, she offered a slight smile

"Give us just a minute," Andy said.

She nodded but her smile dissipated before she turned away from him.

"What's this about, Kurt?" Seth demanded. Kurt's summons to this place had cost them valuable time.

"Can we use your place as a safe house for India?" Kurt leaned out the door, looking up the hall and back down before returning his attention to Seth.

Andy turned his back to them and stared out the kitchen window.

"A safe house? For India? Why?" Seth questioned.

"Cameron tried to break into her home. I want to keep her safe."

"That's ridiculous. Why would he do that?"

"Will you just do it?" Andy spun toward him.

"Not without a better explanation." Seth glared.

"Never mind, Kurt. Just take me home." India pushed past

Seth.

Kurt reached out with one hand and grasped India's arm, pulling her back into the room. "It's either Seth's place or the police station."

"Why don't you ask yourself how I know my friend hurt Emilee?" Andy drew close to Seth.

"Your brother hurt Emilee."

"John?" Andy gave a false laugh. "He traveled all the way to New York, raped, and otherwise harmed his own wife—a woman he's never in the past laid hands upon in violence—and got back here before the call came from the police telling Kurt she was missing."

Raped? Beaten, yes, but raped? "My sister ...?" Seth blinked as comprehension dawned. "India?"

India nodded, holding Seth's gaze for what seemed an eternity. He swam in the desperation he saw there.

Still, his mind wouldn't let him surrender to the truth. "I can't believe it."

"I haven't forgotten what you said to me the other night, Seth New."

Did she believe that he ever would?

"It still hurts, but I can understand it."

She had the advantage over him. He would never understand how he could hurt her that way.

"I even deserve it." Her voice grew louder. "But no one deserves what that monster did to me or to John's wife."

He had abused her with his words, heaping insult upon what she had already endured. *See, God, what You've made of me.* He needed to say so much, but Seth remained silent.

"Oh, Seth." India shook her head, her voice quieter now. "I'd like to tell you where you can shove your self-righteousness, but I'm afraid, and I have nowhere else to go. You heard Kurt. It's either your place or the station. I'm tired, and I want to have a good cry. I'd rather do it in the privacy of your house."

"Let's go then." Seth shoved his hands into his pocket and lowered his head.

"I'll get my purse." She left them.

"What'd you say to her the other night?" Kurt asked.

Seth lowered his head and started toward the door. "I called her a harlot and a home-wrecking tramp."

"Nope!" Kurt shouted, and Seth turned in time to see the chief of police bar Andy from another attack. "If I can't do it, neither can you."

"Let him go, Kurt." Seth brought his hands up, motioning with his fingers for Andy to bring it on. "I deserve whatever he wants to give me."

Kurt relaxed his hold, and Andy moved dangerously close to Seth. "Then maybe you know a little about how my brother must feel. He's not perfect, but he loves Emilee."

Seth nodded, pushing past the woman he once loved—the one who'd suffered the same fate as Emilee.

Chapter Twenty-Four

Seth lifted the fire department's large metal door and watched it follow the track up toward the ceiling. The shiny fire engine seemed to await his return. Why he'd come here after securing India in his home, he didn't know—just a niggling feeling. He reached to turn on the light by the door.

"Seth."

The female voice made him turn. He found no one behind him and stepped out onto the sidewalk. Shaking his head, he re-entered the fire station.

The figure in front of him materialized with his flip of the light switch. He closed his eyes and opened them again.

Emilee's skin paled beneath the dirt covering her face. Her body trembled inside the coat she held together.

"How?" he asked.

"I found the office door unlocked."

Nothing unusual. "Don't run. Okay? I'll do whatever you want." He held up his hands as one would do if someone held a gun on them. Potential injuries, the extent of which he did not know, were the weapons in her hands.

She nodded, and her trembling grew more pronounced. Shock? Infection? Exhaustion? A fever? How had she eluded them this far?

"You said you're a paramedic."

He nodded.

"I need help. Is there somewhere we can go?"

"The hospital." He started forward.

"No, not the hospital, but somewhere that I can assess the situation."

"The situation is you're bleeding, and shock is setting in. I can't understand how you've held it off this long. Look. I know you're afraid of John. He won't find out you're there."

Her violet eyes widened. "I'm not afraid of John. He didn't do this to me. If you know him, how can you think him capable?"

"You ran away when I mentioned him."

"I ran away when you said you were my brother. You have to understand, I'm a little edgy."

"Let me take you to the hospital, please?"

"Not necessary and too dangerous. I'll go somewhere else." She started past him, wincing with each step.

Life consisted of more than simple fate. Everyone except Seth had asked God for Emilee's safe arrival, and God had delivered her into his hands, not once but twice. Seth never uttered a prayer. He never gave God the satisfaction. Still, with Emilee's appearance here at the station, God announced His control of the situation. From some deep recess, the words flowed without conscious thought until they sprang with gratefulness into his heart. *Thank You, Lord.*

The fact that she had been raped needed to be dealt with, but tipping his hand could cause her to scurry away again. "Stop. I have a place." He found his voice.

The woman reached out and placed a dirty hand over his, a

stark contrast against his clean skin. "I trusted you. I came to you. Please don't betray me. We're family."

"If John didn't hurt you, why don't you want to go to him? He and Andy are family."

"They can't know." She swayed, and Seth placed his arm around her.

The trench coat moved slightly revealing a patch of still-moist blood on her shirt. He breathed a sigh of release. At least from what he could see, her blood loss was not substantial.

"Well." She glared at him.

"They won't hear about your arrival from me."

Emilee nodded. Then her knees buckled.

Seth scooped her into his arms. Could he start their newfound relationship off by breaking a promise? He'd still feel better if he did what he knew he should and take her to the hospital to have them look her over.

No. He shook his head. He wouldn't treat her the way her husband had. His sister needed someone to trust. Once he gained her confidence, he'd talk her into going to the hospital—though he suspected she had inherited the stubborn streak that ran deep into his family genetics.

Right now, though, his concern was how to carry her through a town full of men searching for her—including one who was a crazed lunatic. He'd pray, but grateful or not, he was sure he'd used up his last favor with God.

Emilee stood in front of the bathroom mirror after her first shower in two days. In order to take the shower, she'd had to win a heated debate with her cousin over whether she needed to go to the hospital or not. He didn't say, and she refused to admit it, but she'd gotten the impression that Seth was well aware of what had befallen her. The dirt and also the blood, some crusted and some still seeping sluiced down the drain. She wished she could wash the memories, the pain, and the fever away as effectively.

She touched the open wounds and involuntarily gasped. The bandages she had removed before her shower lay on top of the coat she'd worn over her clothes, everything had blood on them much like a map on her body, showing exactly where Cameron had inflicted injury. She bent, with determination to overcome the pain, and picked up her shirt and pants also worn on her long trip.

A soft knock sounded on the bathroom door, and Emilee reached for a towel—large but not big enough to hide the bruises on her arms and legs. "Yes?"

A woman opened the door, obviously cautious at Emiliee's lack of dress. "Seth wanted me to bring this up." She held up a First-Aid kit, looked up, and gasped. The First-Aid kit hit the floor with a clang. Emilee could imagine that the macabre rainbow of putrid purples, blues, and yellows covering her arms, legs, stomach, and back would frighten anyone.

The woman stooped to pick it up as she entered the small bathroom. "Let me help."

Emilee studied the pretty raven-haired woman with the expressive green eyes, the ones she tried to hide from the ugliness covering Emilee's body. This woman was no nurse.

"I can't reach some of the wounds to apply the antiseptic," Emilee told her.

"You're shaking."

"It's a fever mostly, and I'm exhausted."

"You need a doctor."

"I am a doctor." Emilee realized this woman knew nothing of her. "And you are?" *Stop it, Emilee. Pull it out of doctor mode. Act like a normal human being.* "I mean, we haven't met."

The woman met Emilee's gaze. "India."

Emilee nodded. "Like the country." A habit she used, relating names to something she could remember.

"Like the country." The woman nodded. "Cameron did this to you?"

Emilee froze. "How do you know him?"

"Did he rape you, too?" India placed the kit on the counter and rummaged through it.

Too. Emilee drew near. "I'm sorry," she whispered. "I—I didn't realize my family lived here, and that Johnny's moving here would put others in danger. You have to believe me. We never intended for anyone to get hurt. I saw Cameron's cruelty, but I didn't ever believe him capable of this."

"There's a bit of blood's coming through the towel. Sit down." India motioned to the side of the bathtub. Emilee took one look at the thin strip of porcelain and decided to sit on the closed toilet seat.

"Since you're the doc, you can tell me what I'm supposed to do."

"He didn't hurt you like this? Tell me he didn't."

India shook her head. "Not like this. I guess I'm the lucky one."

"No." Emilee sighed. "It's not the wounds on the outside I'll have to live with the rest of my life. It's his whispers in my ear telling me he's going to kill my husband and hearing him tell me if I don't stay away, Johnny will grow to hate me because Cameron touched me."

India busied herself with the items in front of her. "The guy I left isn't capable of hating you."

"Johnny?"

India nodded. "He's worried."

Emilee dropped that conversation. Johnny would have to stay worried if Emilee wanted to keep him safe. "I'll need the topical antibiotic first." She held the top of the towel but lifted the bottom. No room for modesty here. India looked away. Would India be sick? Maybe Emilee could demand professionalism from a nurse, but this stranger was willing to help. Emilee bit her tongue. Whatever her capacity to help heal, India was willing to try.

Seth had married a good one, and his association with Emilee's husband had cost her cousin so much.

Chapter Twenty-Five

The ringing telephone dragged Mickey Parker from his drunken stupor. A moan of pain crossed his dry lips. Even if he could move quicker, he still would not answer the call. Every blood vessel in his brain thundered against his skull.

He managed to sit up and swing his long legs over the bed. Perched on the edge, he propped his elbows on his thighs and rested his head in his hands. The morning sun shined through the window of the bedroom and washed him in the glow of its sticky and repressive heat.

Mickey didn't know how long he'd slept. He remembered leaving the Ryan house after Andy ushered John upstairs to rest. At that very moment, the demons of self-pity had surrounded him as if they meant to tear him to pieces. He wanted Penny to need him the way John needed his wife, to care for him despite his indiscretions. Jealousy had permeated his soul. All the love in the world awaited Emilee's arrival in Serenity. Mickey retained nothing.

Envy was an emotion strange to him—or so he thought. What was it when a man lusted after another woman with no thought to the blessing God had given him? Well, God could just add it to the long list of sins for which Mickey needed to repent.

He wasn't in the mood for repentance, not just now, not with the phone still ringing.

Would the cell phone ever click over for voice mail? When the ding announced that the caller left a message, he picked it up and looked at his calls.

Penny.

He pushed the number, punched in his passcode, followed the prompts, and then listened.

"Mickey, are you there? I need to talk to you?" Penny said.

He bet she did. "No." The word caught in his throat. If she wanted to tell him when to expect the divorce papers, she would need to torture him face to face. "No. No. No."

"Please call me. We need to move on." Strain etched her voice.

He sat up once again and struggled to stand, fighting against the spinning room. His hand brushed against the bottle on his nightstand. He grasped the neck of the whiskey container and dangled it at his side. With one step backward for two forward, he stumbled downstairs.

The cabinet against the wall at the bottom of the stairs seemed to jump in front of him. He fell against it hard and reached to stop it from falling. The feel of the cold steel against his hand almost sobered him. He swallowed, respecting the power of the arsenal gathering dust in the cabinet since his father's death. Dad had been an avid hunter, and he'd been sorely disappointed in his son who never liked the sport.

Mickey paused and brought the whiskey bottle to his lips. The sweet smell of the brown liquid didn't match the burning of his throat as it went down. He wiped his mustache with the back of his hand before grasping the rifle and dragging it with him back upstairs, the barrel thumping against each step as he climbed.

Where was the sweet numbness that greeted him the night before? He remembered Luke's descriptions of his drinking days. "I didn't go to sleep. I passed out. I didn't wake up. I came to."

Mickey had definitely passed out, but before he did, he ceased to feel. Now the ache in his heart overpowered the one in his head, and that wouldn't do.

Life here ever after would continue with the same hurt and remorse. Mickey had lost yet another person who once loved him. This time it wasn't death or another's wrong decisions separating him from others. He lost Penny because of his own foolish mistakes.

Penny had loved him. Even if she had never uttered those three words she considered so important, she showed him in everything she did. She had taken care of his dying mother when his own sister couldn't be bothered, and she had struggled through the hard times with him.

Everything Penny did, she'd done for him, and in his selfishness, he took and thirsted for more, seeking elsewhere for what she didn't know to give him. Revulsion filled him. He hated himself more than he had hated anyone or anything in his life.

The gun slid across the carpet as he moved once again into his bedroom. He would take care of it right here. He wouldn't put Penny through any more of his torment. He had hurt her. Now, he would set her free without the need for a divorce. She and their child would be happier without him.

"Johnny!" The woman's scream jolted Seth from his contemplations. He pushed his mug of coffee away and sprang up the stairs. "Johnny, please." Emilee's voice turned to a soft plea.

Seth ran down the hall. India had finally gotten to sleep. He didn't want her awakened.

"Hey." He bent down to peer into his sister's feverish face. Emotion, like an Atlantic Ocean wave, crashed over him. *His sister.* No matter what Pop had done, in the end, Seth had received a blessing. "Emilee," he whispered.

Her eyes fluttered open, and she tried to spring up. Pain flashed across her face, and she closed her eyes hard then laid back. "Seth."

He touched her hand. She still had a fever. "I don't suppose you'll reconsider going to the hospital."

"No."

"Stubborn as an old New," he said.

"What?"

"Our Grandpa Isaac used to make a twist on the old saying. Every time I didn't want to do something, he'd say, 'Stubborn as an old New.'" Grandpa Isaac would have known what to do with her. He'd always been able to lead Seth to do the right thing.

"I do need to get up. Will you help me? The longer I stay down, the more I'll hurt."

He was a fireman and a paramedic. You'd think he'd know how to help a woman from a bed. Not much space on her body—except for her face—was left with her natural olive coloring. She was bruised all over.

He put his arm around her and lifted her to a sitting position.

"Where's your wife?" she asked.

He blinked. "Wife? My wife is dead."

"India isn't your wife?"

He shook his head. "She's a friend."

"Oh, go on and tell her, you coward." India stood behind him in the doorway. Without looking he could imagine her with her hand on her hips.

What he couldn't imagine is what was next to come out of her mouth.

"We once dated before he met his wife."

Dodged a bullet with that one. Seth sat on the bed beside Emilee and mouthed a silent thank you to India. He held Emilee's right hand and looked down. Her left hand showcased a beautiful wedding set, but on her right hand, she wore an opal with diamonds on each side. A small but elegant piece of jewelry somehow familiar to him. The memory of a similar ring stayed in the corner of his mind, just out of reach.

"Then I dumped him and left him for more exciting pastures," India said.

"You what?" He jerked his head up to scold her.

"Worse mistake I ever made because the stubborn old New won't take me back. He's moving on to greener pastures now."

His sister laughed and paid the price. "Ow." She coughed. "I like this one, Seth. You'll have to be in much greener pastures to find someone better."

Much greener and much more peaceful, but he wouldn't embarrass India. Not this time, at least. "You should be asleep," he said to his old friend and then looked at his sister. "India stayed here last night for the same reason you did. I want her safe from Cameron."

If possible, Emilee's face grew pastier. "Cameron is here?" She shook her head. "Yes, he is. I saw him drive by last night."

"He tried to break into India's home, probably looking for a place to hide."

"Seth, he's trying to kill me." India leaned against the doorframe. "Look what he did to her, and then tell me that it isn't a possibility."

"A very real possibility." Emilee clutched his uniform sleeve. "Are you going to work?"

"I've been asked to attend an emergency management meeting. A tropical storm just became a Cat One hurricane entering the Gulf. Nothing to worry about. If you want, I can call John." Only last night, he'd wanted to kill the man. Now, he was willing to call him for Emilee's sake.

"I know you don't want to tell him you're here, but it's hard to keep a secret in this town, Emilee."

Yet the Ryan brothers had mastered the art.

"I won't lie to you. Everyone is out looking for you. John's leading the pack," he said.

"John and Andy can't know I'm here. If Cameron thinks I've left them, they're reasonably safe."

"That cat is out of the bag. They suspect Cameron has something to do with your disappearance." He patted her hand and stood. "Why don't I take you to your family?"

But she was his family, too.

She gazed up at him. "Please don't make me run again."

He laughed. "You can hardly stand. I'm not worried about that."

"You promised."

"I promised not to take you to the hospital, a promise I'm regretting right now. I didn't promise not to get you back to John and Andy." He crossed his arms over his chest. "Although, I think you could have chosen better. What made you marry someone like him?"

Tears filled her eyes. "You would never say that about Johnny if you really knew him. He's kind and compassionate, so much so that when someone hurts him, he doesn't understand the pain he feels. But even though he strikes out at others sometimes, Johnny is a wonderful man."

"Hmph." India pushed from the doorframe. "If you say so. Andy's the kind one, if you ask me." She glanced out the window. "Any chance that storm is coming this way?"

"You know good and well, any storm in the Gulf has a chance of crossing our path under the right conditions."

India glared at him. "But most times they know where the thing will travel when it's five or six days out."

"There's a front conditioning the path. We're taking the usual precautions." Seth turned his attention to Emilee. "We always do this when a major storm enters our waters."

"What? Argue like stupid children?"

Seth shook his head. From where had that thought process come? He paused for a second and then chuckled at her quick wit. "No." He narrowed his eyes at her. "India and I don't need a reason to argue like kids. But I do need to plan for the landfall of a hurricane."

Emilee smiled but offered no retort.

"What's Luke saying about the storm?" India pressed.

"I haven't checked with him."

"Don't you think you should? After all, Luke's the accurate one, not the weather service."

Emilee held up her hand, asking for more assistance. This time to stand. She wore one of Linda's old nightgowns. "Are you sure you two aren't married?" she asked.

"Quite sure," India smirked. "He's too stupid to marry me."

Seth smirked back. "Too stupid or too afraid?"

Emilee stared at the two of them for a long moment before shaking her head. "Will you be gone long?" She eyed Seth.

"Most of the day. India will be here with you." Again, he put his arm around her shoulder, giving her the brace she needed to get to her feet. "The offer is still open. I can take you to that wonderful husband of yours."

"I'm going to get dressed." India left them.

"These aren't India's clothes I'm wearing?" Emilee ran her hand down the front of the gown.

He put on a fake smile and shook his head. "No, they're my wife's."

"Seth, I'm sorry for your loss. I sometimes forget to say things like that, but I truly mean it."

She was a breath of fresh air.

Seth reached into the closet and pulled out Linda's robe, resisting the urge to drink in the lingering scent of Linda's soap and powder. Lilac.

He draped the robe over Emilee's shoulders. "My wife would love the fact that she could share her clothing with my sister. Though, she wouldn't have rested until I had you seen by a physician."

"I am my own medical doctor."

"What is it they say about a lawyer who represents himself?"

"Johnny always says that at least they can't file against their malpractice insurance."

"I have to admit, it's going to take time to get used to thinking of John as a brother-in-law."

"Cousin," she corrected him. "We're cousins. That's what Cameron said. He told me my mother was your mother's sister. Wasn't your mother Uma?"

"Yeah, but we were both fathered by the same man. David."

She shook her head. "Cameron said that my father was Owen New. Your uncle."

And there was just one more individual in the long line of folks who knew more about him than he knew himself. Seth led her slowly down the stairs.

"Right?" she pressed.

"Let's not argue about it," he told her, weary with the truth. "I left earlier and sneaked back to my place. I have some coffee brewing and some donuts and cereal for the two of you."

"I thought you lived here."

Seth shook his head. "Not since Linda died."

Emilee linked her arm in his, leaning upon him for support as she walked. "It must be painful returning."

"Surprisingly, I'm okay." He leaned and kissed her forehead. "Glad to meet you, Sissy."

She started to say something but clamped her mouth shut.

The beeper on Seth's uniform belt sounded, and he looked at the number displayed. "My reckoning." He winked before he walked out the door. How in the world would he explain where he'd been and what had kept him away from the search for Emilee?

FAY LAMB

Chapter Twenty-Six

Luke finished listening to the last of the weather report then headed up the embankment toward the Ryan house. The news that Emilee Ryan had surfaced in Serenity Key had drawn a crowd. "Good morning," he announced his presence.

David held his finger to his lip, summoning Luke's silence.

Kurt was speaking to someone over the phone. "That's not responsible, Seth. Emilee is your sister after all, and we've seen no sign of Cameron after his attempted break-in at the Thompson place."

"What?" Luke looked from John to David. "I think I missed a chapter or two. When did the plot change?"

Kurt gave an angry shake of his head as he continued the conversation. Kurt's night had probably been a long one. Luke would forgive him.

"Let me ask Luke." Kurt placed his hand over the receiver. "Seth's been called to an emergency management meeting. What're your thoughts on the storm?"

"Batten down the hatches." Luke turned his attention to Andy. "Your buddy Cameron's in town, huh?"

"It's coming our way," Kurt spoke to Seth and then hung up the phone.

"The weather reporters don't think so," John disagreed. "Look at the clear skies."

"Who are you going to trust, the weather reports or me? I'm going to anchor the boat out away from shore later."

Fear registered in the lawyer's eyes.

"You are kidding, right?" Andy's laugh sounded anything but jovial. "You can't predict the weather."

"Luke's usually right about storms," Blanchie advised.

"I see you haven't lost all your faith in me." Luke winked at her.

"But it's only a storm, right?" John pleaded.

"Cat One hurricane, John," Luke answered. "What's going on? Why is everyone here? Is Cameron missing, too? How'd I miss so much?"

"Seth saw Emilee last night. We've been searching half the morning. We believe Cameron's behind all this." Andy ran his fingers through his long hair.

What could Luke say to either brother? And how had he allowed Blanchie to become involved with these men? Through his own stupidity and recklessness, that's how. Now, what could he do to win her back?

"Cat One? That's not bad, right?" John continued to search for an answer.

Luke forced his gaze from Blanchie to John. "With the right conditions, even a tropical storm can cause a lot of damage. There's no telling what we'll have when it gets into warmer waters."

"I don't believe you." John paced away from him.

Luke ignored him, turned, and placed his arm around Blanchie. "Can I drive you to work? The roof on Town Hall needs patching before the storm hits or a good gust will take it off. I'm heading there now."

Blanchie nodded. "Sure." She pulled from his touch and waved good-bye to Andy without kissing him.

Luke sensed some kind of change in the axis of his world—possibly in his favor, but he averted his gaze and faced David. "So, if Mrs. Ryan is Seth's sister, she's your ..."

"She's my daughter, boy." David offered a feeble smile.

"She'll be okay," Luke assured. He could ask so many questions right now, but they'd only serve as fodder for gossip.

"I guess I better get enough plywood for the restaurant," Andy muttered.

"Forget your restaurant," John roared. "We need to find Emilee. Is everyone calling it quits now that it's daylight? My wife's in danger."

"John," Kurt sighed. "Some of us need to take care of our homes and our livelihoods. We'll work in shifts. No one's abandoning the search."

David placed his arm around John's shoulder. "We'll keep searching. Let the others board up."

John shrugged David off. "There's no way he can predict a storm the experts say will probably travel in another direction."

"Sure, John," Luke placated. In his sobriety, he was a lover, not a fighter, and he didn't want to stand around arguing when he could be helping others prepare. "You ready, Blanchie?"

Blanchie sat for some time in Luke's truck outside her salon.

No customers waited, and Blanchie didn't need to hurry.

"Do you think it's right, you staying the night at their place?" Luke beat a drum rhythm on the steering wheel, but he wasn't fooling her. Condemnation had laced his voice.

"They needed me." Blanchie leaned away from him, studying the storm brewing in her ex-husband's eyes.

"All night, Blanchie?"

"Andy stayed out looking for Emilee. And I wouldn't have allowed anything to happen."

"I know." He tunneled his fingers through his hair.

"Come on in. I'll give you a trim."

"Later." He reached across the seat and held her hand.

She stared at his hold without resistance, and the fact she didn't want to resist nagged at her conscience. "What's wrong?"

"I'm jealous, babe."

"What?" She suppressed a laugh and wiggled out of his touch.

Luke stared as she brought her hand to her lap. "I thought I could handle it, but I can't. You don't know how it feels, seeing you with Andy and trying to accept it. It's killing me."

"You think I don't know how it feels? How many nights did I wait up for you knowing what you were doing but not wanting to believe it?" Even now, the heaviness of his long-ago actions weighed on her heart.

But she'd swear his eyes wore a hint of remorse. And the anger in her heart lifted like a long-heavy fog moving away from her.

"I love you, Blanchie. I'm sorry for the past. This is just too hard."

"Nothing is ever easy for you."

"Except you," he remarked.

He really did believe her a fool to have loved him. The anger drifted back toward her. "Excuse me." She threw open the door.

He winced as it slammed out as far as it could go. "No. No." He pulled her back. "You used to make everything so easy."

"And I paid for it, didn't I? I paid for it double, and I'm done paying."

"What can I do to convince you?"

"It isn't in you," she softened. "I need more than you can give, Luke."

"And Andy can give it to you? I haven't seen him step inside the Serenity Key Baptist Church."

Blanchie smarted at the truth in his words. "Luke ..."

"So, you see, you're not getting anything better than you had with me when you settle for Andy Ryan, unless it's the money you're looking at, riches he can give you that I never will."

Blanchie's eyes filled with tears. "Do you honestly think I ever considered our finances when I left you?"

"Didn't you?"

"I considered what you did with the money I set aside to pay bills, but we always had the money to pay those bills until you gambled it away or spent it on some woman or on alcohol. I would have happily lived with you in poverty. If I had satisfied you, Luke, and if you hadn't looked for someone or something to take my place, I'd have remained with you forever."

"Oh, babe, I long to satisfy you; I want to show you how I've changed. Give me another chance. I never pleaded before. I'm begging now." He folded his hands in front of him and held them toward her. "Please." His green eyes held an emotional storm all their own. "Please."

"You can't satisfy me while you're drinking."

"Blanchie. I'm clean. I'm a changed man."

She rolled her eyes. "It takes more than your words to convince me."

"All I want is another chance with you."

"You blew that chance time and time again. I can't make it easy for you again."

"Just don't close the door on us."

"Right now, it's shut." She slipped from the seat and stood on the sidewalk. If only he knew how close she was to opening the door for him to enter into her life again.

If that were true, though, why was she having trouble forgetting Andy's protective touch on India? She had to have feelings for him, too.

She straightened her shoulder, dug in her purse for her keys, and forced herself to take the steps that would separate her from the opportunity to fall into Luke's familiar, strong arms.

"I love you, Flunchie." He called out his pet name for her. "I've learned my lesson. I know there isn't anyone on this earth I love more."

He never admitted that to the world before. She always had to drag those three precious words out of him. She turned toward the truck, but he'd already pulled away.

She entered the shop and collapsed into her salon chair. Her reflection in the mirror stared back at her. She slammed her fist against the arm of the chair, jumped from her seat, and paced like a lion in a cage.

"This isn't fair, Luke. I want to love Andy." She stopped in front of her station and stared at her reflection once again.

"Oh, Lord, open the door or close it for me. I want to live in obedience to Your will. I married Luke once. Should I give him another chance? Once upon a time, I considered divorce the wrong option, so did Luke's dad, but we agreed that Luke needed to wake up. Now, he might be wide awake, but I don't know what to do. Tell me what it is You want from me." She sat in silence for a very long time, waiting. Her prayer haunted her. God had given her His answer in her own words, but she didn't want to listen.

Luke still had a lot to prove.

And so did Andy.

Noah pulled the next-to-last heavy piece of wood from his shed and carried it toward the church. He would take no chances with the stained-glass windows. If the storm didn't arrive, he'd wake up early before Sunday services and remove the plywood.

The clouds were moving in, and the wind was picking up, probably about ten knots, which it did when a storm moved anywhere near the island. If it moved away, it would suck the air away from the place, leaving the island hotter and muggier.

He left John Ryan soon after Andy met up with them outside Liam's Pharmacy. They had searched every possible inch of Serenity and searched it twice more for good measure. John remained silent most of the time. Noah understood why, and he didn't interfere. He spent his time during the search in silent prayer for the missing woman.

Noah sensed the Lord forging a friendship between John and him. If the Lord allowed Noah to choose anyone to be his friend, the last person he'd have picked was that man. John tried hard to hide his warmth, kindness, and deep, abiding love for his wife behind an icy façade, but God had shattered it, giving Noah a look at the real man.

"Got any more over there?" Luke pulled up in front of the church.

"One." Noah said a silent prayer of thanks as Luke jumped from his truck and ran toward Noah's workshop. His friend greeted Belle as he entered their backyard. Belle had already packed their bags in case they needed to head toward the mainland to stay with Noah's sister.

Luke returned with the heavy piece of plywood in tow. "You know there's a cart behind Stewart's Grocery. Would have made this a bit easier," he scolded. "I hear your search failed to turn up Emilee Ryan. It's like she's vanished, huh?"

"Don't say that around, John." Noah moved toward the back of the church and opened the small wooden shed next to the building. He brought out an aluminum ladder, moved to where Luke stood, and set it up as close to the building as he could. Then he shoved down, making sure the loose Florida sand would hold the ladder in place. "When do you predict the storm to come ashore?"

"Depends on that front and where it stalls. They're predicting it won't move forward. I'm sure it will, most likely early tomorrow morning. I'm concerned that the majority of the models are wrong. The only one pointing our way is the correct one, and emergency management isn't going to sound the warning in time."

"How do you know so much?"

"A God-given talent, I guess." Luke ran back to his truck. He returned with hammer and nails and climbed the ladder.

Noah stood gaping at his friend.

Luke laughed. "I like the legend better, you know, my ability to read nature. Truth is, Noah, I love everything about weather. I make a game out of predicting weather patterns. I'm hardly ever wrong."

Noah couldn't control the smile spreading across his face. Didn't his friend already know he was considered Serenity's own eccentric? "I like the legend better myself. Your secret's safe with me."

"I knew it would be." Luke pushed the plywood into place over the window. Their cut was a perfect fit. They would be. Luke had prepared them

Noah had the hard job. He held the wood in place while Luke drilled the screws into the holes of the wood left there for this exact purpose. Luke had completed this task many times over the years while his father shepherded the church.

Before picking up the cordless drill, Luke stuck the remaining screws in his mouth, but he managed to speak. "I guess I'll have to do this to Dad and Mom's place."

"I'll help," Noah offered.

"I thought you would." Luke pressed in the first screw.

"Have you seen Mickey?" Noah asked.

"Not since last night. Why?" The drill whirred again.

"His SUV's been in his driveway all day. I went to tell him he might want to start prepping for the storm, but he didn't answer the door." Noah strained to hold to the heavy plywood.

"Probably sleeping. Depression will do that for you."

"What's going on with him and Penny?"

"You need to ask him." Although Luke confessed many faults, Noah respected the fact that gossip was never one. "But if he isn't going to get up and work, we'll need to board up the law office and his home."

Before the day ended, Luke would likely have a hand in helping just about everyone they knew on the island and possibly a few seasonal residents. Then, if the storm failed to visit their sleepy little island, the town's folks would brand him a fool. It wouldn't matter that Luke's predictions prior to this never failed. Noah would stand beside his friend.

"Are you going to the mainland with Belle?" Luke asked.

Stay here and watch with Me.

Only part of the verse came to Noah. Jesus had taken Peter, James, and John to the Mount of Transfiguration. He left them and asked them to wait. "Then He said to them, 'My soul is exceedingly sorrowful even to death …'"

Stay here and watch with Me.

Again, the words came to Noah. He took a deep breath. Jesus had a reason for wanting his disciples to wait. His earthly ministry would end soon. Did the Lord have a reason for Noah to stay on the island in a hurricane?

He shook his head. "I may stay and look after the church," he said.

"Do you think that's wise?" Luke climbed down the ladder and moved it. They stood in front of the second window of three on the south side of the church. Three more windows remained uncovered on the north side.

"It's what I have to do." Noah placed his faith in the God that sustained him through the years. "But I wouldn't be safer anywhere else."

"The Lord's speaking to you, huh?"

"Yeah. He does that when I listen."

"He's been talking to me some, too," Luke divulged.

"Are you listening?" If so, Noah would praise God for the

answer to his prayers.

"Trying." Luke climbed up the ladder once again. He accepted the wood Noah held up to him. "You'll get Belle and her aunt and uncle out, though?"

Noah didn't intend to leave the subject Luke had opened. "Luke, you thought much about coming back to church?"

"I won't be there tomorrow." Luke let the screws fall from his mouth and into his hand. He took the exact number he needed and placed the others in his jeans pocket. "Unless there's a miracle."

Chapter Twenty-Seven

Emilee opened her eyes, blinked, and opened them once again. At first, her surroundings mystified her. The door of the cherry-wood armoire stood open, revealing a television with the sound obviously muted. Lace curtains adorned the window, and outside, she could see shrubbery with a street beyond.

Somewhere nearby a door squeaked open. Her heart pounded against her chest, and she bit her lip to stifle the pain shooting through her body as she rose from the soft cushions of the Victorian couch and the heavy blanket covering her.

"Shh. Emilee's asleep." She heard a woman's voice. "How'd your meeting go?"

India.

"Emergency Management didn't learn their lesson after the last storm. They're refusing to issue a warning apart from the National Weather Service. They insist Luke's predictions were lucky coincidences."

Seth.

With a slow, deep breath she managed to sit and then stand.

"The reports still say the storm's not coming our way."

India had been sitting in the living room with her. Emilee must have fallen asleep.

"I watched them, too. They're betting the front will stall and keep the storm away. I'd trust Luke's intuition any time. The front's not going to stall, and if it does, it won't stall far enough or long enough to keep us out of its path."

"How are we going to get out of here without everyone knowing?" India's tone held a twinge of fear.

"I have to stay until the last minute, especially since I know the warnings are going to come a little too late. They haven't found Cameron yet, and I don't want you two leaving alone—too much swamp land between here and there. If you turned up missing, we'd never find you. As soon as I can, I'll get you out. We'll use the ambulance. You and Emilee prepare to go."

A chair scooted. "There's John outside," India said.

"Emilee!"

Emilee blinked at the mournful cry of her name. A dreadful terror mingled with joyful surprise made her step toward the front door. He stood on the sidewalk in front of Seth's home, her real-life Heathcliff on the moors, his back to her but looking lost and afraid just the same. She watched as he poked around outside, even looking under the porch. "Johnny," she spoke his name aloud.

"You're awake." Seth entered the living room from the kitchen.

Emilee backed toward him. "I haven't seen him in months."

"Emmy," John's trembling voice came to her again. "Em, it's John. Babe, if you can hear me, I just want to help."

"He won't give up. He's been searching all day. Let's bring him inside and let him know you're safe," Seth urged.

Emilee moved toward the door, but when Seth started around her, she grasped his sleeve. "No."

"This is driving him crazy."

"Send him away."

As Seth started to obey, she held to him. He pulled from her grip and stepped onto the porch.

"John, have you boarded up Emilee's house?"

"Emilee, where are you?" John made a full turn before acknowledging Seth. "Have you seen her again? I need to know she's okay." John stepped out on the street. "Emilee! Honey, just tell me where you are." He thumped his chest with his hand. "I can feel her. She's near."

Emilee backed away from the door, out of John's sight. "I'm sorry, Johnny. I'm so sorry, but you can't know I'm here," she whispered.

India came behind her.

Emilee sighed. "It's so hard to deny him anything when he gives me so much."

"His brother ain't half bad, either," India said, and Emilee looked into smiling eyes.

When Seth opened the door, Emilee did not turn toward him, afraid her resolve would break. She half-hoped John would enter with him. As if reading her mind, India shook her head. Emilee walked away without acknowledging Seth.

"He's going home." Seth held to her shoulders.

"Home." The word poured from deep inside. She covered her face with her hands. "When do I get to go home?"

"You're here, Sis." Seth made her turn and pulled her close to him.

Emilee let the mistruth slide this time. Seth was a cousin, not a brother. She rested her head against his shoulder, though even his light hold caused her broken body to ache.

"I'll bring him back. Just say the word," Seth offered.

"I love him, Seth. I can't risk losing him to Cameron's growing madness."

"The storm's coming our way. I tried to convince him you'd be upset if he lost the house before you could see it. The home belonged to our Grandma and Grandpa New."

Emilee pulled from his embrace and sat on the couch. "It wouldn't take much for me to guess he'd do something like that for me. No matter what he thinks I did, he'd never be able to stop showing his love."

Seth paced in front of her, betraying his nervousness. "Well, I don't much want the old place to vanish either, but somehow I don't believe he'll do much to protect it. He's too worried about you."

"Are we in serious danger?" Emilee asked.

"It depends on the speed of the storm and the tidal surge expected. In case we need to leave the island, I want you and India ready."

"We will be," India assured. "Won't we, Emilee? I hope Cameron stays and drowns."

"Seth, John will stay on this island if he thinks I'm here. Please convince him to leave."

"I'm afraid the only way I could do that is to bring him here, show him you're safe, and he'll leave with you."

Emilee leaned back, the same exhaustion she had experienced all day settling in once again. "Well, then, I guess he's safer in the storm than with me."

Insanity clawed at John with each scream of his wife's name

and the pounding of every nail and the whirring sound of every drill upon every house on the island. Everyone prepared for a storm that by all accounts intended going another direction. They reminded him of ants scurrying to gather the year's supply of food in the event of disaster. Did he alone remember Emilee was injured and missing? Even Seth, who claimed to have personal knowledge of her presence on the island, worried more about the storm than he did Emilee's safety. Still, the man's attitude toward him had changed, but he didn't care what Seth thought of him now or later.

John stomped onto the back stoop, knocking the dirt off his shoes before entering the house. Walking into the living room, he found Andy staring at the television. He had not spoken much to his brother. Andy ran in and out of the house all day, searching one moment and helping with storm preparation the next. John lost track of all the homes his brother reported they had boarded. If John weren't so worried about his wife, he might be envious of Andy, who took so easily to life on the island, and everyone accepted him without reservation.

The weather report blared once more. The newsman reported the same information he detailed an hour earlier. The Cat One Hurricane Pauline moved and still continued on its northwest trek well off the coast and was not expected to threaten the island. Andy shrugged, "Maybe Luke's wrong."

"Maybe." John spit the word. "They say we're not in danger. Are you going to be as quick taking the boards down as you were in putting them up?"

In horror, John watched the next weather report at seven o'clock. The weatherman advised that a front that all but one computer model—and Luke—had predicted to stall farther from the island continued to inch south, turning the storm toward

FAY LAMB

Serenity.

By eight, they expected Hurricane Pauline to stall. Luke had indicated if it did halt, it would gain strength while it sat stationary, and he voiced no doubt it would turn into a Category Two storm within the hour. The meteorologists grew nervous.

At ten o'clock, the storm began to move, and as Luke had forecasted, it moved forward as a Cat Two storm continuing to build strength. "Hang on folks. Stay tuned."

"This can't be happening." John's gaze flitted toward his brother. "If the storm comes our way, what happens to Emilee? She's looking for me. She can't find me. She's out there alone. I can't find her." John moved onto the porch and stared out over the waters.

"John, I don't know what else to do." Andy followed him.

John wanted answers, not excuses. From out on the darkened Gulf, he saw the flash of an S.O.S. He pushed the screen door open and made his way to the dock. The wind whipped around him, and he struggled against the gusts. Luke was attempting to motor toward shore in the small craft he usually kept tied to his sailboat. The larger craft was now anchored offshore, but Luke made little headway in the angry, choppy waters. When he managed to get close enough, he tossed a rope to John, and with several mighty pulls, John drew Luke's craft within easy reach of the dock. John tied the rope to the piling, and Luke climbed from the small boat. He shined the flashlight in John's face. "Appreciate it. The surf's picking up."

John pushed the light away. "No. Really?"

"What's left to do?" Andy came from the house.

Luke turned the flashlight upon Mickey's dark home. "The fool better get back here and do something so Penny's new home

302

stands a chance."

"His car's there." Andy pointed.

"I've pounded on his door. Noah said he knocked. I've called and called. He's not there, and if he's where I think he is, he can face the consequences. I'm not helping his sorry tail this time. He can explain to Penny why her house is ruined." Luke grumbled from tiredness. John saw it in the slump of Luke's shoulder and the slowness of his gait. Luke had worked long and hard along with Andy. His frustration was showing in his words.

"He's not with the person you think," Andy told him. "Maybe he just left town for a few days. Is there anything else needing done?"

Luke thought for a moment before shaking his head and starting up the small hill toward the house. "I helped board up India's house, although I can't say why. Seth called and asked, and I did it. I noticed you and David aren't done boarding up."

"He didn't look too well after he got back from securing Ms. Stewart's store. I told him I'd wait for you to get the boat anchored, listen to the next report, then go get him to finish up."

"This place needs some help. Then I'm getting Blanchie and Penny to the mainland." Luke knocked his boat shoes against the wooden step before entering the porch. "I'm going to shoot Mickey. We sure could have used his help today."

John's short success with curbing his impatience grew to an abrupt end. "Has everyone forgotten Emilee is out there?" He pointed into the growing darkness.

"No, John." Luke fell into a porch chair. "None of us has forgotten. We're trying to save our livelihoods. If sitting around here all day would bring Emilee back to you, I would gladly do it, to heck with the island."

"That's enough." Andy gave Luke a stern look. "John needed to search for Emilee. He hasn't sat around all day."

Luke ignored Andy's reprimand. "We're running out of time. We need to finish and be out of here. Noah's already taken Belle and her aunt and uncle to the mainland, but he insisted upon returning."

"You're sure, aren't you?" John's heart wrenched.

"Very sure." Luke pushed to his feet and placed a hand on John's shoulder. "At the risk of sounding like Noah, you just need to have faith. With every house I boarded up or fixed to stave off the winds, I said a prayer for your wife. God isn't taking your challenge lightly, John, and don't you. Got any food? I'm starving." He walked inside without invitation.

"I'm living in a nightmare," John breathed.

John's nightmare worsened. Luke's predictions proved incorrect, but only barely. John stared in horror and awe as the weather reports indicated that the storm showed its full intention of visiting Serenity Key an hour later than Luke had forecasted. A roaring tempest, it sat out in the Gulf, its millibars decreasing, a sign that it was growing stronger with more wind velocity than the forecasters believed possible. At midnight, while they still struggled with the storm preparations, the weatherman sounded the urgent warning. From atop the fire station in the center of town, a siren wailed. Emergency services received the order with only a small window of opportunity to perfect a swift and mandatory evacuation, and John had seen how efficient Seth New could be in times of danger. Time was at a premium before they'd have to close the bridges over the four bayous between the island and the mainland on the other side.

But John couldn't leave Emilee alone.

"Move it, John," Luke pushed. "We needed to leave an hour ago. Let's finish here and get into town for the girls."

John, finally convinced that Luke was a weather shaman, kicked into action. They finished boarding the windows and secured the remaining items on the porch. John slowed every few minutes to listen for a ringing phone. "Service is non-existent," Luke told him. "And we're going to lose electricity soon. I'm surprised it's held so far. Get a move on. We need to help David and Andy at the restaurants, and I want to get Blanchie and Penny off the island."

"Emilee's out there." John stood in the middle of the yard. His hair lifted in an angry swirl of wind. He turned away as a gust whipped dirt into his face. "She could die in this."

"She's okay, John, and you have to stay safe for her," Luke urged.

John nodded without conviction and climbed into Luke's truck.

As they neared the center of town, the warning siren screamed again. The rain began to pelt them. "We're done here." Andy ran to the truck. "David ran to Seth's house to batten down the hatches. He said for us to go on."

The radio in Luke's pickup announced that the first hour of the morning had ended. The announcer informed them that buoy information from the Gulf indicated the storm had grown to minimal category three strength. With several hours between the storm and the island, it had the potential to grow in intensity. "We have to get out of here." Andy climbed into the back of the truck, and Luke drove to Blanchie's home.

Luke jumped from the truck and ran toward the porch. Andy and John followed.

"I'm not going, Luke." Penny ran to him. "Not without Mick."

"Penny, he's probably off the island. We need to start toward the mainland. Traffic's backing up."

"I'm not leaving without him," Penny repeated. "He hasn't answered the phone all day. If he left the island, you'd know he'd come back to help. You know he would. He wouldn't let us go through this alone, no matter what."

Luke's fist hit the doorframe.

"Where could he be?" John asked.

"Who knows?" Luke screamed into the wind. "I hate him for this. I really do. When I find him, I'm going to kill him."

John slipped his arm around Penny's shoulder. "Can't you see she's worried? Get them to town, and I'll go back and find him."

"No." Luke shook his head. "You two get them to the mainland. I'll find his sorry butt and bring him with me. Just as long as you realize I'm not kidding. He's a dead man."

"I'm not leaving until he's with me." Penny stood firm. "You bring him back, and we'll leave together. And if you touch him, Luke, I'll murder you."

"If your sister was as stubborn, we'd probably still be together." Luke looked to where Andy stood trying to reason with Blanchie.

"And you'd still be cheating on me." She'd heard him. "When you get back here with Mickey, we'll leave together."

"Where do we go?" John asked.

"If I'm not back here in fifteen minutes, you and John carry them to the car and get them off of the island. We'll be behind you. Go to Mainland High School. It's a shelter. We'll meet you there."

John wouldn't argue now. He'd stay here and help settle the girls' nerves, but he wasn't leaving this island without Emilee

Chapter Twenty-Eight

Seth pulled his work truck into the driveway of his home. One long day had just turned into the start of another. Tired. The word played in his mind along with a few others. *Worn and weary. Worried and wary.*

The figure moving up the front walk, though, pumped energy into Seth. He jumped from his truck.

Water fell over the wide bill of his hat and ran down onto the heavy standard-issue yellow slicker he wore. The growing wind threatened to push him backward. Fighting against it, he drew beside his father. "What are you doing here?"

"I'm going to board up the house. We anchored your boat in the bay. I wanted to get this done." Pop's shoulder's sagged and dark circles had formed under his eyes.

Why hadn't Seth taken even a moment of the day to check on his father?

"Leave it. You need to get out of here."

"Fine. I'll leave with you." Pop gave in too easily. Worn, weary, worried, and wary himself, Seth guessed.

The crackle of Seth's radio frayed his nerves. He reached under the rain gear to pull it from its protective sleeve. "Serenity One."

"We're closing the roads to the mainland. I repeat, roads closed," Kurt Davis answered. "Wind is bringing water over the asphalt. Close call with several vehicles."

Seth leaned against the house. Why hadn't he insisted that India and Emilee take shelter on the mainland? Why had he allowed Pop to work so hard that his pallor mirrored that of a corpse?

"Serenity One, you copy?"

Seth raised the radio. "Ten-four. Taking immediate action." As immediate as he could.

"What can I do?" his father asked.

"Pop, I have something to tell you." Seth studied his father's face. Maybe the news would renew the old man's vigor and bring his color back.

"What is it?" Pop straightened. "Is it your sister?"

Seth pushed a smile into place, too exhausted to do it without effort. "She's inside. I had to make sure that both she and India were safe from Cameron Matrai."

Pop blinked. "Emilee is in this house … safe … unharmed?"

"Safe, Pop, but she's not unharmed. Cameron hurt her. I'm worried about her, but she refuses to seek treatment." As stubborn as an old New.

"John has nearly lost his mind …"

"I understand that, but she's frightened that if she returns to John, Cameron will harm him."

Pop stumbled backward, but Seth caught his arm. His father was more fragile than he'd noticed.

"One other thing …" Seth said.

"I don't know if I can take one more thing caused by my willfulness."

"Like John, she thinks I'm her cousin and that you're her uncle. She'll smile politely at us, but deep down, she can't wrap her head around it yet."

Pop shrank back from Seth's touch. He had to keep Pop focused and moving, or he'd never get back to duty.

"I need you to get the girls to safety. Cameron hurt India, too. That's why she's hiding here with Emilee. I've got to get back out there, but Emilee and India have to find a better shelter. Can you do that for me?

Pop nodded but said nothing. Something was wrong, very wrong, but Seth was caught between two nightmarish worlds. Too many people needed him in the other world. His father would have to cope in this one.

Seth opened the door. "Girls," he called, moving aside so that his father could enter.

In seconds, both women came to the top of the stairs. India stepped around Emilee and greeted them. "She's been sleeping on and off. Bad dreams keep waking her," she said before Emilee drew close enough to hear.

Seth nodded and moved up the steps to his sister. Emilee was somewhere between asleep and awake. Her eyes were glassy and feverish. She gripped the banister, her knuckles white, her gaze coming into focus beyond him to their father. Was she trying to stay on her feet or was she afraid of the stranger?

Her thick brown mane was messed. She wore a pair of sweats he hadn't worn in years. She had to be too warm in them, yet she shivered.

"Emilee?"

She looked at him.

"That's our father. He's come to get you and India to a safer place. The hurricane's bearing down on us."

A table scraped, and Seth turned.

Pop had stumbled forward, hand outstretched. "Uma," Pop sputtered. "Uma, is that you?"

India braced him. "No, Mr. New. Her name is Emilee."

What little color Pop had left drained from his face. India struggled with the weight of him as she tried to keep him on his feet. Seth rushed to them, taking Pop from India and leading him to the couch.

"Move."

Surprised, Seth complied with Emilee's command. She picked up Pop's wrist and Seth's at the same time. Studying the second hand on Seth's watch, she stayed silent for a moment then dropped her touch from both of them.

"Are you experiencing pain?" she barked.

"What?" Pop asked, looking to Seth.

"I'm asking you. Do you have pain in your chest, your arms, your jaw, your legs?"

Some bedside manner, but she had all of their attention. Seth had learned that the best doctors cared little for formalities.

Pop shook his head. "No. Not now."

What did he mean by that? Pop never mentioned any problems.

"In the past?" Emilee pressed.

"Don't worry about me."

"Sir, I suspect you ..."

Sir? Definitely not a term of respect, but more an address to a stranger. And just what did she suspect?

"Child." Pop pushed himself up. "Oh, Lord, thank You." He held out his arms, but Emilee scurried from his touch.

Seth's radio crackled. "Serenity One. Serenity One. Requesting assistance. Are you in transit?"

"Ten-four," Seth lied and turned to his sister. "I wish we had time for this, but you need to get to safety."

"With the roads closed, where will we go?" David turned from Emilee to Seth.

"Not here." But Pop posed a good question. Where could they be safe? Where could they stay where he could get back to them— if he could get back to them?

"The school?" India said.

"I stayed in the school during the last blow. The roof nearly blew off. I'm not staying there again." The firehouse came to mind as a viable solution.

The church bells sounded through the wind and rain. "Noah's at the church, Pop. Go there." He might not trust God, but he did trust Noah, and that old wooden church appeared deceptively weak when, in actuality, reinforcements, tie-downs, and storm-rated windows added over the years made the place a fortress against the highest winds. He'd driven by and saw that Luke had helped Noah board up the expensive and not-so-hurricane-proof stained glass.

"Where are you going?" Emilee reached out for him.

"I have a job to do. Go with Pop. He'll keep you safe."

Emilee gripped the sleeve of his raincoat. "I'll stay with you. I can help."

"That's ridiculous." India grabbed her hand.

"Emilee." Seth leaned forward. "You're not in any shape to help. I want you safe inside the church. Noah will look after all of you."

She shook her head, a stubborn glint in her violet eyes.

Seth leaned toward her. "Please take care of Pop for me."

"John and Andy?"

"Emilee, I need to go. They'll be fine. We need to take care of Pop and India. Please? For me, Dr. Ryan. I need you." Would the reminder of their father's condition gain him freedom to go—freedom he despised at this moment?

"Come on, child." Pop motioned.

Emilee looked from one to the other, reminding Seth of a frightened animal wondering if it could trust a human. With a sigh, Emilee grasped their father's outstretched hand.

Luke pulled his truck behind Mickey's Explorer. As he stared at the darkened windows of the house, something Penny had said caused the hair on Luke's skin to stand on end. No matter what, Mickey would never let them go through this alone. No child of the island, even one ensnared in India's web, would fail to rush home during an impending storm.

Not one light shone in the night. "It's dark," Luke muttered. "Too dark." He opened the truck door and jumped out, leaving it ajar despite the rain. He quickened his pace. The home stood like a sinister foe, beckoning Luke toward sorrow, and Mickey's Explorer loomed in Luke's path, a stalwart guard protecting an evil secret.

As he moved past, he noted no sign of recent use. Luke's steps slowed. If he had controlled his anger with Mickey, he might have realized his friend would never place Penny in danger. No. Using his organizational skills, Mickey would have assured everyone's departure hours before the storm's arrival.

If only because Penny stayed there, Blanchie's place would be the first Mickey boarded. Instead, Mick left it for others. *Lord, I didn't offer compassion; I distributed condemnation. Don't let this turn into the biggest mistake of my life. I'm so sorry I failed my friend. He's like my brother. We love two sisters.*

"Jesus, please. I know until today, I haven't been much to pray, but let this situation end without tragedy. Let some good come out of this." He climbed the steps to the front door and banged once, twice, a third time. He turned the knob. The door creaked opened. "Mick. Hey, Mickey. It's Luke. You home?"

The howling wind answered him. Placing one shaky foot in front of the other he shuffled through the darkness until he reached the light switch. With the flick of his finger, the lights came on in a blinding flash of brilliance. Luke sucked in the stale air and listened to the house moan and squeak in the pounding gale. His gaze came to rest on the fancy gun cabinet near the stairs. Luke's hatred of weapons made him cautious when around them, and the empty space where the old hunting rifle always sat—until today—screamed foul play.

He closed his eyes and again asked for strength from above. Avoiding the stairs, he peered into the kitchen. A whiskey bottle's cap lay on the countertop, but no other telltale sign indicated Mickey's presence.

He faced the stairs, his body growing heavy, his legs hard to lift as if filled with lead.

At the top of the stairs, the master bedroom door stood open. Luke let out a breath and eased toward the door, stopping when he saw the toe of Mickey's boot jutting through the doorway. Just beyond, Mickey lay sprawled across the plush carpet. "Mickey." Luke strangled on the whisper. "How will I tell Penny? She'll lose the baby."

He stepped forward then stopped. "You had it all." He held his breath, taking another step but not wanting to see the horror awaiting him. "God, don't let this be happening." Luke wanted to remember Mickey alive and well, an ever-present smile on his face, not dead from a self-inflicted gunshot wound.

The pungent smell of alcohol assaulted his senses. He drew close, pushing back a cry that fought to escape his throat. He kicked hard at the empty bottle beside his friend. It rolled against the wall, hitting it with a thud. He stared down at Mickey's immobile body.

Luke's legs gave way, and he fell to his knees, covering his face with his hands. "You idiot. You fool. Nothing's this bad."

For a while, Luke sat rocking back and forth, listening to the mounting wind and the rain that pelted the windows. Drawing in deep breaths he forced himself to look at his friend, to face the ugliness. He pushed against Mickey's shoulder, struggling to turn over the body.

Mickey smiled up at him with a lopsided, drunken grin.

"Mickey!" Luke's shout pierced the air. "You drunken idiot!" Luke jumped to his feet and kicked his friend in the leg. He reached for the gun and pointed the muzzle in Mickey's face. "I'll shoot your fool head off!"

Mickey struggled to sit up. He placed a shaky hand on the muzzle and pushed it away, his smile fading. "I tried to do it. Only a man with character can pull the trigger." His speech slurred.

"Character! How much character does it take to leave everyone with a mess you made?"

Mickey's laugh mocked Luke's anger. "What type of character does it take to cheat on your pregnant wife? I lost her. I just threw everything away."

Luke flopped onto the bed with the gun across his lap. "The woman who begged me to come and get you isn't the type of woman I think would leave you for long. She's waiting for you so she can get off the island."

"Off the island?"

"There's a hurricane, dope." Luke's body relaxed. "Blanchie and Penny are waiting for us so we can leave together. Can you make it?"

Mickey pushed to his feet, using the bed for leverage. His body swayed. "I'm staying."

"What?" Luke closed the space between them. "You'd leave Penny on the island because you're feeling sorry for yourself?"

"You take her. She doesn't need me."

Luke shook his head. "Maybe you're right. If you can't protect your wife and your children any better than this, you don't deserve any of them. Go off and have another fling with India."

"India means nothing to me."

"Yeah, sure, and the baby you created with her is immaterial."

"You don't have much room to talk." Mickey swung his hand in an exaggerated manner. He swayed like the trees in the wind outside.

Get mad. I need you moving. The storm won't wait on us.

Mickey fell to his knees and remained there. Even if Luke managed to make Mickey angry enough to go to his wife's rescue, Mickey would be unable to walk of his own accord.

"You're right, Mickey. I cheated on Blanchie many times."

"Then don't lecture me."

He refused to argue with him. Mickey was a cheap drunk, and the effect of the alcohol depended on the mood he was in when he started drinking. "Penny needs you right now, and you can prove to her how much you love her and the baby by getting up and moving." He left the gun on the bed and stepped to the door. "Show her, and she'll come back to you."

"Like Blanchie came back to you?" Mickey looked up at him.

"Blanchie gave me many opportunities to choose her. I didn't stop doing those things that tore us apart. Gambling, women."

"Women." Mickey bowed his head. "I had one woman."

"That's all it takes. Think, Mickey. How many men has India been with? You jeopardized more than your marriage when you messed around with her. I thank God every day for Blanchie's health—my health, too—since I was too stupid to realize I could have killed her with my indiscretions."

Mickey lowered his head.

Shame. That would work. Luke would try anything. "You were selfish and arrogant, fulfilling whatever need you convinced yourself Penny didn't provide. I know from experience."

"I want her back, Luke."

"India or Penny?"

Mickey jerked his head upward and glared at Luke, his eyes nearly clear.

Bingo. Now, he'd raised the dead. *Come on, Lazarus. Move it.*

"I don't care if I ever see India again."

"Her child isn't to blame." Luke helped Mickey to his feet this time. "But do you think you're going to win back Penny's affections by hiding in a bottle with a hurricane battering her new house?"

Mickey shook his head, looking like a bobble-headed doll.

"What do you need to do here?"

"Penny, she's frightened?"

"She's afraid for you, but I gave Andy orders to carry her bodily to the car if we weren't back in thirty minutes."

"Forget the house. We can rebuild. I want her off the island."

Luke picked up the gun and checked for ammunition. He sniffed the barrel. "This rifle hasn't been fired."

Mickey shrugged. "Penny hid all the bullets as soon as I put the guns in the house."

The emotions of the last few minutes drained Luke. He lowered the rifle, holding it in his hands, lifting his head toward heaven until laughter from somewhere deep inside emerged through the mixture of fear, frustration, and relief.

"You're laughing, and my world has fallen apart."

"Yeah, people usually laugh at fools. Get a move on."

"I want Penny. I want to live with my wife and baby after it's born." Mickey stumbled forward.

"You have a heck of a lot more character than I ever did," Luke said. "Maybe Blanchie is in better hands with Andy than she is with me."

Mickey opened the bathroom door. "When did that happen? Andy and Blanchie?"

"See what you miss when you climb into a bottle? Let's go."

Chapter Twenty-Nine

The rain fell against Emilee's skin like tiny assaults from the heavens. Her uncle ushered them up the steps of the church where Seth had first found her. India held to Emilee's arm and propelled her forward. David pulled the door open and indicated they should enter. The wind took the door from his grasp, and he retrieved it, pulling with both hands to get it shut in place.

Over the years, when she imagined her father, she'd imagined a younger version of her Uncle David. Had God given her that image to comfort her?

Emilee wiped the rain from the sleeves of the heavy sweats she wore, but excessive movement cost her too much in the way of excruciating pain.

She looked around her at the quaint little sanctuary and then gave her attention over to David, who stood soaked from head to toe. He had insisted she and India remain inside the car until he could open the door. He wanted to make sure they all made it inside.

David wasn't a well man. His pulse had been erratic, his color a sign to her that she needed to pay attention to him, or she'd lose him before she could give him a what-for or before she could get to know him. If only for Seth, she prayed that he'd remain stable until the storm passed.

The ringing bell in the church steeple that lured them stopped, and from somewhere behind the sanctuary, footsteps sounded and a door closed. A second later an entry toward the front of the sanctuary opened, and a man came toward them. "Mr. New." He took off his glasses, looked at them, and rubbed them against his semi-damp jeans. "I thought you left." Replacing his spectacles, the man stopped and stared at Emilee.

Emilee cast her eyes upward toward the ceiling, anything to avoid his scrutiny, though she didn't know why it bothered her.

"Pastor Noah McGowan, I'd like you to meet John's wife. Emilee, this young man has remained a very good friend to your husband since your disappearance."

"Dr. Ryan, you're an answer to prayer—mine and John's and many others. We're glad you're alive and well."

John had prayed? Her self-confident, in-control man, had actually bowed a knee to God? Why did she find that so hard to believe?

"You are, aren't you?" the pastor asked.

Was she what? She tried to focus and thought about what he'd asked her before. Oh, yeah. "Perhaps alive, but not well," she muttered. "Is John off the island?" She took his outstretched hand in hers, giving it a gentle shake, feeling the not-so-gentle pain shoot through her body.

"I left him some time ago. I'm not sure. Haven't you seen him?"

Emilee shook her head.

"Noah, are you sure we're safe?" India broke into the conversation.

"I can't be too sure of much in a hurricane, but I think so. This church has withstood every other hurricane sent our way even before the hurricane standard upgrades. How many more are stranded?"

"Seth's trying to make that determination," David said.

The door opened again, and with a rush of wind and rain, two women entered. David pushed with them to close the door. Emilee started to admonish her uncle. He needed to do as little as possible. Instead, she remained quiet.

The pastor helped one of the women shrug off her heavy raincoat. Static from the hood of the coat made some of her reddish blonde hair stand straight up. She pushed it down, and the air seemed to crackle with the electricity.

Emilee backed against the wall by the door. When she believed she'd be alone with her uncle, India, and this pastor, she'd been fine, but now, apprehension crept over her like Cameron's body, pressing her down, taking her breath. Fear began to rise. Fear that only Johnny could take away.

"They didn't come back, Noah. I don't know what to do." The redhead cried.

"Who, Penny?" Noah soothed.

"Mickey and Luke," she wailed the two names as if she could raise the dead.

The other woman, a petite blonde, turned and touched the crying woman's arm. "They'll be fine. Luke won't let anything happen to them."

"I'm sure they'll be fine. Luke knows how to handle these types of situations." Emilee's uncle touched the blonde's hair, and the woman turned into his arms.

The blonde pulled away and looked up into David's face. "Luke went to look for Mick. We haven't heard from him all day.

They never made it back to the house. John and Andy made us come with them, trying to get to the mainland, but Kurt turned us back. He said the roads were swamped and the bridges unsafe to cross."

John and Andy. In the storm. Her family. Her only family.

Emilee moved toward the door.

"Where are you going?" India blocked her way. "You don't even know where they've gone."

David, still holding to the stranger, reached out for Emilee.

She pulled from his touch.

"Penny, this is Emilee," the pastor spoke to the woman he embraced. "John's wife."

Penny left the comfort of the preacher's arms and stepped forward. "Emilee?"

Emilee turned away from her. In her world, there was room only for John and Andy. She wanted nothing to do with these people.

"My husband is John's law partner. John and Andy are fine," the woman insisted. "They dropped my sister and me off. They're looking for my husband. No one's seen him all day."

For the life of her, Emilee couldn't focus on the woman's problems. All she wanted was John. What if Cameron …? *Oh, God, no.*

"Emilee, there's more out there than a hurricane to worry about," India's whisper echoed Emilee's thoughts.

Emilee looked to her and nodded.

Penny lowered a cool, direct stare upon India before moving away. Something unpleasant stood between these women, and Emilee didn't like the way this Penny treated the woman who'd helped Emilee so much.

"I think you'd be safer in the hurricane," the girl in David's arms snapped at India.

"Blanchie," Penny warned then stepped menacingly close to India herself. "Have you seen my husband?"

"No," India declared. "I've been with Emilee all day."

"While John worried about her? What kind of stunt is that?" Penny stomped her foot.

"I'm sorry, but I don't think that is any of your concern. I made the decision." Emilee learned in medical school that a certain tone of her voice could calm any situation. She placed the sternness into each syllable.

Back off, Red.

The door opened. Wrenched from the man's hand, it hit the wall with a resounding bang. Noah rushed to close it. Emilee's breath caught. Her first instinct said run. She needed to protect him and being here with him wasn't the way to do it.

Yet, it had been so long since she'd seen her brother-in-law.

Andy pushed the long, wet strands of his hair out of his face. He first caught sight of Blanchie. "I think I'll take that haircut now." He smiled as she ran into his arms. He hugged her to himself.

As if having her uncle coo over the woman wasn't enough, Andy's actions rang of betrayal. Andy didn't hold women that way. He was cool and aloof most of the time. This embrace—well, it was more.

Had Andy purposely kept this intimate relationship from her? Had John put this space between them? Emilee touched the wall behind her, wishing she could crawl inside and have it cover her.

Again, the door opened, and the wind tried to have mastery over the building. Johnny? Emilee's heart soared, but only for a moment.

The woman in Andy's arms pulled from him and practically jumped into the arms of this new stranger.

Hurt. She knew Andy's look all too well. John caused Andy enough pain that she'd had her fill of seeing it in Andy's eyes.

"Luke, don't ever worry me like this again." The blonde pulled back but hugged the man again.

"Blanchie, have I ever let you down?" Luke smiled down at the small woman and then kissed her long and hard.

Blanchie pulled back, her face red. She left Luke's embrace and moved back to Andy.

Emilee's insides flamed with anger. No one played with Andy's heart like that.

"Mickey!" Penny's scream pierced the air. She fell against the next man who entered. He almost tumbled backward, none to steady on his feet. Emilee closed her eyes and exhaled to get the stench of the alcohol out of her own lungs. The man was drunk or coming off a drinking binge. Still, he caught Penny and held her against him. "I'm sorry, Mouse. I'm sorry. I'll never do it again."

"Em. Emmy …" Andy said, and Emilee blinked. He reached out for her.

She began to sob, great choking sobs as she took one step and then another toward him. "Andy," she cried his name as he held her against him as though he would never let go. Pain caused her breathing to stop, and she bit her tongue to keep from crying out.

The pain meant she'd survived the nightmare. No matter what awaited them, they were together.

Or were they? "Johnny?" she cried. "Where's Johnny?"

Andy released his hold on her. He looked to Noah, who held to the door while Andy stepped outside. "John," he yelled. Emilee stepped to the door, grasping the frame to keep from being pushed back inside. John gave a stubborn backward wave toward Andy.

"John!" she called against the wind and fought to stay on her feet.

He didn't turn.

"Johnny!"

He spun in her direction.

"Johnny!" she screamed his name again.

He ran toward her, the wind ripping at his shirt. He crashed against her with the force of a tornado loosed from the clouds. "Baby, I thought I'd never hear you call my name again. I'm sorry. I'm so sorry. Thank You, God. Thank You."

The searing arc of excruciation threatened to launch her into unconsciousness.

"Em." He kissed her again and again, bringing her from the edge of darkness. His cries mingled with hers. "I thought I'd lost you without a chance to make things right."

"Don't you know if anything happened, my memory would haunt you until your dying day? You'll never rid yourself of me, Johnny Ryan. I'm Catherine, and you're my Heathcliff." Her hands tangled in his wet hair. She leaned away from him. "Your face. What happened to your handsome face? Cameron ...?"

He tried to speak, but the sobs of relief robbed him of all voice. He could only shake his head.

Emilee forgot the pain and the brink of oblivion. She wanted John to hold her. She should have known she'd never be able to stay away from him—even if his life depended upon it.

"Say my name again," he begged.

"Johnny," she whispered against his ear.

"I love you, Em." He continued to cry. "I'm never letting you

away from me again. If they think I'm possessive, I don't care."
He offered her a sheepish grin. "You know what I've done, don't
you?" He kissed her again.

"And I'm so mad at you." She held to him. "So mad."

The pastor motioned the others toward the hall. "We'll be
safer there. I've got a weather radio to track the storm."

They started to follow, John and Andy on either side of her,
everyone else in front of them.

The wind whipped at their backs, and turning, they watched a
man struggle with the door.

"What does he think …?"

The slamming door cut off John's question.

Emilee trembled at the sight of the man who entered, and John
started to leave her side. "No," she whispered and managed to
move in front of her husband.

Cameron Matrai stood before them. He wiped the water from
his face with a handkerchief and then moved forward, his eyes
boring into Emilee's soul. "John," he greeted. "I thought you might
need some help down here. I see you didn't need me after all."

Emilee blinked. She'd seen the depth of Cameron's madness,
but who would believe the extent of his arrogance, acting as if he'd
done nothing wrong.

John started forward again.

"Cameron, good of you to care enough to get through." Andy
pushed John and Emilee behind him. "Looks to me like we'll be
weathering the storm together. What do you think?"

"I know what I—" John started.

Andy blocked his way, cutting off John's attempt to grab
Cameron's arm.

Andy turned to them. "Mine," he mouthed. "All mine."

Chapter Thirty

The electricity failed at 4:15 a.m. Noah lit a candle and switched the radio current to battery power. The local station remained on the air despite the ravaging winds. The eye of the storm had not yet reached Serenity Key, but they expected it within the next hour.

Noah sat amongst the eleven people huddled in the small center hallway. They lined each side.

A silent unceasing prayer for his wife occupied most of Noah's thoughts. Belle was unhappy with his decision to remain behind, and she'd insisted on staying also. He stood his ground, and she'd left but not before clinging to him much the way John Ryan clung to his wife right now.

Noah smiled at the memory of Belle's sweet face looking up to him. "I'll submit, husband, but only if you agree to stay safe. I have something to discuss with you."

He'd given in, and before she ducked into the backseat of the car, she winked at him. "I love you. Don't do anything foolish."

He looked around at the people seeking refuge with him. Settled close to Cameron Matrai, Andy caught Noah's eye and gave a terse nod.

John and Emilee sat several feet away near the entrance to the hallway. Blanchie sat on the other side of Andy between him and Luke.

Cameron's gaze fell several times upon Emilee. His smile sickened Noah.

Emilee leaned against her husband, her body trembling at times, but she grasped John's arm as if she meant to hold on to him for dear life. She winced each time John hugged her to him. The couple talked among themselves from time to time. John was a different man with his wife in his arms, and Noah could easily see that this woman was loved by the no-nonsense lawyer.

The wind howled and presented a fury most of those in the hallway knew well. A sharp explosion of light just beyond the window of the nursery caused everyone to jump. A muttered curse made him smile. God would understand Mickey's fear.

Noah saw the flash, most likely from a blown transformer, because he sat across from the nursery. He left its hurricane safety-rated window uncovered only because he hated closed-in spaces, and being able to see even the rain battering the window provided some comfort. A rumbling from the ferocious winds shook the church building followed by another bright flash. Could be the storm had spawned a tornado. A loud boom sounded toward the front of the church as something heavy landed against the outside wall. "Hope it wasn't my house," he said.

No one responded.

Fear never entered into the picture for Noah. God meant him to stay behind, and the Lord brought the other ten people in this hall here for a purpose. He would trust God to show him, and if the reason remained veiled, he would rest in faith that God performed His purpose. He closed his eyes to give thanks to the Lord and to pray for Kurt and Seth, who might still be outside in this tempest.

When he opened his eyes, David New offered him a weary but reassuring smile.

David had hoped that Seth would seek refuge with them prior to the storm's heaviest winds. Four hours later, Seth failed to appear. Worry taunted David, but at the same time, Emilee's presence in her husband's protective embrace brought David joy.

Yet, everything within him wanted to take the man sitting beside Andy and tear him into tiny pieces. *Lord, forgive me, but if Andy hadn't placed his hand on my shoulder when that fiend walked into this room ...*

Andy sat with his knees drawn close and his left hand cupped into his right palm. He never heard anything like the moan of the wind as it pushed against the church.

"This is something, huh?" Cameron leaned toward him. "Did you ever think we'd be huddled in a church—a church of all things?"

Andy wanted more than anything to step out into the other room and end this facade forced upon him by Cameron's arrogance. His friend had harmed two people in this room, and he had the gall to put on a show of innocence and concern. He was a coward who terrorized women, and he was egotistical enough to believe they wouldn't tell his terrible secrets. How could Cameron hurt Emilee when he knew how much Andy loved her, and what had India ever done to him?

Andy slipped his arm over Blanchie's shoulder. His hand brushed against Luke, and the other man offered a sympathetic smile.

Luke moved away from Blanchie. In his fear, he failed to notice how close he sat to her. He would protect his ex with his life. Andy's inadvertent touch reminded Luke that though he would never fail her again, she had not offered him the right to such closeness. Yet, he wanted to take Blanchie in his arms in front of everyone and tell her how much he loved her. The declaration got him nowhere before; it had only proven how much she loved Andy.

Luke wouldn't stand in the way of her happiness after he'd brought so much misery into her life. He'd allow her to love someone without the pain he'd always brought to her. Andy already loved her better than he ever had.

God, why didn't I see what she needed before her love passed me by?

Blanchie rested her hand on his knee. Luke placed his hand over hers and squeezed, thankful she at least still cared.

Blanchie offered Luke a tentative smile. His words outside her salon haunted her. They drew her back into his web. Always the cool one in the crowd and the most likely to find trouble, he pushed the envelope. As a teenager, she liked excitement. She enjoyed being his girlfriend, even when he offered so little in return for her love. She'd found pleasure in being his wife until she realized just how little their vows meant to him.

His words spoken to her earlier in this long day had flowed deep from his heart.

Lord, I need to know the truth. Luke is a changed man. He voiced his love in an open, honest declaration, and I turned my back on him. He is the man I promised to have and to hold forever, but he betrayed those vows first, not me. Show me, please, what You want me to do. Do I put trust in this man who threw my heart away so many times, or do I walk away with a man I know I can trust?

Seventy times seven.

No. No. You can't be asking me to forgive and forget. Andy's too perfect, Lord. Don't ask me to walk away from him. Andy will never harm me. Look how even now he's using his body as a barrier between Cameron and me. Show me what I want to see.

Blanchie closed her eyes and bent her head. The Lord had worked with her for years on her stubbornness. She wiped the tears of frustration aside. *Show me what I need to see. I'm waiting. Show me something that will let me know that my decision is the right one, something I can't deny.*

When she looked up, she stared into the bloodshot eyes of her idiot brother-in-law. He sat next to Penny right across from Blanchie, his feet pressed up against her toes in the narrow hall.

Mickey tried to offer Blanchie a smile, but he didn't feel well. His head throbbed. He braced his elbow against his knee and rubbed his eyes with his hands. He would give almost anything for an aspirin and everything for Penny to hold him close. *Lord, I'm a coward. The storm outside doesn't scare me. It's the one in here making me want to run. I'm the wind picking up the debris and throwing it around our lives. Penny doesn't deserve this pain. India's alone, and my selfish fear keeps me away. How do I tell India I care without losing Penny forever?* The truth was, if he wanted to fight for his marriage, he couldn't be anything to India. *Lord, help India. Be the arms that I cannot be, like the protection that belongs only to my wife. Please help her.*

He moved to hold Penny, but she pulled away from him.

"Forgive me." The words came with the tilt of his head. He did not mean others to hear, but in trying to get his voice above the roar outside, his words boomed.

India brought her knees up close and buried her head into her arms. She felt the storm inside the hallway and wondered if it wouldn't be safer running out into the hurricane. She could face the debris easier than the anger and the pity swirling around her now.

An abrupt jar made her fall against David New.

"Whoa." Cameron Matrai gave a startled laugh at the far end of the hall, as far away as she could get from him. "I think the building shifted."

The old wooden building did move, jolted by a strong gust of wind. The building was tied down. Her father's company had donated the labor and materials.

Am I an acceptable sacrifice, God? Will You save the others if I step out into Your fury? They say You're a loving God. Where's Your love toward me?

Enough thinking of me. I always think of myself.

Where's Your love for Emilee? If You love us, why is Cameron here? He can reach out and squeeze the life out of her and out of my unborn child. He can't find out. I won't let him harm this baby.

The tears fell, and she fought to keep herself quiet.

Penny doesn't deserve the pain of thinking my child belongs to her husband. I meant to tell the truth. You know I did.

Please, let me be an acceptable sacrifice? I give myself to You! Just take this all away. Let their world return to normal. I don't know much about love. I have nothing acceptable for You, Lord. Seth painted an honest picture of me. I'm a harlot, and I'm ashamed. If Cameron had only asked, I'd have given him what he stole with violence from me. Is that what You wanted me to admit? Well, there. I've said it. I'm a home-wrecking tramp.

India placed her hands against her face and sobbed into them. *I don't want to live like this anymore. I want to know Your love. Please, God, love me.*

"Come here, child." David's words calmed her. He did not move to embrace her. He simply tugged at her arm. She looked at him, and he opened his embrace. She fell against him and felt the comfort of a father for a daughter.

"'I will never leave thee nor forsaketh thee,' the Lord promises." David's words touched somewhere deep inside of her.

You do love me, Father. I know You do.

India lifted her eyes. Through the dim light from the candle, she saw Cameron's hungry gaze upon her. David's embrace was a gift from the heavenly Father.

Cameron Matrai's hunger seldom called for food, but right now he wanted something to eat. His stomach rumbled, and he pressed his hand against his gut, flashing a smile at his friend. Andy, though, did not return the gesture. Andy feared storms. It went back to the night his mother died. Seeing her beneath a balcony in the rain, beaten at the hands of his father, had traumatized Andy.

At least Andy's mother had died. She didn't endure years of abuse the way his mother had suffered at the hands of Andy's father. She survived only because she knew that after every beating, Zack paid well.

Cameron tried not to look at India. His first plan had backfired. She presented a danger to him, but she remained silent. If he'd made it inside her house, they wouldn't have searched for her body until days after the storm.

He leaned his head back against the wall. With Emilee here, Cameron had to act quickly to get rid of both women before anyone learned the truth of his involvement.

He glanced through the semi-darkness to where Emilee leaned in John's arms. John brushed her hair away from her face, whispering to her the way he used to do. She obviously had not told John. Otherwise, John wouldn't touch her like that.

Cameron's skin crawled. *I can't let you hold her, John, not when it hurts Andy. If you loved Andy, you'd know how sad it makes him. I'm more of a brother to him, not you. Never you.*

Another tremendous boom split the air.

Emilee screamed.

Cameron balled his hands into tight fists.

"Something wrong?" Andy asked.

Cameron focused his attention on John. "No," he said between clenched teeth.

John pulled Emilee even closer to him. Her shriek hung in the air for long seconds. She trembled, and more than anything, he wanted to vanquish her fears. He wished the enemy outside were human and not nature. He would obliterate it and prove his love, just the way he planned to destroy Cameron.

"I'm so sorry," he whispered for the hundredth time. "I love you so much." He kissed the top of her hair. She wore a long-sleeved sweatshirt and sweatpants. Why wasn't she suffocating in them? Instead, she trembled in his arms.

"Johnny?" She stared up at him, his name spoken in a soft whisper.

He smiled at her.

She touched his face. "No matter what, I love you with all my heart. I always have. There has never been anyone else for me but you."

If only he'd remembered her love instead of listening to Cameron's accusations. She never looked at anyone else, not even Andy. John loved her so much more than he ever thought possible. Even when he failed her—and he always failed her—she loved him without condition.

He bent and kissed her, and he felt the old fire burn as if jealousy had never quenched it.

———

Emilee felt John's kiss, not only in her heart but also in the pain ripping across her body. She stifled the cry and reached to hold him closer. She never wanted him far from her again. If Cameron wanted to kill her husband, he needed to get through her first. John shifted his weight, and it placed pressure against her side. She pulled away and laid her head on him. The pain made her wince. The tight hugs from Andy and John broke the wounds open again. The bandages, she feared, wouldn't help her hide what she'd endured at the hands of Cameron.

If the pain wasn't enough, she exhibited all the signs of a fever: sweating while at the same time freezing, headache, and chills so deep she craved a blanket. She looked toward the pastor, needing to focus her attention away from her injuries. *He truly is Your man, Lord. He doesn't seem to realize his faith stands before us like Your beacon. Did You actually cause him to befriend Johnny? John needs Your friendship, Lord. Thank You for the gift of Noah in Johnny's life, and let him see the goodness I've always known You've given Johnny.*

Emilee's nerves settled a bit. The storm outside had quieted even if the storm inside still raged.

"The eye's over us," Noah remarked. "I guess we can expect a few minutes of peace." The preacher started toward the hallway leading to the front sanctuary.

Luke jumped to his feet. "Where are you going?"

"I'm going to ring the bell if there still is a bell. Someone may need refuge."

"I'm going to look outside." Luke stepped over the legs and feet of the people separating him from the doorway. "As the television shows always say, 'Don't do this at home, folks.' No one should step out into the eye of the storm, but I'm looking for the injured within sight of the grounds."

"You stay close, you goof," Blanchie warned. Her gaze followed Luke out of the room, and Andy watched her. Was this girl playing both men? Emilee seethed at the thought of Andy getting hurt.

"Where's the bathroom?" Emilee asked, afraid to move for fear of Cameron and fear that the bandages were long past their usefulness. She needed another round of first aid.

"I'll show you." India got to her feet.

"I'll be back," Emilee told John who held to her hand. "Five minutes."

"No more." He winked at her.

"Your face," she whispered. She realized how much his kisses must have hurt.

"Nothing I didn't deserve." He touched the bruises.

"That's for sure," Andy teased.

"Shut up."

The ripple of laughter flowing through the group was a welcome sound. Above them, the bell pealed forth its anthem of safe haven. India and Emilee waited for the others to make their way into the sanctuary. Emilee stood very still as Cameron exited the room. He reached to pat her cheek, but Andy pushed him forward.

Chapter Thirty-One

Emilee leaned over the sink in the ladies' room. The pain. If only it would go away. A small stain betrayed the injuries beneath the bandages and the sweatshirt. She could hide it from John, at least until they could be alone. She still doubted internal bleeding, but the fever was her body's way of saying something was wrong. She'd admit only to John that she needed medical attention, but John had never been good at handling medical emergencies. His reaction to her admission would only cause worry for him and for her Uncle David. She couldn't add that stress to either man, especially when she suspected that David was on the verge of collapse, and trapped on an island in a hurricane.

"Do you need help?" India stepped out of the stall.

Emilee shook her head. "Who are those other women out there?" And more importantly, what kind of hold did the little petite one have over her brother-in-law?

"Blanchie and Penny are sisters."

"And they hate you, why?"

India breathed deep. "Do you really want to know the truth?"

"I don't like it when people treat my friends with disrespect."

India's eyes widened. Then she looked away. "I'm no great friend. Ask Penny."

"I want to like them."

"They're very nice people. Penny has always been kind to me." India moved away from the door. "I'm carrying Cameron's child." India looked at her.

"Why didn't you seek treatment after the rape?" What a stupid question. Emilee had ignored Yasmin's pleas.

Emilee shivered, and the fever was not the cause. What if she carried Cameron's child as well. Beside her, India kept her gaze on the floor.

Emilee touched her hand. "That was insensitive and hypocritical of me. There are many reasons that women don't report rape. I admire you for protecting your child." She lowered her own gaze. "I didn't even think that an innocent life could be conceived." Her lips trembled. "I don't really know what I'll do if that's the case with me." She took a deep breath and looked at India. "Funny how people argue right and wrong without thinking of the choice they would make if something caused them to make the choice."

"I'm no saint, Emilee. If I hadn't been afraid of what others thought of me, there's no telling what I would have done. But something deep inside tells me that this little baby isn't responsible for its circumstances, and I don't have the right to be the judge, jury, and executioner over the life I carry inside." Despite everything she said, a smile broke the spell of worry that seemed to loom over India.

"What?" Emilee asked.

India covered her stomach. "For the first time ever, I think I've chosen someone's needs over my own desires." She shook her head. "Maybe God is listening … or perhaps I'm hearing Him for the first time."

Emilee understood, pushing aside the possibility that she and India might be carrying the children of their mutual attacker. "I think He has my attention, too. But you feel condemned by these people because of your reputation."

"No." India shook her hand. "They aren't that shallow. I did something else—something terrible."

"Go ahead," Emilee urged.

"I—I got involved with Penny's husband to cover up the pregnancy."

Emilee waited. How would she handle a woman doing that to her? She'd kill her; that's what she'd do. No wonder those women spat so much venom in India's direction.

"I've tried to tell Penny the truth, but she won't listen."

Would the truth lessen the hurt for the wronged wife? What blame did Penny's husband carry in all of this? Penny sure looked glad to see him when he entered the church. If John had done this to her …

Instead, Cameron had taken something from John. And she had no idea what he would do if she did carry Cameron's child.

India bowed her head, and her tears fell to the tile floor. "In all of this mess that I've gotten myself into, I'm thankful that I didn't take action. I want this baby. Funny, Penny and I always debated abortion when it came to rape. I always stood with the mother's choice, even though I couldn't fathom killing a child. Now, I know. God's gifts don't always come in beautifully wrapped packages, but we have to peer inside to find out how glorious they can be. I just wish I hadn't taken the sanctity of Penny's marriage to protect the life within me."

"I don't see Penny's husband as an innocent victim." Now, Emilee's anger churned not at Penny or Blanchie but at the tall, blond, drunken man who'd allowed this to happen.

India wiped her tears with the back of her hand and lifted her gaze to Emilee. "Trust me. I had to work hard at breaking down Mickey's walls of fidelity. He only gave in when I finally stopped sending the battering ram at him and showed my vulnerable side, and me, being me, did what I've always done best—what I think is best for me. So, how do you feel about calling me a friend now?"

Emilee offered India her best smile. "Fortunate. I'll never forget what you've done for me." She looped her arm in India's and opened the door.

John stood, waiting. "You okay?"

"I'm fine." She managed to smile at him. "India and I needed some time to talk."

"How did you run into each other?"

John's curiosity was endless, and she loved to tease him about it. "That, my dear husband, is a secret India and I plan to keep." She smiled over her shoulder at the other woman as they walked out into the hall. "Right, India?"

India nodded, but Emilee noticed India's attention rested upon the wife she'd helped betray. Penny glared in their direction and pulled her hand from her husband's.

The door into the sanctuary opened.

"Seth." Emilee rushed to him.

Seth pulled the yellow slicker from his back. "Some of those gusts blew pretty hard," he said as he greeted his sister.

Did she know what she meant to him? He'd never have taken

a step into this church if it weren't for her. The tolling of the church bells grated on Seth's nerves. Noah needed to stop. He doubted anyone else would venture out of their safe haven.

"Boy." Pop clasped Seth's hand and pulled him into an embrace. "You worried me."

"I stayed huddled in the fire station with Old Eloise's tomcat. She couldn't find him before she evacuated, and he's as ornery as his owner. I left him in the station."

"Mind if I seek refuge?" Kurt opened and then closed the door. "Pretty lonely in the police department."

"Good to see you." Seth held Emilee's hand and brought her in front of him. "Kurt, meet Emilee Ryan."

Kurt stared for a long, silent moment. He did not speak, and his chin quivered.

"Hey, it's okay." Seth grasped his friend's shoulder.

Kurt stepped forward. "Dr. Ryan, it's nice to finally meet you."

John joined them. "Kurt is our Chief of Police, Em. I don't think he's slept since they reported you missing."

"I'm sorry to have worried you." Emilee placed her hand on Kurt's arm.

"Are you okay?" Kurt asked.

Emilee turned her gaze toward the hallway.

Seth looked in that direction. "You'll be fine."

Kurt nodded. "We'll take him out with the rest of the trash once the storm blows over."

Cameron stood speaking with Mickey. He waved to those in the sanctuary, the gesture mocking.

Luke came inside. "Not much damage on this street. Quasimodo's home is still standing."

As if on cue, Noah stopped ringing the church bell.

"Seth, do you think anyone could be hurt?" Emilee asked.

"We won't know until this blows over." In a discreet motion, Seth pointed to a spot on her shirt. His sister was bleeding through her bandages again.

Seth was pretty sure John saw the stain, but except for a quick glance in Cameron's direction, John gave no indication of his feelings. The ones that could hide their emotions were the ones he had to watch, and one look at Kurt told him the police chief felt the same.

Noah stepped through the interior door, coming down from the steeple. "I don't see anyone milling about, just the two of you," he spoke to Seth and Kurt.

"There were no calls, and emergency management directed me to stay inside during the backside of the storm. They say it's going to show us the full strength of a Cat Three," Seth advised.

"Tidal surge?" A chorus rang from the natives. The non-natives and newcomers stared.

"Not expected. The storm came inland south of us and moved a bit west. We're on the good side. Winds and spawned tornadoes are our biggest problems." Seth's words would calm their fears. Everyone but the New Yorkers in the group were veterans of many storms. He doubted he would have ever met his sister if John or Andy had known that Serenity Key held the record for the Florida city hit by the most hurricanes.

"Let's get in the hallway," Noah directed. "I'd like to say a prayer."

The winds picked up quickly. Everyone settled into the hall. Seth took a seat beside Emilee, placing her in the middle between him and John.

Kurt moved toward the end of the hallway, his back against the wall as he faced forward down the corridor, hemming Cameron in between him and Andy. "How's it going?" he asked.

Seth lowered his head and allowed himself a smile. Cameron Matrai had no idea who he sat beside. Even though Kurt had little tolerance for those who would brutalize the innocent, the chief of police also had a reputation for justice. And the innocent victims of Cameron's assaults, including India and Seth's sister, would get their justice the right way. Seth was never more thankful for his friend who would handle the situation well without stepping over boundaries, and he'd save Seth—and probably John and Andy— from a life in prison.

"Lord," Noah began. "Thank You for safely seeing us through the front side of the storm, and we trust You will be with us to see us safely through to the end. Thank You for allowing us to come together, to encourage each other as friends. Thank You for the safety of Emilee and for Kurt and Seth's safe appearance. Be with all of our friends and neighbors who weather this storm, and forgive us everyone our trespasses and let us be ever mindful to forgive others. Amen."

Seth listened to the prayer. He looked at his sister. Her safety was an answer to prayer. He touched her hand, the one she rested on the floor beside him. She laced her fingers in his, and he fingered the opal and diamond setting of the simple ring. Where had he seen it before? He smiled up at her. "It means a lot to me that you're safe."

He had not entered this church since the last funeral on Serenity Key. Attending church allowed God the upper hand, and he refused to concede God's love and goodness toward him. He accepted Emilee's appearance at the fire station as a well-orchestrated tactic by God to lure him out into the open.

I know You expect repentance God, but I never asked my wife for her forgiveness. How can You expect me to seek it from You? Linda died without knowing my sorrow over what I did to her. I was reckless with her passion and her love, and I took both away from her in my demands. Still, she never told a soul, and she said she loved me until the end. Now that I promised not to drink, nothing deadens the pain. I don't want to think of being in Your church. I don't want to think of my sin. Go away, Lord, and leave me alone.

Seth again studied the ring on Emilee's hand laced in his. Trying to remember where he'd seen the exact same setting gave him an escape from the maddening thoughts of God who'd forsaken Seth before Seth had walked away from Him.

———

India covered her ears. The gusting wind picked up and howled without reprieve. The rain pounded against the wood over the windows. The banging and the booms heard only occasionally with the front side of the storm now never ceased.

I can't take any more of the wind and noise. Please take it away, Lord. I'm trapped in a cage with a madman. It's driving me insane, too. "No. No. No." Her repeated whisper grew louder and louder. "No. No. No."

"India," the voice came to her. Someone pried her hands away from her ears. "Look at me. Look at me, okay. It's fine. It's just wind and rain."

India opened her eyes. She pulled back, but Penny continued

to hold her hands.

"You need to calm down. You're not helping the baby."

"Baby!" Somehow above the noise, Cameron had heard. "India's pregnant? Who's the father, or does she know?"

India sat frozen by fear. How could this be happening? She'd asked God to love her. Had He refused?

"It's mine." The voice, a little too loud, too strong, convincing in the lie, made India lift her gaze. Why would he do this for her? Why did he just throw everything away for someone like her?

"She's been trying to protect me, but the baby's mine," Andy declared the untruth.

"Calm down. You need to think of the baby now." Penny stroked her hair. "Mickey's baby," she whispered.

"No, I lied. I lied to Mickey. It isn't. I set him up to hide the truth!" she screamed. Everyone stared at her. "Mickey didn't care for me." India gripped Penny's hand. "He loves you. Please don't leave him because of what I did."

Penny's kindness unleashed the tide of emotions inside India. Penny wrapped India in an embrace. She cradled India like a child.

India sobbed against her. "I'm sorry," she said. "I'm so sorry."

"Penny," the male voice broke in. "I think your husband needs you."

Penny moved and Seth took her place, sitting between India and his father. He held her close to him, and India clung to his compassion. She closed her eyes. *I've told the truth, Lord. They all know now. But why did you let Andy throw away his reputation on me? Forgive me, please. Lord, I need You.*

"Why didn't you tell me it was Andy's child?" Seth whispered close to her ear.

India's eyes sprung open. Still holding to Seth, she looked to where Andy sat.

Andy pressed his forefinger to his lips and indicated with a discreet shake of his head for her to remain silent.

"Oh," India cried against Seth. "I'm so horrible."

"You've told the truth now. That's good. The rest will fall into place." Seth soothed.

———

The pains cut sharp into David's chest both figuratively and physically. He heard every word between the two women, even those not meant for his hearing. He, more than anyone in this room, understood the truth of the situation. He listened as India confessed the affair she pushed on Mickey. He saw the entire picture as if God placed it on a movie screen.

Everything that happened revolved around his sin—his long-ago sin and his failure to confess it to those he'd harmed by his indulgences. His misdeeds were rearing their ugly heads and causing the pain in this room. His actions had left his daughter vulnerable. They brought evil to this island. India and Emilee were together in Seth's home for one reason. The child growing inside of India didn't belong to Mickey or to Andy.

Oh, God, did Cameron rape my daughter, too?

Lord, are You using Mickey as a mirror to my own sin? Don't. Please, don't. Are you showing me Andy's unselfish nature to prove mine so selfish? You can't let him confess to something not true, not because of what I did so long ago that put all of this in motion.

It's too much, Father. I can't bear this burden alone.

Come to Me, all you who labor and are heavy laden, and I will give you rest.

Lord, I watch Kurt and Noah step around each other, brought together in all of this. Kurt must know firsthand the abuse these women suffered. Hasn't the rumor long been that he endured abuse at an early age? My sin has caused him to relive this pain.

David caught his breath, felt the icy fingers of pain squeeze his heart. Why did his chest hurt so badly every time he tried to inhale? He glanced down the row toward the trio at the end.

I poured my sin upon Noah. It must have felt like a knife cutting into his heart. He hasn't been able to forgive Kurt for his closeness to Belle. The compassion he offered to me and to John came at a great price.

Adultery was the name of David's transgression, but it ran much deeper. *Oh, God, I know all sin is equal and condemns us all. I took the greatest gift You gave to this world, and I threw it in Your face. You forgave me, but I never sought the forgiveness of others. You brought me to this church with all of these people, my friends, my loved ones, to show me the truth.*

"Oh, God." He rubbed the area over his heart where the pain now did not cease. "Oh, God, help me." He could not bring himself to utter the words, to tell them what he had done. Seth's touch tingled upon his numbing arm. David looked into his son's worried face. "I think I'm having a heart attack."

A tremendous explosion shook the church. David gasped for air. He was being pushed down. Hands grasped his wrist. His shirt was torn apart just as the ache ripped through his chest. Emilee sat on her knees beside him barking orders at Seth, but David could not hear them. He wanted to tell his children good-bye, needed desperately to tell Emilee he loved her, but the attack rendered him powerless. *Don't take the chance away from me now, Lord. I'll tell them. I promise. Just give me another chance.*

Oblivion separated him too soon from his blessings from God.

———◈———

Emilee looked down at David's face, drawn even in sleep, as if he still felt pain. The wind pushed the rain against the ambulance window, and Seth had trouble controlling the wheel. A loud thump rocked the truck, and he swerved. Caught off guard, Emilee fell on top of David and had to regain her balance.

John offered her a smile. She gifted him with a faint one of her own and again checked David's vitals, thankful they had managed to stabilize him enough to move. A minor victory. Getting David to the hospital, over the wind blowing at high speeds across the bridges and the water-swept roadways was their biggest obstacle.

Something crashed against the roof of the ambulance. All three ducked as if unprotected by the metal surrounding them.

She'd made the call. If they all died, she'd be the blame, but her uncle would not live through the hurricane if they didn't try to get him to a hospital. Hopefully, they had a generator and could be of assistance. If not, Seth would lose his father.

"I can't see anything." John tried to look through the darkness and the rain. A wave of water struck the emergency vehicle, and it hydroplaned for several seconds. Seth fought for control.

Emilee swayed, bracing herself first against the ambulance wall and then against the gurney where David lay. A hot spasm of pain pulsated in her stomach. She pursed her lip.

Hopefully, she wouldn't have survived the torture at Cameron's hand, the pain of reaching Johnny, and hiding from a storm in a church, only to die in an ambulance doing the job that she once thought she'd been born to do.

Seth let out a whoop. "That was the last bridge. We didn't end up swimming with the alligators. We should be home free now."

Emilee sure hoped so.

Chapter Thirty-Two

Andy pushed open the door and stepped out of the church. Morning and sunshine. He hadn't expected to see the sun, but he found no clouds at all, and barely a breeze stirred the oppressive October heat.

Palm fronds, pine needles, and tree branches littered the churchyard and the lawns of surrounding homes.

"How's it look?" Luke joined him.

"Like a powerful storm blew through." Andy shielded his eyes from the sun and looked around for any substantial damage. "Can you believe it? The houses are still standing."

Luke slapped a hand on his shoulder. "Believe me, Andy, when we look closer, we'll find lots of structural problems."

The Billows. What would he do if the storm took down the place? Taking a deep breath, he relaxed. He'd rebuild. He had the money, the insurance, and the time.

One by one, the others emerged like butterflies from the cocoon of the boarded-up church. Even Cameron, who'd been sleeping beside Kurt, made his way outside. Kurt exited behind him. With a short nod of his head, Kurt motioned to Andy. "Wait up a second," Kurt said to Cameron.

Andy waited as the others filed past. They looked like the

survivors of an apocalypse. He hoped they weren't the last people on earth. He'd have his hands full with the two women staring at him, waiting for answers.

He had none.

"Cameron Matrai, you're under arrest for rape and attempted murder. You have the right to remain silent …"

"What?" Cameron spun out of Kurt's grasp before the chief could slip the handcuffs on him. "Andy? What's this about?"

"You hurt someone I love, Cameron." Andy braced himself, ready to tackle his friend if the need arose, but the suddenness of Kurt's arrest had taken Cameron by surprise.

Kurt pulled Cameron's arms behind him. The metal of the handcuffs scraped as Kurt slipped them on his prisoner. Kurt continued to read Cameron his Miranda rights. "Let's go, Mr. Matrai."

Cameron struggled as Kurt pushed him forward. "Andy? Do something."

"Don't add resisting arrest to the charges." Andy raised his hands and moved down the steps out of Kurt's way.

"You can't believe I would hurt …" Cameron looked beyond Andy, and Andy turned to follow his gaze.

India stood, her mouth a small round circle, her eyes wide. She wrapped her arms around her waist.

"You." Cameron pointed. "You told them lies. Why did you lie?"

"No—no—I—you did this to yourself," India countered.

Andy stepped between Cameron and the frightened woman. He narrowed his gaze upon Cameron. "India's name wasn't mentioned."

Kurt pulled back on the cuffs.

Cameron released a primal scream.

"You sound like the animal you've become." Andy stepped forward.

"You're listening to her lies. She told you I hurt her because she didn't want you to believe she's a tramp, Andy. Don't listen to her. She wants your money. That's all, man. She just wants someone to take care of her."

All movement had stopped. The crowd began to draw back together.

Andy grasped Cameron's collar and jerked him toward him. "Emilee, Cameron, why did you hurt her? I want to know."

Cameron stared back at Andy, blinking his eyes. "You think I hurt Em?"

"Take him. This bad actor has played his last role in front of me," Andy said.

With Andy's hold on Cameron's shirt, Andy could see the marks of defense that Emilee must have left. He nodded to Kurt who looked, closed his eyes for a second, and then practically threw Cameron toward the patrol car parked in front of the church. He pushed Cameron inside and closed and locked the door.

"His lawyer's in New York. Make sure he gets to call him. He'll need him to recommend a good Florida defense attorney. The two best Florida lawyers," Andy turned to look at Mickey, "would have a conflict of interest."

Another savage roar split the air. The car rocked with the fury inside of it. Andy blinked. He'd seen that rage before.

From his father.

"You're saying you never noticed this behavior?" Kurt raised a brow.

"He's come undone." Andy watched the caged animal. Kurt

might not be safe alone with the madman. "Do you want me to come with you?"

Kurt shook his head. "I think you have a bigger mess to clean up." He ducked into the patrol car and pulled away from the curb.

Andy swallowed hard, looking down at the puddle at the edge of his foot. His muddy reflection stared back at him. How long had he been looking after everyone in his life, missing the dirty truth? He'd thought that his father's death brought about the end of lies and distrust. Andy had closed his eyes to the actions of John and Cameron, and Emilee and others suffered at their hands.

"What's going on?" Mickey stepped beside Andy. He looked much better than he had when he first arrived at the church hours before.

Andy stared at him for a long moment. "I'm sorry for the problems I caused you and your wife, Mickey. I hope with my confession that Penny will forgive you." He rested his gaze on the two women standing behind Mickey. Blanchie he knew he could love if only she would give him the opportunity to explain. India he pitied.

Blanchie turned her back to him.

India stepped forward.

"I don't understand." Mickey ran a hand through his already mussed hair.

"I'm the father of India's baby, Mickey. I'm sorry that you got caught up in this because of my blindness."

"That's not true." Mickey cast a look toward his wife, who walked toward the end of the street.

"You sound disappointed." Andy shot back. "I'd think you'd be glad."

"I know you didn't ..."

"You have no idea what I'm capable of doing. The baby is mine."

"Mickey, I'm sorry that I let you think you were the father. I was afraid …" India started.

Andy grabbed her hand and gave it a light squeeze.

"Cameron?" Mickey shook his head.

"Yes," India admitted.

"No." Andy cut her off. "The baby is my responsibility."

"But you risk losing Blanchie?" Mickey whispered. "Why would you do this?"

Penny's screams pierced the air.

Mickey ran toward her.

Andy moved slowly. Now, he'd pay for his lie. The god of his nightmare was about to drop the hammer down on his head.

Everything decelerated. A thunderous beat of his heart, and then long seconds where he didn't know if he was breathing or not, hampered his movement.

Penny fell into Mickey's arms.

Luke raised his hands toward the heavens as if issuing a challenge to his God.

Noah bowed his head.

Blanchie fell to her knees in the middle of the road. "No," she screamed. "No. No. No. No."

With each step, Andy's reason returned. Penny would not cry to see his business torn to shreds. Blanchie was so angry with him now that she'd probably dance in the street if The Billows had vaporized.

No, it had to be the law office or …

He stopped in front of Blanchie. She looked up at him, tears streaming down her beautiful face. "Why?" she asked.

Did she want an answer to his behavior or some answer from God as to why bad things occurred? He had no answer for either.

He offered her his hand. She pulled back.

"She's okay." Luke stepped between them. "Come on, baby. We'll rebuild it for him." He helped her to her feet.

Andy turned away from the end of his relationship with the girl he desired more than anything. He forced his gaze toward the dock and inhaled in surprise. The Billows stood tall with only a few shingles off the roof and perhaps some water damage inside. The terrible destruction lay on the portion of Front Street, closer to where they stood.

"God," Penny prayed. "Why? Why did You let this happen?"

Noah McGowan took off his glasses and wiped his tears away.

A chill ran deep through Andy's soul. Very little destruction lay before them, but clearly, one of the explosions rocking the church during the storm was the local's favorite restaurant splintering into nothingness. The area where David's Place had once stood was vacant. Blown apart wood floated in the waves, crashing against the dock pilings and onto the shores of the beachfront on each side of the street in front of the dock.

"He'll rebuild. If I have to, I'll rebuild it by myself," Luke said again and started toward the dock. "God, you've tested us all lately." He lifted his eyes to the sky. "I won't let this beat David New into the ground. Please bring him back to health, and I'll bring his restaurant back to him. He's too good a man."

Andy followed Luke, but he stopped as he heard footsteps behind him. He waited without hope for Blanchie to catch up and walk beside him. Instead, she pushed past.

His heart plummeted to the depths of his stomach. He fought back familiar feelings of rejection and turned away.

He stared up at the bright blue sky that showed no hint that a storm had passed through. Blanchie had asked him to be truthful. He hadn't meant to lie. Protecting Cameron's child and the mother of that child had taken precedence.

Maybe a man who protected others at the expense of the one he claimed to love didn't deserve acceptance.

"Andy." India stood in the middle of the street.

He closed his eyes and forced a smile.

"I'm so sorry," she said.

Andy nodded. "For what?"

"You lied to protect me."

"No." He brushed the side of her face with as tender a touch as he could give to her. "I lied to protect your child—same as you."

"I appreciate what you did, and I don't expect anything else from you."

"But I expect something from you." The little pooch of her stomach frightened him more than anything in his life.

"You're going to make me pay for this, aren't you?"

"India, this is the second time you've asked that. I hope, in time, you learn to trust me. Despite what you've seen in us, the Ryan boys are civilized human beings. We mess up sometimes, but we do try."

She stared at him, her jade eyes large, as if she waited for Andy's god to beat her with the hammer Andy thought would be used against him.

"I guess I should have asked rather than expected." He smiled, but her lips remained pressed into a tight line. "India, would you let me … at the rate my love life is going, I don't think I'll ever get the opportunity to be a dad. Would you allow me to be the father of your child?"

India's eyes filled with tears. "You would do that? Really?" A smile pushed upward on her lips.

He dreaded the possibility that she'd say yes, but he nodded just the same.

"Yes, Andy. Yes." She threw her arms around him. "Thank you."

The woman was spontaneous, if nothing else. And suddenly, the joy of fatherhood spread through his being. He was going to have a daughter ... or a son, a boy or a girl to love the way his father never loved him.

"Blanchie?" She pulled away.

"I promised you I'd protect you, and I'll protect that child from his natural father. No one will ever know as long as you want it that way. Telling Blanchie ..." He closed his eyes. He couldn't tell India that he considered Blanchie a gossip, not when he had enjoyed much of the gossip she'd shared. "One more leak of the truth, and there's a good chance word will get around and somehow, someway, Cameron will find out. We can't afford that." Even if it meant never winning Blanchie's love.

India threw her arms around him again, and Andy held her to him.

"Andy, I believe you are a gift from God." She breathed the words into his ear.

He'd let her believe what she wanted, but he knew better.

Chapter Thirty-Three

The dull ache wouldn't go away. With eyes closed, Emilee brought her hand to her head. She had rounds to do. She couldn't sleep all day, and since when did they give doctors anything other than a hard cot to sleep in. "Mrs. Ryan?" Someone called her name.

"Dr. Ryan," she mumbled the correction. Hopefully, it would stay that way if she could find a new hospital to complete her residency.

"Dr. Ryan, I need to take your temperature."

Emilee jumped at the touch on her arm.

"You're okay," a voice broke through her fear.

Emilee blinked and brought the person into focus—a nurse wearing a pair of blue scrubs with pictures of little dogs and cats all over them. The nurse pressed a thermometer to Emilee's ear.

"Where am I?"

"Dr. Bernhardt wanted you to rest. He ordered you a private room."

The thermometer beeped. The nurse pulled it away and recorded her temperature. "Not bad. We've got you down to 99.5."

Emilee didn't care about that. "My uncle—Mr. New?"

"He woke a few minutes ago. He's asking about you."

"My husband?"

"He's looking in on Mr. New."

Emilee pushed herself up. "Ahh." She lowered herself back down. The soreness had not diminished. She blinked her eyes and shook her head, trying to clear the grogginess. Bringing her hand to cover her eyes, she stopped and fingered the orange bracelet on her arm. "I'm admitted?"

"Dr. Bernhardt and your husband held a heated debate on whether to keep you a few days or not. Your husband won. The doctor has your release papers ready."

Emilee couldn't help it. The smile came unbidden. She had missed her husband. If she lost everything after all the hard work to get to where she was, being together with him was worth the cost.

Then an unbidden thought pressed her smile into a grimace. "Nurse, did they examine me? My cousin, did he mention …?"

The nurse touched her shoulder. "You don't remember?"

Emilee shook her head. She recalled only seeing her uncle, on the gurney, being rolled into a room, a doctor giving orders to the nurses around him. She'd sunk into a chair, and like her journey to Serenity Key, all was lost between the getting there to here.

"You asked to be seen privately. I only know because I worked ER during the storm. You were examined."

"Was I …?"

"You said the incident only happened within the last few days. A test is only accurate after seven days."

"And they …?"

"They did."

Emilee closed her eyes. She must have slipped into clinical mode when assessing her own situation. She'd made decisions based upon her schooling and not her emotions.

She said a prayer for a child she may or may not have been carrying. A rape kit didn't prevent the birth of a child born of rape, not unless the drug was requested. She didn't remember making the request to assure termination of a pregnancy, but her lapse in memory wouldn't let her shift the blame from herself onto the hospital staff.

"Does my husband know?"

The nurse shook her head. "You specifically requested that he not be told about the rape. The doctor spoke to him, per your HIPAA form authorization, only about the injuries you sustained."

The door swung open, and a whistled tune preceded a man in green hospital garb. "Dr. Ryan." He clicked his pen and wrote a few notes on a chart. "I'm Scott Bernhardt. How are you feeling?"

Emilee pushed her remorse aside and pulled the covers up over her. How had they gotten her into the hospital gown?

The dull headache continued to tug at her well-being. "I'm fine," she lied. "You've talked to my husband I've been told."

Bernhardt pursed his lips and nodded. "I've given John a prescription for antibiotics, both oral and topical, for you. He could probably use a little of the topical on his face. He said his brother did that with one punch." The doctor ran a hand over his face as if thinking, but Emilee couldn't miss the mile-long grin. "I can't imagine why."

Emilee laughed, and it cost her. She coughed. "We've been through a lot over the last couple of months. I apologize for his manners."

Again, he nodded. "He's very protective of you."

"David?" Emilee changed the subject.

"Angioplasty. A full recovery and change of diet expected."

"Thank you, Doctor."

"You and Seth saved his life. It took a lot of guts fighting the storm to get him here, but you took very good care of him."

Emilee didn't answer. The praise surprised her. Compliments were very rare in her residency in New York.

"Would you like to see David?" He handed his notes and the clipboard to the nurse.

"Very much." She again pushed up, this time a little slower, and started to climb out of bed. While David's relationship to her was in question, he was still her patient.

"Whoa, not so fast," he said. "You've been admitted. You know the rules, Doctor. Anne, would you mind retrieving a wheelchair?" he asked the nurse.

Anne nodded and left the room.

"Your husband told me you surrendered your residency in New York to move here." Bernhardt stepped to the side of the bed.

"Yes. Yes, I did. Unfortunately, I know how difficult it can be to switch residency." She pulled the gown around her to assure the ends met. Her attention turned to the door, sizing up an exit. Would she ever again feel safe alone in a room with any man other than Johnny? Well, she had felt safe with Seth.

"Are you disenchanted with medicine?" Dr. Bernhardt didn't seem to notice her anxiety as he sat on the bed beside her, crossing his arms and staring at the toe of his dark leather shoes.

Rounds. He was here on his rounds, straight from his office— or maybe he hadn't left the hospital during the hurricane.

She envied him and the career she'd be relinquishing for love. "No," she assured. "I'd give almost anything to complete my residency. I was so close."

The doctor stood as Anne returned with the wheelchair. He offered his hand and helped her into her transport.

"All set?" he asked.

She nodded.

"If you're serious about resuming your career and you'd like to do so here in Florida, look me up. I have some pull. It'll take a little work, a little shuffling of paper, but we can make it happen."

A flicker of anticipation burned within her. If Johnny didn't mind, she'd be knocking on Scott Bernhardt's office door very soon. "Thank you," she said. "For everything."

The doctor walked beside her as Anne wheeled her two doors up. "Look who's awake," Anne announced as they entered.

John stood from his makeshift seat on top of the air conditioning vent perched under the window. "There's my sleepy head."

She'd left him alone. He didn't know the danger Cameron imposed. She peered at him through eyes brimming with tears. The floodgates opened, and the tears streamed down her face.

"Hey." John wiped them away with the tender press of his thumbs against her cheek. "Everything's okay."

"Well, darling, they say my two children saved my life," David said.

Seth stood at David's bedside. Her cousin shared a look with her husband.

"Dr. Ryan, remember my offer." Scott Bernhardt placed a caring hand on her shoulder. "I'll check in on you later, David."

"Thank you, Scott," David called as the doctor left.

"The doctor gave you a good report," Emilee said.

"I'm going to recover, and I'm going to live a full life surrounded by my children."

Why wouldn't they listen to her? She wasn't his daughter. "I was told you were my uncle." She placed firmness into her tone.

"Who told you?" John's tone was even firmer.

Emilee squeezed his hand, the name coming forth in a whisper. "Cameron."

"How could he know? No one knew but me."

"Zack." Again, her voice was a mere whisper. "Zack and Cameron were closer than you and Andy ever knew. He became the son he couldn't have in you or Andy. Cameron was malleable."

John pulled away from her touch. Emilee grasped for his hand. "Don't be angry with me, Johnny. Don't shut me out again."

"Oh, babe." John brushed a tender touch across her cheek. "No, never again."

"I know it hurts you to hear the truth."

"It's Andy I'm thinking about."

Emilee lowered her head. "And I know when I tell Andy about Cameron and your dad, he'll tell me he's worried about you."

John held both her hands in his. "Em, what David says is true. He's your father. Seth is your brother."

Emilee looked at David. She studied his somehow familiar features. "Della?" she asked. "Do you know Della?"

David furrowed his brows, looked to Seth, who shrugged, and then back to her. "No, darling. I don't think I do."

"She told me about Serenity Key. A long time ago. She told me that Serenity wasn't just a state of mind. It was a real place. I never understood." She turned her gaze to Johnny. "I think—I think Della is my mother."

"No child," David said. "Your mother was Colleen. She was the wife of my brother." He wiped his eyes. "I'm not proud of what I did, but she and I—"

Emilee held up her hand. She could not bear to have this man say that she was born of a mistake. "I need time to come to terms with this. I've lived a life of secrets and lies."

"Em, I'm sorry." John bent in front of her wheelchair.

She loved him for his remorse, but they had to move on. Still, she leaned into him. "I don't want to be a mistake," she whispered. "It hurts too much."

"You take all the time you need," David said.

John kissed her hand before standing and turning her chair so she could face her father.

David held his hand out toward her, and Emilee clasped it in hers.

"But please don't leave. Stay around and get to know us," David said.

"I'll ask you to do the same."

"I don't plan to go home for a long while. The Lord has granted me a new chance to know my daughter."

"Why did my mother take me from you and from Seth?"

David looked to Seth and back to her. "What we did was wrong."

"Pop," Seth warned.

His words seeped into her parched heart. These were no words of comfort, no balm for her. They reverberated and pained her. *Oh, Lord, no.* She dropped David's hand and studied the lines on her palms, not looking up. *I'm alive because of sin. I can't even justify my existence.* She pushed from her chair.

"Em, what are you doing?" John asked.

She found her footing and stepped away from the chair and toward the door, ignoring the pain.

John started to follow, but she raised her hand to stop him. "I need a minute. Just give me a minute."

He stepped forward, refusing to listen.

"John, a minute." She placed the sharp edge into her voice on purpose. "Can you give me that?"

John stopped. The familiar question had to resonate with him. He used it every time he wanted his way.

She opened the door and let it close behind her, moving down the hall.

Her whole life was a mistake. Her mother betrayed her own sister, and Emilee was the result of their betrayal. David and her mother—this Colleen—were ashamed of her.

She pressed her hand against the wall to keep herself on her feet. When she reached the corner at the end of the hall, she leaned her back against the wall and covered her face with her hands. *God, why? I find my family only to discover my birth a terrible, ugly mistake.*

...The Lord has called me from the womb. He has made mention of my name.

Oh, God, help me see how You could even stand to look at me. You hate sin. She turned her face to the wall, and using her arms as a pillow, she cried.

"Emilee." Seth came from nowhere. He grabbed her arm and tugged at her.

"No," she uttered the panicked whisper and spun forward, falling against the wall, hands outstretched, trying to protect herself from the blows that burst into her memory.

Cameron had caught her against the wall where she'd run after his attack. He pummeled her there at first with his fist, and when she fell to the ground, he kicked her and stomped upon her.

When the beating failed to start, she opened her eyes.

Seth's face had paled. He stood without words.

She fought to breathe without the catch in her throat.

"Emilee, it's me," Seth reasoned.

She held up her hand, taking in a little more air.

"I know you're upset, but you have to listen to me." He placed even more space between them.

"I was a mistake, Seth," she managed. "No one wanted me."

"That's not true."

"My mother left me with Zack Ryan. By the time I was seventeen, I was desperate to get away from him. I even asked my teacher, Della, to let me stay with her." She waved her hands, trying to make sense of it all. "No! I wouldn't have stayed. I was so in love with Johnny, and Andy is my best friend."

"Our dad and your mom, they were two scared people trying to cope with something—"

"Something that made them ashamed." In a slow cautious movement, Emilee slid to the floor, feeling the tug of the bandages on her body.

"The situation, Emilee, only the situation caused them shame, but never you. I know Pop, and the emotion I see on his face each time he looks at you is pride. It's not shame."

Emilee shook her head. "I am the situation, Seth. Can't you see? My mother never came back for me."

Seth sat in front of her, folding his knees Indian fashion.

"Could she have asked this Della to look after you? Pop doesn't know her. Maybe she's a friend of your mother's."

Emilee leaned her head back and looked at the ceiling. "I don't know."

"Maybe Della wanted to give you a hint about your birth?"

"She told me about Serenity, told me it wasn't only in my mind. I remember her saying it, and she told me about attending church. She told me about David and Owen." She widened her eyes. "Seth, she said her husband died while she was pregnant. That he never knew about the child she gave away. She wouldn't tell me the father's name. She said she knew my mother thought of me every day, but she lied. Della Croix. Doesn't that even sound familiar to you?"

Seth straightened. "What was her last name?"

"Croix. Della Croix."

Seth leaned his head back for a long, excruciating second. Then he looked at her with a smile. "Emilee, Dellacroix is the maiden name of both of our mothers."

Emilee bit her lip and heavy tears began to fall. "She talked me out of running away from Zack. She reminded me how much I cared for his sons. At the same time, she said she loved me." She hiccupped, feeling the pain in the pull of the gauze. "But she didn't. She couldn't have."

"Why do you think that? Maybe there's a reason."

"If you love your child, how can you leave them behind?"

"I don't believe for a minute your mother left you behind. I think you remained with her the way you never left Pop's heart. In fact, there's a letter at Pop's house I want you to read when we get home."

Emilee answered him with silence.

"It makes sense now. Pop has a letter from your mother. She wrote Pop about you about the day Zack took you from her again."

"Why did she let me go? She promised to keep in contact with me, but she never called or wrote."

"I'm angry with your mother right now myself, but I think her failure to contact you has everything to do with John's father and nothing to do with what she wanted."

"Mr. Ryan ..." She started to speak but chose silence instead.

Some things were only meant to be shared with John and Andy, the ones who'd endured them with her.

Strength left her. She slumped forward and buried her head in her hands. Silence stretched between them for a few moments while she gathered her thoughts. "John is so much like his father." She betrayed her husband with her words.

A knife of emotion twisted in John's gut. Emilee plunged it toward him with the truth.

John touched Seth's shoulder and waited for him to move back before taking his place in front of Emilee. "Keep talking," he mouthed.

"Give him one more chance, Em," Seth said. "John loves you very much. I've never seen a man so crazy when he thought you could be hurt or lost. I didn't help matters much."

Emilee never lifted her head or took her hands from her face.

"Maybe he has an excuse for not telling you," Seth offered.

"There is no excuse. He handled situations the way his father would have. He must have the upper hand."

"You have always held the upper hand." John touched her soft hair.

Emilee lifted a defiant chin.

He'd forgotten how much he loved that feisty look on her. "Don't you know that?" He brushed her bangs from her face. "You're right, though. I allowed lies and my own hurt to dictate my actions. Andy had to beat sense into me. I handled my pain the way my father handled his anger. I wanted to hold all the cards."

"Why, Johnny?" She knocked his hand away from her.

"Why do animals raised in the wild have instincts that allow them to survive? We inherit them. Andy inherited everything I would like to have. He has Momma's wonderful loving nature. He can soothe and calm even when his heart is breaking. I inherited our father's desire to destroy what hurts me, but if you think back, I handled you differently. I wanted to hurt you, and I know I did, but Emilee I can no more live without you than I can live without air." He rubbed his eyes with the palms of his hands. "I tried, and I can't do it. You are everything that makes me whole."

"Did you know they were my father and my brother? Tell me the truth this time. Did you keep that from me?"

"No," Seth answered. "He didn't. I was with him when Pop told him."

"How do you feel about that?" she asked him.

"I'm glad you have the one wish I know you always wanted and I couldn't grant. I'm sorry my stubborn disposition kept me from telling you even the little I'd learned."

"You're happy in Serenity?"

"I'm happiest wherever you are."

Emilee tried to stand, but she winced and sat back. John stood and helped her.

"What's going on?" Andy's long stride brought him toward them.

"Where's Cameron?" Emilee asked.

"He's behind bars, Em. He can't hurt you or John any longer."

"I'm going to kill him." Anger laced John's voice.

"Let it go, buddy."

Those words washed over John like rain falling from the sky. He jerked almost as if the bolt of lightning were real and not in his mind.

Let it go, buddy. Nine-year-old Andy had led him down the hallway.

Let it go. Andy tucked him into his bed, and Andy had lain on top of the covers cradling him.

Let it go, buddy. Andy had repeated, but his voice cracked under the strain.

Let it go. Was Andy speaking to himself or to his frightened little brother? Just what was he supposed to let go? Was he supposed to forget the truth of that awful night? Was he supposed to forget his mother was dead, and his father had killed her?

Let it go, buddy. Even years later, Andy said those words to him. The seat in the funeral home was hard, and John just wanted the service finished. The old man's heart had given out. What heart?

John had cried from relief, but Andy mistook it for love. It had been easier to allow Andy to believe he loved their father. He despised Zachariah Ryan, at the same time knowing he was too much like his father for comfort. The one gift they all wanted from Zack, they never received.

Zack was incapable of displaying love, his soul a cold, dark stone.

"Let it go, buddy," Andy said again. "Come on, John. You don't want to do this to Emilee. She needs you to be strong for her, not vengeful."

John pulled free of Andy's grasp. Emilee fell against him, and he held her in his arms.

She was the one possession he could not give Andy, though he always knew his brother loved her. He refused to step aside and let Andy love her as his brother wanted. Andy's reaction to John's claim on Emilee's love only strengthened the conviction of Andy's devotion for him. John held his arm out, and Andy enfolded both Emilee and him in an embrace.

When they parted, John met his brother's tender eyes.

Andy clasped his shoulder. "You're a jerk, you know it, don't you?"

"I only make you look good." John had never known laughter to be so freeing.

From the area by the elevator, out of sight of everyone, Colleen Dellacroix New stood with her friend who'd come so far to lead Colleen home. Colleen shared a look with Verity.

The heavyset woman wiped her eyes. "I think David's free from all his secrets."

Colleen smiled. "And so is Emilee." She turned away.

Verity followed. "Where are you going? Don't you want to see your daughter?"

"Now is not the time, Verity. She's in better hands than mine."

Chapter Thirty-Four

A ringing phone brought Emilee from a deep sleep. Morning sun was pouring through the window. She reached over John to answer his phone before it woke him. "Hello," she whispered.

"Emilee, thank goodness you answered. This is India. There's something wrong. Can you come to my house?"

Emilee pushed herself up in slow increments and brought her feet over the side of the bed, careful not to jar Johnny awake. First-time mothers often got anxious over the little things. "What you don't want to do is to tense up. It's probably nothing."

"But you will come? I need you to come. Please come."

"Are you experiencing contractions? Spotting? Tell me what has you worried."

"Something's wrong." India began to cry. "Ow," she screamed into the phone. "Emilee, please help me."

"Just lie still with your feet propped on a pillow. Don't get up and move around except to unlock the door if you have it locked. Where do you live?"

Emilee listened to the directions "I'll be alone. John and Andy are still asleep." She set the phone down.

A smile turned her lips as she stared at her husband. Exhaustion left him deep in sleep. She brushed a strand of wayward hair from his forehead and kissed his lips. When he slept, John still reminded her of a spoiled child. While awake he could wreak so much havoc. "I love you, Johnny."

"Love you, Em." In his sleep, John reached out and touched her.

She stood from the bed and fumbled through his clothes for something to wear. They would definitely need to find some clothes for her before they made another visit to see David.

She found Johnny's gray sweats and a worn t-shirt and struggled against the pain to put them on before moving downstairs.

A notepad lay on the table in the kitchen, and she scribbled a note as to her whereabouts.

Then she stepped out onto the back steps and took a deep breath. Palm fronds and broken limbs cluttered the lawn. The only other sign that a storm had plundered the area were large puddles of water surrounding the home. Stepping away from the house, she gave a prayer of thanks for Cameron's arrest. Emilee could not remember when she'd felt safer.

Luke threw the pieces of splintered wood into a pile and turned at the sound of his name. He squinted in the brightness of the sun as Noah McGowan headed toward him. The morning was humid, the air stagnant as it always was after a storm system blew through. Luke wiped his brow as the sweat poured down.

"Have you seen, Kurt?" Noah asked.

"No, not since he carted Andy's friend off to jail."

Noah scanned the area on the other side of the water separating the dock from the main section of town. When he looked back in Luke's direction, his lips formed a worried frown. "His patrol car isn't at the station. Tank says he's not answering his radio."

"What did Cameron Matrai say about him?" Luke picked up a board with nails showing and waited. Why did he feel like a hammer was about to fall?

Noah shielded his eyes from the sun by cupping his hands over his forehead. "That's what's got us worried. Cameron Matrai isn't in the jail. He's missing, too."

Luke dropped the board as he spun back toward Noah. Without another word between them, they hurried toward town.

———— ≈≈≈ ————

Before David woke, he sensed her presence even through the drug-induced haze. She stood beside him, and he wondered why he remained in a hospital bed. His vision blurred at first, and he tried to focus. "Uma?" He reached for the figure beside him. "Uma, is that you?"

"Shh, you need your rest." The hallucination spoke to him. "You need to get strong for your son and our daughter."

"I'm sorry," he apologized for a lifetime of ills. If he was dead, as he was beginning to believe, he wanted to tell her before they reached Heaven together. "I hurt you. I hurt everyone with what I did."

"I helped you do it," she spoke. "I'm as much to blame. I hope you'll forgive me."

"You had nothing to do with it. I betrayed you and my brother. I betrayed everyone."

"David, I caused the separation from Emilee with my actions and my pride."

David closed his eyes. "I don't understand." When understanding dawned, he opened his eyes. "Colleen?"

The woman nodded. "You have a special friend who brought me here. She said you needed me."

"I thought you were Uma." David turned away from her. He didn't need his wife's sister. After all these years and all the remorse, he only wanted his wife.

"I know Emilee's been told the truth. It happened all in God's time. You understand, don't you?"

"I could have told her long ago. I should have told her."

"I could have told her, too, but the Lord accomplished it in His time. He had other plans for our little girl. Seems He knew you'd need a doctor to save her father's life."

He didn't look at her, surprised by his feelings of deep loss. For a moment, he had believed he had a second chance to redeem himself in his wife's eyes. His sister-in-law didn't deserve the anger brewing inside him. Still, the question burned for an answer. "Why did you give her to him?" He stared at the curtain separating his bed from the empty one on the other side. He tried to remind himself that Colleen may not know his daughter's recent fate, the brutal attack at the hands of a madman.

"Because he convinced me he loved me. I felt wronged by you and evil for my hand in Owen's death. After what we had done, turning to another married man didn't seem so terrible, until I met his wife."

"Oriana Ryan had the heart of an angel." David would never

forget the kindness of that woman.

Colleen stared at him. "Emilee once gave the same description about her son."

"She's right. Andy is a compassionate young man."

"She wasn't talking about Andy. She said that about John."

David looked at his hands. "I've learned over the past couple of days how easy it is to misjudge."

"Our daughter loved him very much even as a child."

"About the Ryans …?"

"I met Oriana once before Emilee was born, and I felt so terrible for what I'd done to her. I told Zack I didn't love him. I couldn't love him, not after meeting Oriana. He convinced me that even if I didn't love him, Emilee would benefit from a home with a mother, a father, and two children to keep her company. I didn't realize his ruthlessness until he made sure I lost my low-paying job. He evicted me from the apartment he provided. He left me with nothing to offer Emilee except the good fortune of his family."

"Why didn't you call me?" He turned toward the woman, wanting to close his eyes against the very likeness of his own beautiful wife.

"When I thought about it, I remembered Uma. You know I told her the truth."

"I know."

"She still came to me when I needed her."

"And she died because of it." The words flowed, and the edge of bitterness he held inside surprised even him.

Colleen winced. "Uma convinced me to return home with her. We slipped out of the hospital—out of Zack's grasp."

"Then you—"

"Emilee and I were in the car when Uma wrecked. I don't know how we survived, but I knew when you discovered Uma gone, you wouldn't want to suffer through life with the causes of her death. Zack once again became my only option, but I made one demand upon him. I told him I would never agree to his adoption of our daughter. I left the option open for you."

David grew silent. He weighed each of her words. She offered him only truths that he'd failed to grasp so long ago. If he'd only taken the hard road and opened up about the sin he harbored.

"You have a wonderful friend in Verity Stewart. She told me how you've shared everything with her even when you couldn't share it with anyone else. She tracked me down. It took her a long time, but she found me."

"Why?" He tried to sit up.

Colleen reached over and pushed the button allowing the head of the bed to rise. She straightened his pillow. "She told me with the arrival of the Ryan boys she worried how you would handle the situation. She predicted the stress could kill you."

"That's ridiculous."

She smiled for the first time and spread her hands out as if introducing him to his situation. "Is it?"

David chuckled despite himself. "Where is the old girl?"

"Outside. She insisted I see you alone." Colleen walked toward the door.

All anger vanished. "Colleen, are you going to see Emilee?"

She turned. "Not right away, but I won't leave town before I do."

"Don't leave town, okay?"

"We'll get you out of the woods first," she assured. Sadness seemed to fill her eyes as if she knew something he did not.

Had something else occurred because of his self-centeredness?

"I'll get Verity." She gave him a slight wink before going out the door.

John woke with the ringing of the phone. He reached for his nightstand before realizing the ringing came from the device laying beside him on the bed. "John Ryan."

"Mr. Ryan, I'm so glad to hear your voice," a woman greeted.

"Sorry, I don't recognize ..." John wiped tired eyes.

"I'm Yasmin Garcia, Emilee's friend."

"Dr. Garcia." John sat up. "You're okay. With everything going on here I forgot to ask."

"I spoke with the dispatcher at the police station who told me Emilee made it home. She provided your number. I hope you don't mind."

"No. That's fine, and yes, Emilee is here."

"When I saw the hurricane heading toward you, I worried she'd be in danger. The news reports said the storm trapped residents on the island."

"We were among the few." John pushed himself up, drawing his knees toward him, resting his head in his hand, still too groggy to comprehend much.

"Is everyone okay?" she asked.

"My father-in-law suffered a heart attack and lost his business."

"Emilee's father is there?"

"Yes, it surprised us all."

"Well, I'm sure she can use all the support she can get right now. Rape is a terrible ordeal to face, and she worried about how you would react."

The knuckles of John's hand turned white as he gripped the receiver. Rape? No one told him Cameron had raped his wife. Cameron beat Emilee. He did not rape her. "Rape?" He said the word almost too filthy to utter.

Yasmin Garcia remained quiet for a few moments.

"Cameron raped her?" John looked to the door of his room where Andy now stood. Andy nodded. "Cameron raped my wife?" he repeated, wanting confirmation from the person on the other end of the phone line.

"Emilee didn't tell you. Mr. Ryan, I'm so sorry."

John stared at his brother, the pieces falling into place—Emilee's fear for him, Andy's willingness to turn on his friend, Andy's false confession. "India?"

Andy nodded once again.

"She wouldn't tell me who did it but I suspected," Yasmin answered.

He dropped his free hand to the bed and clenched the bed sheet until his fingers ached. Fool. Fool. Fool. He should have known. He should have protected her.

"Please let her know that I miss her already. We all do. I'll get in touch with her soon."

"I will." John pushed the button and stared at the phone. Then he tossed it with all his might against the far side of the room. It left a dent in the wall but otherwise did little damage to the encased device.

Andy jumped but didn't leave the doorway. "I thought you

understood. I'm sure Emilee thought so."

John looked for the first time to the empty side of his bed. "Where is she?"

"The phone woke me. It rang earlier this morning, and I assumed you answered it."

"I didn't hear it." John sprang from the bed, pushing Andy out of his way.

Both men ran downstairs. Andy hurried toward the kitchen and dining room. John sprinted toward the porch.

They met back in the living room. Andy carried a note. "India worried with pregnancy. Don't think there's much of a concern, but I wanted to ease her anxiety. Be back soon. I need clothes. Love, Em." Andy handed John the piece of paper and, yawning, ran a hand through his messy hair.

"John, Andy? You home?" Luke called and then knocked.

John answered the door, surprised to see Noah with the handyman.

"You guys are up early," Andy said.

"Kurt's missing," Noah said. "We can't find his patrol car. He doesn't answer dispatch, and Cameron Matrai has vanished."

"Emilee." John's sharp whisper cut the air. "India's house. He's got them at India's place."

Chapter Thirty-Five

Andy should have gone with Kurt to the police station instead of seeing India home. No matter the precautions Kurt took, Cameron's madness could make him capable of anything.

Andy ran across John's property and through Mickey's yard, cutting through the patch of woods blocking the view of India's huge home and splashing into pockets of water left behind from the hurricane. He barely noticed the pain as the sticks and burrs cut into the flesh on the bottom of his bare feet, and he didn't want to think about a displaced alligator or venomous water snakes. Stopping to catch his breath before he reached the clearing, he found the evidence he needed to convince him Cameron had gotten to both women: Kurt's car sat hidden in the brush.

He halted and moved toward the car, opening up the driver's door and then a back door. Blood on the seat. He moved for the latch by the driver's door and popped the trunk, holding his breath, he took slow steps toward the cracked opening at the back of the car. He exhaled and lifted the heavy metal at the same time.

Then he bent forward.

Relief poured from him.

No Kurt. He had to be with Emilee and India, a prisoner.

He made his way through the woods to the road, flagging

down Luke's truck as it came into view. "Kurt's car is in the woods. There's blood. He's probably with them."

Noah looked to the skies and then seemed to bolster himself up. Even in the midst of all of this, the preacher showed tremendous courage. Andy had to admire the man.

Andy tugged on Luke's driver's door. "Everyone out."

Luke's eyes widened, but as he climbed out of the truck, they widened more. Luke looked at Andy's feet and back to him. "You could've …"

"I made it, didn't I?"

"What are you doing?" John demanded from his perch in the back of the pickup. His stubborn brother had not listened. Noah was already approaching Andy from the passenger side.

"I'm going to check on the mother of my kid and on your wife."

"I'm going with you." John climbed down.

Andy didn't have time to argue with his little brother over chain of command. "John, you stay put."

"We need to get a call in to dispatch," Luke reasoned as he unlaced his work boots and tugged his feet out of them. He kicked them over to Andy with his socked feet. "And if you show up barefooted, Cameron will know you're on to him."

Noah pulled out his mobile from his pants pocket.

Andy nodded his thank you and slipped on Luke's lace-up boots. They were a size too small but loosening the laces gave some relief. He didn't care. He'd make them work.

"Let's go." John stormed forward.

Andy grasped his arm. "You need to stay here. I have to get in the house. I may be the only one who can talk to him."

"I don't care—"

"John, where has your hot-headedness gotten us so far?"

John took a deep breath and stepped back. He felt for the truck with his hand.

"Let it go, buddy. You can beat me up later and show Emilee what a manly man you are." Andy smacked John's cheek with a brotherly tap. "Believe me, if I thought you'd get away with it, I'd step aside."

John nodded. "Save us, Andy, like you've always done."

"Wait," Noah said. "Let's pray to the only One capable of saving us."

Luke bowed his head.

Andy stared at John before closing his eyes.

"Lord, we pray for Your grace and mercy. Bring all involved through this ordeal safely and keep us ever mindful that it is only in Your hands that we have strength. In Jesus' name. Amen."

"Amen."

Andy nodded and started down the road, trying his best not to limp in the tight shoes. The curtain covering the glass panel portion of the front door moved. Andy pushed a smile into place as he rang the doorbell.

Emilee opened the door. "What are you doing here?"

"I found your note. How are India and my baby?"

"They're fine. I need you to go home right now." Emilee held to the door as if his life depended upon its remaining in the same position. "She's sleeping now. You need to come back later."

"If she's sleeping, why don't you come on home?"

Emilee shook her head. "Please," she mouthed. "Go home."

"Not a chance. It's my baby she's carrying, and I want to make sure they're both okay."

"It's not the time," Emilee sighed. "She's resting."

"Where?"

Emilee moved her eyes to the left.

Andy shouldered the door from her grip. His movement pushed Emilee to the right and slammed the door against something solid.

"Stop!" Cameron commanded. "Andy, stop."

Andy faced his sick, demented friend.

India stood in front of Cameron, his arm around her neck. Her lip bore a cut and a bruise, and the cold steel of a gun barrel—Kurt's gun—rested against her head.

"Let her go." Andy raised his hands in surrender. "She's not in any condition for you to mistreat her."

Cameron threw India away from him. She fell hard against the floor. Emilee dropped beside her and with a lot of effort, she helped India to her feet.

"Where's Chief Davis?" Andy looked from the girls to Cameron.

"He's where no one can find him. Hard as it was to get him there, it was worth the trouble—added protection for me."

"It's kidnapping."

"Security."

"Why do you feel it necessary to do all of this?"

"Necessity is the mother of invention," Cameron laughed.

"We've always been so close. What changed?"

Cameron repositioned his grip on the gun.

Andy feared it would fire, but he wouldn't flinch.

"You are my best friend," Cameron announced.

"Then tell me why."

"Zack made promises to me. He said I'd always be a member of his family. Zack wanted it that way. He promised my mother, and my mother went through so much with him. He beat her, and he lied to her. Did you know that Andy?"

"No, I didn't." But he could believe it. Zack was a sick man. If Andy could see it so easily in his father, why hadn't he recognized it in Cameron?

"John never told you Zack left me money in a trust—a trust John controls."

"No, he never told me. Zack kept your best interest in mind. You must have meant something to him. Even Emilee didn't receive a dime." How did one reason with a madman? He'd never learned to reason with Zack.

"It doesn't matter what Zack thought of me. He owed me."

"But it did matter that Zack put John in control of you."

"John takes and takes, doesn't he, Andy? I know how much it hurt you when he stole Emilee."

Andy glanced to where Emilee sat on the couch with India. "It stung a little, but Emilee was never mine or yours. She loves John." Andy never wanted her to know the true depths of his feelings. "Emilee loves John, not me, not like that."

"She should have loved you." Cameron turned the gun toward the women.

India cringed beside Emilee who stared without any apparent emotion.

"She isn't blind, Andy. She had to see what she meant to you; she hurt you."

"It wouldn't have been love on my part if I imposed upon Emilee what she didn't feel for me. Life goes on. As far as Zack and the control he placed in John's hands, he was the master of evil deeds. Zack probably did it to pit you against John."

"I get a monthly stipend John allots to me because Zack had

the freedom to abuse my mother." Cameron's body trembled. "I hate John. I hate him." Cameron's face contorted. His voice deepened with rage. The frayed ends of Cameron's insanity unraveled in front of Andy.

"So, you hate John. I hate him sometimes, too."

"He doesn't deserve it," Cameron spit the words, "but you love him!"

"Yes, I love my brother. I love you, too, Cam. You and I are friends. Real friends. I'm sorry if I haven't been there for you."

Cameron raised the gun barrel to the ceiling, squeezing the trigger three times.

The bullets blasted and plaster fell in front of Andy. He moved forward.

Cameron leveled the gun in his direction.

Emilee screamed, rising from her seat, fighting off India's hold on her. "No, Cameron. Please. It's me you want to shoot, not Andy. I'm the one John can't live without. He told me last night. You need to shoot me. It's the way to make Johnny pay. Can't you see? If you take me away from him ..."

"No." Andy shook his head. "Cameron, no one needs to die. No one needs to get hurt, not Emilee, not India, not my child, not Kurt."

Cameron looked between the two of them. "She's right." He turned the gun on Emilee. "Without her, John will live in misery. If I have to go to prison, at least I'll know I've placed John in one, too." Cameron's finger played with the trigger. A smile crossed his face. His finger tightened.

"No!" Andy pushed forward, frantic to get between the bullet and the women. "Get out of here, Emilee. Get out!" He grasped Cameron, spinning him to face him. The bang shook the air. The loud noise produced a burst of pain against Andy's temples. The door behind him burst open.

Andy held Cameron's hand as they struggled. He fought to keep the gun from the direction of the girls, pounding Cameron's hand against the wooden floor until he relinquished his grip on the weapon. Managing to get the upper hand, he pounded his fist against Cameron's face. "Enough," Luke's voice broke through to him. "Enough, Andy. He's not got any more fight in him."

Andy pulled away. Cameron's face was bleeding, but he remained conscious.

Luke jerked Cameron to his feet.

"Kurt!" Andy demanded. "Where is Kurt?"

"You'll never find him." Cameron spit blood from his mouth. "He'll die where he is."

John pushed Andy aside. He grabbed Cameron's shirt collar. "Tell me, or so help me, you'll die right here."

"I don't care." Cameron laughed. "I know you don't like to share. Emilee won't mean anything to you now."

Andy closed his eyes as all the anger and pent-up frustration roared from his brother. He wanted neither to see nor to stop John's fists from pounding against Cameron's face.

With each blow, laughter rang from Cameron, the mirth of the insane. "Kill me, John, and I'll have my ultimate revenge."

"Johnny." Emilee soothed. "Johnny, we've won."

Andy opened his eyes but doing so was a struggle.

John lowered his arms. "I want to kill him." His fists remained clenched.

Cameron swayed but refused to fall.

"I know you do, and I know it's only because you love me," Emilee continued her plea.

"I love you." John's fists remained tightened.

"And you've never denied me anything I've ever wanted."

"Never."

"I want Cameron to go to prison for a very long time."

"It's too good for him."

"But it's what I want." Emilee placed her hand over his closed one. "Can you give me that?"

John unclenched his fists and released his grasp on Cameron's shirt.

Cameron sank to the floor.

"I'll give you that." John wrapped Emilee in his embrace.

For a second, Andy thought he could see the fountain where John had taken Emilee's love from him, kissing her first, telling her he loved her.

He shook his head. He could feel the warm water of the fountain splash on his face, over his head.

Fountain? There was no fountain in India's home.

Andy told himself to move, but his body refused. Instead, he fell back against the wall, his hand pressed to the searing pain at the back of his head. Flashes of color burst in front of his eyes.

He pulled his hand back as the warmth ran over his fingers. Deep red blood covered his hand. "Emilee?" He held it toward her. "I think I've been shot." He slid down the wall.

Chapter Thirty-Six

John stood in the back of the small break room of the Serenity Key Police Department.

Officer Tank Williams stood by a map stapled to a board and slanted over a microwave. He pointed to Serenity Key and its barrier islands. The chart had been divided into five sections.

The deputies from the mainland arrived only minutes before. Many of the islanders knew them by face and name. John didn't care for introductions. They were all strangers to him. He wanted his wife and his brother. He grinded his teeth as emotions threatened to overwhelm him.

He'd pushed Emilee and Andy away because of Cameron— because of his own need for self-preservation.

He felt for the wall behind him and fell against it. An old projector screen leaned to the side then hit the wall with a thud. John managed to find his balance.

"Are you okay, Mr. Ryan?" Tank raised worried eyes in his direction.

John nodded. But he wasn't okay. The glimpse of life he'd seen through his father's viewpoint frightened him. How could a man live like his father had—never trusting, always afraid someone would take from him before he could take it from them?

Abusing women with his fist ... and worse.

How could his father have looked beyond Andy and set his sights on John? Andy was the most capable, the most dedicated, the most caring—Zack's finest legacy of goodness.

And that's why Zack Ryan couldn't stand his oldest son.

John was the machine, the one who moved when Zack pulled the right lever, the one manipulated by greed, hurt, hatred, and ... evil.

He leaned back so that the top of his head found the wall. Cameron used the same tactics as Zack. Divide and conquer. Yet John never realized it.

"Hey, John, it's okay if you want to go to the mainland."

John turned his head to the side. Noah McGowan was beside him.

"I'm going to help find Kurt Davis. He worked so hard to find Emilee. Andy wouldn't understand if I didn't do this."

"He's in good hands with your wife and Seth. India will help them, too. We have enough volunteers, though."

The angry retort stopped at the edge of his heart. He had to cease being a younger version of Zack Ryan. That part of him would die today. "I'll be fine."

Noah nodded to Tank. Had they really stopped the meeting because of their concern over his well-being? John breathed in slow and deep. These people—they would be easy to love.

Fifteen people, including John, ten deputies, and the handful who'd been trapped on the island during the storm or had been close enough to return, gathered to search for the missing Chief of Police. Verity Stewart sent over supplies of water and drinks from her grocery store, and she promised to provide meals from the non-perishable items in the store for all the volunteers. Penny and

Blanchie helped with dispatch and coordination over old-style walkie-talkies. They would monitor and coordinate the location of all the volunteers.

Tank turned to the girls now. "If anyone else makes it back to the island and wants to help, send them over to the church. Tell them we have a group in prayer. I don't want more folks walking over what could later become ..." He stopped, his muscular body rising and falling in a heavy sigh. "Tell them that Mrs. McGowan is leading the prayer group. They also may want to assist Mrs. Stewart with the meals."

John lowered his head.

"John, honestly, if you're not okay ..." Noah pressed.

With head still lowered, John turned his gaze to the side. Concern laced the pastor's eyes. "I'm fine," he whispered. "It's just that only a few days ago, I'd have laughed at the thought of a group of people gathering to ask a god to deliver someone from a terrible situation. Now, I know prayer to God alone can save Kurt and Andy."

"Prayer to God can save you as well," Noah said.

John straightened, giving Noah his full attention. "Then why can't I offer up even the tiniest plea?"

Noah started to speak, but Tank interrupted him. "Groups of three, one deputy in each. First group here."

Luke and Mickey were a part of that group if only because they owned boats unharmed by the ravishing winds. Tank pointed to Devil and Angel Keys. "They're small and should be easy to traverse."

If he had the energy, and if his heart wasn't battling within him to remain civil, John would have offered up the suggestion that Cameron didn't have a boat or time to get to either island.

Instead, he remained silent.

"Second group." Tank hit his own chest before pointing to John and Noah. Tank circled the city proper, indicating their search detail. "We'll knock on doors. Group three, you have the Bayou. Group four, here." He pointed to the area the locals called the outland. "Group five, here." He indicated the area between the outlands and the mainland. "The uniforms will help ease the concerns of the residents who are already on edge because of storm damage." The big man paused for a second, pinching his trembling lips together. He shook off his emotion. "Listen, this man is more than the chief of police. He's a friend to everyone in this room. Let's find him quickly."

Movement at the door attracted John's attention. Two deputies nodded in Tank's direction. "We're here for the prisoner."

Tank led them down a short hallway. A muffle of voices reached the crowd. "Get up now, Mr. Matrai! Move!" Tank's angry voice rang out. The clang of metal chains and the scrape of a heavy metal door preceded Cameron's walk through the room flanked by the three officers.

Cameron shuffled under the burden of leg irons and handcuffs attached to waist chains. Good to know they weren't going to underestimate him this time. Cameron held his battered face high, looking straight in front of him. John tightened his hands into tight fists. He shouldn't have agreed to Emilee's request not to kill Cameron. He'd never have to look at that man again and be reminded of what he'd done to Emilee—what he may have done to Andy.

Two deputies walked alongside Cameron. One leaned and whispered in Tank's ear. Tank stopped, his face hard as stone.

The deputies stopped, turning their prisoner to face those

waiting to find his victim. "The prosecutor will be filing murder charges against Mr. Matrai."

John's knees buckled, and he fell to the floor hard.

Cameron's glare pierced John.

John swallowed hard. Andy was gone? No. If he had died John would know it. Noah helped him to his feet.

Or had his unnecessary anger pulled the plug on their brotherly connection? John straightened, but he didn't move.

The officers seemed to be fixed in their spot, non-moving, waiting for John's reaction—or maybe they hoped Cameron's will would be broken at the news. Then, again, maybe they wanted John to rid the world of Cameron. Yet, that's not what Andy would have wanted.

"He's gone, Cameron." John's word began as a whisper. He cleared his voice. "You have one death on your hands. Don't add Chief Davis to it. Andy was an accident. It isn't first-degree murder. They'll put you in the electric chair for killing the chief of police."

Noah placed his hand on John's shoulder. He'd never forget the action. John sensed a complicated undertone to the pastor's relationship with Kurt Davis.

Now, he and Noah were brothers in arms, and John suspected that Noah's grip was meant to keep them both in place.

Tank brought his large frame between John and Cameron, facing away from John and towering over the other man. "You want to tell us where to find the chief?"

"Tell the officer, Cameron, so we can save Kurt's life," John demanded. "Do this one unselfish act for Andy." John softened his tone.

"The cop dies, too. Their blood is on your hands." Cameron

shrugged, pulling the deputies with him. "Come on, boys. Take me away."

John straightened his back, steeled his emotions, and waited for the deputies to push Cameron into their vehicle.

All he wanted was to hold Emilee in her arms. Instead, he walked to the front of the room, passing the burly officer who now led the search to save the chief's life.

"Mr. Ryan …" Tank said.

"It's John," he said. "Let's not waste time on condolences. "Let's find Kurt. That's what Andy would want."

"Can you give me a minute?" Tank pressed.

John shook his head and walked alongside Noah. "Kurt may not have minutes." All he wanted to do was to give as much devotion to Kurt as the chief had given to finding Emilee. Once Kurt was found … dead or alive … John would then bury his sorrow deep into the soft scent of his wife's hair, the caress of her hands against the small of his back, the taste of her skin on his lips. The thoughts of Andy's death and the desire to hold his wife brought to mind the vow he'd made to the Lord. God may have taken his brother, but He did bring Emilee safely back into his arms. He'd never expected the Lord to replace one person he loved and take another. Still, God had answered the prayer, and true to Noah's petition on the dock when John had no idea if he'd ever see his wife again, God was pressing him for a response to that vow. Yet, John couldn't understand a God who would want him after all the wrong he had done.

Chapter Thirty-Seven

John had refused yet another attempt by Tank to offer his condolences. John needed to keep it together for Kurt and for Andy. He couldn't do that with someone offering him their sympathies.

They needed to get a clear picture of the man they were trying to outfox. He had, and the arrow of truth pierced his soul. Kurt had to be lying face down in the stagnant water of the bayou, as lifeless as Andy. If Cameron hadn't murdered him, the hot October sun, the wildlife, or the insects were eating away on him.

John reached out and braced himself against the corner of the house. He could hear Tank inside speaking to the owners. Andy would know where to look. They'd have found him by now if Andy took charge. He lowered his head and closed his eyes against the emotions threatening to overcome him.

No. He wouldn't shame his brother. He'd cry later—alone with Emilee.

Emilee. She was facing the loss of Andy alone as well. He needed to get to her.

The crackle of Tank's radio split the air. John wandered through the yard, drawing close to Noah, fighting the urge to give up and run into the arms of his wife. "They won't find him here—

not in the open like this."

Noah stooped to look under the house. "We need to check everywhere."

"Think about it." John turned in a circle, looking beyond the houses. "He wasn't in the patrol car. Cameron stashed his body away …"

Noah coughed and looked away.

"I'm sorry." And he really did mean it. Only an insensitive idiot could lose his brother in one moment and in the next tell another that his friend was most likely dead.

"Noah, he put Kurt somewhere before he went to India's place. We searched the area around her home, and we found nothing. The only other answer is—"

Noah held up his hand and shushed him.

They both listened.

John heard the faint sound of a bell—the church bell.

The pastor's eyes grew large with inquiry. "You hear it, too?"

John nodded.

"The church," Noah muttered. "Lord, thank You."

John stared at the preacher. "What are you talking about?"

Without a word, Noah took off.

John followed Noah, sprinting between the yards, hurdling fences, and springing into the churchyard and up the steps. They both fell upon the door at the same moment. It crashed back against the wall under their weight, and they tumbled onto the foyer floor.

Those gathered to pray screamed with alarm as John helped Noah to his feet and ran after him to the door in the hallway leading up to the now silent bell tower. Noah clamored upward while John waited below.

"Noah?" Belle McGowan came beside John and called up the

stairs to her husband.

Noah pushed against the hatch. Sunlight and fresh air flooded the dark mustiness of the stairwell.

Noah turned a worried look to John. "He's here, but I'm not sure he's alive."

Mrs. McGowan gave a small whimper of alarm and started to climb the stairs.

John held her back.

"Please, Mr. Ryan. I need to get to him."

Noah poked his head over the hatch. "Come up, Belle. He's alive. John, we need 9-1-1. With Seth at the mainland, ask them to send the group from the outlands."

Belle didn't look behind her as she scurried up the stairs. He patted his pockets.

"Don't you worry," a dark-skinned lady beside him said. "I'll call my husband. Tank will be praising the Lord that we found his friend alive. The chief sure means a lot to us, like a member of our family."

"Mrs. Williams?" John asked.

"Fran," the woman said as she turned away, phone to her face.

John climbed the stairs. Mrs. McGowan cradled the unconscious man in her arms, her hand tenderly stroking his cheek. "Kurty. It's Belle. Wake up, sweetie." She turned to her husband. "He's got to be okay," she whispered through tears.

John watched the preacher's face. Noah touched his wife's hand. "The EMTs are on their way, Belle."

As if the sound of the preacher's wife's name seeped into Kurt's subconscious, his eyes fluttered open, failing to focus for a moment but then zeroing in on Noah's wife. "Belle?"

"It's me." She touched her forefinger to his parched lips.

"You're okay." She rocked back and forth. "You're okay. What would I have done without you?"

Kurt tried to sit but fell back.

"Be still." John placed a hand on Kurt's shoulder. Dried blood covered the floor where the chief's head had lain, reminding John of Andy. The last time he saw his brother, blood covered Andy's hand as he held it out toward Emilee.

That picture would be his last memory of his brother.

"Lay still, Kurt. Pretty smart of you to ring the bell," Noah said.

Kurt shrugged off grogginess. "I didn't ring any bell. I—how did I get here?"

Noah shot John an inquiring glance.

"I heard it ringing," John answered.

Belle continued to touch Kurt's face with unashamed tenderness. "The bell didn't ring, Noah. You know how loud it sounds in the church."

"God works wonders." Noah winked and offered his wife a smile.

How could Noah offer such kindness and warmth? If Emilee ever touched another man in such a loving way …

He'd do just what he'd done to Andy and to Emilee.

Belle smiled at John. "Thank you for helping to find him. He means so much to both Noah and me."

"I just returned the favor." John took a quivering breath.

"Belle, go on. Let John and me get Kurt downstairs. Gather the folks for a prayer of gratitude." He leaned over and kissed her cheek, but Belle hesitated.

"Go." Kurt reached for her hand. Belle held it as she climbed through the hatch.

"Sorry for the worry," Kurt told her.

"Just don't do it again," she scolded and released her hold.

"Kurt." Noah stood. "We need to try to get you downstairs."

"I can do it," Kurt promised, but he had trouble getting to his feet. "He must've hit me pretty hard."

"I believe he meant to kill you," John said. "He may even think you're dead."

"Where is he?"

"The sheriff took him to the mainland on a murder charge." John would not let his emotions show, not in front of strangers. "He killed my brother."

The cry of the ambulance sirens split the air. John climbed down three steps and waited to brace Kurt as Noah helped him through the hatch.

"I'm sorry, John." Kurt managed, and they both simultaneously took one step at a time. "Andy was a good man."

John nodded, though no one but John knew the depth of Andy's goodness. His brother's well ran deep, and it always overflowed with compassion.

I survived Zack, John. Surely, I can survive you.

Andy had lied.

At least you love me.

Andy's words sprang from memory and hit him as hard as the punch Andy threw a few days before.

His selfishness killed Andy just as assuredly as Cameron pulled the trigger.

They reached the hall, and John held Kurt upright, but as if declaring his territory, Noah took hold of the chief, letting the injured man lean on him for strength.

A crowd had gathered at the good news, and as Noah helped

Kurt through the church, laughter, cries, cheers, and applause greeted them.

John held back, waiting until the crowd slipped through the church door.

Forced beyond his own control, he sat in the front pew. He bowed his head, his body trembling uncontrollably. "I can't go on without him. He made me laugh." John touched his face still sore from the beating Andy gave him. "I never want this pain to end. I need it as a reminder that I didn't love him enough to move aside and let him show Emilee his love. He loved me enough to move aside, and I accused him of betrayal."

He rocked back and forth. "Oh, God." He stopped and leaned forward, falling to his knees in front of the pew. "Bring him back." He looked toward the heavens. "Take me. I deserve to die." He coughed out the words. "You can have my life. Take it. Andy's the good one." He raised his hands in petition. "Take me. Let my brother live and take me."

John waited long, hard moments for the Lord to speak to him.

"God, why won't You listen? I don't want to be here without him. I'm not half the man he was. I don't know how to go on." He leaned back, lifted his head and released an animal-like cry from deep within his soul. The beast within—the one Zack had created of him.

"I love him, and I never told him!" John screamed. "You have to give me the chance to tell him." He covered his face with his hands.

Someone—was it Noah—bent beside him. Hands grasped his shoulder.

"Leave me alone." He pulled from them.

"Everything's okay, buddy."

"No ..." John let loose the mournful cry. "No ..." He dropped his hands.

A smile met his gaze.

He caught the man in an embrace. "Andy, I thought you left me."

"I'm fine. The bullet just grazed me." Andy touched the gauze that encircled his head.

John held tighter.

"Everything's okay, buddy. Let's go home. Em ..."

"Tank!" Anger hardened John's heart.

Boots clomped across the hardwood floors. "Now, you want to talk to me, huh? I tried to tell you. I would never have tried to have insinuate that your brother had died, man. I wouldn't do that to you. I wanted him to think we'd found Kurt. Men with his arrogance usually don't like to be bested. I was hoping he'd say something to give us a clue. You jumped in and assumed. My heart felt for you, but you wouldn't let me tell you what I had to say."

The anger subsided, and John slumped forward.

"You big dummy. Here in Serenity Key, we don't treat people like that. I'd have told you if that was my ploy." The officer turned and stomped out the door. Then he looked back in. "But I'm sorry I put that off on you after all you've gone through." He walked through the door.

John wiped his eyes and pulled Andy to him once again. "Don't ever do that to me again. Don't ever ..." He thought of Tank's words and half-laughed and half-cried. "You big dummy." He pushed Andy away with a playful action. Then he tugged him toward him again. "I love you," John choked out the words. "I do, Andy. I've never said that to you before, but I love you."

"Obviously." Andy smiled, stepping backward toward the

door.

"Where's Em?" John asked.

"She and India are filing affidavits. Seth brought me back. Good thing. He got the call about Kurt. He said he'd bring the girls home. Kurt, too, since he knows the guy won't let them keep him overnight."

Noah entered. "Seth's had a busy day." He ran the back of his hand over his wet eyes.

"I'm glad we found Kurt." John stopped in front of him.

"If anything more had happened to him, I'd feel the same way you did about losing Andy."

John nodded.

"Excuse me, I have some prayers." Noah started down the aisle.

"Noah?" John called.

The pastor stopped.

"About Kurt and Belle—"

"John, God has graced you with the love and presence of two people you love very much. He has just given me the same mercy."

"Whatever it is between them—"

"John," Andy warned.

John stepped toward the pastor. "Whatever it is, I have to tell you, I don't think you have to worry about your marriage. I know I haven't done a lot to earn your trust. I've treated you badly, and I can't believe I'm asking this. I've never asked it of anyone." John held out his right hand.

Noah continued to stare.

"Thank you for being a friend to me. Will you allow me to return the favor?"

Noah shook John's hand. "In Serenity Key, John, you don't

have to ask. You just become a friend, but I'm honored."

"In becoming your friend, please let me assure you that whatever Belle feels for Kurt, it's not as deep as her love for you."

"How could you tell?"

John had him flustered—something he never thought he'd be able to do. He almost let the smile of satisfaction play on his face, but that was the old John. This John wanted to share the same type of compassion Noah had shared with him. "Because the way she looks at Kurt is the way my wife looks at Andy. Emilee loves Andy—as a brother. I suspect the three of you have been as close as we have been. Don't ruin your love for her with jealousy that has no reason."

Noah pointed toward the door. "I'm sure Belle wants to go to the hospital to be with Kurt, but I need to take a moment to pray."

"Hold her close," John returned Noah's own advice, given when he thought he'd lost his wife. "Like precious gold."

Chapter Thirty-Eight

David thanked the nurse and waited for her to leave the small hospital chapel. She left him without a word, and David maneuvered his wheelchair between the rows of pews. The plain room showed no partiality to Christian denomination. Simple flowers adorned the front of a podium and an unadorned wooden cross graced the wall.

Unable to begin, but knowing the Lord called him to prayer, David bowed his head in silence. *Answer me when I call to you, my righteous God. Give me relief from my distress; have mercy on me and hear my prayer.* The beginning of a sweet Psalm of David came to his mind. Over the past few days, David's thoughts constantly turned to the king. He recalled the words of David's wise son, "For God will bring every deed into judgment, including every hidden thing, whether it is good or evil."

The tears falling down his face surprised him, if only for the reason they flowed. "I'm so happy." The words poured from deep within. "You are such a wonderful Father, and Your rod of correction is much less than I deserve." He looked to the cross. "That You, Father, could love me when I wasn't worthy of love, and that You would send Your Son to die on the cross for me, and even when I continue to disobey, You love me enough to show me the way." He lowered his head once again, the cries washing over him. "Thank You for my son. Thank You for my daughter. Thank You for everything You have given to me in my life, most importantly for the truth You have delivered. Forgive me for taking so long, and please put back together what I destroyed." For a very long time, David sat with his head bowed.

Someone cleared his throat, and David wiped the tears away before turning. "Mr. New." Noah sat in a pew behind him. "You asked me to pray like I believed Nathan would pray for David."

"Yes."

"But I think your prayer just now mirrored so many of David's prayers."

"Not so eloquent."

"God isn't looking for eloquence. He's looking for words from your heart."

"Seth told me you found Kurt." David smiled.

Noah nodded. "John and I."

"You were a good friend to my son-in-law through all of this. I would have hated for it to end with you losing your best friend."

"I did what God called me to do."

No words passed between them for some time. David moved closer to the preacher. Noah did not speak, and David marveled at the maturity in the young pastor God called to leadership. Many others would have tried to fill the awkwardness with talk.

"You realize my sin brought everyone to the church the night of the storm?" David asked.

Noah remained silent while David recounted his every transgression. When he finished, he allowed the preacher to sort the information he provided. Noah's eyes grew large behind his wire-rimmed glasses, and David worried that the young man would turn away from him; his sins were so atrocious. Noah swallowed hard. "Even Kurt suffered. He almost lost his life."

David closed his eyes. "And you, Noah. Haven't you looked at John, Andy, and the lies coming between them? It hasn't crossed your mind that there is a parallel to your relationship with Kurt?"

Noah's cheeks burned red. "Yes, this whole incident has made me realize how unfairly I'm treating Kurt, and I'm asking for your prayers. I want to put it all aside, but it's very hard for me to do. I'm a stubborn man."

"Son, don't wait for God to get your attention the way he's gotten mine."

Noah nodded.

Even a preacher would sometimes have to learn God's lessons the hard way. "Kurt could have died," David reminded Noah of what he'd declared himself.

Noah shuddered.

"Andy could have died," David reminded the preacher.

"There's one person you didn't mention. Your son could have died getting you to the hospital, trying to save your life."

"But he's the one I hurt the most. Seth watched me for an example of how to accept what life has to offer and to trust God completely. My example pushed him so far from God I don't think he'll ever return."

Noah stood. "Is anyone ever too far from God? Doesn't He reach out for us? We're incapable of turning to Him on our own. Did you wake up one day and think you needed Him without feeling His touch on your life?"

God called David from the pew that day so long ago when he had no one else he could trust. Seth had called on Jesus as a young boy. Life had thrown his son just as many curves, and Seth was angry with the Lord, questioning God's sovereignty. "You think God's working on Seth?"

"Hey." Noah smiled for the first time. "He worked on you for thirty years."

<hr />

John stretched his arms upward and gave a deep, satisfying yawn as Andy walked onto the porch. John lifted his cup of coffee to his lips.

"Morning." Andy held up his own cup.

Serenity basked in sunlight with just a hint of cool in the air, and John found it hard to believe it was still October. A smile turned his lips as Andy sipped his coffee and coughed at the bitter taste.

"I made it," John confessed.

The distaste on Andy's face continued to show. "Well, that one sip will keep me running for five days. Em still sleeping?" Andy sat in the chair across the table from him. A spot of red showed on the gauze tied around his head. Emilee would take care of it once she woke.

Andy sat.

"Like a baby." John pushed the creamer and sugar toward his brother. "This might help. I used three sugars and half the creamer."

"You'll be able to pound nails for ten days running."

"Luke wants David's Place rebuilt by Thursday evening," John said.

"He'll get it done, too."

"He's already gone, sailed over to the dock behind what's left of the restaurant. Apparently, these friends who offered to help are early risers."

"Maybe we should get going." Andy started to stand.

"Give me a minute." John set his coffee on the table. He swallowed, staring into the mud in his cup. "I owe you an apology."

"I thought we went through this at the church yesterday."

"No." John looked up. "You heard I love you, but you didn't hear that I'm sorry for all the harsh words and accusations I threw your way. Even my silence spoke anger, something you never deserved."

"It all worked out. Let's not worry about it."

John's hand fell with a slap against the table. "I have apologies to make. Please, let me do this."

"I'm listening." Andy leaned back.

"I know what happened the night of the storm."

Andy shifted in his seat. "Cameron can't know about India."

"Not that storm." John searched Andy's face. It hadn't occurred to him until this moment that two separate storms, many years apart, altered their lives completely. He ran his hand through his hair. "The night Dad killed Mom."

"You couldn't. You just think …"

"I could hear Mom crying as Dad hit her, and I heard her screams fade away as he threw her over the balcony. Dad threatened you that night, and I realized you chose Emilee and me over freedom from him."

"I didn't want you to remember."

"That's why I never told you. I knew your silence protected us. You had so much on your shoulders all those years. I wanted to make life easy for you. That's why I worked with him until I couldn't—until I had to think of Emilee first. Then, you still cut me slack by taking over the company business so I could stay with the firm. I have so much to thank you for."

"Maybe I need to thank you."

John blinked. "I've never done anything for you like you've done for me."

"We both did what came naturally to both of us. We protected each other and safeguarded Emilee as much as we could."

John shook his head. "I didn't shield her as well as you did. I know that, too."

"What do you mean?"

"Dad got to her. He hurt her. I could see the bruises and the cuts on her lips. I knew each time Dad whispered something and made her doubt her self-worth."

"Why didn't you ever tell me or do something about it?" Andy asked.

"Because my wife trusted you with those secrets, not me."

"Is that why you believed Cameron's lies about us?"

"I've been thinking about it." John stood and moved to the screen door. He looked out over the water to the dock where Luke's boat usually sat. Surprisingly, John felt the emptiness. "I think I believed Cameron because Emilee was the one possession in my life I couldn't give you. I know you've always loved her, but I loved her, too. Cameron told his lies, and I felt betrayed by my selfishness more than anything else."

"You can erase the guilt." Andy stood beside him. "I knew from the start how Emilee felt about you. Being Emilee's friend is a cross I have to bear."

Both brothers looked out over the water. "We have another

cross to bear," John said. "I don't want you to handle it all alone. I know what it has cost you."

"Cameron." Andy took a deep breath. "We'll need to make sure he gets the best help."

"The best help behind bars." John searched Andy's face.

Andy nodded. "He'll be there for a long time, John. You don't have to worry. He's dug himself a very deep hole."

"Emilee won't push to prosecute," John said. "I've talked to her about it." He'd stand beside his wife whatever the decision, and she'd done, again, what they'd always done for each other, but now their circle of influence had grown by one. He smiled at Andy. "She won't put you or India through it."

"India agreed to the same for obvious reasons, but I know that Kurt isn't going to let the attempted murder charge drop."

"You're going to see Cameron today, aren't you?"

"I don't have a choice."

"You'll understand I can't. I'll stand behind you in whatever treatment you want to provide, but I can't see him right now."

"Emilee needs you to let go of the anger, John. She's very sensitive, and she'll know if you hold it inside."

John could only nod his answer.

"It's okay to feel hurt and angry, but you have to show Emilee you're hurting for her and not because of her."

"I love my wife more than I've ever loved her, if that's possible."

"Just don't go stupid on us again." Andy chuckled but sobered quickly. "I'll deliver any message you want to Cameron."

"Dad set aside a trust for him. Let him know I'll be turning it over to you. That way he can contact you if he needs funds while in prison. Otherwise, we'll just let it gain interest. He might want to designate a beneficiary in case something happens to him."

"Why didn't you ever tell me about the trust, John?"

John remained silent.

"Why do you feel the need for secrecy all the time? Why can't you just open up and let Emilee and I know what's going on with you?"

"How would you feel if Zack left your inheritance in the control of someone else? Would you want others to know?"

Andy stared, his mouth opened.

"Before you start hating yourself, I should tell you that I enjoyed holding it over Cameron's head the last couple of months. I despised him for telling me about you and Emilee."

"John, answer me one question, and tell me the truth. I'll know if you're lying."

"Sure." John nodded.

"How much did Zack really leave me?"

John winced, hating himself for making the promise. "Andy, I don't think that's relevant."

"I want to know, and don't think it's going to hurt me. Zack can't harm me any longer."

John swallowed and shook his head.

"Nothing?" Andy's laughter filled the air. "He didn't leave me one dime." He pointed at John. "You—I went to work for Zack's company trying to help you out so you could stay with the law firm, and I didn't own a piece of it."

"Dad didn't leave you anything, but I gave you what I thought you would believe came from him."

"Why?" Andy grew solemn.

"Because you deserved it all. You're the oldest and the one responsible for our survival. I would have given it all to you, but you wouldn't have believed it. But through it all, haven't we always pooled our resources? With everything, I can't remember a time when we thought about where the money came from or who paid what."

"I thought I knew you so well, little brother, and it turns out I didn't know you at all. Emilee always swore you have the heart of an angel, and I laughed at her."

"Emilee said that about me?"

"She said it, and I thought her a fool, but she's right."

John walked away from his brother, uncomfortable with the praise. He'd treated Emilee as if he'd never loved her. He allowed lies to come between them and left her vulnerable to Cameron's madness. They had it all wrong. He was no angel.

"What are you going to do about India?" John changed the subject.

"I'm going to stand beside her and help her raise our child."

"You'd jeopardize a possible relationship with Blanchie over a baby that isn't really yours?"

"I don't believe the world should know the truth. It isn't fair to India, and it sure isn't fair to the baby."

"It isn't fair for you to take the responsibility of a child you didn't bring into this world."

"Cameron came here with me. I exposed India to him."

"But you didn't make him do it."

"John, if Emilee became pregnant with his child, would you throw her to the wolves?"

Andy's words brought a shudder. John had tried to block out the fact Cameron harmed her. "Emilee is my wife. India isn't even someone you thought of until the storm."

"Until I learned she became pregnant with a child that's going to take my name. I want to know you'll stand beside me on this. I'd rather take care of Cameron alone, but India will need this family's support."

"She has a reputation."

Andy smiled and started inside the house. "And you don't?"

———

In disbelief, Penny pushed the screen door to her sister's house open. "India, I have nothing to say to you. Our friendship is over."

"You've always been a good friend to me. I don't think you'll ever stop. I'm the one who has a lot to learn about friendship." India stepped back to the edge of the porch, her hand resting over her stomach. She leaned back against the post.

"Is something wrong?" Penny asked.

"I feel these little pushes against my stomach. Have you felt them?"

Above India's hand, Penny saw the movement. Despite her anger, she smiled. "I believe your baby's beginning to kick."

India smiled also. "Then he or she is very strong."

Penny lost her humor. The baby inside India had a tie to the baby inside her. They were siblings. "Again, I have nothing to say to you, and I'm not going to accept an apology from you right now. The wound runs too deep."

"I understand."

"Then why are you here?" Penny stood beside the post opposite the woman.

"Because I know you still believe Mickey's the father of my baby."

"It's not Andy."

"How can you be so sure, Penny? Everyone knows how loose I am."

"I never said anything like that to you."

"Yes, and you sure didn't deserve what I did."

"I said I don't want an apology."

"Then I won't offer you one." India pointed toward the porch swing. "Can we sit down?"

"This isn't a social visit."

"Fine. Look, I just—Andy said we shouldn't, but you deserve the truth."

"I know the truth. Andy's protecting Mickey for some unknown reason."

India looked beyond Penny, and she turned to see what gained India's interest.

Mickey took a couple of steps toward the porch and stopped.

Penny turned her glare back toward India.

"Andy isn't protecting Mickey," India said. "He protected me, and he safeguarded my child from his real father. I used Mickey as a pawn. He didn't love me. He told me as much. I needed him, and I pushed him into what I thought was my only solution. I wronged you both, but at the time I thought I had no other choice."

"You're not making sense. You had no other choice but to sleep with my husband and carry his child?

"I'm telling you this baby is not Mickey's child. I was pregnant before I trapped Mickey into something he tried to fight."

"Then who is the father?"

"You're right. It's not Andy's baby, at least not his natural child. No one else can know. Mickey, you understand, don't you?"

Penny whirled around toward her unsuspecting husband.

"You told her to come here and tell these lies."

"No." Mickey nodded. "I thought Andy covered for me, too."

"Cameron." India let the name stand between them. "Cameron raped me. I didn't report it. I used Mickey to cover the truth."

"What a convenient excuse. You take what happened to poor Emilee Ryan, and you use it to get out of one scrape and in the process, ruin other lives as well."

India pushed away from the post. "Think about it, and you'll know it's the truth. I understand you don't want an apology, but I am very sorry. I hope I haven't destroyed the two of you. Your baby, Mickey's child, needs a father."

"Did he hurt you like he hurt Emilee?" For only a second, Penny could not believe the words flowing from Mickey's mouth until she realized, yes, Mickey still had a heart.

"Emotional pain." India's voice quivered. "I think his hatred of John caused him to rape me. Even though it was wrong, I hope you can see I was trying to protect myself and my baby."

"And you do that by taking my husband and by taking away the opportunity for my sister to have happiness. Andy and Blanchie had a real chance, and now that's gone."

"Andy made that choice," Mickey said. "I didn't hear India ask him to protect her. You can't control lives. Not everything turns out like we want. I'm sure India would rather not carry Cameron's child, but she did do something valiant. She spared her child's life. The world certainly wouldn't blame her if she ended her pregnancy."

"All this at the risk of our marriage." Penny fought back.

"That baby isn't to blame for this. What happened to you, that was me, all me. My restlessness and insecurities got the best of me. Grief wrapped around me, and I put myself into a position where I could hurt you. You're getting a very hard heart, Mouse." He stepped away. "A very hard heart."

"You don't have any right to lecture me!" she screamed. "You have no right at all, Mickey Parker. You turned to the arms of another woman and made me feel worthless. If I ever wanted to mean something to someone, it was you."

"Mouse, you mean the world to me. There are so many reasons I'm sorry. I came between two friends who could sure use each other right now. India says she seduced me, but I used her vulnerability in an attempt to gain something I thought missing in our marriage. I'm sorry I didn't tell you how I felt. Since Mom died and my sister left town, I've struggled. I didn't know how to cope with the loss. At times, I wanted to die. Maybe if I had ..." He started away without finishing the sentence.

"Oh no, you don't, Mickey Parker." Penny flew down the steps after him. "Luke told me about your little stunt with the gun. You're not getting off that easy. I'm going to make you pay. I'm going to make you pay for what you've done to me. Do you understand? I'm not letting you think about killing yourself because then I won't be able to get my revenge on you every day of your life."

There, she accomplished what she intended. Mickey stood before her dumbfounded, unable to comprehend her words. *You ponder that a while, buster. Sit in it and stew. I understand your hurt more than you know.*

"What are you saying, Mouse?" He started back toward her.

She held up her hand to stop him. "Your mother died and your sister left you, Mickey, but you still had me." Tears sprang to her eyes. "I was right here." She shook off the emotion and stared into his blue eyes. "You give me two days, and I'll have my answer for you. I'll let you know what I intend to do, but whatever I decide, you have a debt to pay."

"I'll gladly pay any debt as long as I have you."

"Two days, and you'll know whether you have me or not." Penny whirled back on India. "You always fall out of the frying pan onto a plate of pure gold. I hope you and Andy have a happy life."

India blinked back tears.

Penny softened. "But I only wish the best for the baby."

"I wish the same for you, and I hope that in the two days you're thinking about your husband's punishment, you'll remember something."

Penny did not give India the satisfaction of an inquiry.

"Even when he feared losing you, Mickey told me he wouldn't let me down. He would be here for this baby. There aren't too many men like him out there, Penny. Despite his mistake, you have a good one."

"And you have the other. Andy doesn't even belong to you, does he?"

"No, you're right, and maybe if Blanchie wakes up and looks at the truth, she'll have him. Although, I don't believe Blanchie knows whether she wants Andy or Luke, and neither of the men deserves that."

"She doesn't want your leftovers. That's for sure."

Mickey straightened. He walked down the street, head bowed, leaving without saying a word.

"That was a low blow," India whispered. "Tell me why you were so willing to forgive me all those years, but now you can't give Mickey even one chance. You better wake up before you end up like your sister and like me—in love with the man you threw away." She turned on her heels and started in the opposite direction from Mickey.

Chapter Thirty-Nine

Noah watched as Kurt shuffled the paperwork on his desk without really working on any of it. According to Tank, Kurt assigned himself to desk duty for the three weeks Dr. Scott Bernhardt prescribed bed rest. "Should you be here?" Noah stepped into Kurt's office.

"Look, I have everyone and their brother telling me what to do, and if that isn't enough, Tank has the mainland deputies offering to cover for me. I don't like being fawned over, and I don't need any more out of you."

Noah raised his hands in defeat. "I just wanted to see how you were doing."

"I have a headache the size of Texas that the doctor said would leave gradually."

Noah ran his hand over the back of the chair sitting in front of the desk. He both wanted and dreaded Kurt asking him to have a seat.

Kurt said nothing.

"You'll let me know if you need anything."

"Belle's already offered." Kurt picked up a handful of papers and tapped them against the desk to get them aligned. He did not look to Noah as he spoke.

Noah swallowed the hard knot rising in his throat. Neither Kurt nor the Lord planned to make this easy for him.

"You know, you're a lucky man." Kurt turned deep green eyes toward him.

"I know." A sharpness Noah didn't intend edged his voice.

"You better wise up and know Belle never did anything to make you ashamed of her. She loves me, Noah, but it's something you can't understand."

"And neither of you will tell me."

"I'll tell you this, old friend. Your wife loves me in much the same way I love you."

"And how's that Kurt?"

Kurt stared at him for a long second before speaking. "I love you like a brother. I have and I always will."

Noah stared. Kurt spoke of love as if he mentioned it every day. Before Kurt had arrived in Serenity Key, life had toughened him with a past he never shared with anyone.

"I love you," Kurt repeated. "Does that surprise you?"

"Not that you do but that you would say it so bluntly."

"Well, I do." Kurt went back to his work. "And maybe someday when you finally become convinced of it, we can begin our friendship over. I really miss you, Noah."

Kurt would not look at him again. Noah understood him all too well.

"I'm glad we found you safe."

"I'm glad you found me, too. I'm glad it was you."

Noah nodded and walked away. Kurt had sewn a few stitches in the torn seam of their friendship. He passed the needle to Noah, and Noah failed to even make a stitch.

John entered the bedroom, but Emilee, sitting on the edge of the bed, didn't seem to notice. "Hey."

Emilee startled to her feet. She fell back toward the wall.

John nearly dropped the tray of food he carried but managed to set it on the bed without too much damage. "I'm sorry." For the first time, he could imagine some of the terror she must have suffered at the hands of Cameron Matrai.

She dropped her hand from where it had clutched at her chest. Her breath calmed. "It's okay." Her lips turned into a smile only for a fleeting moment.

"What is it?"

She moved toward him now, touching his arm. "Nothing. Why? You just scared me."

"When I scared you before, you'd yell at me. You were too frightened of me just now to do that."

"You're making more of this than there is."

"More of what?" he asked. "More of what you're feeling? You cried out in your sleep last night. When I tried to hold you, you curled up into a little ball like a small, frightened child until you cried my name. Only then did you allow me to comfort you."

She waved his words off with her hand and stepped away from him.

"Were you dreaming about the rape?"

"Stop it," she demanded.

"I don't think it's anything we can sweep under a rug and pretend it didn't happen. He hurt you."

"He hurt you." She surprised him. "That's why he did it to

me."

"Only because it caused you pain."

"Don't be ridiculous." She stamped her foot, and pain sliced across her face. "It's going to stand between us. It's going to act as a wall just like the wall I created between my father and mother."

"What?" He could have laughed at her correlation had he not known she was so serious.

"It's something that's going to keep us apart."

"I don't want anything to separate us. I want to hold you and protect you."

"But I'm not the same Emilee."

"I know that." But he didn't want to know it. He didn't like the thought of another man harming her, taking from her what she didn't want to give.

"You'll never be able to look at me again without thinking of him."

"Don't."

"Don't what? State the truth? Look how you were when you thought Andy and I had an affair."

He hated that he'd made her feel this way. "That's different."

"It isn't!" she screamed. "It isn't any different at all. I know you. I know you don't like to share."

They all mistook his concern for possessiveness, even Emilee. He thought she understood. "I didn't share you. He took you, and you had no choice. Baby, if I couldn't understand that, then I don't deserve you."

"I can't forget his hands on me. I can't forget him holding me down. I can't forget any of it." She trembled. "And neither can you. You will never let it go."

"No, I won't let it go." At his words, she jerked her head up toward him. "Because I allowed Cameron to get to you. You tried to tell me about him, and my jealousy made me such a fool that I couldn't hear."

"Johnny."

John closed his eyes. He treasured the sound of his name on her lips.

"Johnny, you're not to blame."

"What about the times Dad hit you, Em? I feel responsible for that, too."

"I knew you would. That's why I never told you." She lifted his hand and placed her hand over it, measuring the size of his against hers. Then she laced her fingers in his. "You've always looked after Andy and me, and I didn't want to add more problems to the ones you were trying to solve."

John sat hard on the bed, and Emilee scrambled to save the contents of the tray. She moved them to the window seat and sat beside him.

"Didn't you think I knew?" She touched his face. "Johnny, you have such a caring, warm, wonderful soul."

"You have me confused with the other Ryan."

"Oh no." She shook her head. "Both Ryan brothers are good men, but the one I married, he's the special one. He's the one I told Della about so long ago."

He had almost forgotten her ability to undermine all of his defenses. It seemed a very long time since he'd given her a reason to care to try.

"Didn't you ever wonder why I couldn't see past you to Andy?" She leaned against him. "Because you shined so much brighter just because you tried to hide your light."

He laid back on the bed and brought her with him, careful of her sore body. "We'll make it. We'll take one day at a time. And you're wrong."

"About what?"

"When I look at you now, I don't see what Cameron did to you. All I see is the woman I love. She's a little fearful and a little emotional, but she's my Emilee." He kissed the top of her head, felt the soft strands of mahogany against his face. "And I'm so happy your biggest wish has come true."

"You're so arrogant," she teased, holding to him.

He laughed. She couldn't hide her dry sense of humor if she tried. "Your father," he feigned aggravation. "You found your father."

"And my brother." She used his chest for leverage and looked down at him. "Did you get along with Seth when you first came here? And don't lie to me, Johnny Ryan."

He made a face as if caught at being bad. "I never much talked with him," he admitted. "I thought he was your cousin. I should have tried to make conversation, but I always pulled away."

"Guilty conscience?" She eyed him.

"Very guilty." He reached up and pushed her long hair behind her ear.

"Well, Mr. Ryan, there's one other member of my family missing, and I expect you to find her for me."

John laughed aloud. "Like you said, I've never denied you anything."

She kissed him passionately and then pulled away. "Find my momma."

"How do you know I haven't already found her?" He pulled her back toward him for another kiss. His time in the desert of loneliness had lasted far too long, and Emilee's love was the sustenance he needed for survival. "Make a list, I'll find anyone on earth you want."

"Find me, John."

He held her, knowing exactly what she meant and wondering if it was possible.

Luke walked with Blanchie to the end of the dock, listening to all she had to say.

She swatted her tears away. "Are all men like you and Andy?"

"We're all fools, yeah." He gave a half-laugh. "None of us really knows what we want. Some of us just stick to what's given to us better than others."

"Wrong words to say to me, Luke Crum." She turned upon him. "So, you were just sticking to me while you looked for something better."

"Do you want the truth, or do you want a lie?"

"I want the truth."

"I was a stupid teenage kid who had a girl who would do anything for me. Even when I treated her badly, she forgave me. Why would I want to give that up? I foolishly believed we could make it work because you loved me."

Blanchie's opened mouth told him he'd dealt her a hard blow.

"But I wasn't ready to love. The harder you held to me, the more I tried to prove we'd made a mistake."

"Oh." Her mouth snapped shut. "That's what we made, a mistake."

"We made a big mistake getting married so young."

"The day of the storm you told me you loved me. What was that? Did you know the truth about Andy? Were you trying to brace my fall?"

Luke reached out and grabbed her shoulders. "Here's the truth, Blanchie. I'm getting ready to pour it on you, and I want you to listen to me carefully because I won't have the opportunity to spell it out for you again. Are you ready?"

She struggled to pull away from him. Everyone working on the dock stopped to stare at them. Still, he refused to release her. "We made a big mistake in thinking love could conquer everything. We were stupid kids, and we wouldn't listen, not to your parents or to mine. Your mistake came from loving me. My mistake was in not realizing how much I love you. I wasn't ready to settle down and play the good husband. I thought you took my life away from me, so I searched for another life. Then you woke up, and you did what you had to do. You left me, and I crumbled. Do you know what finally made me see just how much I do love you?"

"I can't imagine." Sarcasm rolled off her tongue.

"Because, baby, when Seth lost Linda, I couldn't breathe for a week. I caught a glimpse of what life would be if God took you out of the picture altogether. I discovered I love you more than I have ever loved anyone or anything in my life. I can't bear to lose you, not forever, not like Seth lost Linda." He touched her hair and saw her face fill with the admiration he'd taken for granted for so long.

Part of him gladdened at the sight. The other part cursed the words that placed it there.

"Andy Ryan loves you." He purposely broke the spell. "I've made a decision, and I'm going to stand by it. I have to let you have the happiness I could never provide. Andy offers you love with security. He's the man you deserve. I'm the man getting what I deserve."

"But he and India, they're having a child. Do you know how often I prayed God would give us a child?"

"What would a baby have done for us?" He turned from her, closing his eyes as he spoke. "I would have been trapped more than ever."

"And you couldn't stand to be trapped with me and our child?" She stamped her foot on the wooden dock.

He didn't answer for some time. He wanted no sympathy to show on his face, and when he turned toward her, he offered her none. "Not then, no."

Blanchie reached out and grabbed for the railing.

Luke watched her fight against the new tears threatening to fall. "Sometimes I wondered what having a kid would be like for us. Other times, I broke out in cold sweats, knowing I wasn't daddy material." He hadn't been. Not back then.

"Oh, Luke." She leaned over the railing as if in great pain. "All the time I thought you were making me miserable, and I was actually doing the same to you." She turned and one single tear fell. He would never vanquish the memory of the sadness on her sweet face.

"Andy won't make you miserable."

"I never want to think of Andy Ryan again."

"Why? Is it because he's doing an honorable deed?"

"It's not so honorable to sleep with India and leave her in the condition she's in. What he did—what he didn't do—it caused a lot of pain for my sister and Mickey."

"What he didn't do was sleep with India." Luke leaned close

to her, his voice barely a whisper.

"It's hard to have a baby when you didn't sleep with the woman."

"It isn't impossible to take the responsibility of another man's actions."

Blanchie shook her head to tell him she didn't comprehend.

He stepped even closer. "Cameron Matrai raped India."

Blanchie's eyes grew large. "Cameron's the father."

Luke placed his finger to his lips. "You're not supposed to know, and, my favorite little gossip, if you ever tell Andy I told you, I'll deny it." Again, his voice lowered to a whisper. "He doesn't even realize I know." And he hated this talebearing, but Blanchie needed to know the truth.

"Why would you tell me this? Do you want so completely rid of me that you're willing to go this far?"

"I'll never be completely rid of you." He would always hold her in his heart. He intended to keep his vow to God. If the Lord didn't want to give Blanchie back to him, Luke would never touch another woman.

"Luke, I don't understand."

"I've hurt you enough, Blanchie, and if I can risk my friendship with Andy by telling you the truth and making you happy, I'm going to do it." He walked away from her. "I've got a job to do, and I don't have much time to do it."

Chapter Forty

Seth sat beside the hospital bed. Only the monitor measuring his sleeping father's heart rhythm broke the quietness of the hospital room. He wanted to tell Pop so much, but one subject they would not discuss was the ruin of the restaurant. Dr. Bernhardt warned both Emilee and Seth against it, and over their father's protest, the doctor kept Pop in the hospital to allow Luke time to get some work done, anything to lessen the blow.

The door to the room opened, and Seth stood, thinking the nurse would need room to take his father's temperature or other vitals. The woman who entered hesitated. Then she stepped forward. "Seth?"

"Yes, ma'am." Seth watched her. There was something strangely familiar about her. He moved forward, held out his hand. "I'm sorry, but have we met?"

"Seth." Pop awoke, his voice hoarse from sleep. "Is that you?"

Seth turned away from the woman, and as he did, realization hit him like a ballistic missile. "I'm here, Pop," he muttered.

"How long have I been asleep?" Pop pushed himself up on the bed. He smiled at the woman as if not surprised by her presence at all. "Is your sister with you?"

"No. I came alone. Emilee's resting."

Pop motioned the woman closer. "Colleen, you've met Seth."

"I was just about to introduce myself." Colleen Dellacroix New stepped forward.

"This is your sister's mother," Pop told him. "Your mother's sister."

"I know who she is." Seth moved away from the woman's outstretched hand. "You knew she was in town?" He looked to his father for an answer.

"I came back to town with Verity," Colleen answered

"That's why Verity left so suddenly on their mysterious vacation," Pop advised.

"Verity wouldn't hurt me like this." Seth refused to believe in a conspiracy.

"I'll be back, David." Colleen moved toward the door. "Seth, you enjoy your visit with your father. I'll wait until you leave."

"I'll be here for a while."

"I'll wait." She pulled the door open.

"Colleen, don't," Pop called after her.

"Let her go, Pop."

The door closed with the woman on the other side of it.

"I thought I raised you better than this," Pop snapped.

"I won't forgive her for what she caused me to lose."

"The blame for that belongs to me, boy. I caused your mother to die in that car wreck. She was going to her sister to make sure my child had a chance in this world. Your mother was bringing Colleen and Emilee back to Serenity when the accident occurred."

"And after she killed my mother, she put my sister in the hands of strangers." He'd told Emilee her mother loved her, but he couldn't really believe it.

"Indirectly, Seth, I put her in those hands. I could have taken her away, but I left her."

"But she left her there in the first place." He'd told Emilee she had a good reason. Seth couldn't really think of any.

"Stop it," Pop commanded.

The monitor behind him beeped and silenced both of them for a moment.

"Before you start hating her so much, why don't you ask Emilee if she would have traded lives? Seems to me she loves John Ryan very much."

Yes, she loved John. Seth wasn't entirely sure how she could, though.

"Colleen made decisions, but she based those decisions on my behavior toward her. If you still need to place any blame, I want you angry with me and not at her."

Seth didn't want any more anger toward his father.

"I'll give you something to think about."

"What?" Seth spat the question.

"Without her, you wouldn't have your sister."

Pop was wrong. Seth would have a sister, and she would be a whole part of him and not half. Emilee would have been his mother's child.

"Yes, your mother and I could have had another child, but not Emilee." His father read him too well. "In just the little while I've spent with her, I found her uniquely refreshing."

"Well, I didn't have her for thirty years, did I?" Seth was unwilling to let this go. He'd been lied to—denied a relationship with his sibling.

"All because of me." Pop stared at him. "Seth, you still hold Linda's death deep inside of you. Before her, it was your grandparents. I suppose it's because of the ultimate loss of your mother."

"Death is permanent. I do hold on to it. I've suffered it a lot in my life. Just because I didn't know my mother doesn't mean I can't love her. She did give me life."

"But Emilee is one loss that you've recovered. She's here with you now. A gift from God. For both of us. And the woman to whom you were so rude gave life to your sister. Colleen knew your mother better than anyone on earth. I'm sure she'd be happy to tell you all about her. She seemed very eager to meet you, and you just pushed her away. You know, she hasn't even talked with Emilee yet. I knew you would be here, and I asked her to talk with you first."

"Why?" His father's confession perplexed Seth.

"Because I think you need her more than Emilee needs her."

What was the old man thinking? Had the heart attack damaged his brain? He didn't need Emilee's mother. He wanted nothing to do with the woman.

"Does it take her falling on the floor with a life-threatening disease to gain your forgiveness?"

"It would probably take her dying." Seth moved toward the door.

"What about me, boy? Do you want me to die, too?"

Seth had been waiting for Pop to awaken so he could tell him, and now Pop gave him the opportunity. "I forgave you before you had the heart attack. I forgave you when I found Emilee curled up by the church sign. I fell in love with my sister, and there wasn't any room for anger with you."

"Colleen wants the moment she sees her daughter to be special, and you need to ponder how much it would mean to your sister for her brother to at least appear to appreciate the fact she's found the woman that had to let her go so many years ago."

"She didn't have to let her go. She chose to let her go. There's a big difference. Colleen abandoned Emilee."

"I abandoned both Emilee and her mother."

Seth reached for the door. He opened it and turned back to his father wanting to know the answer to the same question Emilee asked of him. "Was she such an awful mistake that you didn't want her around?"

"She was a mistake, and no, in my youth and in my stupidity, I didn't want to own up to my errors." A smile crossed the man's face. "But God does turn our mistakes into wonderment, doesn't he? She's a great kid, and I'm never letting her go again."

"She's no more a kid than I am." Seth smiled. "But she's taken to calling you Daddy. She says she doesn't like Pop."

"Daddy or Pop suits me fine."

Seth let the door close and came back toward his father. He folded him into an embrace.

"Just as long as it's said with love," Pop whispered into Seth's ear. "Later, when I earn it, I'll expect the respect to return."

"I respect you, Pop." Seth released him. "Just not your choices."

"You can't find it in your heart to give Colleen the same benefit?"

"That woman didn't raise me or my sister."

"I'm asking you to think about it."

"Well, I've got an important date with a carpenter."

Pop gasped.

Seth winced at the cruel joke he unintentionally played on the man. "Luke, Pop. Luke and I have a very important project."

"Damage from the storm?"

"Yeah. I'd say." He waved as he again pulled open the door.

Seth looked for Colleen in the waiting room, but she wasn't there. Her absence suited him just fine. He left the hospital, pleased his anger could remain intact.

Andy tugged on the tail of Blanchie's shirt. The beautiful blonde was busy wiping down the tables one of the island residents had donated to the cause of bringing David's Place back to life. Blanchie paused and swiped her arm across her forehead to push the sweat away. The dark streak the dirt made caused him to smile. Andy was official photographer of this expedition. They'd designed the job for the purpose of keeping his activity level down, treating him like an invalid, but someone had to do it. The picture of Blanchie was just too irresistible, and he snapped it before she could protest. "I haven't had a chance to talk with you since the other day."

"Since you were shot." She reached up and touched the bandage.

He winced and pulled away. "It really hurts. Are you okay?"

"I'm fine, Andre." She patted his cheek tenderly.

He wondered if she left a smudge on his face as well.

"How is Emilee?" she asked.

"She's doing well. She's a little ticked at John because he won't let her help with the cleanup."

"Well, Luke has Kurt looking over the invoices to make sure he and his friends weren't double-billed for any materials. Maybe she could help there. We have to make the money work for us."

"What the insurance doesn't cover, I'll pay the difference." Andy looked back toward Kurt, who diligently pored over the paperwork as he sat at a makeshift picnic table.

Blanchie puffed out a breath. "Do you always have to make life work out even when things that happen aren't your fault?"

Andy shrugged. "It's a fatal flaw of mine."

"It may be the one quirk about you I can't overlook. It's a good attribute, but sometimes you do it at the expense of others."

"What are you talking about?"

"I think you know exactly what I mean."

Andy studied his hands, realizing Blanchie knew the truth, but he'd decided never to speak it aloud to anyone outside the family. He wouldn't betray India. "What does it mean?" he pressed.

"It means that we've hit a fork in the road, and I think I want to go the rest of the way alone or maybe with someone different from you."

The dismissal stung. "I'm sorry if I hurt you. I didn't know about it before we started dating."

"What didn't you know?" She tilted her head, one eyebrow arched.

"I didn't know about the baby."

"But you knew of the possibility. Isn't that why you gave her the job at your restaurant so easily? Didn't you want to provide for the baby, even if it isn't yours?"

"It's mine. The baby is my child, but it shouldn't stand between us."

"The baby's not standing between us." She rose on tiptoes to plant a kiss upon his cheek. "Because I'm heading down that opposite fork in the road." She stared beyond him, and he turned.

Luke.

"I believe God has another direction for me to travel. Eventually." Blanchie returned to her cleaning.

He leaned forward, placing his hand over hers. "I don't want to part on bad terms."

They were so close. All Andy had to do was lean forward, and he'd taste those sweet lips again, maybe convince her that they could work out all of their problems.

A smile so warm and loving crossed her face, filling Andy with desire.

"We're not parting on bad terms. We're just not coming together quite as closely as we might have liked. I can't deal with what you've chosen to do. It doesn't mean I don't believe it's honorable."

"I care about you." His whispered plea hung between them.

A crane lifted a piece of wood from the ground and swung wildly.

"Whoa. Hold up!" Luke's booming voice, calling to the machine's operator, filled the air as he continued to supervise the building.

Blanchie's warm smile blazed as she turned to look at her ex-husband, softening when she gave her attention back to Andy. "I'm sorry."

"Every time I try to make the right choice, it just comes down on me." He turned from her.

"I know this won't help right now, but someday maybe you'll understand. I'm going to be praying only good to come to you, Andre Ryan, because you are so generous and kindhearted. Only a man so full of love could sacrifice the way you do."

Her words were of no consolation to him, but he nodded and walked away. Too many times in his life, he'd reached for something outside of his grasp.

"Hi. How are you?" India walked toward him, but as soon as their eyes met, she dropped her gaze to the ground.

"I should be asking you." Andy looked to her midriff where she held her hand. "Everything okay? You've been through a lot."

"The baby's moving. I really do need to set an appointment."

"May I?" He nodded to her stomach.

She blushed. "Sure."

Andy placed his palm there over her clothing. The baby must have stretched because Andy felt it move across his hands. He smiled and looked up, but again, India was staring at the ground. He lifted her chin with his fingers. "Hold your head high."

Tears ran from her jade-green eyes.

"This baby isn't anything that should make us feel ashamed." He drew her close to him and grazed her forehead with a light kiss. "Set the doctor's appointment, and if it wouldn't be too awkward for you, I'd love to be with you."

More tears.

"I don't have to if it would make you feel uncomfortable. I just thought I'd like to be a part of the birth."

"Oh, Andy." India threw her arms around his neck. "I'd love to go through this with you. I don't want you to feel like you have to."

He hugged her. "Thank you for giving me the privilege. I won't ever take it lightly."

"You will still let me work at the restaurant? I need to learn. I have to support the baby."

He wouldn't tell her that support for the baby—or her—would never be a problem, but Andy sensed that the job was important to her. "We're staying closed until David's Place is restored. Most of the folks who provide my stock are taking care of other business anyway. Kurt said our closure would help with a traffic problem, so if you could set the appointment before then, that would be good. If not, we'll work it out."

She pulled from his embrace. "I won't make you regret it—any of this. I'll stay in the shadows. I know the baby is your main concern."

"What task do they have you doing?" He pointed the camera lens at her and took a few pictures before she realized what he was doing.

"I thought I'd see if they'd let me help." She offered him a nice pose to go with her genuine smile. "Surprise them, you know?"

He clicked one more picture of the mother of his child. "Find Emilee or John. You're family now. We stick together." He winked. "This invalid has to get back to his job."

Again with the tears.

What had he said?

John worked alone repairing the small bit of damage the storm caused to the end of the dock behind what was beginning to look a lot like a reborn David's Place. He knew nothing about using a hammer. He considered himself a thinking man. The excuse kept him from admitting his actual ineptness with tools.

Already, he felt the blisters on his palms, but the work proved cleansing, allowing him time in the sun where the fresh Gulf breeze regenerated his tired body. "John, there's another way to do this." Mickey came from behind him. "Let me show you."

"I'm doing fine."

"Yeah, sure," Mickey stepped back. "How's Emilee?"

John nodded. "Penny?"

"Angry and hurt."

"It must help knowing Andy's the father and not you."

"I've been told the truth. You don't have to lie."

"I think it best for us to pretend to see it Andy's way, don't you?"

Mickey nodded. "The baby isn't the problem. It's the fact I even entered into an affair."

"You saw how I behaved when I thought my wife and brother betrayed me. I can't say I blame Penny."

"I never thanked you for taking her to see the doctor."

John stopped his hammering and studied his partner's face. "I think I'm responsible for her finding out the truth. I pointed out your car to her on the way back from the mainland that day."

"No. I was somewhere I shouldn't have been." Mickey leaned against the railing John just finished repairing. The wood gave way. John reached out, grabbing Mickey's outstretched hand before he could fall into the water below.

Once Mickey steadied himself, John stared at him in disbelief before laughing. "I guess you can teach me a trick or two."

"Just think of it as payment of a debt owed. I've learned more from you about the law than I ever learned in law school."

"You're learning from hands-on experience, not from me."

"How did you learn?"

"I had a corporation to represent and a brother to oversee. I needed all my legal ends nice and tight."

Mickey laughed. "Andy's a handful, huh?"

"Andy's something else." John looked down the dock to where his brother sat with Emilee and India. "And I wouldn't want him any other way."

"It must have been tough when you thought he died."

"Tough isn't the word."

"Did you ever keep that promise you made to God? He did bring Emilee home to you, and as an added bonus, He kept your brother safe."

"I haven't seen you going to church much since I moved here. Are you a member?"

"Oh boy, my mother was the best Sunday school teacher in Serenity. I attended church every Sunday morning, Sunday evening, and Wednesday night prayer meeting to boot."

"You haven't been lately."

"No, John. I moved away from God when my mother died and my sister left town again. I guess I felt abandoned by them, and I just assumed God didn't care." Mickey bent down to show John how to correctly mend the railing. "You didn't answer my question. Have you kept that promise?"

John shook his head. "No, I haven't."

"Don't wait too long."

"Why? Will He rain down fire on me?"

"God loves us, John. He's not sitting in heaven waiting to punish us, but 'When you make a vow to God, do not delay to pay it. For He has no pleasure in fools; pay what you have vowed.'" Mickey said with a pride John could not understand. "God defines a fool as someone who doesn't believe in Him. Don't be a fool. God showed Himself to you by answering your prayer." Mickey held the wood and indicated where John should place the nail to hammer. "Noah's around somewhere. Why don't you let me work here? You go talk to him."

"Mickey, I'm sorry I didn't tell you about Emilee."

"Believe it or not, I understand. Someday when it doesn't hurt so much I'll tell you how hard Penny had to work to pull the truth out of me."

John used his law partner's shoulder to push himself up. "I hope I haven't lost your friendship. I haven't said it to you at all, but I've enjoyed working with you and your wife. I've learned a lot from you, too."

"Like what?" Mickey continued to work.

"How to love without conditions. And now, I'm going to find Noah. I have a vow to keep." John walked away before Mickey could disagree.

Chapter Forty-One

Thursday hadn't come soon enough.

David searched the room one last time. He didn't want to forget anything because he didn't plan to return for it. He never wanted to see the inside of a hospital again. His first admittance was much different than he assumed it would be. All his life he thought this type of institution designed for the sick to seek rest. Instead, they prodded him at least four times nightly to take his temperature and his blood pressure. The monitors would keep him awake, and if he did sleep, a nurse would wake him to see if he was alive. He couldn't wait to get out into the fresh air and away from the overly large torture chamber.

As if summoned, the door to his room opened. "Hey, Pop." Seth wheeled in his transport, his sister sitting in the wheelchair. "We've got your ride."

John and Andy stood behind them. Emilee lifted herself out of the chair with careful movement. She leaned forward and hugged him, and he noted his daughter had not quite gained her full strength.

"Are you ready to go home?" she asked.

"I'm ready, willing, and able."

"We saw Dr. Bernhardt out front. He's signing the discharge

papers."

"Well, it's about time. My time's just as valuable as the doctor's"

"Daddy." The word slipped from Emilee's mouth for the first time in his presence. She blushed.

"Did you call me Daddy?" David demanded.

Emilee looked not to him but to her husband.

"I'm asking the question," David reminded her.

"I—I didn't think you'd mind. I could call you David."

"Daddy sounds find to me." He opened his arms to her again. *Thank You for this blessing, Lord. I'm sorry I took so long to claim it.* She was his daughter, his flesh and blood, as much a part of him as Seth. "Daddy sounds just perfect."

Emilee held to David for some time. "I'm so glad to be here with you," she whispered against him.

"And Daughter, I'm glad you're here." He kissed her cheek. "Have you seen …?"

"Pop, we need to make sure you have everything." Seth brushed past David. "No," he muttered, and David understood. Colleen had not talked with her daughter.

"Have I seen what?" Emilee asked.

"I was going to ask you if you've met Verity Stewart."

"Actually, it's been very busy. We talked but not at great length."

"She's looked after your brother and me for a long time. I hope you'll get to know her."

"I'll make sure they do that," Seth assured.

David moved toward the wheelchair. "Well, we need to get out of here so I can make sure my restaurant weathered the storm."

Everything seemed to stop around him until Emilee spoke.

"Let me go see if Dr. Bernhardt has the papers."

"Dr. Bernhardt is right here." The door opened. "And here are those discharge papers I promised."

"Thank you, Scott." David reached out for them. "Why don't you plan on stopping in at my place for a free meal or two this weekend?"

Scott Bernhardt released the papers to David's hand. "I just might do that, but you're not to lift a hand in the way of work."

"I'm going to supervise." David would concede only slightly to the doctor's orders.

"Supervision is work. I expect to see you in three weeks in my office." Dr. Bernhardt ordered then turned to Emilee.

John drew closer to his wife.

"Dr. Ryan, I'll be waiting to hear from you about your residency."

Emilee nodded. "I always keep my promises, and I appreciate the opportunity, Scott." She shook the doctor's hand.

"What promise is that?" John asked.

"To continue my residency. Remember?"

John leaned forward and shook the doctor's hands. "Thank you."

"I've already called Cornell, and they have only good reports on your wife, Mr. Ryan."

"It's John, and I could have told you that."

"We're getting my dad home where he belongs." Emilee placed her hand on David's shoulder. "I hope you'll stop in later tonight."

The doctor nodded. "Any eligible women left on that island since I escaped, David?"

David laughed. "I thought they all ran away pining for you."

"Then I might find some peace there, huh?" Scott walked out the door.

"Let's go, old man, before I decide to leave you." Seth laughed as they proceeded down the hall toward the exit.

Mickey rubbed Verity Stewart's ample shoulders as she wrung her hands in nervous anticipation of David's reaction to the surprise. "Relax."

"He could have another heart attack," she said. "I want everything perfect."

The plumbers and the electricians were putting the finishing touches on their work.

"Where's Luke?" She looked around her. "Where's that boy? I want to give him a big hug for what he's pulled together here."

"No one's seen him," Mickey told her. "His boat isn't docked at the Ryan's or here. He and Noah worked until early this morning pulling it together."

"David's going to be upset his place isn't open tonight."

"Well, he'll have to understand. We pushed the miracle department by getting the county to approve the rebuilding, we took advantage of the town council's absence, and the Ryans paid double for the equipment and the industrial generators. We'll just have to wait for the inspections. But they can't keep us from having one heck of a continual weekend celebration." Mickey stepped in front of Verity. She indulged him in a small dance.

"Now, I have to get back to work." Verity spun away. "Colleen!" she bellowed as she turned. "Do you think we should put the cake out now?"

Mickey held up his hands in exasperation. "Do you ever listen to us?" he asked.

Verity turned around. "Only to people who have grayer hair than mine."

Blanchie entered the restaurant. "Mickey, where's Luke?"

Mickey shrugged and pressed his lips together as if to tell her he had not one clue. "Where's Penny?"

"She's still at your office writing up something for you. I think John dictated it. She said something about you're needing to sign it."

"Me?"

"Something to do with an agreement between you and Penny." Blanchie shrugged her shoulders. "Why don't you go see?"

Mickey stumbled backward before being able to move forward again. "I'm not signing anything." He blinked. "I won't agree to anything." He ran out the door and sprinted the short distance down Front Street. He took the steps up onto the dock with one leap, pulling the door to his office open just as Penny yanked a paper from the desk

"What are you doing?" he demanded.

"Excuse me." She wrinkled her nose "What happened to good morning? You're gaining some of John's bad habits."

"Is it a good morning?" He stood by the door. "What are you doing?"

"I told you two days."

"And?"

"And I'm ready to give you my decision."

"I'll fight a divorce."

"You will?" She acted as if his revelation was news to her.

"On what grounds? Do you have any grounds to deny me my freedom?"

"You know I love you. You know I want to work this out with you. I can't lose you. How could you and John do this behind my back? I won't sign anything."

"You may want to discuss this with your lawyer. He knows what's in it." She stood like a statue taking in his discomfort with what appeared a bit of smugness. "Because this is going to change your life."

He scuffed his tennis shoe on the carpet like a boy facing his punishment. "I don't have a lawyer." He fought to control his emotions. "I don't want a lawyer."

"John's your lawyer."

Mickey frowned. "Penny, the first lesson you learn in law school is ethics. John can't draw up divorce papers for you and represent me." He didn't even know if the courts would accept a handwritten document these days.

She held the papers out to him. "If you would like, you could take these in your office and read them over."

He hesitated.

She shook them at him. "I promised to help Verity get the food set out for David's welcome home."

Mickey snatched the papers from his wife's hands. As Penny picked up her purse, he walked back toward his office. How could John do something like this to him? He smiled at him one minute and pushed the knife in the next.

Mickey slammed his office door as he walked inside and threw the papers on his desk. They floated over the pile of files and papers already there. "I should have shot myself when I had the chance." He cursed Penny for hiding the bullets and slumped in his chair unready and unwilling to look at his future.

———∿∿———

The fancy sedan John owned intrigued David. He told John so and admitted that maybe he had missed out on a few of the luxuries in life.

"David, believe me, you have more good in your life than you know," John replied.

"We share a few of those, don't we?" David turned to look at the three in the back. They were not listening to the conversation. Emilee and Andy teased Seth about something. Seth played the role of one highly agitated with their remarks, but David saw the gleam in his son's eyes. Seth's arm fell over Emilee's shoulder, and she leaned against him. There was a joy in David's heart that he could never have comprehended only a few days earlier.

As they reached Cutter's Bridge, John pulled off the road. David watched with interest but said nothing. John killed the engine and turned toward the backseat. "It's time," he announced.

"It's time for what?" David asked.

"Daddy." Emilee leaned forward. She maintained the middle seat in the back, and when he turned, David could look her in the face and see her sincerity. "We want to let you know something before we get to town."

"What's wrong? What's happened?" David searched each face.

Emilee was the only one wearing a sympathetic smile. The others appeared stoic. "You've heard about good news and bad news, right?"

David turned further to look closely at his son. Now, Seth smiled back at him. "Listen to her, Pop."

"Was someone hurt in the storm?"

"Your restaurant received a lot of damage," Emilee confessed.

David leaned back in his seat and stared out the window. "Is that all?"

"Well, the damage was rather severe."

"I have insurance."

"Yes, you did," Andy spoke.

David turned. "What do you mean, I did?"

"Well, we sort of used it." Andy shrugged.

"Used it?" David looked to each of them again. "How could you use it?"

"To rebuild." Emilee's fingers tightened on his shoulder. "Luke Crum came up with the idea, and he wouldn't let us rest until Seth got the insurance company's authorization to go forward. Luke brought his construction friends around, and even put us all to work, and we rebuilt your place."

"That bad, huh?"

"There was nothing left," Seth told him.

"I don't believe that." David looked to his son. "Nothing left would be losing all of you." His eyes clouded over with tears. "God has been so wonderful." He looked out the side window. Let's go see what Luke Crum has done." He shook his head. "That boy always has had a special place in my heart even when he shot Old Sheriff Tompkins."

Seth coughed. "Since you brought it up, there's something you should know."

"About Luke?"

"No, about Sheriff Tompkins."

"What in the world could you tell me about old Tompkins?"

"Well, Noah and I—we—the pellet rifle went off by accident. Luke wasn't around, but he got the blame."

Andy roared with laughter.

"Noah and I shot him."

"How could you both shoot him?" Emilee joined in Andy's laughter.

"We were holding the gun trying to see how it worked. One of us hit the trigger, and the sheriff got it right in the rear." Seth snickered then straightened at the severe look his father cast him. "Are you okay, Pop?"

"I thought you'd take that one to the grave with you, boy."

"You knew? Why didn't you say anything? Noah and I ..."

"I think you both learned the bigger lesson from my silence. Skeeter McGowan thought for sure when he gave that belt to Luke's dad, the two of you would 'fess up." David offered a slim smile before looking out the window. "I realized Luke's character that day when he didn't give the two of you away." He lowered his head.

"Are you okay?" John asked. "We don't want you to stress."

"I am at complete peace. Complete and wonderful peace. Drive on, Johnny. I want to see the Lord's mercies toward me." He saw the look his son-in-law gave him, and David decided he would have a lot of fun calling John by the name he apparently only gave Emilee permission to use. Sometimes a parent's greatest joy in life was the ability to playfully aggravate a child.

Chapter Forty-Two

Mickey read the words John dictated for Penny. Those covered only the first paragraph of the legal document. The rest Penny pulled from her memory. She took the most important day of her life and set down on paper the most meaningful words either of them had ever spoken.

He always knew his wife took so much to heart. Why hadn't he realized she would have memorized each word from their wedding vows? It wasn't even that she remembered them; she lived them. Every day, those vows were a reality to her, and he'd hurt her so badly by breaking them in such a hideous way.

Now, she offered him a second chance to take their mutual covenant to heart. Before God and his family and friends, he once promised to love, honor, and cherish his wife. They swore whatever God put together they would never tear asunder. His actions ripped those vows apart. He tore their love to shreds, and she, with her handwritten piece of paper, sewed it back together. He understood why she needed two days. It would have been so easy for her to walk away. The choice she made was the toughest.

He stood from his chair and stumbled toward the door, wanting only to sign the paper in front of her and begin the healing. He would let everyone witness his redemption. "Lord." He stopped in the middle of the hallway leading from his office. "Forgive me, and help me keep this promise." He ran out of the office.

"Penny." He pushed the door of the restaurant open. She stepped out of the kitchen wiping her hands on a towel as if what he needed to say held no importance to her. "Verity, Blanchie," he called the two women over and laid the document on the table in front of his wife. He dug in his pockets, realizing he had forgotten a pen. Penny reached out and handed him the pen she pulled from her pocket. She came prepared, and he smiled as he took it from her. "All of these promises, I will keep. I'll love you as much as you've loved me." He started toward her to kiss her, to hold her, but she backed away.

"Sign it." She pointed. No emotion played on her face.

"Witness this." He signed with a bold stroke and pushed the document first toward Blanchie and then to Verity. They signed, and he picked it up and held it toward his wife.

"You keep it," she whispered through tears. "You remember it. Because when I said I'd never let you forget, that's what I meant. I will remind you of those vows every day. I'm going to make a copy, and I'm going to frame one for our bedroom and one for your office."

"I'll repeat them right now if you want."

"Oh, Mickey." She fell against him. "I've missed you so much for so long," She clung to his neck, and the realization of how long this journey had been for her was all he needed to keep him from ever straying from her side again.

Blanchie placed the chairs around the table and stood back to take in the place. The workers had rebuilt the restaurant, returning it to its glory. The few tables and chairs that sat in the middle of the floor, surrounded by booths rebuilt against all the walls, had been donated. Blanchie had taken special care to get them scrubbed and in order.

Noah slipped into the restaurant, but Luke wasn't with him. She'd heard that Noah and Luke had worked until very early in the morning putting the finishing touches on the place.

Blanchie started toward the kitchen but paused at the wall where a dozen pictures hung in frames. The old memories had been taken by the storm. These were new ones, and they included those David loved and never really knew until recently.

"Luke wanted me to give this to you." Noah held out an envelope.

Blanchie stared at the paper in his hands. "What's he up to?" she asked.

"David's on his way. Let's make sure we're all together." Verity clapped her hands.

Noah ignored Verity. "I know very little, just what he wanted to tell me. He wouldn't answer all my questions, but he assured me everything's okay."

Blanchie took the envelope. "Where is he?"

"Come outside with me." Noah motioned.

Blanchie shook her head. "David and his family just arrived."

Noah looked through the window. "Luke did a great job here."

"That's just it. He did this. He should be here." She looked toward the group of men, the members of several construction crews and companies that Luke had worked with just to make ends meet only to spend the money on selfish pleasures.

Luke had not been selfish or self-serving in helping David. The boy she had always loved had turned into a caring and selfless man.

"He's told me what to tell David, but he's anxious for you to read your note."

David was taking his time getting out of the car.

Blanchie led Noah out onto the dock. Her hand holding the envelope trembled. "What are you doing?" she questioned Luke as if he stood near, and then she ripped the envelope apart. Pulling the card out, she opened it.

Blanchie,

When all else failed, I always turned to you, and I'm afraid that what you perceive as a failure in Andy will cause you to turn back to me. Give the man a chance. I told you we were very foolish when we married as kids, but what I didn't say was that sometimes the happiest people on earth are fools and those who don't know any better. I long for what we shared as teenagers, sitting on the porch swing making those memories you mentioned to Andy that night on the boat. You see, I do watch, and I do listen. I take in everything about you. I always have, even when I fail to show it.

Noah worked with me this morning until I thought everything was perfect. He talked to me about God, and I did rededicate my life to Him. I didn't do this for you or my parents. I did it for me. I was tired of feeling like God peered over my shoulder, and I just couldn't get it right. I've decided if I work with God, maybe He can direct my life. I'm off, Blanchie, to the great waters beyond Serenity Key, and if the world isn't flat, and the Good Lord is willing, I'm going to write on the boat this winter. I'm going to wing it. I cleaned out my savings, and you know what a paltry (see the writer use the big word) amount that is. I'm trusting God. It's just Him and me for a while, and I do expect prayer, lots and lots of prayer.

You have a chance for happiness with a good man. Given that chance, Andy could possibly love you as much as I do, and he'll never put you through anything like I did. Give him a chance to show you what a good man is like. He won't let you down. I do love you, you little nut, and I'm carrying you with me in my heart. I want the best for you. I'll write in a few days or maybe weeks, or maybe months. It'll take some time for me to write like a friend and not an old lover, but I will write eventually. I can't stand to not communicate with you. You have always been my lifeline.

Your Once Wayward Husband.

Blanchie bent over the railing. *Oh, God, don't let him go. Bring him back.* She wanted to scream the prayer aloud, but she held it inside. As badly as it hurt, she knew Luke was only doing what he felt he must do. It had to be the hard way, and she would wait for him. Still, she wondered if he knew how much she wanted him to return to her, to sail back into her life.

Noah placed a comforting hand on her shoulder, and she

turned toward him. "Pray for him. Pray with me daily that he discovers what he's looking to find."

"He's looking for you." Noah obviously betrayed some of the conversation he held with his friend.

"He didn't need to leave to find me. I'm right here."

"But he has to find himself first. He said if you were here when he returned, he wanted to be the man you have always asked of him. He doesn't expect you to remain available, and he just wants time with God to deal with the hurt."

"Look at what he did here. Look at his accomplishments. He's so full of love, Noah. He always has been."

"But he's made some bad decisions in his life. He needs to come to terms with them."

Blanchie wiped her eyes. "Can I ask you a question?"

"I'll see if I can answer it."

"When you and Luke were teenagers, did he ever talk about me, and was I a joke to him? Did he think it was funny how I tried to make him happy?"

"Luke once told me that you were a star in the night, and he depended upon you for direction. He just didn't heed it too well."

Blanchie nodded. "I'll give him as long as he needs, but I will be that star that guides him back here where he belongs."

Blanchie dried her eyes and walked inside. Stopping in the door, she turned.

Noah raised his hand in the air waving to the boat that was nestled close to Angel Key.

Luke stepped up and waved. Had he actually waited to see if she accepted his plans? He was leaving without knowing that she would be waiting when he returned.

She shivered. He'd told her there would never be another

woman for him.

If Luke sailed away and found love somewhere else, it would kill her.

"Oh." The realization of what her dalliance with Andy cost both her and Luke hit her in the gut.

If only she had waited for the Lord to give her clear direction.

Instead, she'd hurt two good men, and neither of them deserved the pain she'd caused.

Noah opened the door, and she moved out of his way. "Pray for me, too, Noah. I'm going to need it. I've just learned that walking away from God's path puts us on some rocky roads, and I'm afraid Luke's journey is going to be a rough one for me."

Emilee entered first and held the door open.

"What kind of joke is this?" David bellowed from outside. "Looks the same to me."

Although no one yelled surprise, as her father entered the restaurant, Emilee saw that seeing his friends and loved ones around to support him had the same effect. "Are you okay?" she asked.

David offered no more than a nod. He moved past her and began greeting everyone with a handshake and a word of thanks. Seth came to stand beside her, and Emilee leaned against him. "I'm so jealous of you," she said.

"He isn't always this easy to please," Seth joked.

"I think Emilee envies all your friends." John slipped his arms around his wife's waist. "I know I do."

"Ditto." Andy came beside them.

"Look around." Seth waved his hands. "You've been working right alongside them. They're your friends, too."

David finally reached the last person in line who congratulated him on his recovery of both health and business. Having never seen the restaurant before its demise, Emilee's heart went out to her father. According to Seth, it was David's Place rebuilt as before. Still, Emilee suspected the restaurant was such a part of her father that he could tell every minor difference.

David walked to the portion of wall to review framed pictures hanging there. For some time, no one spoke. Emilee followed Andy to where David took his time reviewing each photo. He beamed at the picture of Blanchie with the smudge on her forehead. He touched the one of Seth and Emilee standing at the edge of the dock. He laughed aloud at the picture of Andy Ryan and Kurt Davis standing together like embattled soldiers with their bandages wrapped around their heads. There was one of Seth, Emilee, John, and Andy. "My family," he whispered before continuing to look over the others depicting the workers at their various tasks.

"Who took them?" David searched the faces waiting for his response.

"They gave the job to me." Andy smirked. "Since I couldn't do much of anything else."

David patted the young man on the face. "Andy, I knew you were something special."

"A competitor." Andy laughed.

"A son." David winked.

Emilee turned away from the scene, and John caught her in his arms. After so many years, Andy had received the greatest gift anyone could offer him: acceptance by a man he respected. In many ways, Andy remained the small boy who only wanted a father to love him. "Em," John whispered against her. "Do you remember the person you wanted me to find for you?" He turned her with his hands on her shoulders. "Do you know this woman? She says she knew you when you were in prep school."

Emilee stopped breathing. Her heart pounded against her chest. She hadn't decided how she should act toward the woman who brought her into this world. As if pushed by some invisible force, she took one step then another stopping only when she noticed the woman not moving toward her. "Della," she cried the name.

The woman ran forward and caught Emilee in an embrace.

"Momma." Emilee's entire body shook with the release of years of longing for a mother's touch. She held to Colleen, afraid to release her. When she did, she looked to where her brother stood apart from them frowning. "Seth, meet my mother, your aunt."

Still, no smile came to his face.

"Seth," Emilee pleaded.

Seth stepped forward and held out his hand. "Aunt Colleen and I met already."

"You've turned out to be such a handsome man," her mother offered. "Seth, I'm sorry for any pain ..."

"I'm fine. I have my sister here and her family. That's all I can ask."

"I wish it were your mother standing here," her mother continued. "She loved you very much."

"I know she did."

"Sometime, if you want, I'd like to tell you about her."

Seth said nothing. He looked to Emilee.

"Please," Emilee whispered.

Seth nodded. "Someday, that'd be nice."

"You still wear the ring." Her mother held up Emilee's hand. She touched the ring with her finger. Wearing it was second nature to Emilee.

"I've never taken it off. Over the years, it kept my memory of Della Croix alive."

"I'm glad," her mother said.

"Seth." Emilee pulled the ring from her finger. "Your mother gave this ring to Momma." She turned to look at her mother. "I'm right, aren't I? The story you told me, this is what you meant?"

Her mother wiped away tears and nodded.

Emilee turned back to Seth. "Daddy gave it to your mother, and your mother gave it to mine as a token of forgiveness and love on the night I was born." Seth looked at the ring Emilee held toward him. "I want you to have it, and please forgive me for causing your mother's death."

"Emilee, you didn't cause her death." Seth took the ring from her. He closed his eyes tightly then opened them wide. "Now I remember where I've seen the ring before. My mother's wearing this in her portrait."

"Yes, she is," Colleen nodded. "She insisted the artist depict it. Isn't that right, David?"

David nodded, his attention riveted onto Seth.

"There's an inscription inside. *Beloved.*" Emilee took the ring back from him and turned it so he could see it. "Your mother was our father's beloved. Your mother forgave my mother for what happened, and she gave the ring to her. It proved she loved my mother, and one day, the saddest day in my life, my mother gave the ring to me as a token of her love. Now, I'm giving it to you, because I love you so much."

Seth gripped the ring.

"Beloved." Emilee touched his face. "You are so loved."

Seth brought Emilee's hand down and slipped the ring onto her finger. Andy clicked the picture. "And you are so loved by me." His hand curled over hers. "Aunt Colleen, I'd like to hear all about my mother."

Emilee's mother nodded.

She reached and touched Seth's face. "You remind me so much of her. I'm not only thankful to find my daughter once again. I'm overjoyed to see Uma's son because I know the love she had for you."

Seth hesitated. Then he stepped toward his aunt, wrapping his arms around her. "Pop reminded me that you're the reason I have my sister. From the bottom of my heart, thank you."

David placed his arms around his children, drawing Seth back to him. "Where's the boy that brought you all together to do this for an old man who doesn't deserve it?"

"He's off on one of his adventures," Noah announced. "But he wanted to tell you that he's rededicated his life to the Lord and that he hopes that the Lord will be as good to him as He's been to you. Oh, and he said something I don't think I've ever heard him say of anyone but Blanchie. He loves you, and he wants you to take care of yourself because he doesn't know what Serenity Key would be like without you in it."

Emilee swiped at the tears that fought against any attempt to keep them at bay.

This was what she'd always thought home should be. Not just family, but also friends who loved and supported you.

She embraced her husband. "Thank you for this. Thank you

for all of this," she whispered in his ear.

———✦———

We hope you enjoyed the first glimpse of Serenity Key. Please stay tuned for the second book, coming soon! And please consider leaving a review for the author at Amazon.

Character Name and Relationship

Scott Bernhardt, M.D. - Physician at the mainland hospital
Blanchie Crum - Ex-wife of Luke Crum, Penny Parker's sister
Luke Crum - Ex-husband of Blanchie Crum
Kurt Davis - Serenity Key's Chief of Police
Queen Edwards - Belle McGowan's aunt
Yasmin Garcia, M.D. - Friend and co-worker of Emilee Ryan
Cameron Matrai - Family friend of the Ryans Belle McGowan Wife of
    Pastor Noah McGowan
Noah McGowan - Pastor of Serenity Key Baptist Church
Colleen New/Della Croix - Sister-in-law of David New; wife of Owen
    New, mother of Emilee New
David New - Father of Seth and Emilee New; husband of Uma
    Dellacroix New
Owen New - Brother of David New; husband of Colleen Dellacroix New
Seth New - Son of David New
Uma New - Mother of Seth New; wife of David New; sister of Colleen
    Dellacroix New
Penny Parker - Mickey Parker's wife; Blanchie Crum's sister
Mickey Parker - John Ryan's law partner; husband of Penny Parker
Andy Ryan - Brother of John Ryan; brother-in-law of Emilee Ryan; son
    of Zachariah and Oriana Ryan
John Ryan - brother of Andy Ryan; husband of Emilee Ryan; son of
    Zachariah and Oriana Ryan
Emilee Ryan - Wife of John Ryan; sister-in-law of Andy Ryan
Oriana Ryan - Mother of John and Andy Ryan
Zachariah Ryan - Father of John and Andy Ryan
Hannah Stewart - Daughter of Verity Stewart
Verity Stewart - David New's best friend; mother of Hannah Stewart
Chelse Thompson - Wife of Xander Thompson; mother of India
    Thompson
India Thompson - Daughter of Chelse and Xander Thompson
Xander Thompson - Husband of Chelse Thompson; father of India
    Thompson
Tank Williams - Officer on the Serenity Key Police force
Fran Williams - Wife of Tank Williams

About the Author

Fay Lamb writes emotionally charged stories with a Romans 8:28 attitude, reminding readers that God is always in the details. Fay donates 100% of her royalties to Christian charities.

She has always taken joy in forming words that tell stories that will enrich the lives of others. She tackles issues that she has had to face. She isn't afraid of the hard issues and takes delight in weaving humor into the lives of her characters, even in the direst of circumstances.

Fay also loves teaching the art of fiction and has taught at several conferences over the last five years. She and her husband, Marc, reside in Titusville, Florida, where multi-generations of their families have lived. The legacy continues with their two married sons and six grandchildren.

For more information or to schedule an interview or a workshop, contact Fay Lamb. She loves to meet readers, and you can find her on her personal Facebook page, her Facebook Author page, and at The Tactical Editor on Facebook and on Goodreads. She's also active on Twitter. Then there are her blogs: On the Ledge, Inner Source, and the Tactical Editor.

Recent releases by Write Integrity Press

Latest Romantic Suspense

Evil doesn't take a holiday.

Haven Ellingsen has escaped the man who relentlessly hunted her in the Cascade Mountains. But when an old friend from her dangerous past shows up unexpectedly to warn her that Dade Colton is determined to recapture her, Haven makes the only safe decision: to go into hiding once more. But where? Who can she trust? If only she could tell someone about her tragic secret. But Dade's threat to kill anyone who helps her would put that person's life in jeopardy, too.

Sometimes you hide; sometimes you stand and fight.

Latest Romance

Annalee Chambers:
Poised, wealthy, socially elite …Convict.

Annalee Chambers floated through life in a pampered, crystal bubble until she smashed it with a single word. Dealing with the repercussions of that word might break her, ruin her family, and land her in jail.

True, Annalee's crime amounted to very little, but not in terms of community service hours. Her probation officer promised an easy job in an air-conditioned downtown environment. She didn't expect her role to be little better than a janitor at an after-school daycare in the worst area of town. Through laughter and a few tears, Annalee finds out that some lessons are learned the hard way, and some seep into the soul unnoticed.

What can a bunch of downtown kids teach a Texas princess?

Thank you
for reading our books!

Look for other books
published by

Write Integrity Press
www.WriteIntegrity.com